"Muffin's gone," she screamed, tears pouring down her cheeks.

"What?" he asked.

"My dog," she sobbed, rushing past him to go back outside. "Muffin! Muffin!" She continued shouting that one word as she frantically searched her front yard.

He stepped onto the porch, wondering what kind of mess he'd gotten himself into. But what kind of guy would leave a woman alone in a situation like this?

"Hey!" Callum called, still having no clue of her name. "What's Muffin look like? I'll help you look."

"He's a golden cocker spaniel. About this high." She gestured to just above her knee. "He's wearing a red collar with a gold heart ID tag on it, and he has a lot of fur."

"Okay." He nodded and shoved his phone back into his pocket. "I'll have a quick drive around. Why don't you go check if any of the neighbors have seen him?"

"Thank you," she said, her voice choked as she rushed over to the house on her right.

When he'd woken up that morning he'd been engaged and planning a wedding. Now it appeared he was single and looking for a stranger's dog. What wild thing could happen next?

A Matter of Trust

Rachael Johns & Christy Jeffries

Previously published as *A Dog and a Diamond*
and *The Makeover Prescription*

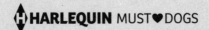

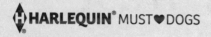

ISBN-13: 978-1-335-00801-5

A Matter of Trust

Copyright © 2020 by Harlequin Books S.A.

A Dog and a Diamond
First published in 2016. This edition published in 2020.
Copyright © 2016 by Rachael Johns

The Makeover Prescription
First published in 2016. This edition published in 2020.
Copyright © 2016 by Christy Jeffries

Recycling programs
for this product may
not exist in your area.

This edition published by arrangement with Harlequin Books S.A.

For questions and comments about the quality of this book, please contact us at CustomerService@Harlequin.com.

Harlequin Enterprises ULC
22 Adelaide St. West, 40th Floor
Toronto, Ontario M5H 4E3, Canada
www.Harlequin.com

Printed in U.S.A.

CONTENTS

Rachael Johns is an English teacher, a mom and a chronic arachnophobe as well as a writer. A lover of romance and women's fiction, Rachael loves sitting in bed with her laptop and imagining her own stories. She was voted in the top ten of Booktopia's Australia's Favourite Author poll in 2013. Rachael lives in the West Australian hills with her husband, three mostly gorgeous heroes in training, two cats, a cantankerous bird and a badly behaved dog. Visit her at her website, rachaeljohns.com, and Facebook and Twitter.

Visit the Author Profile page
at Harlequin.com for more titles.

A DOG AND A DIAMOND

Rachael Johns

For Beck Nicholas and Jackie Ashenden—
two awesomely talented writers who have been with
me almost from the beginning of this crazy journey
and have become great friends in the process.

Chapter 1

"You have arrived at your destination," announced the deep, monotone voice of Chelsea Porter's GPS.

She slowed her car, frowning as she looked up at the sign that loomed above the private bridge to her right: McKinnel's Distillery—Oregon's Best Whiskey since 1977.

Definitely not a place of residence. Perhaps she'd misread the name and address on the client form. Before continuing, she grabbed her cell out of her purse, pulled up her email and checked the details that one Miss Bailey Sawyer had supplied.

Mr. Callum McKinnel, and then what she'd assumed was a residential address in well-to-do Jewell Rock but appeared to be the home of the renowned McKinnel's Whiskey. She didn't drink herself but her grandfather had sworn McKinnel's was the best whiskey in the world. And, like most other members of her family, he'd drunk enough of the stuff to know.

You couldn't live in these parts without having heard of the McKinnel family. Rumor had it the great-great-grandfather of the current McKinnels—and there were a lot of them—had once been a bootlegger. It was his face on the bottle's famous label. Criminal or not, he'd been a handsome devil and, from what she'd heard, his descendants had inherited his good looks.

Now that she was here, staring across the bridge, she couldn't believe she hadn't recognized the name. There'd been an obituary in the newspaper a month or so ago for Conall McKinnel—he'd been the big boss at the distillery for almost forty years until his recent death thanks to a sudden heart attack. Then there was Lachlan McKinnel—a chef who had won numerous awards, he occasionally appeared on local television and blogged his unique recipes online, all while single-handedly raising his disabled son. Callum—whom she guessed to be one of Lachlan's brothers—was probably as close to a celebrity as she'd ever get and her stomach clenched with uncharacteristic and ridiculous nerves.

A horn sounded and she realized she'd stalled in the middle of the road. She waved a hand in apology at the car behind her, turned right and then started over the bridge toward the cluster of rustic-looking buildings in the distance. The lake on either side of her sparkled and she shivered, imagining that at this time of the year it would be icy cold. As she emerged on the other side, the sight before her took her breath away. The building sprawled almost the length of the lake and the word *quaint* came to mind when she looked at it.

Although the exterior was brown, there were so many windows that it didn't look dark. The pine trees in the back and the immaculate, stone-bordered garden beds at the front reminded her of a postcard of a holiday resort. When the snow came in a month or so, this place would be magic.

Such a pity she wouldn't have reason to return.

She'd never imagined a place that produced whiskey to be as beautiful and classy as the grounds and buildings that she admired now as she followed the signs to the parking lot around the side. Nope, she associated alcohol with shouting matches, slurred words, bad breath and prayers her parents wouldn't kill each other.

Instead of white lines, the parking lot was marked out with old barrels, which made her smile as she turned off her ignition. Someone, or more likely a whole family of someones, had put in a lot of TLC to ensure this old building continued to sparkle.

Breathing in the crisp cool air that carried a hint of liquor as she climbed out of her car, Chelsea almost forgot to grab the chocolate bouquet off her backseat. Determined not to be distracted by her surroundings, she held her head high as she strode toward the main building, which obviously housed a café if the folks sitting at tables out the front were anything to go by. It wouldn't be long before it would too cold for outdoor dining. She had to sidestep a couple of obvious tourists taking selfies to get inside and contemplated asking if they'd like her to take a photo for them, but reconsidered when she remembered why she was here.

Not to tour or dine or admire the scenery but to be the bearer of bad news to one of the illustrious McKinnels.

That thought made her feel as if she'd swallowed a brick. *Why?* This wasn't the first time she'd done this. Even before she'd started her business, doing what she was about to do had been a gift. She was determined to get in and get out, because no matter how lovely this place was, it also made her uncomfortable. Chelsea strode the few more steps to the massive, glass-front doors and pushed one open.

If the outside of McKinnel's took her breath away, the inside filled her with warmth as if someone had just wrapped her in a heated blanket. In addition to a number of fall decorations—gourds and pumpkins and whatnot—the walls hung with hundreds of whiskey bottles, black-and-white family photos and old prints related to whiskey drinking. And as she'd predicted, a massive fireplace roared away on one wall. It felt more like she'd stepped inside a cheerful family home than a business. She loosened her scarf and undid the buttons on her coat as she started toward the counter.

As she queued alongside the people waiting to buy or taste whiskey, she looked at the wall behind the counter and smiled as she read some of the many quotes scrawled on a massive chalkboard.

What whiskey will not cure, there is no cure for.

I'd rather be someone's shot of whiskey than everyone's cup of tea.

Too much of anything is bad, but too much of good whiskey is barely enough. —Mark Twain

She might not agree with any of the sentiments but she liked the way all the quotes were in different handwriting as if lots of different people had scribbled their thoughts.

"Hello? Can I help you?"

At the deep voice, Chelsea spun round, tightening her grip on the bouquet as she came face-to-chest with someone. Then she looked up into the face of possibly the best-looking human she'd ever laid eyes on. And not in a clichéd way. Tall, dark and handsome didn't begin to describe him. He was all those things and then some, with an element of something else she couldn't quite put her finger on. And his sea-green eyes just happened to be her favorite color. Although he wore charcoal business pants and a lighter gray shirt with the distillery logo on the breast, his strong, muscular physique and the scar just above his right eyebrow told her he didn't spend all his time behind a desk.

"Are you after a gift or…" His voice trailed off and she realized she'd been openly gaping at him.

Ignoring the strange dizziness that came over her—maybe she'd spun around too fast—she straightened, held her head high and addressed him in her most professional voice. "Hi. I'm looking for Callum McKinnel."

He couldn't be the man standing in front of her because no woman in her right mind would dump someone who looked like *that*. Not even her.

"Then look no more. You've found me." The man's illegally sexy smile didn't falter as he offered her his hand. "And how may I help you?"

He *was* Callum? *Oh, shoot.* Heat rushed to Chelsea's cheeks and she shuffled the chocolate bouquet she held in her right hand into her left, then slipped her hand into his, reminding herself she was here as a professional, not to ogle the produce.

"Can we go somewhere a little more private?" she asked, hoping her voice didn't sound as strained as it felt.

Callum raised a deliciously dark eyebrow and a hint of amusement crossed his lips. "Do we have an appointment?"

She shook her head, trying not to stare at his lips, which were perhaps even more delicious than his eyebrows. Very kissable indeed. "No appointment, but I need to talk to you. I have a message from Bailey, and you might prefer to be alone when you hear it."

At the mention of the other woman, recognition flashed across Callum's face, his smile faded and his eyebrows knitted together. "You'd better come this way."

Before she could ask which way he meant, she felt his large hand across her back and she bit down on her lip to stop from whimpering. What the heck was wrong with her? There were a number of layers between her skin and his; she could only imagine how her body might react if there were not. As Callum led her across the slate-tiled floor, she took a few deep breaths in and out, trying to regain her equilibrium. She told herself this weirdness must be due to where they were, but feared this wasn't actually the case.

"We can talk alone in here," he said as he pushed open a door with a gold sign on it that read Director— Callum McKinnel. The sign looked shiny and new as if it hadn't been in place very long and, when she stepped inside, the office didn't seem at all to Callum's taste.

And how would you know that?

"Take a seat," Callum said, gesturing to a shiny, dark leather armchair as he shut the door behind them.

"It's fine, I'll stand." She rushed her words. "But you might want to sit down."

"That bad, hey?" She couldn't quite interpret Callum's tone, but was glad when he walked around the massive desk and sat in a luxurious leather office chair on the other side. His elbows perched on the desk, he folded his hands and he looked up to her expectantly.

She took a quick breath before launching into her speech. "I come on behalf of Bailey Sawyer." She cleared her throat and continued, forcing herself to look at Callum, despite the fact that looking at him put her all off-kilter. "Bailey acknowledges that you have been in a relationship for five years and that you have both invested a lot of time and energy into each other. She's had a fabulous time with you, but I regret to inform you that she would no longer like the honor of being your fiancée. You're more like a brother or a best friend, and although you had a lot of fun together in other aspects of life, when it comes to sex, the attraction has faded for her."

His eyes widened and Chelsea couldn't meet his gaze, heat flaring in her cheeks. The whole sex thing came up frequently in her line of work—not being physically compatible was one of the top reasons for dumping someone and she prided herself on delivering this news with the utmost tact. She wasn't a prude by any means, but just saying the *S* word in front of Callum

McKinnel made her feel like a teenage girl who'd just discovered *The Joy of Sex* in her parents' bedroom.

Jeez, it was hot in here. She mentally gave herself a cold shower as she tried to remember the next part of her spiel. Bailey Sawyer hadn't paid good money for Chelsea to make a mess of breaking up with her long-time boyfriend.

Oh, that's right. She focused. "You are a great guy but Bailey has realized you're just not her type. She doesn't think you want the same things she does and wishes you the best in the future. She thinks one day you could make some woman a very wonderful husband, but she is no longer prepared to come second to your work."

Her heart racing now, Chelsea stepped forward and thrust a bouquet made only of the finest Belgian chocolates across the desk. "These are from Bailey. Your favorite, apparently."

He glared at the chocolates like they were soggy roadkill. "Not anymore, I don't think." He blinked and then ran a hand through his thick, dark hair. "I'm sorry…is this some kind of joke?"

Callum stared at the woman across his desk, waiting for her to say "Smile, you're on *Candid Camera*" or whatever the hell the latest incarnation of that ridiculous show was. She was almost as tall as he was, which was rare in a woman, but she was definitely all woman. Despite the fact she'd just delivered him the news his engagement was over and she was wearing a heavy winter coat, he couldn't help but notice the way her body curved in all the right places. She'd tied her caramel-blond hair back in a high, professional-looking knot, but he could easily imagine what it would look like if she let it all hang loose. Had she even told him her name?

It felt like hours but was probably less than a minute before she replied, "No, I'm sorry, but it's not."

He raised his eyebrows, kinda stunned by this whole bizarre situation and, if he were honest, more than a little annoyed. "What exactly does my relationship with Miss Sawyer have to do with you?"

She cleared her throat again and then glanced back at the door as if contemplating her escape, but he didn't plan on letting her leave until she'd given him a reasonable explanation. "I am a breakup expert," she announced as if this wasn't an alien profession to him.

"A what?" He couldn't help his scoffing tone. Maybe this really was a joke. Bailey liked to think herself a bit of a comedian; then again, he doubted she'd interrupt his work for a laugh. She knew how important the distillery was to him, even more so now that his father had died and he was running the show.

"I'm a breakup expert," she said again. "I handle the difficult task of ending relationships for people who don't feel up to the job themselves."

"You mean gutless people who like an easy cop-out?" He shook his head before she could reply. "I can't believe what the world is coming to. What kind of person does that?"

"Someone who cares deeply about their partner and feels they may end up staying in an unsatisfactory relationship because they don't want to hurt the other person. Bailey had your best interests at heart when she hired my services."

"I meant, what kind of person does *this* for a job?"

"Oh." Color bloomed in her cheeks and she dropped her chin to her chest, staring at the floor a few seconds before looking up again and crossing her arms. "My reasons for my career choice are no concern of yours, Mr. McKinnel. And now I'm afraid I have another appointment. Good day."

She'd turned and fled the room before he could call her bluff on another appointment. Did she actually get enough of these gigs to earn a living? He stood and hurried after her, weaving through the customers milling in the shop area—the time leading up to midday was a busy one, loads of tourists looking for a place to lunch—but she was fast and he saw no sign of her. Cursing under his breath, he emerged outside just in time to see a little red car reversing out of the lot.

"Dammit." He patted his trouser pocket to check for his keys, then without another thought jogged around the back to his own parked car. Wondering what had come over him but unable to stop himself, Callum started his SUV and screeched after her, narrowly missing a whiskey barrel in his haste. He caught up just as she was turning onto the road in the direction of Bend, the nearest city to Jewell Rock.

As he drove focused on the car in front, he called his sister on speaker phone.

"Good afternoon, McKinnel's Distillery, Sophie speaking. How may I help you?"

"It's me," he barked. "Look, I've had to go out. Can you handle my calls for the next hour or so?"

"Out?" Sophie's disbelief came across loud and clear. "Out where?"

"Never mind. Something's come up. Call me if there's an emergency."

"I may be young and I may be a woman, but I'm more than capable of holding the fort for a couple of hours. Enjoy your mystery rendezvous."

He snorted. Hah! If only she knew what he was really up to. "Thanks, Soph. I owe you one," he said as the traffic lights in front turned amber. Breakup girl zoomed through and, determined not to lose her, Callum pushed down on the accelerator and just scraped through the intersection before the light went red. He checked the rearview mirror in case there were cops, then let out a puff of breath. He could just imagine the look on a police officer's face while they asked him why he'd gone through a red light. Admitting to stalking the car in front could get him into all kinds of trouble and his father would turn in his grave if he garnered any bad publicity that could sully the McKinnel name.

As they drove past the boundaries of town and headed onto the highway toward Bend, Callum glanced at his fuel gauge, hoping he had enough gas to get to wherever she was going. Thankfully it was near full. He supposed he should call Bailey, if only to clarify that the woman he was currently trailing wasn't some kind of lunatic. She'd seemed legitimate but one couldn't be too careful these days.

Bailey *always* answered her phone but today the number went straight to voice mail. "Hi there, you've reached Bailey Sawyer, event planner extraordinaire— leave a message and I'll get back to you soon. Bye."

"Bailey, what the hell is going on? Call me."

He'd been acting on some sort of adrenaline until

now, but as he followed the little red car, navigating the country roads between Jewell Rock and Bend, realization dawned on him. What would he tell his mother if his relationship with Bailey had actually ended? She'd been so pleased when he and her best friend's daughter had announced their engagement…and annoyed that they'd taken years to get to the stage of almost tying the knot. This, so soon after the loss of her husband, would devastate her. Anger surged inside him at Bailey and he almost missed the moment when breakup girl turned down a street on the outskirts of Bend.

He slammed on the brakes and swerved to follow. He'd been a teenager with a brand-new license the last time he'd driven this recklessly and he was out of practice. About three minutes later, she swung into the driveway of a little house that looked in dire need of renovation.

Callum parked on the street out the front. Should he confront her now or wait until she was done with the next lucky recipient of her "work"? He waited and watched a moment, but when he saw her unlock the front door and go straight inside instead, he realized she must live here.

In that case… He climbed out of his SUV and beeped it locked, all psyched up to confront her, to demand more of an explanation. And, if he were honest, to tell her what he really thought of her career choice. But his bluster cooled the moment he stepped into her doorway. Either her housekeeping skills were dismal, or while she'd been delivering him the breakup speech, some scumbag had broken into her house. The smashed glass panes on her door indicated the latter.

Standing in the middle of the disarray, she bent down, grabbed some kind of vase off the floor and then spun around and held it as if she were about to hurl it at him. "Stay right there!"

He froze and held his hands up in surrender.

Recognition dawned in her eyes. "You! What are you doing here?"

"I…um…" For once in his life he was lost for words. Now didn't seem the time to pay out on her.

"Never mind." She shook her head, threw the vase onto the couch and headed down a hallway, wailing "Muffin, Muffin!" as she went.

Frowning, Callum stepped inside and surveyed the mess. Whoever had done this had left no stone unturned. What a violation. He dug his cell out of his pocket, about to call the police when she returned.

"Muffin's gone." Tears streamed down her cheeks.

"What?"

"My dog," she sobbed, rushing past him back outside. "Muffin! Muffin!" She continued shouting that one word as she frantically searched her front yard.

He stepped onto the porch. What kind of mess had he gotten himself into? If he were sensible, he'd head back to the SUV, climb inside and phone this in to the police on his way back to the distillery. But what kind of guy would leave a woman alone in a situation like this?

"Hey!" he called, still having no clue of her name. "What's Muffin look like? I'll help you look."

She froze a moment, looking at him as if she couldn't tell if he meant it or not, then said, "He's a golden cocker spaniel. About this high—" she gestured to just above her knee "—he's wearing a red collar with a gold heart ID tag on it and he has a lot of fur."

"Okay. Got it." He shoved his phone back into his pocket. "I'll have a quick drive around, why don't you go check if any of the neighbors have seen him?" She appeared more worried about the dog than the house and the culprit was probably long gone, so he decided to focus on the mutt first, as well.

"Thank you." Her voice was choked as she rushed over to the house on her right.

Callum jogged back to his SUV, climbed in and, shaking his head, turned the key in the ignition. When he'd woken up that morning he'd been engaged and planning a wedding, now it appeared he was single and looking for a stranger's dog. What crazy thing could happen next?

Chapter 2

"Did you find him?" Chelsea asked as half an hour later Callum climbed out of the SUV he'd just parked behind her car.

He shook his head. "I'm sorry." He sounded genuinely so and a prick of guilt jabbed her heart that she'd dumped him without hanging around to offer support. The services of The Breakup Girl included counseling of the dumpee and it wasn't unusual for her to spend up to an hour with the brokenhearted after she'd done the main part of her job. She let her clients' exes pour out their hearts to her, and by the time she'd finished, most of them had decided getting shafted was the best thing that had ever happened to them. As her old friend Rosie often said, some people could cook soufflés that didn't flop in the middle, some people could play a musical instrument and Chelsea's talents lay in the art of dumping people. But she'd failed dismally in being a professional where Callum was concerned; being in the confined space of his office had flummoxed her.

And instead, here he was helping *her*.

"I guess you didn't either," he said as he walked toward her.

She shook her head, sniffing as the tears threatened to fall again. She hated crying and rarely did so—especially in front of other people—it made her feel weak. But there was only one thing in the world that truly mattered to her and that was Muffin, so these were exceptional circumstances. How would she survive if he didn't come back?

"Let's get you inside," Callum said. And before she realized what was happening, she felt his arm close around her shoulders as he ushered her toward her front door. He was so warm, so solid, and she had a crazy urge to lean into him but instead she pulled away and headed inside, conscious of him following behind her. Chelsea was unsure why he was hanging around, but not in the head space to question. She'd barely noticed the mess the first time—so focused on Muffin—but now she hardly recognized her home. Living alone it was easy to keep things tidy as she liked them, but her little house looked as if she'd moved in a year ago, emptied everything she'd owned onto the floor and left it there.

"I don't understand what they were looking for," she said, surveying the mess. It would take her days to clean this up, but her first priority was finding Muffin.

Callum came up behind her. "Probably just kids, but either way, we should call the police before you move anything."

"I need to do up some notices about Muffin and hang them around the neighborhood." She glanced over at her little desk—or rather where her little desk was usually set up in the corner—and promptly burst into tears. They hadn't taken her laptop or her printer but the desk had been upturned, her laptop looked to be broken in two and her printer lay in a number of smashed up pieces.

Callum cursed as he followed her gaze. Two seconds later he was right beside her. "Here." He offered her a crisp white handkerchief. She took it, surprised—she didn't know men still carried such things.

"Thank you," she whispered and then used it to wipe her eyes.

As if a mind reader, he said, "My mom makes me carry it. She says you never know when you'll need one and I'd never admit it to her, but it does come in handy every now and then."

She almost smiled. "I'm Chelsea Porter, by the way. And tell your mom thanks."

"I will. I'd tell you my name but I think you already know it. Can I fix you a drink? A coffee or maybe something stronger? I'd offer you a whiskey but I left in a bit of a hurry and didn't bring any."

Wasn't she supposed to be the one offering him a drink? She shook her head. "Thanks, but all I care about right now is finding Muffin."

And she didn't drink—not that he needed to know that.

"I know you're concerned about your dog," he said, his tone soft and understanding, "so let me call this in to the cops and then I'll help you work out what to do about Muffin."

She sniffed and looked up at him properly. Lord, he was delicious, but she didn't even know him. "You're being very kind to me, considering...considering what I did to you."

He shrugged. "I have two little sisters. I'm used to female hysterics."

She noticed he made no comment on his now *ex*-fiancée. "I can guarantee I'm not usually like this."

His lips curled up at the edges and she couldn't help but smile a little too. "Besides, my mom would have my guts for garters if I left you alone to deal with this."

"I like the sound of your mom."

"She's not bad. But if you'd prefer, I could call a friend to come and be with you."

She *should* tell him that he could go and she would call a friend herself, but the truth was she hadn't made any real friends in her time in Bend. Acquaintances yes, but no one she'd call on in an emergency, and however pathetic it made her, she didn't want to be left alone right now. This burglary had shaken her up, reminded her that no matter how hard she worked to achieve the things she wanted, she still didn't have complete control over her life. "I haven't been in town long enough to make many friends." Then she added, "But you don't have to babysit me. I'm a big girl."

"You *are* tall," he said. "I haven't met many women who are up to my chin without wearing heels, but I wouldn't call you big."

He'd noticed she was wearing flats? She couldn't help being impressed—in her experience most men noticed nothing unless it was naked—and also a little flattered. Which was ridiculous. He'd just been dumped by his fiancée and Chelsea's priority right now was finding Muffin. Her heart rate quickened again and she swallowed, trying to halt another wave of tears.

"But," he continued, hopefully oblivious to her thoughts, "you shouldn't have to deal with this alone. Let me call the police and then we'll work out what to do next." Without another word, he stepped back outside onto her porch and a few moments later she heard his illegally sexy voice on the phone.

She sighed and flopped down onto the sofa, unable to believe this had happened. It felt surreal—Callum whom she'd only just met here helping her, yet Muffin achingly absent. Since she rescued Muffin from a shelter almost three years ago, he'd always, without fail, met her at the door with his tail wagging and his tongue hanging out when she'd returned home. It was true what they said about no one loving you quite as much as a dog did; she'd never had anyone who even came close.

She'd tried to make this house a home by filling it with bright cushions, bookshelves, funky ornaments and life-affirming, happy quotes, but without Muffin, it felt empty.

"A patrol unit will be here as soon as they can," Callum said, coming back into the room.

"Oh, thank you."

He sat down on the other end of the sofa and her belly did a little flip at his proximity. She hadn't had a man in her house for... Well, not since she'd moved to Bend actually.

"Now," he continued, not at all affected by *her* proximity to him, "the police suggested you make a list of what's been taken for when they arrive. They don't want you to move or touch anything, if possible. While you do that, I'm going to call the local vets and animal shelters and give them Muffin's description. Have you got a photo?"

"Um…" She nodded and gazed around the mess, looking for her framed photos, but in the end, gave up and dragged out her cell. "Here," she said after a few seconds of scrolling through photos. The majority of her photos were selfies of herself and Muffin—walking in the park, chilling on the couch—but she didn't want to show Callum those photos. Eventually she found one of Muffin standing on the front porch looking out onto the street at something. It was one of the rare moments that her hyperactive dog had stood still.

"He's a cutie." Callum took her phone to look at the photo and his fingers brushed against hers in the exchange. Something warm and tingly curled low in her belly but she tried not to show it on her face.

"He is." She sighed. "I guess I'll go make that list."

The first call Callum made was to a local security firm, asking them to stop by Chelsea's house ASAP to fix her windows and change her locks. He hoped she had insurance to cover this disaster, but if not, he'd foot the bill—call it his good deed for the day. Then, he called every refuge and vet clinic he could find on the internet in the vicinity of Bend, leaving his cell number as a contact because, as he realized when speaking to the first place, he had no idea what Chelsea's was. Besides, he guessed her contact details were on Muffin's collar, so if anyone found him, they'd likely call her first anyway.

As he was disconnecting the final call, a police patrol car rolled to a stop on the curb. He shoved his cell in his pocket and went over to meet the cops.

"You call in a burglary?" asked cop numero uno as the two officers climbed out of the car.

"Yes, I did," he said, trying not to smirk as he eyed the pair who were each other's opposites in almost every possible way. One was short and fat with gray hair and smile lines around his eyes. The other was tall and thin, looked like he'd gotten his police badge from the toy section in Kmart and wore a scowl on his face as if a mere neighborhood burglary wasn't at all the excitement he'd hoped for when he'd signed up.

"Your place?" asked the young guy.

"No," Callum explained as he led them through the sparse front yard to the house. "It's owned by Chelsea Porter. She's a…" What the heck was she besides a woman who'd walked into his workplace and dropped a bombshell on his world? Or what should feel like a bombshell but after the initial shock didn't make him feel anything much more than annoyed. At Bailey, not Chelsea. "She's a friend," he concluded, deciding the officer didn't need to know their exact relationship as it had no bearing on the case.

They stepped in through the front door to find Chelsea staring at the mess in the living room, a notebook in her hand, a pen caught between her lips and a frown on her face. Even with this expression, she was gorgeous, and the fact he could think such thoughts made him wonder if perhaps he owed Bailey a favor. While he loved her—they'd known each other since they were in diapers and had a lot of fun together—he couldn't deny he'd gotten engaged to show his dad he could settle down. Also because he wanted a family and was traditional in the sense that he believed children should be raised within a marriage. He didn't believe in the type of love his mom and sisters gushed about while watching sappy made-for-television movies, but he did believe any relationship could work if you put in the hard yards.

"Jeez, what a freaking mess," commented the younger man, echoing Callum's thoughts as the two officers surveyed the crime scene.

Chelsea looked up and took the pen out of her mouth.

"Good afternoon. I'm Sergeant Moore and this is Officer Fernandez. You must be Chelsea," said the older officer. "I'm sorry this has happened and I know you probably want to get things cleaned up as soon as possible, so—"

"Frankly, I don't give two hoots about the mess right now," Chelsea interrupted. "Ask me what you need to and then tell me you can help me find my dog,"

"Your dog's missing?" questioned Sergeant Moore. She nodded.

"And—" Officer Fernandez gestured toward the notebook in her hand "—is that a list of the things that were taken?"

"That's just it." Chelsea glanced down at the notebook as if she'd forgotten she was holding it. "I don't think anything was."

Officer Fernandez frowned. "Except the dog?"

Shock flashed in Chelsea's eyes. "You think they

stole Muffin? I just imagined he got scared and ran away."

She sank down onto the sofa and Callum found himself crossing the room to sit beside her. He glared at the young cop.

The older one offered Chelsea a sympathetic smile. "Let's not jump to conclusions. I'll ask you a few questions and we'll go from there."

"Okay," Chelsea whispered, her voice shaky.

The sergeant ran through the usual questions—how long Chelsea had been out of the house, what time she came home, had she touched anything, et cetera, et cetera, et cetera. Callum could see her getting more and more agitated as the questions became more and more repetitive.

"Do you think they could have been looking for something?"

She quirked an eyebrow at the cops. "I earn an honest living, but I haven't got any family jewels lying around if that's what you're insinuating."

Callum couldn't help but smile at her sass.

"Okay. And what do you do for a living?" asked the tall, young cop. The way he spoke made it sound as if *Chelsea* was the one who'd committed a crime and Callum fought the urge to say so.

"I'm a breakup expert," she said, in much the same manner she might say she were a hairdresser or a nurse.

Like Callum had done earlier that day, the officers raised their eyebrows and adopted mutual expressions of confusion at this reply.

Chelsea offered a short explanation. "I break up with other people's partners, via phone, email or in person, so they don't have to do it themselves. But I really don't see what my career has to do with this."

"Hmm…" Sergeant Moore pondered. "Could any of these men you've broken up with bear a grudge? Could they want to hurt you like you hurt them?"

"First," she said, her eyes sparking, "it's not just men I dump, and second, I am good at what I do. So no, I think that is a highly unlikely possibility. Are we almost finished? While we're sitting here, none of us are out there looking for my dog. What exactly are you going to do to try to find Muffin? Can you register him as missing?"

Officer Fernandez smirked and spoke in a patronizing tone. "Missing dogs aren't actually our area of expertise. I suggest—"

"But," interrupted his superior, "as Muffin may have been stolen he *is* our responsibility. I assure you we will do our best to find him and return him to you and get to the bottom of all this." He gestured around him at the mess.

"Thank you," Chelsea said, standing. She saw the two men to the door and then grabbed a ball cap off a hook on the wall near the door. It appeared to be the only thing in the whole place left untouched. She tugged it down onto her head and was about to step through the front door when she turned back, as if suddenly remembering him.

"And thank you for everything too, Callum," she said. "You've been beyond generous with your help and if there's anything I can ever do to you to repay the favor…"

"Forget it." He waved his hand. "You going out looking for Muffin again?" *Stupid* question.

"Yes. I want to have a thorough search of the neighborhood on foot before it gets dark."

"I'd offer to help," he said, "but someone should stay here and wait for the security guys instead."

Her face fell and it was obvious she hadn't given one thought to her unsecured house. "Oh. No, you don't have to do that," she said quickly. "You've helped enough already."

Damn straight he had and he couldn't really explain why he'd offered, but neither could he just walk away. He liked animals as much as the next guy, but he'd never seen anyone quite so distraught over a dog as Chelsea appeared to be. She really shouldn't leave her house unattended the way it was or someone might come in and loot the place. "My conscience says otherwise. Now go find Muffin. Unless you don't trust me."

She narrowed her eyes at him. "I don't trust anyone, but I also care little about the contents of this house." And with that, she turned on her heels and hurried down the front steps, the sight of her cute ass in her tight business trousers making his gut clench.

Alone and cursing his red blood cells, Callum called his sister again and told her he'd be out longer than he'd first imagined. Although he heard the curiosity in her voice, she didn't pry and for that he was thankful.

His life had suddenly become very complicated, and he wasn't sure he could explain everything that had happened today even to himself.

Chapter 3

Callum glanced at his watch, hoping the security company he'd called wouldn't be too long, and then once again looked around the cottage-sized house surveying the mess. The cops had done their thing—although he didn't think they were taking this burglary as seriously as they should be—so he could start the cleanup without fear of disturbing evidence. Although this wasn't his house, he'd never been the type of guy to sit around and twiddle his thumbs. Putting his phone and keys down on the kitchen counter, Callum pushed up the sleeves of his shirt, wondering where to start. Not wanting to overstep the mark by rifling through Chelsea's possessions, he chose to begin with gathering up the broken glass and other damaged goods.

He found plastic trash bags in a drawer in the kitchen and a vacuum in the cupboard in the hallway. Taking

his time not to throw out anything that looked important or of sentimental value, he went through the house
collecting the big bits of unsalvageable debris. On the
kitchen table were a few pieces of a jigsaw puzzle. He
glanced down and saw hundreds of other tiny pieces
scattered on the floor. Collecting them back up into
the box took a while and he hoped he'd found them all.
Next he righted the furniture that had been upturned
in the invasion and put the pieces of her computer back
on her desk. As he did so, his gaze caught on a photo—
miraculously it didn't appear to be a victim of the car-
nage—and he realized something that had been bugging
him about Chelsea's home since he stepped inside. The
one-and-only photo Chelsea had on display was of an
old man sitting in a tattered armchair with a teenage
girl standing behind him, her arms wrapped around
his neck. To him, it seemed almost unfeminine not to
surround yourself with photos of memories and loved
ones; it was just something he'd taken for granted as
part of the female way. Until now.

Without thinking, he picked up the frame and stared
down at the photo. The young girl had to be Chelsea,
all that unruly caramel-blond hair hanging over her
shoulders. Yet, although her mouth was stretched into
a massive grin, her eyes weren't smiling—instead they
harbored an anxious, unsettled look, exactly the same as
the expression she'd been wearing today. He frowned in
response and found himself wondering what her story
was. Why didn't she have other photos? Was this man
her only family? There were all these prints of affirma-
tive quotations on the walls—All That I Seek Is Already
within Me, Allow Your Soul to Sparkle, You're Never

Too Old to Wish Upon a Star—as if she were trying
to create a safe happy haven, but there was something
missing here. Something warm, something real.

A knock on the open front door startled Callum from
his reverie. "Hello! Anyone home?" called an overly
chirpy male voice.

Callum rolled his eyes. Exactly how many people left
the door open if they went out? And if they did, well,
they probably deserved to be burglarized. "Yep. Come
on in," he called, putting the framed photo back down
on the desk and turning toward the front door.

A short but very buff guy, dressed in a tight-fitting
uniform stepped inside and raised his eyebrows as he
looked around. "Someone sure went to town on your
place."

Callum didn't correct him or comment that he'd already tidied up a lot of the mess. He just wanted this man
to leave again. Instead, he nodded. "I need you to replace the locks on all the doors, replace the glass that's
broken and," he added almost as an afterthought, "can
you also install proper locks on the windows?" Chelsea's current locks wouldn't even keep out a small child,
and for some reason, knowing what she did for a job, he
didn't like the idea of her living in an insecure house.
Even he, a relatively levelheaded man, had felt a surge
of rage toward her when she'd first "dumped him," so
he could imagine there were men out there who might
get a little heavy-handed after such mortifying rejection. He didn't like the thought of that one bit.

"No problemo," said the security man, dropping a
toolbox to the floor and then stooping to open it. He
started immediately, and although he whistled while

he did so, he worked quickly and efficiently and of that Callum approved.

While the worker changed the old locks and installed new ones, Callum continued tidying up. The noise of the security man's machine blocked out his whistling and Callum experienced a sense of achievement when he finally switched it off and examined his progress. Callum's mom would be proud—she always harped on about raising new-aged heroes—and Bailey didn't know what she'd lost.

Bailey. He was beginning to wonder if she hadn't done him a favor. She was right—he didn't have the time at the moment to give her what she wanted as all his energies needed to be piped into reviving the distillery.

He simply wished she'd had the guts to tell him to his face.

Callum sighed at that thought. His dad had done a stellar job of pretending everything was okay, but the truth had startled him when he'd finally gotten his hands on the business's books. McKinnel's Distillery wasn't in dire straits but it was pretty damn close. He put this down to the fact his father refused to move with the times, despite the number of other boutique distilleries and breweries that were popping up all around them. Every time he'd raised this issue when his dad had been alive, every time he'd suggested a new idea that could raise revenue, Conall had pooh-poohed whatever the latest proposal was and reminded his son who was in charge.

Sometimes Callum couldn't believe he hadn't cut and run from the family business years ago, but the truth was, he loved the distillery almost as much as Conall had. You had to wonder though whether the stress of declining business had contributed to his father's fatal heart attack.

If only you'd let me help, Dad. If only you'd given me the chance to prove myself.

But Conall McKinnel had been a hard man, almost impenetrable to anyone except his wife, for as long as Callum could remember. Mom put it down to the tragic loss of his twin brother, Hamish, which had happened not long after the two had established the distillery.

"I'm all done," announced the security dude, appearing suddenly beside Callum in the living room and offering him a bunch of shiny, new keys. "You've done a good job of cleaning up here too."

At the other man's tone, Callum almost expected him to give him a pat on the back. "Thanks," he said, referring to the work done, not the compliment. He dragged his wallet out of his pocket. "How much do I owe you?"

The man quoted what sounded like an exorbitant amount, but Callum handed over his Amex without question. "Can you give me a receipt for the insurance company?"

"Sure thing, buddy."

Callum flinched at the term of endearment and bit his tongue, which wanted to say that they weren't "buddies" at all. According to his mom, sisters and even Bailey, he had a tendency to be unnecessarily grumpy. Quite frankly, he thought much of the population had an unnecessary tendency to be jovial.

When the workman realized Callum wasn't the type for idle chitchat, he left, beeping his horn and waving as he reversed out Chelsea's drive. Once again Callum found himself alone at this stranger's house. Standing on her front porch, he looked up at the darkening sky and then down at his watch. Chelsea had been gone a few hours now and he guessed this meant she hadn't found her mutt, but surely she couldn't stay out all night looking. He'd called the shelters, the cops and neighbors knew the dog was missing—what more could she do?

With this thought, he decided to go look for her himself. Callum found a scrap of paper, scribbled down his cell number in case she returned before he found her and needed to get inside her house, then stuck it onto her front door. Ensuring her house was indeed secure, he locked the door, popped her new bunch of keys into his pocket and then jogged toward his SUV. Although he'd grown up in Jewell Rock, he'd never spent much time in Bend and he'd certainly never driven around this end of town.

He drove slowly down the surrounding streets, getting the occasional odd look from locals who wondered who this stranger patrolling their neighborhood was, but the only woman he wanted to pick up was the intriguing Chelsea Porter. A rush of blood shot south at this thought, catching him off balance. He wasn't in the market for a hookup. All he wanted was to get Chelsea home safely, so he could get on with his life.

Finally, he saw her and let out a breath he hadn't realized he'd been holding. Miss Porter was a damn sexy woman and he was defenseless against his pounding red blood cells. *Calm the hell down*, he told them, as he pulled his SUV over to the side of the road and wound down the window.

"Chelsea!"

She turned and blinked at him as if he was the last person she expected to see. Although she didn't speak, her eyes were bloodshot and mascara was streaked down her cheeks. His heart turned over in his chest at the sight.

"You've got new locks on your house," he said, hoping this might give her a lift. It didn't. She blinked as if wondering what that had to do with the price of eggs. "How about I take you home? It's getting dark." Left unsaid was the fact that if she hadn't found the dog by now, it was unlikely she would.

Chelsea shook her head, a few golden locks that had escaped her ponytail swishing across her face in the process. "I can't. Muffin is out here somewhere. All alone. He needs me."

Her desperation told him she likely needed the dog more than the dog needed her. Callum curled his fists around the steering wheel, but refused to let his frustration show on his face. What was he supposed to do now?

"How about you get in…" He leaned over and opened the passenger door. "And I'll drive you around a bit more." Maybe once she was in the confines of his SUV, he could convince her to go home and call it a day.

She looked at him skeptically a few moments, then sighed and climbed into the vehicle. "Why are you being so nice to me?" She asked as she tugged the seat belt over her breasts and clicked it into place. "After what I did to you today?"

"That wasn't personal. Besides, I'm a nice guy," he replied, although the thoughts he was currently having about her breasts contradicted this statement.

She shrugged as if she didn't believe in the fairy tale of nice guys—smart chick—but at least she was in the car. He didn't need to win her approval, he simply needed to get her home and hand over her keys, so he could leave in good conscience.

As he steered the SUV back onto the road, Chelsea spoke again. "You can take me home and I'll grab my car," she said matter-of-factly. "I'll be able to cover more ground that way."

"It's fine," he said. "Two sets of eyes are better than one. I'll help you."

"Thanks," she whispered, almost too quiet to hear, and then settled back into the seat.

"How long have you lived in Bend?" he asked as they circled her extended neighborhood a few times. So far they'd witnessed two fat cats having it out in someone's front yard and a teenager who was learning to drive reverse into a fence, but they'd seen no sign of her cocker spaniel.

"Just over a year," she said, as if that was the end of the conversation, but stuff it, he was playing chauffeur here and for some bizarre reason wanted to know more. His mom always said he was like a bear with a bee in his bonnet when he wanted something.

"Where was home before?"

She mumbled the name of a suburb in Portland, her gaze never veering from out the window.

"What brought you to Bend, then?" he asked. "Family? A boyfriend?" There hadn't been any signs of either in her house, and he found himself hoping it was because the latter didn't exist. Which was ridiculous. It's not like he wanted to play the part.

She turned her head to glare at him, her nostrils flaring slightly. "Are we playing a game of twenty questions that I don't know about?" Even with bloodshot eyes and all that runny mascara, *especially* with the edge of irritation in her voice, she was gorgeous. Quite simply one of the most stunning creatures he'd ever laid eyes on.

His mouth quirked at the edges. "Sorry. You don't have to tell me anything."

She sighed and crossed her arms over that delicious rack as he kept driving. "My grandfather—the only family that mattered to me—died fourteen months ago and I needed a change of scenery. I had no boyfriend, a dead-end job, no family, so I saw no reason to stay in Portland. I decided to get in my car and drive until something inside told me to stop and put down roots. I had plans to go much farther afield, but something about Bend got to me. Maybe it was the fact that apparently 49 percent of people here own dogs? Besides, I found out Muffin wasn't big on road trips."

He chuckled. Despite being obviously distraught, she had a sense of humor.

"I'm guessing you've lived in these parts all your life," she said, indicating discussions about herself were done.

"Yep. Born and bred in Jewell Rock. I was recently considering spreading my wings a little, but then my dad died and, well, now I'm needed at home. At the distillery." Which was what he'd always wanted—he just hadn't wanted his dad to be pushing up daisies in order to make it possible.

"Were you and Miss Sawyer going to move?"

Truth was, Chelsea was the first person he'd confessed to about the fact he'd been considering leaving the family business. Guilt made his gut heavy at the thought. "We were in discussions," he lied.

Silence reigned a few more moments as they both kept their eyes on their surroundings, then, when they neared a famous chicken fast-food joint, Callum's stomach rumbled so loudly he felt certain Chelsea must have heard it too. He hadn't eaten since breakfast and he guessed she hadn't eaten in hours either.

Without a word, he pulled into the drive-through.

"Hey," she exclaimed, "what are you doing?"

"Ordering us some dinner. What do you want?"

All Chelsea wanted was her dog back and she thought she'd made that perfectly clear, but now that Callum mentioned it, she was starting to feel a little light-headed. Maybe she needed food. Or maybe the dizziness was because of being in a confined space with six-feet-plus of sexy McKinnel. Either way, she found herself asking for a fried chicken sandwich and a serving of french fries. Callum ordered the same, but added some coleslaw. The teenager behind the speaker who took their order giggled ridiculously at the sound of his deep sexy voice.

"Did your mom tell you that you should have veggies with every meal?" Chelsea asked as they waited in front of the window for their food. She thought it kinda cute the way he'd mentioned his mother a few times.

"Something like that." He almost smiled and something inside her quivered so that she had to glance away. Looking out the window made her realize she hadn't thought of Muffin in all of two minutes. Not that she wanted to forget him—she desperately wanted, needed to find him—but Callum had given her a few moments' reprieve from her anxiety.

When their orders were ready. Callum took their food from the teenage attendant and passed it over to Chelsea. The smell of hot, greasy goodness filled the car, making her want to moan out loud. She rarely ate takeout—years of not being able to afford such luxuries had become a habit.

"Let me give you some money for this," she said, snapping back to reality and realizing she was sitting in a stranger's car—a client's ex's car more to the point—and he'd just paid for her dinner.

He waved a hand in dismissal as he drove away from the restaurant. The warmth of the food seeped through the paper bag, making her thighs hot. She inhaled again and her taste buds begged her for a fry, but Callum couldn't eat while driving and she couldn't very well eat hers in front of him.

"We can pull over somewhere a few moments if you like so you can eat," she suggested.

"Or we could go back to your place and eat there." His tone was innocuous and it wasn't that she thought he was about to take advantage, but the idea of eating dinner with a guy in her house was so alien it made her nervous.

"But we haven't found Muffin yet." She hated the neediness in her tone but couldn't help it.

"Look, Chels," Callum began, turning to look at her so that his deep green eyes sought hers and made her skin hot. Or that could simply be the way he'd used a nickname for her, as if they were friends, rather than recent acquaintances. She was loath to admit it, but she liked it. "I know you're worried about Muffin, but we've both searched high and low. I've called every dog refuge in a three-hundred-mile radius of Bend. I think maybe it's time to call it a night. What if Muffin comes home while you're not there?"

And with that one simple question, he got her. The thought of her dog finding his way back to the house and her not being there to welcome him tore at her heartstrings. "Okay." She gave one nod of defeat. "If you could take me home, that would be great."

He gave her a warm smile and turned the SUV in the direction of her place. The closer they got, the more nervous she began to feel. Not nervous that maybe she would never find Muffin, but nervous about Callum McKinnel coming into her house. Granted, he'd already spent a good deal of time there earlier in the day, but this now felt like the closest thing she'd had to a date in months.

Don't be ridiculous, came a voice inside her head. *The man just got dumped by his long-term fiancée.*

Actually you dumped him, said an opposing voice, but she blocked her ears—that was simply semantics. Besides, he likely wouldn't stay long—just enough time to scarf down his dinner and, as he was a guy, that could be merely a matter of minutes.

Ten minutes later, Callum parked in her driveway for the third time that day. Chelsea got out of the vehicle and carried their takeout up the path to the front door, all the while trying to act calm, cool and collected. Callum was a few steps behind her and only when she read the note he'd stuck to her door did she remember he had her new house keys. She spun around and almost slammed right into him.

"Sorry," she mumbled as his hands shot out to steady her.

"Not a problem." That smile again. Quite aside from the fact Callum was a client's ex, as a McKinnel, he was also *way* out of her league.

She swallowed a groan of disappointment as he let her go and then retrieved a bunch of shiny keys from his jacket pocket. Stepping past her, he selected a key and slid it into the lock, then turned it and opened the door to *her* house for her. Bamboozled by his touch, she let him usher her inside and take the lead.

"Shall we eat in the kitchen or do you prefer the couch?" he asked, shutting her door behind them.

Silence echoed around the house, reminding her of Muffin's absence, but in spite of the aching hole in her heart, she couldn't help notice the state of her house. All clean and tidy now, barely any evidence of the burglary. "Did you do this?" She gaped around and then turned her attention on him.

He nodded and shrugged. "Had to do something while I waited for the security company."

No, actually, he did not. He owed her sweet eff all, but for some reason unknown to her, he'd gone out of his way to look out for her today. That Bailey Sawyer needed her head read. Who cared if Callum wasn't *all that* between the sheets? He was kind and thoughtful, not to mention hotter than the sun itself; these traits weren't ones to be scoffed at in a man. All she could think to say was "Thank you."

"You're welcome."

She looked away because she could no longer handle his intoxicating smile. "Let's eat in the living room. It's more comfortable there."

He followed her to the couch, where he sat beside her as she handed out their food. She'd taken a bite into her sandwich before she remembered her manners. Dammit, she wasn't used to hosting guests. "Can I get you a drink?" she asked, putting the sandwich on the coffee table and shooting to her feet. "I've got club soda or cola."

"I'll have a cola, thanks." He smiled again and then sank his teeth into his own sandwich. It was the sexiest thing she'd ever seen in her life. *Maybe I'm the one who needs her head read?* With that thought she scuttled away to the kitchen, wishing it was farther away so she'd have a little more time to pull herself together.

Chelsea opened the fridge, pulled two cans of cola out and pressed one against her forehead, thankful Callum had his back to her. She could see him from the kitchen, sitting back against her couch as if it were the most natural thing in the world. She shook her head— was this some kind of weird dream? Nightmare? Maybe she'd wake up and discover Muffin sleeping by her feet as he always did and find out Callum McKinnel was nothing but a figment of her imagination. Yet the pain when she pinched herself to check this spurred her into action and she carried the cans and two glasses back over to him. No one in her family had ever drunk soda out of glasses—unless the soda was mixed with something stronger, which it usually was—but Callum had a mom who made him carry a hanky, so the glasses felt necessary.

"Thanks," he said as she cracked open a can and poured it into a glass for him. She tried not to drool as he lifted said glass to his lips and took a sip, the thick columns of his neck muscles flexing as he did so.

Right, time to get a grip on reality. She poured cola into the other glass and downed approximately half of it. Although she hadn't eaten since this morning, the butterflies dancing in her stomach put her off eating. She racked her brain for something to say and then re-membered how she'd fled from his office without of-fering her full service.

"I'm sorry about this morning," she said.

Callum raised an eyebrow. "About dumping me?" He made it sound like they'd been in a relationship and she'd ended it.

She shook her head. "Usually after I've delivered a message to someone, I hang around to chat and see if they're okay."

His other eyebrow lifted. "Good customer service? I approve. So why did you not follow through on that promise this morning?"

The way he spoke, the way he looked at her, made her think he knew the reason and heat rushed to her cheeks. "I'm…not…sure."

"It's okay," he said, half chuckling. "I'm not a big talker and Bailey probably did me a favor."

"Really?"

"Sure, I wouldn't want to be with a woman who didn't consider me Mr. Right."

Callum sounded so lighthearted, but she guessed there had to be pain behind those words. She was about to offer to talk about it now, but he asked a question before she could.

"This breakup business? Is it seriously what you do for a living?"

Surprisingly, she detected none of the repulsion he'd had earlier in his tone.

"Yes. Until recently I also waited tables." She named a well-known establishment in Bend. "But it was either hire another employee to take on some of the breakup load or quit my second job. I chose the latter."

His eyes widened. "No offense, but I'm surprised breaking up with other people's partners is such a lucrative profession."

She couldn't help but laugh. "I wouldn't say lucrative, but I take pride in my work and my reputation is spreading. Breaking up is never easy to do. My service is much like hiring someone to clean your house or mow your lawn. Only cleaners and landscapers don't usually offer counseling, as well."

"How many of these gigs do you get a day?"

She did a quick mental tally. "One or two in-person breakups a week—I only offer that service to customers in Bend and surrounding areas, but I do a lot of online work. Emails, et cetera. Follow-up phone calls for the brokenhearted. Business is good enough that I'm thinking of expanding and looking for freelancers to do face-to-face breakups in other areas."

"You learn something new every day." He popped a french fry into his mouth and she ate one, as well. Then he said, "How exactly did you get into this business?"

Chelsea took a deep breath and surprised herself by telling him pretty much the truth. "My best friend,

Rosie—she lives back in Portland—actually suggested it. I have this thing where I can't manage to hold down a relationship for long. Rosie believes I'm just dating the wrong guys, but whatever the reason, at about the three-month mark, I always lose interest and we break up. But we always manage to stay friends. So far this year, I've been to five weddings of ex-boyfriends. Anyway, Rosie once joked that I was the queen of breaking up and could do it for a living and then a friend of hers actually asked me to do so. I only did it as a favor, but it went so well someone else asked me to do it. And…"

"The rest as they say is history?"

She smiled as she nodded. "Yes. I'll admit it's not a very common profession but I honestly think I'm doing a necessary service. Do you know how many people stay in bad relationships because they're too scared to get out?"

He shook his head and she guessed he came from one of those perfect families. She didn't know much about the McKinnels, but his father's obituary had definitely painted him as the ideal family man. And Callum had *how many* brothers and sisters? She racked her brain but couldn't come up with the number. It was a lot, anyway, reminding her again what different worlds they came from.

"Well," she said, "it's a lot." Then she said, "Thanks for the dinner. It was good." Hopefully he'd take the hint that it was time for him to leave. That she no longer needed babysitting, even if a tiny part of her wanted it.

He nodded toward her sandwich still sitting on its grease-proof paper on the table. "You barely ate."

"Sorry." She bit her lip. "I'm too worried about Muffin."

He nodded grimly. "Fair enough. I guess I'd better be going." But he didn't make a move to stand—for some unfathomable reason, he didn't appear in a hurry to abscond.

"Thanks for everything," she said, trying to encourage him. She just wanted him gone so she could ignore her hormones and get back to worrying about Muffin.

Callum reached out and wrapped his long fingers around hers, then gave a little squeeze. "I'm sure he'll be okay. You'll find him."

"Thanks," she said again, slipping her hand out of his for self-protection and then standing. If the guys she'd dated before had all been as lovely as him, maybe she wouldn't have felt compelled to dump them.

He stood, as well, and awkwardness buzzed between them. What was the protocol here? This wasn't a date. He wasn't going to kiss her good-night and ask when they could see each other again. Likely they'd never see each other again and tonight would become some distant memory and she would one day wonder if it had ever actually happened.

"Well." He cleared his throat and looked down at her—not many men looked down on her and she liked the thrill it gave her. "Maybe call me when you find Muffin. Just so I know."

She rubbed her lips together, loving the confidence in his voice that she'd find her dog but also joyful at the prospect of an excuse to call him. Her tongue twisted at the thought, so she nodded.

"You'll need my number," he said.

"I think it's on my front door."

"Right...of course it is." He shoved his hands into his pockets. "In that case, good night."

Chelsea followed him out, waved as he reversed out of the drive and then closed the door behind her, the thud echoing around the now empty house. Having Callum here had been so bizarre, it had given her a few minutes' pardon from missing and worrying about Muffin, but now that he was gone, she had nothing left to do but worry. She retreated to the couch, collapsed into a heap and wished there was something more constructive she could do than cry.

Chapter 4

It was late by the time Callum returned to the distillery and all but the security lights were switched off. He contemplated going home, but he wouldn't be able to sleep without checking that everything had gone okay this afternoon. Although Sophie had a good head on her, his sister was only twenty-six and had rarely been left alone with the responsibility of the office and the tasting room. Sure, they had a couple of employees to help serve customers, but this had always been a family business and they were the ones with their hearts and souls invested in it.

He parked out the front, let himself into the building and then, happy everything looked as it should, he headed into his office where he poured himself a generous shot of bourbon and took a much-needed sip. This had been, without a doubt, the weirdest day of his life and he scratched his head as he leaned back in his chair and thought over it.

Leaving Chelsea shouldn't have been as difficult as it had been. Sure she was hot and sexy as all that, but so were heaps of women. They'd never made him want to look after them the way she had. It felt more like a compulsion than a want.

The sound of the main distillery door opening broke into his thoughts and Callum sat forward, his muscles immediately on edge. Who the hell would be coming in at this time of night?

"Hey, baby boy, it's just me," called a voice he recognized better than his own. A voice that still insisted on calling him "baby" even though he was thirty-five years old and her eldest child. "Mom," Nora McKinnel clarified a moment later, just in case he'd forgotten.

He rolled his eyes, chuckled and prepared himself for something halfway between a lecture and a sympathy speech. "In the office," he called back, as he stood and retrieved another glass from the shelf behind the desk.

His mom appeared in the doorway as he was pouring her glass. She was wearing a pink fluffy dressing gown, a scarf, a beanie, Wellingtons and her cheeks were flushed from the cool outside air. She still lived in the main house, which was a hundred yards or so behind the distillery buildings, with his brother Lachlan, Lachlan's son, Hamish (the second), and his other brother Blair, who'd moved home a couple of years ago after his divorce. Officially Callum lived in a cottage also on the property but he often stayed at Bailey's apartment in town. He guessed that wouldn't be happening anymore. And dammit, he'd have to go collect his stuff.

"Oh, thank God you're okay." His mom rushed at him, her boots thumping against the solid floor, and threw her arms around him. He just managed to put down the bottle in time.

"Why wouldn't I be?" he asked, although he'd already guessed the answer.

She pulled back slightly and looked into his eyes. Hers were a little puffy as if she'd been crying. "I thought you might have…you know…driven off a bridge or drowned your sorrows in the merchandise."

So she'd heard about him and Bailey. How good news traveled fast. "I'm fine, Mom," he said, escaping her embrace and gesturing for her to take a seat and a drink. Perhaps he shouldn't be okay, but he was. Not that she'd probably believe him anyway. Thanks to Bailey, he could guarantee Mom would be fussing over him for weeks.

"Are you sure?" She frowned as she lowered herself into Dad's leather recliner; he'd called it his "thinking seat."

Callum nodded, sat back in his own seat and lifted his glass again. "Damn, we make good bourbon," he said, trying to distract her. Flavor wasn't the distillery's issue, it was the fact that the younger generation of drinkers were into boutique beers instead. He had a few ideas about how to attract them; he simply needed to convince the rest of his family.

Nora took a sip, then, cradling the glass in her hands, nodded. But the expression on her face said he hadn't succeeded in diverting her thoughts. "Marcia called me this afternoon and told me you and Bailey had split up."

Although he knew she wanted him to tell her it wasn't

true, he saw no point in delaying the inevitable. "That's right. We decided we weren't right for each other. Better now than later, right?" Not exactly the whole truth, but he didn't think Bailey should take all the blame when she'd been the one with the guts to end it.

His mom sighed and downed the rest of her drink. "I was so looking forward to the wedding after the awful year we've had."

"I'm sorry." He looked down into his glass.

"Is it too much to want another grandchild?"

Here we go. "Of course not," he said merely to placate her. Currently she had two—a granddaughter and a grandson, both his brother Lachlan's kids—but as she herself had seven adult children, she believed this number vastly inadequate.

"I had so much hope for next year with you and Bailey getting married and I'd thought that Mac and Sian would follow soon after. Now all my hopes and dreams have gone up in smoke."

Used to his mother's drama-queen tendencies, Callum tried to offer a sympathetic smile, but she barely paused in her rant.

"Now you and Bailey have followed Mac and Sian instead of the other way around…" Mac had also recently been dumped by his long-term girlfriend. What a sorry lot they were. "Lord knows Quinn can't keep a woman longer than a weekend, or he doesn't want to—either way, I failed dismally with him. Lachlan married a selfish cow, who broke his poor heart, and as much as I adore Hamish, not many women are prepared to become a parent to a special-needs child. Annabel seems destined to mourn Stuart forever." She sighed and took a quick breath. "Why the heck Blair and Claire got divorced is a mystery to us all considering they still live in each other's pockets. I love her like she were my own daughter, but he'll never meet someone else if he stays best friends with her, and Sophie doesn't show any interest in men whatsoever. Do you think she's a lesbian? I have been wondering quite some time if that's the issue."

Callum almost choked on his last sip. "What? No. I don't know. Maybe?" He shrugged. To be honest, he'd never given it much thought. Sophie was almost as much of a workaholic as him and that left little time for dating.

"Not that I would care," Nora said, waving her hands dramatically as she spoke. "Homosexuality runs in the McKinnel family, after all…" She was referring to his father's twin, who'd died before Callum was old enough to remember him. "And I haven't got a problem with lesbians. I just wish she'd open up to me. I am her mother!"

"Yes, indeed, you are." Callum stifled a smile, knowing his mom didn't think this conversation amusing whatsoever. She continued on, lamenting her children's foibles, but his thoughts drifted elsewhere. He hoped Chelsea would find her dog and wished there was something he could do to make sure of it. He wondered how she was coping now she was alone, and once again, his ribs tightened as he regretted leaving her by herself. Maybe he should call and check in on her? But it was late—what if she'd managed to fall asleep and he woke her? They didn't have the kind of relationship where he could phone at all hours; they didn't have a relationship at all. Tomorrow; he'd call tomorrow. And then, goddamn, he remembered he'd given her his number but he hadn't asked for hers.

His mom's heaving herself noisily off the recliner brought him once again back to the moment. "I guess if you're okay, I better head home to bed. Don't stay up too late working though. Promise me? All work and no play makes Callum a very dull boy."

"Are you calling me dull, Mom?"

She came toward him, grabbed his face between her hands and kissed him on the forehead. "You are a number of *D* words, my son—*determined, driven, discerning, droll, dependable* to name a few—but you could never be dull." She frowned a moment. "Is that what Bailey said? Because if it is, my best friend's daughter or not, I'll have to kill her."

Callum chuckled. "Thanks, Mom, and no, Bailey didn't say that." Although she had said he was bad in bed, which irked him, especially since she'd said it to Chelsea.

"Just as well." Nora started toward the door but turned back as she got there. "So if you weren't off plotting your own death, where *have* you been all afternoon and evening?"

He swallowed, not wanting to answer this question for fear he wouldn't be able to explain why he'd gone out of his way to help a stranger. Also not wanting to go into the whole Breakup Girl thing. Such a concept would fascinate his mom and then she'd want to spend all night hearing about it.

"I was checking out some business…stuff," he lied.

She sighed and shook her head sadly, buying this excuse immediately. No doubt she blamed his obsession with the distillery for his split with Bailey; perhaps to a certain extent she was right.

After waving Callum McKinnel goodbye, Chelsea had tried to distract herself with a little TV. She now lay on the couch, mindlessly flicking through channels—something that had always irritated her when her granddad did it—but nothing could take her thoughts away from Muffin. And Callum. Both the couch and the house felt awfully empty without them here.

Missing Muffin she could understand—it had been years since she'd watched TV or gone to bed without his furry body to keep her warm and his heavy breathing as background noise. But missing Callum? What the heck was that about?

She'd known the man less than twenty-four hours and he was head of a freaking whiskey distillery. After the role it had played in her childhood, there wasn't much in the world she despised as much as alcohol, and whiskey, bourbon, whatever you wanted to call it, was one of the worst offenders. Interestingly enough, Callum hadn't smelled of whiskey, and she should know. She'd sat close enough to him in the car and again on the couch to have memorized his unique and delicious smell. Closing her eyes, she tried to conjure it now— something woodsy and sweet. She licked her lips and took a quick breath, then aimed the remote at the TV and switched it off.

Perhaps going into her bedroom where she hadn't been with him, would help exorcise him from her mind. Besides, she needed her sleep so she could continue looking for Muffin first thing. Standing, she stooped to gather their takeout wrappers, empty soda cans and glasses from the table and then took them into the kitchen. Although exhausted, going to bed and leaving such a mess was something Chelsea would never do. Not after a childhood of living with drunks who couldn't care less about hygiene or tidiness.

In the kitchen, she dumped the trash in the can and the glasses in the sink and then her eyes came to rest on a piece of paper on the countertop. It was an invoice for the locksmith. She eyed the price and... *Hells bells!* Was her new lock made of pure gold? Picking up the receipt, she took a closer look, noticing that, not only had the front door lock been fixed, but Callum had also had the back door lock and all her window locks replaced. Without her consent.

Who does he think he is?

She screwed up the paper in her hands, knowing her insurance company would only see fit to pay for a fraction of this. How on earth would she pay him back? Her business made a good living—she managed to pay her bills and tried to put a little aside for rainy days— but she hadn't asked for this! Fury pacing through her, Chelsea turned and stormed into the living room where the piece of paper Callum had left with his contact details now resided.

She snatched it up and was halfway through punching his number into her cell when second thoughts stopped her. She may not have been raised well— manners were always an afterthought used only to get something you wanted in whichever household she lived in—but she knew getting angry at Callum tonight wouldn't be fair. He'd set aside his own pain of being dumped and gone out of his way to help her today. Getting angry at him, although she was furious, would be like a slap in the face.

Instead, she took a deep breath, left the receipt in the room and went off to ready herself for bed. She'd call tomorrow when she'd calmed down a little (and was hopefully a little less physically aware also) and arrange some kind of payment plan. But, as predicted, sleep didn't come easily. Chelsea tossed and turned all night, worrying about Muffin and, much to her annoyance, dreaming dirty thoughts about Callum.

Callum stared at his computer screen, pondering the best time to talk to his siblings about rolling out a rescue plan for the distillery. The ringing of his cell interrupted his thoughts and he snatched it up off the desk, glowering at the unknown number.

He cleared his throat and pressed answer. "Hello, Callum McKinnel speaking."

A pause followed, which made him think this was one of those annoying, automated telemarketing calls. Then, just as he was about to disconnect, a soft voice sounded. "Hi, Callum. It's Chelsea. We met yesterday."

His gut tightened in recognition as awareness flared through the rest of his body. As if he could forget. "Hi." He cringed at the way his voice sounded choked and a tad needy. "Have you found your dog?" That was the only reason he could imagine she'd call him, even though he had secret wishes that she'd called for another reason entirely.

"No," she whispered, her disappointment heavy in her tone. "I went out again first thing. I've called all the vets and shelters again and put up signs around the neighborhood but, nothing so far."

"I'm sorry. But it's still early. I'm sure he'll come back or someone will find him today." He wasn't sure of any such thing—if the intruder had taken Muffin, Chelsea might never seen him again, but he knew better than to say so. "Anything I can do to help?"

"I think you've already helped enough."

He blinked and frowned at her terse tone. "Excuse me?"

"I found the receipt for the new locks." She cleared her throat. "Replacing every one in the house was quite unnecessary."

He leaned forward and rested his elbows on the desk. Was she *mad* at him? "I disagree. In your line of business, you can never be too careful. You should be living in a more secure house. Those old window locks might as well have been bought in a toy department because they'd never keep out an intruder."

"Maybe, maybe not, but my safety *and* my house are no concern of yours. You should have checked with me."

"It's not a problem, I'll pay for them."

"No way. I will pay you for the work, but I'm going to have to do it in a few installments."

He didn't want her money and he resented the tone she'd taken. "As you said, I had the locks fixed of my own accord, so if you can't afford it, don't bother."

"I didn't say I can't afford it." She sounded pissed and that made him pissed. So much for going out of his way to help someone.

"Okay, then. Whatever." Shit, now he sounded like one of his sisters in a mood. "Pay me whenever you can and good luck finding Muffin." He disconnected the phone before she could say anything more, dumped it on his desk and stared at it.

Well, that was a first. He'd never hung up on anyone in his life. Especially not a woman. But something about Chelsea had him doing crazy things. He ran a hand through his hair and groaned, fighting the urge to call her back and apologize.

Chapter 5

"What do you want?" Callum looked up from his desk a couple of days later at Sophie, who was standing in his office doorway glaring at him, her arms folded across her chest.

"A promotion. To win the lottery. Prince Charming to whisk me off my feet. A never-ending supply of cake. But for you to stop acting like a moody bitch for a couple of days would be a nice start."

He leaned back in his seat and held his hands out in surrender. "What's that supposed to mean?"

Sophie stepped inside, closing the door behind her. "Big brother, I know your heart is breaking and all that and Mom said we all need to treat you with extra TLC. But the way you spoke to that customer you just served…" She paused and raised her eyebrows at him.

"Not acceptable. I don't want to have to give you a written warning."

He rolled his eyes but thought back to that customer. "She had no idea about whiskey, and I didn't have time to listen to her uncle's life history to find out what bottle she should buy him for his birthday."

"Callum, Callum, Callum…it is our job to *teach* people about whiskey and also to listen. Listening is a skill anyone involved in the selling of alcohol must fine-tune or did you learn nothing from our dear dad?"

"Fine." He sighed. "You're right. I was a little terse with that woman. Sorry."

"You're forgiven. Just don't come into my tasting room and act like such a grump again."

He nodded his acquiescence. Sophie was right, they couldn't afford to lose customers. "Is there anything else?" he asked, when she still didn't make a move to go. Maybe she really did want a promotion; although he wasn't sure how that would work. He guessed he could give her a better title—director of sales and marketing or something—her own office, maybe a gold plaque on the door?

"No, except I just want you to know that I am here if you want to talk. You know…about Bailey and everything. If you ask me it's a crappy time to dump someone, right before Thanksgiving, not long till Christmas."

"It was a mutual breakup."

"That's not the way Bailey tells it." Sophie shrugged. "Look, maybe you should take a few days off to tend your broken heart?"

"What? And leave you in charge?" he scoffed.

She picked a pen up off his desk and hurled it at him.

Grinning, he ducked just in time. "Thanks for your concern, little sis, but I promise you my heart is not broken. I'll be fine. I've been grumpy because of work, not Bailey." Another lie; he'd been grumpy because he couldn't get that woman—that Breakup Girl, Chelsea Porter—out of his head. He'd lost count of the number of times he'd almost called her these past few days to see if she'd found her dog yet.

"What we all need is to sit down and have a proper meeting about our options," Sophie said, switching from sister mode to professional mode. "You know I'm on your side and think your new ideas are fabulous; we just need to convince Mom, Blair and Quinn." Their other siblings, silent partners in the distillery, would go along with whatever the majority decided. That said, Callum had big plans to get Lachlan a lot more involved in the family business, as well.

He nodded. "Do you want to set a date and gather the troops?" Blair and Quinn were more likely to listen to Sophie; as the youngest in the family by three minutes and twenty-seven seconds, she had certain privileges.

"Sure. Consider it done."

Sophie stood up to leave but as she put her hand on the doorknob to open it, Callum couldn't help telling Sophie what his mom had said. "Do you know Mom thinks you might be a lesbian?"

"What?" She spun around, her eyes sparkling at this news.

He merely nodded, amused.

She rubbed her hands together in obvious glee. "I could have a *lot* of fun with this. Thanks, brother dear."

And then she opened the door and practically skipped through it.

Callum let out a heavy breath and turned back to his computer screen, wondering which idea he should push on, or rather *sell to*, his family first. Some of his innovations would require more time and planning, like expanding the restaurant and also starting to grow their own grain; others wouldn't take much to get started but could increase revenue almost immediately. If they acted quickly and launched a McKinnel's Distillery merchandise line, they might even be able to cash in on the upcoming festive season or maybe that was rushing things.

Still, he'd start with that idea. It wouldn't affect Blair in the production department or Quinn in their warehouse as sales would be made in the shop—Sophie's domain—where they already sold their various types of bourbon.

He'd opened PowerPoint to start a presentation for the meeting when his cell rang. Not planning to answer, he glanced nonchalantly at it to see another unknown number. It wasn't Chelsea because, against his better judgment, he'd saved her number after the last time she'd called. But dammit, he was curious and thus snatched it up to answer before it rang off.

"Hello, Callum McKinnel speaking," he barked down the line, irritated by the interruption.

"Hello," came a hesitant voice. "I'm Lee, calling from the animal shelter in Sisters about your dog. Someone found him wandering in a field not far from here and has just brought him in."

His heart shooting to his throat, Callum sat bolt up-right. "You've found Muffin? Is he…okay?"

"He was a little ravenous, so we fed him, and a little dirty—he's obviously been living rough for a few days—but aside from that, he's healthy. Would you like to come in and pick him up?"

"Are you sure it's him?" Callum didn't want to call Chelsea with the good news if he wasn't 100 percent sure. "Is he wearing his name tag? He's not actually my dog, he's a…friend's, but there's a contact number on his collar." Probably best if they called Chelsea directly. Probably best if he stayed well clear of the dog and its owner.

"I'm sorry, he wasn't wearing a collar when he was found. But he matches the description you left with us perfectly."

Callum sighed and tapped his pen against the desk. "I'll be there in half an hour."

"We'll see you then," said the woman before disconnecting.

Wondering what the hell had come over him, Callum ran a hand through his hair and stood, grabbing his keys and checking his wallet was in his pocket as he headed out. He went through the tasting room on his way outside and called to Sophie who was counting stock.

"Can you put any calls through to my cell?"

Sophie glanced up. "Where are you going?"

He winked at his little sister. "Taking a few hours for my broken heart. Back soon." And then he left before she had the chance to ask any questions.

Forty minutes later, Callum parked his SUV in the lot at the front of the animal shelter. As he climbed out of the vehicle and strode toward the front entrance, a cacophony of barks, squawks and mewls grew louder.

"Hi, how may I help you?" asked a woman behind a counter the moment he stepped inside. He recognized her voice as belonging to the person who'd called him.

"I'm Callum McKinnel, here to collect... Muffin." Why couldn't Chelsea's dog have a more masculine name?

"Fabulous." The woman beamed. "I'll go grab him."

As he waited, Callum glanced around the reception area. There were a couple of cages on one wall with kittens inside and across the other side of room, one entire wall was plastered with pictures of animals in need of adoption, all of which looked bedraggled and lonely. Their sad eyes felt as if they were looking directly at him and a lump formed in his throat. He found himself speaking to the photos on the wall.

"Sorry, but I'm not in the market for a pet. I'm rarely home and I wouldn't have the time to walk you."

"You could always adopt a cat," said the woman, startling him as she returned. "They are quite content with their own company for a few hours a day and don't require you to exercise them."

Ashamed to be caught talking to himself, he ignored her words, lowering his gaze to the mutt at her feet. A gorgeous golden cocker spaniel that looked up at him with wide, wary eyes.

"Muffin?" he said, and the dog cocked his ears up slightly. Well, as much as was possible with those long, floppy, furry things. Callum dropped onto his haunches and held out his hand. "How you doing, buddy? Ready to go home?"

The word *home* seemed to win the dog over and he launched himself at Callum, almost knocking him backward as he started licking his face. The animal-shelter woman laughed as she handed him the dog's lead. "Someone's happy to see you."

He'd be even happier to see Chelsea, Callum thought, his heart rate accelerating at the thought. Once he'd signed a few papers and made a donation to the shelter in lieu of adopting half a dozen strays, he and Muffin were finally in his car ready to go. The moment he turned the ignition to start the SUV, Muffin leaped across the gearbox and into his lap, once again slobbering all over Callum's face.

"Buddy," he said, pushing the dog away. "Boundaries."

But it appeared Muffin didn't have such things and somehow Callum managed to drive all the way back to Chelsea's house with her dog sitting in his lap. By the time he arrived at her place, he was halfway to falling in love with the stupid mutt, not that he'd ever admit that to anyone.

"Come on, you," he said, holding tight on the lead as Muffin jumped down from the SUV. He closed the door behind them and they started up the short path to Chelsea's door. Only as he was about to ring the bell did he consider the fact that she might not be home. She could be out, busy dumping some other poor dude. He found he didn't like that idea, and not because of the actual task, but rather because some other guy would be spending time with her.

Shaking his head of that thought, he jabbed his finger into the doorbell. Approximately ten seconds later, the door opened and Chelsea appeared. Their eyes met, and heat washed over him at the sight of her in skinny jeans and a fitted sweater, but she did not seem so happy to see him. Then Muffin yanked forward and assaulted his owner in much the same manner he'd assaulted Callum at the shelter. The annoyance in Chelsea's eyes was quickly replaced with joy and delight as she wrapped her arms around the dog. Tears, he assumed of the happy variety, streamed down her face as she and Muffin reacquainted themselves.

Callum stood awkwardly on the porch, feeling like a third wheel, yet at the same time pretty pleased with himself for reuniting Chelsea with her beloved mutt. Finally, after what felt like a couple of decades at least, she looked up and the smile she gave him almost knocked him off balance.

"Thank you," she said, her tone dripping with genuine appreciation.

He steadied himself on the doorjamb, feeling as if finding this dog was the best thing he'd done in all thirty-five years of his existence. "My pleasure."

"Where was he?" She straightened, but kept one hand caressing Muffin's head. The dog made a sound almost like a cat purring and Callum couldn't blame him. Who knows what kind of noises he'd make if Chelsea ran her hands through his hair.

He cleared his throat. "At a shelter in Sisters. A jogger found him this morning in a field. He wasn't wearing his collar and I didn't know your number the other day when I called all the shelters, so they rang me." Why the heck did he sound like he was trying to explain himself?

"Oh thank God. That must have been the only shelter I didn't call." She looked almost as if she were about to kiss him, but...no such luck. "And thank *you*. Again. I'm sorry I was a little rude the other day when I called. It's just... I'm not good with needing people. I don't like to feel indebted, but that was no reason to be awful to you when you were just trying to help. Can I blame my rudeness on being worried about this boy?"

"What rudeness?" he asked with a smile.

"Thank you. And it looks like once again I'm in your debt. How am I ever going to repay you for reuniting me with Muffin?"

It was possibly just one of those things people said, but his mind couldn't help conjuring all sorts of ways she *could* repay him. Heat crept to his cheeks and other less visible parts of his body; at least he hoped they weren't visible but with the effect she had on him, who could tell?

"Come to lunch with me on Thanksgiving," he blurted.

She blinked. "Where would we go?"

Jeez, he hadn't thought this one through at all. He'd be ostracized from the family if he didn't show at home for their traditional lunch. Then again, maybe bringing a date would prove to his meddling mother once and for all that he really wasn't too cut up about the whole Bailey thing. "My parents' place. Mom's house now, I guess. You'd be doing me a massive favor as Mom is hell-bent on finding me another girlfriend ASAP. I want to show her I can get my own dates."

She rubbed her lips together. Then, "So this would be a *date*?"

A big part of him wanted to say yes but he didn't want to lead her on. "A fake one, to keep my mother from worrying about me. I'm not ready for another relationship yet, but she can't seem to get that into her head." This part was true—he needed to put everything he had into the distillery for the foreseeable future and that didn't leave time for love and romance.

"Oh. Okay. Because I couldn't date a client."

He smirked. "Isn't Bailey technically your client? And is that a yes?"

She shrugged. "You have a big family, don't you?"

"Pretty big, but don't worry, they're not too scary. My little sister hasn't bitten anyone since she was three."

Chelsea laughed at that and he honestly couldn't recall anything ever sounding quite so beautiful. He wanted to tell her a joke and hear that sound again. "Okay."

"Okay?" he asked.

"Okay." She nodded. "It's the least I can do for you after everything you've done for me. But I'll only come if I can bring Muffin. I'm never letting him out of my sight again."

An unbearable urge to kiss her came over him, but he shoved his hands in his pockets instead. "I'm sure that would be fine. We McKinnels love animals, especially dogs."

"Right. Good then." She met his gaze and then quickly looked away.

"Yep. Good." He should make a move but his legs didn't seem to get the message. "I'll pick you up about noon on Thursday, then?"

She nodded. "Can I bring anything?"

He shook his head. "Just yourself. And Muffin of course. Between Mom and my brother Lachlan, we'll have enough food to feed an army anyway."

She smiled and then they stared at each other a little longer. Until it started to get embarrassing. Until he told his legs if they didn't start walking, he'd chop them off. "Okay. Thursday then."

"Thursday," she repeated.

And, before he did something really pathetic, like lean forward and kiss her, he turned and jogged back to his car.

Chapter 6

As Chelsea waited for Callum to pick her up, she nervously paced the length of the front porch with Muffin chasing at her heels, thinking this was some kind of new game. Perhaps he was right, because she had no idea why she'd agreed to go to the McKinnels' Thanksgiving lunch. It was like she'd rolled a dice and it had told her to go, so she'd said "sure, why not?"

But now she was harboring serious second thoughts.

She should have bought him a box of chocolates as a way of saying thanks for finding her dog. Problem was, Muffin was worth way more than a few sweets. It would have to be a very big box to come close to showing her gratitude, and anyway, there was no way she'd have been able to say anything but yes when Callum McKinnel hit her with *that* smile. It was lethal. Especially set in that sexy, short beard thing he had going on. Chelsea hadn't thought herself a fan of beards, but simply thinking about his had all the organs in her body doing gymnastics.

With a sigh, she sank her teeth into her lower lip and stopped pacing. No point in getting all hot and bothered. What was done was done. This was nothing but a fake date and it would pay for her to remember that. Callum had made that 100 percent clear when he'd asked her. And because of Muffin, she'd felt obliged to help out.

Yes, right, you keep telling yourself that's the reason, Chelsea.

A horn sounded and she turned to see a black SUV pulling into her driveway. *Callum's SUV.* Seconds later he jumped down from the driver's side and Muffin flew off the porch and galloped toward him. Chelsea's stomach did a final tumble turn as she forced her hand up to wave. He grinned and waved back as he opened his arms to receive her dog. Stupid, but her throat clogged with emotion as Callum let Muffin slobber all over him, and then, she snapped out of her silliness.

"Muffin! Leave Callum alone," she called as she grabbed her purse and the bouquet of flowers she'd bought for his mother off the porch chair.

"It's fine. We're old friends." He looked over the top of Muffin's head as she approached them and met her gaze head-on. "Isn't this how you greet all your old friends?"

She couldn't help but grin. He had a way of making her feel comfortable and skittish all at the same time. "Thanks for picking me up. Sorry for putting you out. I don't know why I didn't offer to drive myself." Something she'd been wondering all morning, but she'd been so flummoxed by the idea of a date with him—albeit a fake one—when he'd asked, that she hadn't been thinking straight.

"Nonsense." He stood up and Muffin made a tiny pining sound. "That would have made Mom suspicious. A gentleman *always* picks up his date. You look lovely by the way."

She swallowed and her skin slowly caught on fire as he gave a subtle glance up and down her body. "Thanks."

"That color suits you." He was of course referring to the red, which was the predominant color on the dress she'd spent all morning umming and ahhing over. A dress not really practical for the cool November weather but which she'd paired with some leggings and boots to make it more so. The look on his face made any temperature discomfort worth it. She just hoped she wasn't overdressed. Or underdressed. She'd totally forgotten to ask him the dress code for his family lunch.

"Thanks," she said, resisting the urge to pull her winter coat tightly around her. She liked the way he looked at her but it also terrified her. Callum was wearing smart, navy blue jeans and a marled gray crew-neck sweater with the collar of a flannel shirt peeking out the top—a unique combination of smart and casual, with a massive dose of sexiness to boot.

He strode around and opened the passenger side door for her but Muffin jumped up first. They both laughed.

"He's been a little clingy since he came home," she explained. "I think he's scared we might go without him."

"Never," Callum said as Muffin jumped over onto

the driver's seat. "In the back, buddy." He tried to encourage the dog to do as he asked, but Muffin refused to budge.

"Maybe we can put these flowers in the back and he can sit with me in the front?" Chelsea suggested. She'd be squashed, her dress and coat would end up covered in golden fur but…anything for Muffin.

"Let's give it a shot." Callum grinned as he took the flowers from her. "Are these for me? You shouldn't have."

"I didn't. They're for your mom, to say thanks for having me to lunch."

"Good move." He winked. "She'll like you." Then, he opened the back door and laid them carefully on the seat.

A few minutes later the three of them were settled in the front of the car—Chelsea in the passenger seat, Callum in the driver's seat and Muffin happily perched on his lap. She'd protested and tried to encourage the dog onto hers, but Callum had insisted it was fine.

"We drove like this all the way back from the shelter the other day," he told her.

She gave in and they started their journey toward Jewell Rock, which was if anything even more beautiful than the picturesque town of Bend.

"Have the police found out anything about your burglary?" he asked.

"No. They followed up on a few names I gave them, but as we suspected, they're pretty certain it's just kids fooling around."

"Little shits." Callum shook his head and Chelsea found her eyes lingering on the way his hands caressed the steering wheel. To try to distract herself from this sight and also in an attempt to alleviate some of her nerves about attending a big family Thanksgiving, she tried to make useful conversation. "So, can you give me a quick 101 on your family?"

He glanced at her with those big soulful sea-green eyes. "101?"

"You know, a quick course in everything I need to know."

"Ah." His smile widened and she wasn't sure it was because of what she'd said or thinking about his family. "Okay. Well, I'm the oldest—but you already know me."

Not as well as she wanted to, but she pushed that thought aside because this was a fake date and everything.

He continued. "Next is Lachlan. He's divorced but has two kids. Hallie lives with her mother in California and Hamish lives with Lachlan and my mom."

Chelsea frowned. "They took a child each in the split?"

"It's complicated. Hamish has cerebral palsy and his mom couldn't handle that he wasn't perfect. It put a great strain on the marriage and when they split, she only wanted to take Hallie with her."

"That's awful." Her eyes watered as she spoke, her heart aching for that poor little boy. She knew all too well how it felt not to be wanted, especially by a mom who should love you unconditionally.

"Yeah, I know. It turns out not all moms have that maternal love-your-child-no-matter-what thing built in."

"No, they don't." Chelsea hoped he didn't hear the

bitterness in her tone. "Lachlan sounds like a good guy though."

"He is. The best…and an amazing chef too. You haven't eaten until you've tasted one of his creations." Callum cleared his throat. "Then there's Blair—he's our head distiller and makes whiskey almost as good as our dad did. Then again, he did learn from the best."

"Is Blair married?"

"Divorced," Callum said. "Only his split was much more amicable. And no kids involved, which I guess helps."

"Hmm."

"What about you?" he asked. "Do you have many siblings?"

"Nope. None." Although she'd always wished differently. Watching endless episodes of *The Brady Bunch* when she was little had made her crave a big warm family of her own. Or rather, a warm, loving family— she had enough aunts and uncles and cousins, just none who wanted her. "Who's next?"

"That'd be Owen, although he's been called Mac since high school. You've probably heard of him."

She hadn't until the last few days when she'd been Googling the hell out of his family. "The soccer player?"

"That's the one. After kicking that own goal against Brazil in the Centennial Copa, which stopped the US making the finals, he's a bit of a mess at the moment. Mom should be putting her energies into worrying about him more than me."

"Is he going to return to soccer?"

Callum shrugged one shoulder. "Who knows? He doesn't want to talk about that, or anything else come to think of it, with any of us. He might not even show up today. Surely, you'd rather talk about something more interesting than my dysfunctional brothers."

She laughed. "Don't you have sisters too?"

He didn't ask how she knew—she guessed he just assumed that everyone knew the McKinnels, which was probably true if you were a local. "Yes, Annabel and Sophie. And they are gorgeous. But don't tell them I told you, or I will have to kill you."

"I bet you're one of those really protective big brothers, aren't you?" she said, trying not to grin from ear to ear. Callum loved his mom, his sisters and her dog... She was heading into danger territory and needed to get a grip.

"Muffin, stop licking my ear. I can't see the road."

Chastised, Muffin desisted, slumping down and falling promptly asleep across the gearbox and the two of their laps. Chelsea absentmindedly fondled his fur, wishing it was just Callum she was spending the day with. In spite of his massive sex appeal, she felt comfortable with him. The thought, however, of sitting around a table with all his siblings made her palms sweat almost as much as it intrigued her. She had no experience whatsoever with big, close-knit families.

"Sorry, I'm probably boring you senseless talking about my family," he said, as if sensing her nerves. "Tell me something exciting about yourself."

She snorted in a quite unladylike manner. "There is absolutely nothing exciting to tell. I am the definition of boring."

"I don't believe that for a second." He paused, then said, "Who is the old man in the photo on your desk?"

A lump formed in her throat making it impossible to answer.

"Sorry. I wasn't snooping that day. I saw the photo when I was tidying up."

"It's okay." The thought of him overstepping boundaries had never crossed her mind; he'd been nothing but kind and honorable in their interactions so far. She inhaled deeply. "That's my grandfather. He died just before I moved to Bend. I lived with him from when I was about fifteen until then. I was his caregiver."

"I see. I'm sorry." He looked at her with an expression that made her heart swell. "You must miss him. What was his ailment?"

She swallowed. "Alcohol."

Awkward silence reigned for a few moments as if Callum didn't know what to say to that. She felt a little bad because her family's alcohol issues weren't his fault; then again, if people like *his* family didn't make their living from alcohol, then others couldn't buy it. They weren't much better than tobacco companies in her opinion.

Finally, he said, "That must have been very hard on you."

"Yes, but he loved me the best he could, so I wanted to be there for him." Being with Grandpa had been far better than living with her parents and then being shifted from one family member to the next, which is what she'd done until she'd finally landed with him. The easygoing mood that had hung in the air while he spoke about his family had evaporated and she racked her brain for a way to get it back. Her fingers in Muffin's fur gave her an idea.

"You said your family love animals. Does your mom have any at her place?"

"Not right now, but there was always at least one four-legged creature hanging around while we were kids."

For the rest of the drive to the distillery, they spoke about the various pets the McKinnels had owned over the years. She loved listening to the anecdotes Callum shared about the scrapes he and his siblings had gotten into with their furry friends and it also relaxed her, so that by the time they arrived at his mom's house, her hands weren't sweating quite so badly.

"Gorgeous place," she said as Callum opened the passenger door for her and offered her his hand. It was warm and he was such a gentleman; she'd honestly thought they were extinct, like dinosaurs. Muffin had already leaped out the driver's side after Callum and was now snuffling around the garden in the shallow layer of snow that had fallen overnight.

She gazed widemouthed at one of the prettiest houses she'd ever seen. Huge, but not showy. It was in the same style as the distillery, which they'd passed on their way in. There was a beautiful swimming pool right out front. She shivered at the way the water glistened icily right now, but in summer it would be lovely.

"Yeah, I guess it is," Callum said, not letting go of her hand as he shut the door behind her. "One of those things you take for granted when you see it every day. Now, you ready?"

No. But it was too late to chicken out, so she nodded and let him lead her up the garden path toward the front door, Muffin bounding ahead of them and then lagging behind when he found something else new to investigate.

The door was flung open a few steps before they reached it and in the doorway stood a middle-aged woman who had to be Nora McKinnel. She was petite and thin, well groomed in bright clothes. When she threw her arms around Callum, Chelsea could see the love in their embrace. Three seconds later, Nora caught her off guard by throwing her arms around Chelsea, as well.

"You must be Chelsea. Callum said he was bringing a *friend*. Any friend of Callum's is always welcome. So glad you could join us."

"Thanks," Chelsea said, flummoxed and a tad uncomfortable in the stranger's arms.

Nora pulled back and glanced down at Muffin who had inserted himself between the two women. "And who is this delightful thing?"

"This is Muffin. I hope you don't mind, but Callum said I could bring him."

"Mind?" Nora's eyes gleamed. "I'm delighted. Come on in, little fella."

Muffin didn't need to be asked twice, he bounded inside, following the noise of conversation and laughter. Nora stepped aside so that Callum and Chelsea could enter, and as he closed the door behind them, Chelsea's gaze lingered on the large, framed, happy-family snap on the wall. Beneath the photo hung a sign: *This house runs on love, laughter and a lot of whiskey.* Funny, the houses she'd lived in as a kid had been pretty much the same, just without the love and the laughter.

Nora followed her gaze. "Not a bad-looking bunch,

my tribe, are they? Of course this was taken a few years
ago now. We're all a little more wrinkly these days. I
think it was taken on the twins' twenty-first birthday."
She reached her finger out and touched it on the man
that had to be Callum's dad, and Chelsea didn't know
whether she could offer sympathies or not. "Anyway,
come along. Everyone else is already here."

Nora took her hand and led her down the hallway
into a massive country-style kitchen flooded with people, the biggest table she'd ever seen sitting right in the
heart of it. As she took in the beautiful decorations on
the table that had already been set, the din died down
as everyone else stopped talking to look at her. For a
few seconds, Chelsea felt like a new exhibit brought
into the zoo, but Nora introduced her as "Callum's new
friend"—again accentuating the *friend*—and everyone
rushed forward to greet her, introducing themselves and
talking right over the top of each other.

It was hard to hold on to her nerves when they were
all so warm and welcoming. She found herself falling immediately in love with each and every one of
the McKinnels, although she didn't know how she was
going to keep track of them all. Callum took her jacket,
asked in her ear if she was okay and then went off to
hang it somewhere as the youngest McKinnel said, "You
can sit next to me if you want, Chelsea."

She smiled at the boy who looked about ten years
old and whose speech was slightly slurred. "That would
be wonderful."

He scrambled off his seat and pulled back the chair
next to him, crashing it against his own chair in the
process. "I'm Hamish," he said as they both sat back

down. "Is this your dog?" Muffin had finished doing
the rounds and come to sit between them. "I love dogs."

"He sure is. I think he likes you."

"Everyone likes Hamish, don't they, buddy?" Callum
said, returning and taking the seat on the other side of
Chelsea. The little boy beamed at his uncle's approval,
and Chelsea lost another tiny piece of her heart. It had
been a mistake to come here.

"Can I get you a drink?" Callum asked, gesturing
to the beverage options already laid out on the table.
There was wine and beer like at most celebrations but
it was a bottle of whiskey, alongside the pumpkin decorations, that took prime spot in the middle of this table.
She got the feeling the wine and beer were there more
for the benefit of the *non*-family—herself and Blair's
ex-wife, Claire, who was sipping a glass of wine. Yes,
that situation was weird.

Chelsea shook her head. "I'm fine right now."

Conversation flowed easily around the big table
as the family members took turns taking orders from
Lachlan, who wore a white apron and gave directions
as if they were in a Michelin-starred restaurant. The
only person who didn't say much, the only person who'd
merely nodded in greeting at Chelsea when she'd arrived, was Mac, who sat at one end of the table nursing
a glass of bourbon. He caught her looking at him and
threw her a dirty look.

"Can I do anything to help?" Chelsea asked, glancing away from Mac to Nora.

"Don't be silly," said the sister who had introduced
herself as Annabel. She had a lovely smile and a face

like a pretty pixie, similar but not quite the same as Sophie, her twin. She looked very fit, which was likely
down to the fact she was a firefighter. "Guests don't
have to lift a finger in this house, do they, Mom?"

Nora smiled and shook her head.

At the mention of guests the doorbell rang and perplexed expressions were exchanged among the family. All except Sophie who shot up from her seat and
clapped her hands together. "That'll be my *special
friend*," she said, looking at her mother and then winking at Callum as she shot out of the room.

Chelsea leaned close to Callum. "What was that
about?"

He leaned even closer and she tried to focus on his
reply, rather than the warm, lovely tickle of his breath
against her ear. "Sophie's having a bit of fun with
Mom," he whispered. "I'll fill you in later."

She shivered at the way he said *later* and then told
herself to get a grip. It was simply a figure of speech—
fake dates didn't do *later*.

Sophie returned, her big eyes sparkling and her face
lit up with a smile as she glanced at the beautiful redheaded girl attached to her hand. "Family," she said, "I'd
like you to meet Storie. Isn't she just, something else?"

Once Storie had been welcomed into the fold and
fussed over by Nora McKinnel, the food was brought
to the table. Granted the McKinnels were a large family, but Chelsea reckoned this feast could feed the entire
population of Jewell Rock and half of Bend, as well. At
the sight and aromas in front of her, she worried about
her taste buds going into cardiac arrest.

Lachlan, obviously in his element, gave a rundown of what he'd made, listing classic Thanksgiving cuisine—such as roast turkey and green bean casserole—as well as contemporary dishes that sounded amazing...well, all except the baked ham with bourbon glaze. She'd be steering clear of that. He seemed particularly proud of his fall harvest squash salad and later, when she tasted it, Chelsea could see why. The man truly was a genius in the kitchen.

"I want to thank you all for coming here today," Nora began before anyone touched any of the dishes. She sighed, a bittersweet smile on her face. "As our first Thanksgiving without your dad, I know it might be hard to find things to be grateful for, but looking around this table at your father's legacy, I consider myself very lucky. You are all my blessings."

Chelsea blushed when Nora looked her way, seemingly including even her. What would it feel like to be loved like that?

"Anyway," Nora continued, bending and picking something off the floor by her feet, "you might need to think a little more creatively when you fill this in this year, but remember, there is always something to be thankful for. I can't wait to read your entries. Callum," she said, looking to him, "can you please say grace?"

He nodded and then reached out to take Chelsea's hand. Hamish took her other one and she followed the family's lead, closing her eyes as Callum led them in Thanksgiving prayer. She'd never been much of a God person but the way Callum sounded when he prayed almost turned her into a believer. She knew his voice would be haunting her dreams—*read, fantasies*—when she closed her eyes that night.

Callum tried to keep his voice normal as he went through the motions of saying grace, yet inside his chest tightened because he shouldn't be the one doing this. Mom had taken Dad's place in welcoming everyone and now he was taking over in the traditional prayer. Everything felt wrong.

"Amen," he finished, unable to recall what he'd actually said and hoping it made some kind of sense. He looked up to see a tear strolling down his mom's cheek and accepted her smile of approval by offering one back. Firsts after the death of a loved one sucked big-time and as his father had only died a couple of months ago, they still had many more to get through. Christmas. His parents' wedding anniversary. Dad's birthday. He blinked, not wanting to think further than today, and then he realized everyone was staring at him in expectation.

"What?"

"Aren't you going to carve the turkey?" Annabel asked.

He shook his head. Feeling the burden of being the head of the business was one thing, but Lachlan, as second oldest, could help shoulder some of the familial responsibilities at least. "I think our esteemed chef should do the honors."

Lachlan was all too happy to oblige and they all watched, mouths watering as he did so. When he was done, it was everyone for themselves as dishes were passed around the table and food served onto plates.

Chelsea appeared a little bemused and also somewhat terrified by the way everyone attacked the lunch. Callum smiled, guessing that as an only child she'd never had to fight for her share of much.

"Can I get you a drink now?" he asked Chelsea, gesturing to the wine and whiskey on the table as he realized she was the only person at the table without a glass. Except for Hamish of course; he drank his orange juice from a plastic tumbler.

She smiled but shook her head. "No thanks. I don't drink."

"What? *Ever?*" He hadn't meant to sound so startled and regretted his outburst the second it left his mouth, especially because it drew the attention of his entire family. They all ceased chewing and looked at her.

"Never." Chelsea, crimson rushing to her cheeks, shook her head. "I come from a long line of alcoholics. It's not worth the risk."

Awkward silence descended across the table. Callum could have kicked himself, but his mom did the honors for him, no doubt thinking he should know this about his date.

"Fair enough," he said, reaching under the table and squeezing her hand to show he understood her decision. And strangely he felt a prick of guilt, as if somehow her family's addiction was on him. Which was ridiculous— the McKinnels produced whiskey for people who appreciated good flavor and enjoyed a social drink. It wasn't his fault if some people couldn't hold their liquor. "Can I get you a soda or something instead?"

"Thanks." She squeezed back and then extracted

her hand, reminding him this wasn't real. "A club soda would be great."

He stood, went to pour her a drink and was thankful that by the time he returned, chatter had resumed around the table. Claire, who sat across from Chelsea, had engaged her in conversation and they were talking about their favorite chick flicks or something. He'd always liked Claire, from the moment Blair had brought her home in high school, and he had no idea what had gone wrong with their seemingly perfect marriage.

The meal progressed as it always did in the McKinnel household—everyone talking loudly, multiple conversations taking place across the table like multiple games of tennis on one court. Chelsea appeared to be enjoying herself, smiling at the jokes and politely answering all the questions asked of her, not that they were all that personal. The only hiccup was when Mac spoke for the first time in at least an hour and asked how the two of them had met.

She looked to him for clarification and Callum cleared his throat, buying time. "Through Bailey actually. Chelsea worked with her once." And he left it at that, despite the few raised eyebrows. Let them all think what they wanted to think; he was simply glad her presence meant his mom hadn't used the opportunity of having everyone around to harp on about his needing to find another girlfriend if he didn't want to end up old, gray and alone. There was no such thing as letting the grass grow in his mom's mind, at least not when the possibility of grandchildren was involved.

In between the clearing of the main meal and the bringing of dessert to the table, Mom's Thanksgiving journal landed in Chelsea's lap. She shook her head and made to pass it on to him, but Mom objected loudly.

"Oh, Chelsea, you have to fill it in too. It's tradition that whoever eats at this table does so."

Callum knew it was futile to argue.

Chelsea looked uncertain, but then raised the pen and, after a few moments, started scrawling something. He was glad he was next in line as he found himself curious to see what she had written. Normally he wasn't much of an inquisitive soul—unless it involved work— but for some reason he wanted to know anything and everything about her. While eating he'd kept thinking back to their conversation in the car and wishing he'd jumped on the chance to ask about her parents, to find out what had happened to them and why she'd ended up living with her grandfather.

When she passed him the book, their fingers brushed against each other. He smiled as he took it and then looked down at the open page. She had beautiful handwriting. Neat and easy to read yet flowery at the same time.

I'm thankful for the opportunity to share a meal with this wonderful family.

Hah! She might not think they were so wonderful if she spent much longer with them, but her comment warmed his heart nonetheless. It took him a lot longer to decide what to write.

I'm thankful that I'm finally controlling the reins of the distillery, seemed in bad taste and would break his mom's heart. Besides, he wasn't thankful for his dad's death. He glanced at Lachlan. *Thankful for a brother who can cook?* Then to Sophie, who was now practically sitting in Storie's lap. *Thankful for a sister with a sense of humor?* Finally he turned his head and found Chelsea watching him. He settled on "I'm thankful for life's surprises and unexpected twists," and then passed the book to his mom.

She read all the entries, a massive grin on her face. After the thankful journal came dessert and, once again, Lachlan had outdone himself with far more food than necessary: pumpkin and ginger aqua fresca to drink and grilled stuffed caramel apples, pumpkin pie and, the best dish of all, bread and butter pudding with bourbon glaze. Tasting it only confirmed what Callum had been thinking these past few months, and he couldn't contain his excitement.

"I think this could be one of the signature dishes in our new restaurant," he said to Lachlan. "Would you consider quitting your job in town and expanding the distillery's café into something truly special? Sophie and I have been talking and we believe a proper restaurant at the distillery could really take us to the next level."

Sophie gave him a look that said, Is now really the time or place? But he ignored it. Sometimes you had to follow your gut.

Lachlan leaned back in his seat and considered. "A restaurant?"

"You'd be in charge."

"I always wanted my own restaurant. Do you really think the distillery can support one?"

Callum shook his head, speaking honestly. "I'm hoping this restaurant will support the distillery, but it could be really good for you too. Being the boss will give you much more flexibility in your cooking. Say you'll give it some thought."

Lachlan gave a quick nod. "I definitely will."

Quinn cleared his throat. "And do the rest of us get any say in this new venture? If we're struggling, shouldn't we be focusing on what we already do well? Improving that even more? We're supposed to be about whiskey, not food."

"I love the idea," Annabel said. "Lord knows this town needs more good places to go eat."

Quinn glared at her. "You could always learn to cook."

Annabel shrugged. "And why would I want to do that when there are people, like Lachlan, who do it so much better?"

Nora piped up, a tight smile on her face. "As much as I love the distillery, let's leave business to after Thanksgiving, shall we?"

"Sorry, Mom," Callum said, secretly stoked by Lachlan's initial response.

At that moment, Hamish squealed in delight and everyone looked to him.

"Are you feeding that dog under the table?" Lachlan asked, his tone half amused, half reprimanding.

"I love him," Hamish exclaimed, shattering the tension brought on by discussing business at the table.

"That accounts for why he's been so quiet," Chelsea said. "I did think he was being unusually good."

Everyone laughed and then dug into the dessert.

"I can't eat another mouthful," announced Blair later, when only a few crumbs were left on the serving plates. Desserts didn't stand a chance when the McKinnel clan got together.

"Me neither," agreed the twins, speaking as one as they were frequently prone to do.

"Shall we go into the living room and get on with the fun and games?" Sophie added.

All agreed this was a good idea, so, after a joint effort of clearing the table and stacking the first load into the dishwasher, they retreated into the other room.

"Are you a movie or a board-game person?" Callum asked Chelsea.

She looked confused.

"It's our family tradition," he clarified. "Some of us play games and the others watch a movie. The choice is yours. I'll do whatever you want."

She chose the movie and so he led her over to the sofa and tugged her down beside him. It was so easy to pretend she was his date; half the time he forgot it was an act. Muffin collapsed at her feet, also full from lunch and Hamish, still besotted with the dog, sat beside him on the floor at Callum and Chelsea's feet. As usual, Hamish chose the movie—*The Avengers*—and Callum couldn't help but notice and admire the way Chelsea listened intently to his rambling commentary. Although he and Chelsea didn't speak much, Callum found himself playing the part by stretching out and wrapping his arm around her shoulder. She gave him a brief surprised look and then leaned into him and rested her head on his shoulder. It fit there perfectly.

As the credits rolled up the screen, Nora announced, "It's time to Skype Granddad. Quinn, can you go grab my laptop and set it up?"

"Is that your mom's dad?" Chelsea whispered as everyone soon gathered around the coffee table, the computer perched on it, while Quinn placed the call.

"Yep." Callum nodded.

"Where does he live?"

"He's permanently cruising with a bunch of old friends these days it seems. He lived in the cottage here until my grandma died a few years back. He couldn't bear the emptiness and hasn't lived anywhere as such since."

"That's sweet," she said, then added, "in a sad way. If you know what I mean."

"I do." He squeezed her hand again as Granddad's face appeared large-as-life on the screen.

"He's quite a character," Chelsea said quietly to Callum when everyone had taken their turn speaking to the older man. "I can see where you all get it from."

"Are you calling my family eccentric?" he asked, not at all offended.

Before she could reply, bagpipe sounded across the room and she turned her head to follow the sound. There Blair stood, his elbow heaving and his cheeks red and puffy as he played. "Let's just say I don't know many people who can play the bagpipe, but I'd say cool rather than eccentric," she said.

Quinn heard her and came over to butt in to their conversation. In typical Quinn fashion, he flirted. "We are indeed a family of many talents. Well, some of us are—" he dug Callum in the side "—but you've chosen the wrong brother. Callum is as boring as they come. Do you want me to tell you what *my* talents are? Or maybe I could show you?"

"Or maybe you could take a hike." Callum glared daggers at his brother and then whisked Chelsea away.

"Sorry about Quinn," he said when he had her safely across to the other side of the room. "He thinks himself amusing and is the biggest flirt ever."

"I'm sure he's harmless."

Maybe, maybe not. Quinn had flirted with Claire before and after she and Blair got married and still did now that they were divorced. He'd been the same with Bailey—always leaning in to kiss her cheek or say suggestive things, trying to provoke Callum into explosion. Strangely, it had never bothered him as much when Quinn tried it on with Bailey, but today he'd seen red.

He'd kind of wanted to punch Quinn in the face.

As if his thoughts of Bailey had conjured her into existence, the doorbell rang again. This time Nora flitted off to answer it—more than a little tipsy after her fair share of whiskey—and returned a few moments later with Bailey and her parents, Marcia and Reginald, in tow.

Dammit. What were they doing here?

Of course, Callum guessed the answer. He hadn't told his mom till this morning that he was bringing a date, and she and her best friend had obviously been plotting to get him and Bailey back together. If it weren't for their moms' meddling ways, they'd probably never have become a couple in the first place.

"Who are they?" Chelsea whispered. At the same time Bailey glanced over and saw them alone in the corner.

He swallowed. Talk about awkward. Things were about to get interesting indeed.

Chapter 7

"As in Bailey *Sawyer*?" Chelsea tried to stop the wild beating of her heart but this was very, very bad. No wonder the woman was now glaring daggers across the room at them. Even if she had been the one to end the relationship, no female liked to think she'd been replaced quite so easily, and so quickly, as well. Chelsea only hoped Bailey wouldn't find out exactly who *she* was. "As in Bailey your ex-*fiancée*?"

Callum cleared his throat and nodded. "Yes. I assumed you two would have met, but I'm sorry. I didn't know Mom had invited her."

Chelsea felt sick—as if she were in danger of losing the massive lunch she'd devoured. "She's beautiful." In fact, Bailey was the absolute definition of perfection in a classic Audrey Hepburn kind of way. The big bright blue eyes that were still staring at them were framed with the longest, blackest eyelashes ever and set in a milky, blemish-free complexion. Ms. Sawyer had perfectly shaped eyebrows and the same could be said about her body, which was neither skinny nor fat. Curvy, that was the word—totally the opposite of the beanpole that Chelsea was.

Deep breaths, deep breaths. It would be fine—she and Bailey had never actually met, they'd only spoken on the phone, so hopefully the other woman wouldn't put two and two together. "She doesn't look very happy to see you with me."

"Hmm." Callum put his hand gently on her arm and gave her a distracted smile of apology. "Look, do you mind if I go over and have a quick chat?"

She found that she minded immensely, a spark of jealousy she'd never felt before kicking up inside her, but she nodded all the same. "I think that would be a good idea." He started to go and she reached to grab him back a moment. "If possible, could you not mention exactly who I am? My business reputation is on the line."

"Of course not."

He strode to the other side of the room where Hamish was currently wrapped around Bailey, offering an exuberant hug. And here Chelsea had been thinking she was special. Torturing herself, she watched as Bailey let go of Hamish and then stepped into Callum's embrace. The hug was quick, perhaps a little uncomfortable, and he kissed her on the cheek in a purely perfunctory manner, but still the action tore at Chelsea's heart.

"This is fun," said a droll voice coming up beside her. She turned to see Mac, looking on with a bemused expression. "The old and the new under one roof."

"So you do actually speak?" Chelsea blinked at him, trying to feign an apathetic attitude.

"When it amuses me." Mac took another sip from the glass that appeared to be permanently in his hand.

She'd lost track of the number of times he'd refilled it. Strange thing was he didn't have that smell of booze that had permeated her father's and grandfather's skin. And apart from his three-day stubble, he looked like he cared more about his appearance than either of them ever had. He wore his long chocolate brown hair in one of those man buns that were all the rage these days and, although they weren't her cup of tea, Chelsea had to admit that on him, it worked.

She couldn't help herself. "How long were they together?"

"Too long. Maybe since he was two and she was a few hours old."

When Chelsea's eyes widened, he elaborated, amusement twisting his lips ever so slightly upward. "It was practically an arranged marriage between our 'rents. Mom's handling the breakup a lot better than I thought."

Until Bailey's arrival, Chelsea had been enjoying herself far more than she'd imagined possible, enjoying the fantasy that she was part of this world, this family, actually someone Callum might look twice at. But Bailey *looked* a part of this family, as if she belonged here and had only briefly lost her way, and everyone, except maybe Callum and Mac, appeared happy to see her. Chelsea felt like an intruder, standing in the corner with Mac. She wanted to leave and regretted not bringing her own vehicle so she could do so. Wasn't the first rule of first dates to have an escape plan? Not that this *was* a first date, but she should have thought of all the possibilities.

Turning again to look at moody Mac, she considered asking him if he'd drive her home but decided she didn't want to crash at the hands of a drunk driver.

Finally Callum made his excuses to Bailey and her parents and returned to Chelsea. "Sorry," he said, his soulful eyes searching hers. "You okay?"

"Yep." She held her chin high as she nodded. "But I think Muffin is ready to go home. Could you take us now, please?"

Before Callum could reply, Quinn spoke loudly enough that everyone heard him. "Bailey, Callum tells us he has you to thank for an introduction to Chelsea. How exactly did you guys meet?"

And right then Chelsea wished the floor would grow teeth and gobble her up. Bailey looked over at Chelsea, meeting her gaze head-on for the first time, her impeccable eyebrows coming together in a frown. And at that moment Chelsea knew Bailey knew. So much for maintaining her professional reputation. What must Bailey be thinking? That Chelsea took advantage of clients' exes, swooping in to prey on the poor men when they were heartbroken and vulnerable. Not that Callum had seemed either of those things, but perhaps he was a very good actor.

"Um…we have a mutual friend," Bailey said, totally contradicting what Callum had said earlier about them knowing each other through work. She tossed Chelsea a phony smile and then turned her attention back to the game she was playing with Hamish. The other McKinnels frowned and looked from Chelsea to

Bailey and then back to Chelsea as if wondering what was going on.

"Muffin," Chelsea called softly, and he awoke from his post-prandial meal slumber and trundled across to her. Then she turned to Callum. "I'll go thank your mom and Lachlan for lunch."

She started across to where Nora was sipping whiskey with her two old friends and could feel Callum and Muffin following her.

"Excuse me, Mrs. McKinnel? I'm going now, but I wanted to say thank-you for a lovely lunch. Happy Thanksgiving." She dared not even glance at Bailey's parents.

Nora rose from her armchair and pulled Chelsea into a hug. "It was lovely to meet you. And please, call me Nora. I hope we'll be seeing a lot more of you in future."

Chelsea smiled through gritted teeth—she doubted that very much. Next she said a speedy goodbye to Lachlan and, although she felt bad escaping without talking to Hamish, he was still with Bailey so she snuck out with Callum into the icy, early-evening air.

"Your jacket," he said, when she shivered on his mom's front porch. In her haste to escape she hadn't even thought of it and he'd been distracted also. "I'll just go get it."

"Thanks." She waited on the porch, stooping to hold Muffin close for warmth and comfort. How lethal could Bailey's spreading rumors be for her business? Not wanting to think about that, she forced her thoughts to the McKinnels and had to admit they weren't what she'd expected. It was hard to reconcile the warm, friendly, playful tribe with a family whose name was famous for its world-class bourbon. Each and every one of them had drunk their fair share, yet no one had gotten rowdy or abusive.

"Here you are." Callum's voice was warm as he stepped close to her and held out her jacket. She lifted her arms and slipped them inside. Although she couldn't see his face as he lowered the jacket onto her, she felt his warm breath against the back of her neck and prickles of awareness flared in that spot. She had a crazy urge to turn around, knowing that if she did so, she'd be perfectly positioned to kiss him on the mouth. How she could think such thoughts after what had just occurred inside she had no idea, but it was like her hormones and her brain were two entirely separate entities.

They stood there, glued to the spot a few moments, and then Callum put his hands on her shoulders, before slowly sliding them down her arms and capturing her hands. "Thanks for playing my date today," he whispered right into her ear. It was freezing outside but her insides sweltered. "I'm sorry for Bailey's unexpected arrival."

"It's fine," she lied, her whole body rigid like a statue. What *was* going on here?

"I really enjoyed your company," he continued, still holding her hands, his body still pressed against hers. Her eyes widened as she felt a hardness pressing into her back.

"Yes," he breathed, reading her thoughts, "I don't think my libido got the memo about this being pretend."

She swallowed. What was she supposed to say to that? *How about I give myself to your libido on a platter then?* Her nipples tingled and tightened at the thought—thank God for the cover of her jacket. "Oh," she squeaked.

He chuckled, the sound flowing through her body like hot chocolate through her veins. "*Oh?* Is that all you have to say?"

She turned her head so she could look at him properly. "What exactly…do you…want me…to say?"

He released one of her hands and then lifted a finger to touch her chin. His touch felt soft and hard all at once, exactly how a man's touch should. "I was kinda hoping you might agree to taking this charade a little further."

Her mouth went dry, but she managed to ask, "How much further?" She wanted him to spell it out so she didn't make a fool of herself.

"To your bedroom."

Those three words were like a match against her skin. This would be a gift to herself. An early Christmas present that she very much deserved. Bailey no doubt already thought the worst, so the damage was already done; doing this couldn't ruin her reputation any further. Still, she wanted to set Callum straight— she wasn't about to enter a relationship with a man who made whiskey. "It can only be once. And no one can know. It's bad enough already that Bailey—"

He interrupted before she could finish. "Honey, that's more than fine with me. I'm not looking for a rebound relationship. My priority right now has to be the distillery. And don't worry about Bailey. I'll talk to her. I'll explain I asked you to lunch to do me a favor. She's a good person and she knows Mom so she'll understand. She won't tarnish your name."

Although part of her wondered why he didn't seem

that broken up about their breakup if Bailey was such a good person, another part of her didn't much care right now. All that mattered was the desperate need coursing through her. She was crazy, utterly, certifiably insane but she wanted this more than she'd wanted anything for as long as she could recall.

"Okay," she whispered, then leaned forward and pressed her lips against his to seal the deal. His mouth melded to hers, Callum spun her around so their bodies were also pressed against each other. There was no hiding the desire in his jeans and as Chelsea opened her mouth and welcomed his tongue inside, the illicit taste of him fueled her own desperate need even further. He tasted of the sweet desserts he'd eaten but also of what she guessed must be the whiskey he'd consumed over lunch. He hadn't drunk as much as the others as he knew he'd be driving her home, but the taste was still there and she found it strangely appealing. Intoxicating. Surprisingly delicious. Dangerous.

His hand slid down her back, holding her close as he deepened the kiss. Pleasure flowed through Chelsea and anticipation built within her—if her body reacted this way with a simple kiss, she could only imagine the fireworks that would explode once they got naked together. That couldn't happen fast enough.

As if reading her mind, Callum pulled back slightly and she saw heat and desire in his eyes as he spoke. "We'd better make a move, before we make a scene right here on my mom's front porch."

Chelsea gasped and bit her lower lip. She'd almost forgotten where they were; being around Callum affected her senses, primarily her common sense. The sooner she got him out of her system the better.

"Relax," he whispered, smiling down at her as he brushed his thumb against her cheek. "They can't see us out here, but let's get going anyway. I'm tired of sharing you."

More shivers slid down her spine at his words. She nodded, letting him take her hand and lead her over to his SUV. Tired from all the eating and socializing, Muffin didn't object to sitting in the back. He sprawled across the seat and fell promptly asleep, unaware of the sexual tension buzzing in the air around him. Callum drove the whole way back to her place with his hand on her knee, drawing tiny circles on her skin with his thumb. The material of her leggings did little to numb the effects of his touch and by the time they arrived at her house, she was a writhing bundle of need, desperate to rid herself of her clothes and jump his bones.

Alarm bells sounded in her head—getting involved with Callum McKinnel wasn't a good idea on a number of levels—but she ignored them because this wasn't getting involved. This was getting off. Just once.

She almost whimpered when he parked the car and removed his hand to open the door and climb out. He let Muffin out next and although she knew he would come around and open the passenger door for her, she couldn't wait. Didn't want to. As Muffin bounded up toward her little house, Chelsea met Callum in front of the SUV and took his hand, sending another jolt of desire right to her core.

They didn't speak as she fumbled with her key and let the three of them inside, but their eyes spoke vol-

umes. She could almost see the chemistry that sparked
between them. Chelsea switched on the hall light, and
the moment he shut the door behind her, Callum's hands
were on her waist, spinning her to face him again. For
a few long moments they stared into each other's eyes
and Chelsea found herself admiring his cheekbones.
She wanted to touch them, she wanted to touch every
little last bit of him.

And then they were kissing. Kissing like she'd never
kissed or been kissed before. His hands were in her hair,
caressing the base of her neck as his lips and tongue rid
her of her ability for rational thought.

Despite his declaration that he wasn't looking for a
relationship, Callum didn't rush things. He treated her
as if she were a princess, seducing her slowly but at
the same time with an urgency that sent her blood racing through her veins. As he dropped kisses along her
jawline and down her neck, he moved his hands to her
jacket and gently eased it off her. As it thumped onto
the floor, he moved his head lower, pressing his lips
against the exposed strip of skin just above her cleav-
age. Her breasts swelled at his proximity and he cupped
one in his hand, testing its weight and teasing her nipple
through the fabric of her dress. She arched against him,
feeling like a wanton hussy but unable to care about
anything but acting on the feelings pulsing through her.

"Take my dress off," she whispered and, without a
word, he slipped his hand around her back and obeyed.
She shivered as the zipper came down and his fingers
brushed against her bare skin. He didn't wait for an invitation to remove her bra and she sucked in her breath
as he lowered his mouth around one exposed nipple. He

circled it with his tongue and desire tugged deep in her core. Need burned there; if he didn't remove her panties next she might actually combust.

Totally attuned to her needs, he eased one hand inside her panties and her knees almost buckled as his fingers touched her in the most intimate place.

"Oh God," she panted as he stroked her toward further insanity. "Bedroom. Now."

"Invitation accepted," he said, his voice a low growl that only made her more desperate. Then he picked her up and she instinctively wrapped her legs around him as he carried her down the hallway and shut her bedroom door.

Callum knew two seconds after he lost himself inside of Chelsea that once was never going to be enough. He just wasn't sure how to broach the subject of wanting more—he'd meant it when he said he wasn't in the market for a relationship right now. Everything he had to give needed to go into reviving the business and he wasn't about to neglect another woman the way he had Bailey. Then again, Chelsea had been the one to suggest only one night—she'd made it perfectly clear that was all she wanted from him—so maybe she'd be amenable to just a little bit more.

"Can I get you a drink or something?" she asked, breaking into his thoughts as she spoke for the first time since they'd tumbled into her bed. She now lay in his arms, her head resting against his shoulder, her fingers trailing across his bare chest, and he didn't want to let her go just yet. He could do with a postcoital bourbon though and hopefully one drink would lead to another and then… And then he remembered she didn't drink alcohol so she wouldn't have any in her house.

"What are you offering?" he asked, his tone a lot more provocative than he'd intended.

"I make a mean hot chocolate. I'll even share my marshmallows with you." And that sounded provocative also, whether she meant it to or not.

He dipped his head and captured her mouth again, kissing her hard. The kiss wasn't the only thing that was hard. A torturous moan escaped her lips as his erection pressed into her stomach and then, instead of going for a drink, she reached down between their naked bodies and curled her fingers around his hard-on.

Just once turned very quickly into twice, which was just as explosive as the first time. If not more so. Chelsea took the lead and he watched, mesmerized, as she rode him. It had to be *the* single most erotic thing he'd ever seen. Their gazes glued to each other, they came together in perfect harmony, the sex totally blowing his mind. Callum tried to tell himself this was because he hadn't had any in a while, but that wasn't true. He and Bailey had done the deed on a fairly regular basis, ticking it off on their weekly to-do lists. He hadn't realized that sex had been so perfunctory for them, that their love life had become routine like everything else. But being with Chelsea made him realize just what had been lacking from his previous relationship.

As she collapsed on top of him, her heart racing against his, the heat of their skin slick against each other, he hugged her close and banished all thoughts of his ex from his mind. When they finally recovered from round two, he still didn't want to let Chelsea go.

The thought of crawling out of bed and going on his way, never to return, left his heart cold, frozen.

"How about that drink?" he asked, when she finally pushed herself up off him and wiped her brow with the back of her hand. Her breasts hung naked a few inches from his face and desire reared again inside him. He itched to touch and taste some more, but he didn't want to cause Chelsea discomfort.

"The hot chocolate?" She cocked her head to one side and her golden hair fell across her chest. She was prettier than a painting. Her nakedness was far more appealing than anything the pages of a dirty magazine could offer.

"Yes, please." He pinned his hands beneath his thighs to stop from pulling her back down.

"Coming right up." With those words, she rolled over and slid out of bed. He watched as she picked up a robe that was hanging on the end of the bed and tugged it around herself. All very well, but he'd seen every last inch of her buck naked and the image was imprinted on his mind.

"Need any help?"

She smiled over at him and shook her head, peeling a rubber band off her wrist and then capturing her hair into a ponytail. "Nope. I'll be right back."

Good, Callum thought as Chelsea opened the door and Muffin rushed in; she didn't seem in a hurry to throw Callum out and he decided he'd hang around as long as she let him. Who needed sleep anyhow?

As she headed down the hall into the kitchen, Muffin launched himself onto the bed and attempted to lick Callum's face. He wrestled the dog into obedience, and then rubbed his tummy as they both waited for Chelsea's return.

She came back into the bedroom a few minutes later and smiled at the sight of them in bed together. "Doesn't look like there's much room for me anymore."

"Shove over, buddy," Callum said, nudging the dog to the bottom of the bed and then patting the empty space on the mattress beside him. Chelsea laughed and stepped toward him, two steaming mugs of delicious-smelling hot chocolate in her hands. She stopped at the bed and passed one to him, putting the other down on her bedside table as she climbed back into bed. In a divine act of God, her robe gaped open, giving him the perfect view of her breasts as she settled beside him.

He took a sip, trying to be on his best behavior, when what he really wanted was to kick Muffin out and go for round three. "Hmm, this is delicious. How'd you make it?"

Her eyes sparkled as she wriggled her eyebrows at him and stretched over to get her own mug. "That is my secret, but I'm glad you like."

"Oh, I like very, very much," he said, taking another sip.

She licked her lips. "Tell me about Sophie," she said, leaning back against the headboard. "Why did she wink at you when she went to meet her girlfriend?"

He chuckled at the recollection. "I told you our mom is a mad-keen matchmaker. She won't rest until all her babies are happily married off and having babies of their own, but for some reason she thinks Sophie is a lesbian. Of course Sophie thinks this is hilarious and has decided to play along."

"Ah I see. So Storie isn't her girlfriend?"

"No. I don't know where Sophie picked her up but I think their act was pretty damn convincing, don't you?"

Chelsea nodded and then met his gaze. "As convincing as ours?"

"Probably not quite," he said, reaching out and wiping away a little chocolate smudge on her top lip. She rubbed her lips together and the heat between them flared again. Maybe now was the time to broach… What exactly did he want to ask of her? A fling or an affair sounded salacious and he didn't want to cheapen her in any way, but neither could he bear the thought of walking away. Of never having her legs wrapped around him again.

"What happened with your parents?" he asked, biding his time and also hoping he didn't scare her off.

She took her time replying, as if deliberating whether or not to do so at all. "What do you mean?" she asked eventually.

"You said you lived with your grandfather starting when you were fifteen. I assumed you meant on your own or did your parents live with you, as well?"

She shook her head and stared sadly into her mug. For a moment he regretted prying, not wanting to cause her any pain. "They died. In a car accident when I was eleven. My father was driving and he'd also been drinking, as he usually was. I was only lucky I wasn't in the car, I guess. It was a total wreck, they both died on impact."

"I'm sorry," he said, reaching out to place his hand against her thigh; this time to offer comfort not sex.

She shrugged. "These things happen."

"Maybe," he agreed, "but they still suck. Who'd you live with between when they died and when you moved in with your grandfather?"

"Who *didn't* I live with, more like. I was shipped from relative to relative, but no one really wanted me. I think the only reason they didn't give me to Granddad in the first place was that he was almost as much of a drunk as my parents, although he was a happy drunk, unlike my mom and dad who were violent with each other and whoever was around after a few drinks."

Oh God. His heart went out to her. She spoke with such detachment but he could see through her bravado to the hurting little girl inside. His family might have its faults, but he'd never been made to feel like a burden on any of them. Sure his dad had pushed him to achieve his best, but he'd always known this was down to love and wanting the world for his kids.

"No wonder you don't drink," he said.

"Yes." She sighed. "Although your family appear to be able to have a few drinks without yelling and screaming at each other."

"We have plenty of screaming matches, don't you worry," Callum said, "but we respect whiskey too much to abuse it. My dad taught us all that whiskey, any alcohol really, should be drunk and appreciated with good friends. Drinking should be a social event, not something you come to rely on."

She nodded. "You must miss your father a lot."

"It's complicated," he admitted. "Of course I'm devastated that he's gone—so many times I think of things I want to tell him and then realize I can't—but I have to admit, it feels good to be able to follow my ideas and dreams for the distillery. Dad didn't see that if we are to survive, we need to expand and move with the times. He thought making good whiskey was enough."

"And Quinn agreed with him, is that right? I sensed a little tension between the two of you about the distillery today."

"There's always been tension between us. Of course I love him as I do the others, but we've always rubbed each other the wrong way and I don't think he has the same passion about distilling that Blair, Sophie and I have. It's like he's doing it because he doesn't know what else he wants to do with his life."

"What's his job again?"

"He manages the warehouse, fills orders from suppliers. Most of my ideas will have no effect on his role whatsoever, except that we'll hopefully turn over more whiskey, which in turn means he might earn a better living. I think he objects simply because he can. Anyway, enough about Quinn. I don't want to bore you."

"You're not. Honestly. I must admit, I find big families fascinating. I'd also like to hear your ideas for the distillery."

"Really?"

When she nodded, Callum didn't hold back. He told her about his thoughts for expanding the simple café they currently had into a restaurant, about wanting to have more McKinnel merchandise for sale, about the possibility of introducing a white-dog label and also how he'd recently spoken to an agent about buying some nearby land and actually starting to grow their own grain.

"Do you know anything about farming?" she asked.

He smiled. "Not the first little thing, but I am an expert at delegating. I'd hire someone to oversee that side of things."

"Pity," she said, a twinkle in her eyes as she smiled back at him, "I think you'd totally rock a flannel shirt, a pair of denim overalls and a big floppy straw hat."

He raised an eyebrow. "I think you're confusing farmer with scarecrow."

She laughed. "Maybe." Then she said, "Have you thought about hosting events at the distillery? Like weddings, birthday celebrations and such. You've got the room for it and your surroundings are so beautiful that I'm sure it could become a very popular venue option in Jewell Rock."

"No, I haven't," he said, the idea already taking root. "What an awesome suggestion." He leaned over and kissed her on the lips to show exactly how much he appreciated it.

"If that's what I get for making suggestions," she said when they finally broke apart, "I'll keep them coming."

"Please do."

They spent the next hour or so—Callum lost track of time—talking and fooling around. He'd never been one to chat much postsex, but sitting in bed doing so with Chelsea seemed like the most natural thing in the world. He enjoyed her company as much as he did her body, and that was saying something.

When Muffin roused at their feet and scooted toward the bedroom door, their bubble of bliss broke. "Dammit," Chelsea said, scrambling after him, "I haven't taken him out for his evening wee."

Callum glanced at his watch as the girl and her dog

hurried out of the room. It was much later than he'd imagined—early hours of the morning later—and he should make a move. He didn't want to overstay his welcome, and spending the night had certain connotations. Reluctantly, he climbed out of bed and dressed again.

He found Chelsea outside, standing on the porch, shivering in her robe while Muffin did his business on the grass in front. Every cell in his body wanted to step right up to her and pull her into his embrace to warm her, but he resisted, because if he did so, he wasn't sure he'd ever be able to leave.

And Chelsea Porter was exactly the kind of distraction he didn't need right now.

Instead, he cleared his throat. "It's late. I guess… I'd better be going." He hesitated because although his head told him this was the right move, all his body wanted was to jump back into bed with her.

"Oh. Okay." She turned to meet his gaze, surprise in her eyes, despite the fact they'd agreed this was only going to be one night. *One time.* It was on the tip of his tongue to suggest they arrange another rendezvous, but he simply couldn't bring himself to do so. Whatever way he phrased it, a proposition of the kind he had in mind sounded tawdry. Chelsea didn't deserve to be cheapened in that way. It would be much better to leave things at one mind-blowing night.

Still, this left him with the dilemma of how to actually leave. Should he kiss her goodbye? Seemed stupid to be deliberating about such a thing when they'd already been intimate. In the end, he shoved his hands in his pockets, gave a curt nod, said thanks and then strode over to his SUV and climbed inside, cursing himself as he slammed the door behind him.

Chapter 8

"Thanks?" Chelsea whispered into the cold darkness as the lights of Callum's SUV disappeared into the night. She shivered and pulled her robe tighter around her, but it did nothing to warm her up. What exactly had she expected him to say? Not that she'd had many one-night stands—tonight, with Callum, brought her total to one—but she guessed the goodbye part was always awkward. Then again, it was better than having to give him the breakup spiel three months down the track when the shine wore off their relationship as it would inevitably have done.

She sighed and called softly to Muffin, not wanting to wake the neighbors. The dog obeyed and once they were both back inside in the warmth, she locked the door behind them.

It was long past midnight, but Chelsea felt wide-awake. Wide-awake but also deflated after what was un-doubtedly the best night of her life. She shook her head, wondering if Bailey had been speaking about the same man when she'd said their sex life wasn't the best. Not that she wanted to think about Bailey, because doing so reminded Chelsea that what she'd just done was not only unprofessional but that to Callum she was likely nothing more than rebound sex.

She sighed. But it hadn't only been the sex— al-though that was off the Richter scale, toe-curlingly amazing—it was everything about Callum, from the way he smiled when he looked at her to the passion in his voice when he spoke about the distillery. In spite of her own feelings toward alcohol, she could have lis-tened to him talk all night. If the insides of her thighs weren't a little raw from being up close and personal with his beard, she would think the last few hours had been a dream. The kind of dream where you woke up and then wanted to fall immediately back asleep. Of course, you never could, and even if you did manage to, the dream had always been lost.

She headed back into her bedroom and picked up their empty mugs, deciding it would be a good idea to erase all evidence that Callum had ever been here. She would pretend it was a dream after all. In the kitchen, she dumped the mugs in the sink, turned on the tap to rinse them and then, out of the corner of her eye, no-ticed the voice-mail light flashing on her home phone. Without thought, she stretched over to press Play and then frowned at the strange noise that drifted out into her otherwise silent house. She stilled, the little hairs on her arms lifting as she listened.

Is that heavy breathing?

Before she could be certain, the message ended, but another followed almost immediately. "I'm watching you. Don't think you can get away with what you've done."

Chelsea gasped at the sinister tone and then instinctively glanced around the kitchen, checking that she was alone, aside from Muffin who'd put himself to bed in her room. She shivered, now thankful that Callum had insisted on getting all her locks changed. What would be even better was if he'd stayed the night, if he were still here to protect her against bogeymen or crazed stalkers or whoever had left those messages. She immediately retracted this thought—disgusted with the neediness in it. She didn't need a man to keep her safe—she'd looked after herself practically since she could walk—but perhaps she should mention these calls to the police. What if they were related to the burglary?

At this thought, her whole body trembled, and once again she racked her brain for anyone who might want to harm her. Coming up blank, she took a deep breath. Perhaps the two things were unrelated? But that didn't necessarily make her feel any better.

It was late now but she'd called the number Sergeant Moore had given her and left a message. Then, unsettled by the thought of someone wanting to harm her, she doubled-checked that every door and window was securely locked—*thanks, Callum*—before retreating to her bedroom with Muffin to attempt slumber. She doubted she'd get much sleep with the fear rippling through her, but when she climbed into bed, thoughts of a possible psycho battled with the scent of Callum on her pillow and the raunchy acts of the evening on replay inside her head. Chelsea's body ached in places she'd forgotten existed and she couldn't decide what was worse—fear of a stranger or the fear she might never feel as alive as Callum made her feel tonight ever again.

Callum rubbed a hand over his beard and stared at his computer screen. It was taking him much longer than it should to get through his morning emails and what did it matter anyway? Most of the country took the Friday following Thanksgiving off as an extra holiday and so he doubted anyone would read his replies until Monday morning, but he figured trying to work might keep his mind off Chelsea.

Realizing he'd read the same line of the same email ten times and still had no idea what it said, he pushed back his seat and wandered out onto the tasting floor. Perhaps a walk in the garden would clear his head. He'd had a late night and, despite not drinking since lunchtime, he'd woken with a hangover from hell. He left the office and walked through the tasting room, which was open with a skeleton staff due to the long weekend.

"You look like you haven't slept for a month," Sophie said cheerily as she polished the American oak bar where potential customers could taste their wares.

"Just a night," he replied, heading for the door.

"Can't you keep up with your new woman?" Sophie teased. "Must be getting old, big brother. I've heard there's something you can take for that."

He glared at her, channeling a little of Mac's perpetual grumpiness. "Not a conversation I'm having with my little sister. Call me if we get an influx here and I'll come help you with tastings."

"Okeydoke." She gave him an irritating little finger wave and he went out through the side door in the direction of the actual distillery. He didn't think Quinn would be working in the warehouse today, so he was surprised to see the door open. Deciding that maybe he could try to win Quinn over to his ideas one-on-one rather than waiting until the family meeting, Callum was almost at the door, when Bailey came out, her eyes red as if she'd been crying.

"You okay?" he asked, instinctively reaching out to touch her arm. They'd been officially together five years and friends long before that; it was hard to break the habit of looking out for her. "What's going on?"

"Nothing." She blinked. "I was just…" She shook her head. "It doesn't matter. How are you? Do you think we could talk? I feel like I could have handled our breakup a lot better."

By handling it yourself? He swallowed this response and nodded.

"Sure." He wanted to talk to her about Chelsea anyway. "Want to come into my office or would you prefer to head over to the house and have a coffee?"

"Your office will be fine."

He nodded and escorted her back to the main building. It wasn't that late, but she'd been in the McKinnel world for decades, so he offered her a bourbon and she accepted, downing the entire contents of the glass in a few seconds. They both opened their mouths to speak at the same time:

"I want you to know I never wanted to hurt you," Bailey said.

"I wanted to talk to you about Chelsea," Callum said.

Then they frowned in unison.

"You're not serious about her, are you?" Bailey asked.

He shook his head, because that *should* be the truth, even if he felt his conscience calling him a damn liar. "No, of course not."

Last night with Chelsea had been better than anything he'd experienced in as long as he could remember, but could he trust those feelings right now? He'd been one half of a whole for a long time and he came from a big family—he was used to having people around him. Maybe he'd reached out to Chelsea, simply because he couldn't bear another night of going home alone.

Bailey raised a clearly skeptical eyebrow as if she could see right through him.

"I'm sorry," he said, "I never would have invited Chelsea if I'd have known Mom had invited you. You know what she's like. When she heard we broke up, she was devastated, and to get her off my back, I asked Chelsea if she'd be my date for Thanksgiving."

"You two must have had quite the chat when she… you know, ended things for me."

Bailey sounded accusatory and he was about to say that he'd never have even met Chelsea if she'd done her own dirty work, but she spoke again before he could. "Anyway, it doesn't matter. I should have talked to you myself, but I thought if I did, I might chicken out?"

"What do you mean?"

"You're a wonderful friend, Callum, and I don't want

to lose that. Our families go way back. I enjoy your company and I love you but I'm not *in* love with you."

He nodded, understanding because, now she said it, he realized that was exactly how he felt about her, as well.

"For a long while," she continued, "I've been trying to convince myself that all that was enough. I wasn't sure I could actually go through with ending things, even though I thought it was the right thing to do, so that's why I hired Chelsea. To make sure I did it. Mom thought I was insane breaking up with you and maybe I am but…"

"No." He shook his head. "You were right to do what you did. I think we both know that. You deserve a lot more than I can give you and getting married to keep our moms happy…"

"I know." She half smiled. "Not the right reason at all." She sighed. "Why does love have to be so damn complicated?"

There was something in the way she spoke about love that made him think she wasn't talking about him and something in her eyes made him ask a question he'd never considered before. "Was there another reason you broke up with me?" he asked, finding the idea didn't bother him as much as he thought it would; he was simply curious. "Another man perhaps?"

The way she glanced down at the ground told him all he needed to know.

"Who is he?" he asked.

She shook her head. "It doesn't matter. He doesn't feel the same about me anyway." Then her face crumpled and a sob escaped her mouth. "I'm sorry, Callum, I never meant to hurt you."

"It's okay." And he found he meant it. Not that he liked the idea of being cheated on, but he knew that no one strayed if they were already where they were meant to be. "And, Bails, if this guy doesn't realize how lucky he is to have your love, then he's as big an idiot as me and he doesn't deserve you either."

She half sobbed, half laughed.

"You deserve a good man," he continued, "I'm sure you'll find the lucky Mr. Right very soon. Just be patient."

She sniffed, wiped her nose with the back of her hand and nodded. "Thanks for the drink, Callum. I guess I'll see you round."

"About Chelsea," he said, hoping his voice didn't crack on her name.

"Yes? What about her?"

"You won't tell anyone about her coming over for Thanksgiving, will you? She really was just doing me a favor, and I wouldn't want to hurt her professional reputation."

Bailey stared at him a few long moments, her gaze penetrating. Then, finally, she nodded. "I won't say a word. You have my promise on that."

"Thank you. I'm glad we had this conversation." He didn't want things to be awkward with them going forward. "Our families will always be friends and I hope we will too. We were good as friends."

She smiled, then came around his desk, leaned down and kissed him on the cheek. "We *are* good as friends."

As she turned to leave, he remembered one more

thing. "Can I come around tonight to collect the last of my things?" He'd grabbed some of his stuff from her apartment the day after the breakup but there were still some books, CDs, that kind of thing. They'd never officially moved in together, but had rather lived a little at her apartment and a little at his cottage.

"Sure. I'm going round to Mom and Dad's for dinner, but you can let yourself in. Do you think you can bring over anything of mine left at your place?"

He nodded.

"Cool. And then leave your key on the kitchen table." She'd brightened considerably since he'd run into her outside, and he was glad they'd had this conversation.

"I will. Goodbye, Bailey."

"Goodbye, Callum."

His listened as her high heels click-clacked down the corridor and then, determined to focus on the business and forget about women, he turned back to his computer and threw himself into work.

For the next few days, he barely left his office and every time his mind drifted to Chelsea—as it was irritatingly prone to do—he added another task to his to-do list, reminding himself where his priorities lay. If he were to bring McKinnel's back from the brink, he needed to focus and resist the ridiculous urge to pick up his phone and call Chelsea. An urge almost as strong as the one to take breath.

With Sophie's collaboration, he drafted a five-year plan for the distillery with areas left where Mom, Blair, Quinn and the others could add their ideas at the meeting. He felt ready to wow the unbelievers in his family and take McKinnel's Distillery into the twenty-first century.

In addition to introducing merchandise—stuff like glassware, tea towels, hats and T-shirts, which he'd delegated to Sophie to organize—his number one priority was a start on expanding the restaurant and for that he needed to get Lachlan on board. He could hire any old chef but Callum believed having a McKinnel in charge of the restaurant would enhance their family-run image. People liked that stuff, especially journalists, whose attention he was hoping to attract with the new ventures. They could do with all the good publicity they could get. He also hoped to lure Mac into helping with the expansion of their current café space. In addition to being a superstar with a soccer ball, Mac had a talent for building things and Lord knew he needed something to focus on now that he'd quit playing professionally.

On Wednesday, almost a week from the day he'd left Chelsea in the early hours of the morning, it was with all *this* forefront in his mind, that Callum drove into Bend to meet Lachlan for a late lunch. They'd arranged to meet at a café in the Old Mill District, rather than the fancy restaurant Lachlan currently worked at so the owner wouldn't hear them plotting. As he climbed out of his SUV, he looked over and did a double take at the sight of Muffin sitting outside the front of the café, his leash looped around a fire hydrant. At least he thought it was Muffin, but maybe he was hallucinating. He'd certainly been imagining Chelsea all over the place. Twice in the last few days he'd gone out to the tasting floor and mistaken a customer for her.

Trying *not* to think about her was almost as bad as thinking about her.

He strode toward the dog, half hoping he'd see Chelsea inside the café, half hoping he wouldn't.

"Hey, buddy." He stooped to ruffle the fur on Muffin's head and the dog leaped about like a total lovable lunatic. No doubt about it, there was no welcome so wonderful as that of a dog; maybe he should detour via that shelter on his way home and adopt one. Something big like a German shepherd that would require a ton of exercise—running with it could help burn off the pent-up tension that had set up residence inside him these last few days. A dog would also keep him company on lonely nights and likely be less stress than a woman. This thought led him into the café, but the moment he spotted Chelsea it evaporated. His heart caught in his throat and muscles all over his body locked up at the sight of her sitting at a table with *another* man.

A bell above the door sounded, announcing his arrival and Chelsea looked up. Her mouth opened and color rushed to her cheeks; she held his gaze that fraction too long before blinking and then turning back to her date. That thought sent his blood racing, but then he realized that she could simply be in the middle of one of her professional breakups. Even still, Callum couldn't help the rush of jealousy that hit him like an actual physical blow.

He stood in the doorway like a total idiot, glancing around for his brother, wishing they'd chosen someplace else to meet. They lived in the same damn house for goodness' sake, but Lachlan had a strict rule about not taking his work home. All his free time he spent with Hamish.

Speak of the devil. A hand landed on his back and shoved him forward right into the café. Lachlan spoke far too loudly. "Hey, bro, isn't that your new girlfriend over there? Who's the dude?"

Callum met his brother's gaze, glowered and then hissed, "She's not my girlfriend. Just a...*friend*." He almost choked on the last word, like it were a fur ball in his throat.

"Sorry. My mistake." Lachlan didn't sound apologetic in the slightest. "You guys seemed pretty tight at Thanksgiving. Do you want to go talk someplace else?"

While that might be a sensible move, Callum couldn't bring himself to leave. He hadn't expected to see Chelsea today, and now that she was only a few feet away, he couldn't keep his eyes off her. "No, this is fine. Shall we sit?"

Lachlan nodded and the two of them crossed over to a table in the corner. Unfortunately—or perhaps fortunately—his brother sat first, taking the seat with a direct view of Chelsea. Ignoring the disappointment in his gut, he sat down and pulled out his iPad, ready to hit Lachlan with some of his ideas about the restaurant.

Lachlan glanced down at the menu. "Are you hungry? I think I might just grab a coffee."

"Coffee will be fine," Callum replied; he didn't have the mental coordination to eat and talk to Lachlan with Chelsea a few yards away, whose presence was a major distraction.

A waitress arrived and Lachlan ordered for them both. Then he looked directly at Callum. "Before you start, I just want you to know I love the idea of opening a proper restaurant at the distillery and I'm 99 percent on board."

"What's the 1 percent that's holding you back?" Callum asked.

"I want full control."

Callum raised an eyebrow. "That's it?" He chuckled, feeling as if a weight had been lifted off his shoulders.

"I mean it," Lachlan said. "I know you're struggling, trying to get everyone behind some of your ideas, but I have complete faith that you can turn the distillery around. I don't want McKinnels to die a slow death. I believe a restaurant will help immensely, but not if everyone feels they have to put their mark on it. We all need to stick to what we do best."

Callum nodded. "I completely agree. Just one thing—I don't know how we'll convince him, but I'd like to try to get Mac involved in building the extension. I'm worried about him. It's not good to sit around all day doing nothing. The guy needs purpose in his life."

"You're just scared he'll drink all the profits if he doesn't snap out of his funk."

"Damn straight I am," Callum said, resisting the urge to twist his head to see if Chelsea was still with that guy.

Lachlan smirked. "She's still there. The poor dude looks quite cut up, though. I wonder who he is."

"She's dumping him," Callum said, before thinking better of it.

"What?" Lachlan frowned, disgust flashing across his face. "So you're dating a woman already in a relationship?" His ex-wife had betrayed him before she left and he couldn't abide cheaters.

"No. I told you, we're not dating and she's not dumping him because of me. She's dumping him on behalf of someone else."

"Whoa!" Lachlan leaned back in his seat and held up his hands. "You've lost me."

Callum inhaled in frustration and quickly filled Lachlan in on Chelsea's bizarre career, so they could get on with what they were supposed to be talking about. As predicted his brother thought this both surprising and hilarious.

"So let me get this straight," Lachlan said, his voice thankfully low enough that only Callum could hear. "Bailey hired Chelsea to dump you and then you hired her to pretend to be your date?"

"I didn't hire her and it doesn't matter. We're not here to discuss Chelsea."

"Thank God Mom thinks I'm a lost cause when it comes to relationships, and I don't have to go to the extremes you do," Lachlan said, shaking his head.

Callum thought about just how far he'd gone with Chelsea the other night. And then he succumbed to the burning need to turn his head to look at her. His chest tightened as she stood, her caramel hair swishing across her back as she offered the poor man a sympathetic hug, patted him on the arm and then started out of the café. She didn't look at Callum and something inside him squeezed. Was she annoyed? Was that how things were going to be between them? He wanted to be a good memory, not one she regretted. Feeling bad about the way he'd left things the other night, he suddenly needed to apologize more than he needed oxygen.

He shoved his chair back and stood, barely even

flinching as it scraped against the floor, sounding like nails scraping down a blackboard. "Be right back," he said to Lachlan, and then he turned to hurry after Chelsea, almost bumping into the waitress as she carried over their drinks.

"Sorry," he apologized and then hightailed it out of there.

Chelsea was speedy, and by the time he stepped out of the café, she'd unlooped Muffin and was striding down the sidewalk like she couldn't get out of there fast enough. For a brief moment, he thought about letting her go, but he couldn't bring himself to do so. Instead, he jogged the few yards to catch up with her, calling her name as he tapped her on the back.

She spun around, the terror in her eyes surprising him. "Callum!"

Did she think he was going to hurt her? He held up his hands. "I'm sorry, I didn't mean to frighten you."

She bit her lip, glanced from side to side as if checking their surroundings and then finally met his gaze. "You didn't."

Muffin jumped up at him and although Callum scratched the dog's neck, giving him the attention he craved, his gaze stayed on Chelsea. They stared at each other a few long moments and, finally, she broke the silence.

She nodded back toward the café. "Were you and Lachlan discussing the new restaurant?"

"Yep." But that's not what he wanted to discuss with her. "Chelsea, I…"

"Yes?" She prompted when he stalled.

Damn she was beautiful. Her cheeks were a rosy

red—whether from the cool air or something else he couldn't tell but he'd never felt so tongue-tied in his life. "I just wanted to say I'm sorry about how I left things the other night."

She raised her eyebrows and reached up to tuck some flyaway hair behind her ear. "Why? We were both perfectly clear on what we were doing. You don't need to feel bad. I had a great day. And night."

"Well. Great. It's just…" He wasn't a one-night-stand kind of guy. They were only a few feet apart and he knew he couldn't walk away again. "I was wondering if you'd like to get together again sometime?"

Thank God no one but Chelsea could hear him. His brothers would never let him live it down if they heard him fumbling over asking a woman out.

Her tongue darted out to moisten her lips and then she rubbed them together. "You mean, like a date?"

What was the correct answer here? He didn't want to scare her off. "If that's what you'd like or we could just, you know, hang out."

"Hang out?" she echoed him as if she'd never heard of the concept before.

His pulse picked up. "Yes. That's if you want, but if you'd rather not."

"Oh, I want to," she admitted. The way she looked at him and the tone of her words indicated she understood that when he'd said "hang out" he'd imagined doing so without any clothes on. "I think hanging out is a good plan. When were you thinking?"

"Does right now sound too desperate?"

Her whole face lit up and sparkled as she laughed. "Right now sounds great, but, what about your brother?"

"Who?" For a second Callum forgot there was anyone else in the world except the two of them. "Oh, him. Right. We're pretty much done. He said yes to opening the restaurant, but he's a control freak and wants to do it all himself."

"That's great. I think."

"It is." He nodded. "I have plenty to keep me busy, and I know Lachlan will do a good job." But he didn't want to talk about Lachlan, the restaurant or the distillery. He didn't want to talk period. "Did you walk? Do you want me to give you a lift back to your place?"

She grinned and looked at him in a way that turned his insides liquid. "What about Lachlan?"

"What about him?" Callum asked as he closed the distance between them and gave in to the compulsion to kiss her.

Chapter 9

It was official. Chelsea needed her head read. So much for one night, so much for not getting involved with Callum McKinnel. Fate be cursed for throwing them into each other's paths again. How the hell could she say no to that delicious face asking if she wanted to hang out with him? How could she keep any kind of clear head when he was kissing her like the world would end if he stopped?

Summoning all the willpower she had, she grabbed on to the single cell of common sense in her body and palmed her hands against his lovely, solid chest. "Someone might see us," she hissed, trying to summon some kind of care factor when all she could think about was kissing him again. And then some.

Callum pouted as he looked down at her. He was sexy when he smiled, but damn near irresistible when he scowled. "Ah right, your business reputation and all." His tone said he had little respect for what she did and while perhaps she *should* care about that, she didn't; what he thought of her career didn't matter. All that mattered right now was getting naked with him again, but doing so on the sidewalk would be unwise on a number of levels.

"Yes, my business," she whispered. "And the fact I don't want either of us to get arrested."

He chuckled at that, then took Muffin's lead from her hand and grabbed hold of it with his other hand. "I'd say your place or mine, but yours is closer."

Her hormones wouldn't have let her argue even if she wanted to. Which she didn't. She'd been jumpy and on edge these last few days—feeling someone was watching her—and when Callum had tapped her on the back, she'd almost jumped a mile. She welcomed the chance to take her mind off her paranoia for a couple of hours.

Callum all but dragged her to his parked SUV. As if they'd done this a hundred times before, he opened the passenger door for her and Muffin jumped in first. They laughed as the dog crossed over to the driver's seat and settled in for the ride. Chelsea climbed into the SUV and, as she clicked her seat belt into place, he closed the door and jogged around to his side. She dragged Muffin over to her long enough for Callum to climb into the car, but the moment he sat down, the dog scrambled onto his lap.

Once again, Callum navigated the short distance to her place with Muffin hindering his view. It was the funniest, yet most endearing, sight she'd ever seen.

The nosy old lady from next door was out front in her

garden when Callum parked in Chelsea's drive. Knowing what it felt like to be lonely, Chelsea often stopped to chat, but not today. Today she and Callum all but ran to the front door, trying not to trip over Muffin as he wound in and out of their legs, catching their excitement. On her porch, Callum took her key from her hand and unlocked the door—a little voice inside her considered objecting to this controlling action, but it could barely be heard over her screaming hormones. Sometimes scruples weren't worth the effort.

They stepped inside, and Callum had barely kicked the door shut before he spun her round and pressed her up against it. She felt his firm body mold against her as he smashed his mouth over hers. If she'd thought their previous kisses hot, they had nothing on this one. Ravaged, *beautifully ravaged*—these were the words that entered her head as he slipped his hands inside her coat and roved them all over her body. Her head fell back against the door as he slowly, tantalizingly rid her of her clothes until she was standing in her hallway naked and he was still fully clothed.

"You're freaking gorgeous," he said, his voice low as he looked and touched his fill. Shivers flooded her entire body, yet she was hotter than she'd ever been before.

"I was thinking the same about you," she whispered back, "but I do think you're slightly overdressed for the occasion."

"Am I? Sorry." Callum chuckled and gazed hungrily at her. "What do you suggest we do about that?"

In reply, she reached out and yanked his jacket off him, hurling it onto the pile of her own clothes at their feet. It looked and felt expensive, but she didn't care and he didn't seem to either. Next she stripped him of his shirt and pants, and her breath hitched as she stopped to admire him. Not sure if she'd ever be lucky enough to have him like this again, Chelsea took a moment to admire every chiseled muscle. His hands hung at his side as she reached out and ran her finger over his lips and then down his strong neck over his hard chest and even lower. His muscles tightened beneath her touch and when his erection flared large and proud, she had to bite her lower lip to stop from whimpering. She dropped to her knees, wanting to taste him and wanting to drive him crazy as he had done to her.

Callum groaned as she took him into her mouth and she glanced upward to see him palm his hands against the wall. She smiled around his penis, loving the taste and the feel of it in her mouth. It wasn't long before she felt him twitching inside her and then his hands were in her hair, yanking her back. He wasn't gentle but that only enhanced her arousal.

"Stop," he growled, "before it's too late."

"Too late for what?" she asked, looking up at him and smiling like the Cheshire Cat. Knowing what she could do to him was like a heady drug and she didn't *want* to give it up.

"This," he said, hauling her up and into his arms. He kissed her hard on the mouth as he lifted her up and dragged her legs around his waist. He slammed inside her and she cried out in surprised pleasure, loving the feel as he filled her completely. He was strong and had stamina and he took care of her, refusing to let go himself until she was a writhing, needy mess. And then he took it home, thrusting hard one final time and taking them both over the edge.

She clung to him, their skin hot and sweaty despite the temperature outside, as her heart rate slowly returned to normal. Or as close to normal as it could be with a naked Callum still in close proximity.

"Jeepers," he muttered after a few long minutes.

Chelsea laughed. "That's one word for it."

"Sorry," he said, "I got a little carried away. Next time I'll try to make it to your bedroom."

Sorry? Carried away? She had no complaints whatsoever. But, *next time*?

"Is that too presumptuous of me?" he asked as if he could read her mind.

She swallowed, unable to think straight with him still inside her. "Shall we take this conversation to the kitchen? Do you want a drink or something?"

"Sounds like a good idea." He gently eased her down his body and she thought again how strong he was to have been able to hold her like that for so long.

"Do you, uh…need to use the bathroom or anything?" She nodded toward his groin.

He grinned. "Do you? We could save water."

And man, it sounded like a line but she fell for it anyway.

Much later, once they were both dry, dressed and sitting on the bar stools at her kitchen counter sipping hot chocolate, she broached the issue of next time. "Did you mean it about seeing each other again?"

His lovely long fingers wrapped around her favorite mug—with a cocker spaniel that was almost Muffin's doppelganger painted on the front—he looked right into her eyes again. "Yes. I don't know what it is about you, Chelsea, but I've spent the last week trying not to think about you so I could focus on my work. Problem is, trying not to think about you is almost as distracting as thinking about you."

Heat rushed to her cheeks and she pursed her lips together to stop the ridiculous smile that threatened to burst onto her face. It might not have been your standard sweet nothing—he'd almost made her sound an inconvenience—but no one else had ever said something that made her glow so much inside. She should run a mile in the opposite direction.

"So yes," he said, "I meant it about seeing you again. I'd like that very much. What do you say?"

Lord, it was tempting. But was it worth the risk? To her or his heart she wasn't sure, all she knew was that she didn't do relationships.

He raised his eyebrows as he gazed down at her. "It's not algebra, sweetheart. I'm simply asking if you want to hang out with me on a more regular basis?"

"Like a relationship?"

He nodded. "If you're asking if I'll be monogamous then a 100 percent yes, but I'll admit, I'm not looking to rush into marriage or anything."

"Well, good," she said, "because I'm warning you now, I'm not great with commitment. You should know that I'll probably get sick of the sight of you within a couple of months."

He laughed as if he found this notion hugely amusing. "Then, let's agree to take things one day at a time. What do you say?"

Oh shoot, what am I getting myself in for? "I guess

I say, yes, but what about your family? What about my business? Do you think—"

Callum put his index finger against her mouth to silence her. "I think you're overthinking this. Let's just have fun together, okay?"

She sighed. "Okay." And then he smiled and kissed her again and she forgot why this wasn't such a good idea after all.

When they finally came up for air again, Callum gestured to the half-finished jigsaw puzzle on her small kitchen table. "You like puzzles?"

She remembered how she'd had one on the go the day her house was broken into and how he'd picked up the scattered pieces and put them back into the box.

"Yes. My granddad always had one on the go and I used to help him. It was our thing." She smiled nostalgically. "Stupid but it kinda makes me feel close to him even though he's gone." And it gave her something to do on long lonely nights when she thought she'd go insane if she had to watch any more crap television.

"That's not stupid," he said, pushing back his stool, then standing and walking the few steps to the table. He glanced down at the puzzle, then looked back over to her. "May I?"

"Please, go ahead."

Callum bent over the table and his brow furrowed as he studied the pieces. "Got one," he shrieked after a few moments.

Chelsea couldn't help but smile at his joyful expression.

She slid off her own stool and went over to join him,

immediately finding a piece she'd been looking for. She pushed it in between four other pieces. "Bingo."

Callum grinned at her. "I reckon this could be addictive."

"It is. Trust me."

For a few minutes they sat in comfortable silence, shuffling through the puzzle pieces, congratulating each other and sharing the joy when one of them found a bit they could place. Finally, the dog she'd been working on for days started to take shape.

"This dog is a dead ringer for Muffin," he said.

She nodded. "I know. I couldn't resist it when I saw it. Just as I couldn't resist him."

"I'll bet he was cute as a pup."

"I wouldn't know; I got him from a shelter when he was a few years old, but I'm sure he was adorable. The hardest part was leaving all the other homeless animals behind."

"That was a charitable thing to do. Most people can't resist getting a puppy."

"Most people don't know what it's like to be passed from pillar to post all their lives. I do. I never want to feel like that again."

She didn't know why she was telling him this—it had taken her years to open up to Rosie and she'd never confessed her feelings to anyone else. "Anyway, I wanted to give a dog who really needed me a home."

Callum didn't say anything, but he reached out, took her hand and squeezed it. The simple gesture had tears pricking at the corner of her eyes, but she blinked them back, not wanting to cry like a big baby in front of him. After a few moments, he let go of her hand and looked at his watch. "I guess I'd better be heading back to the distillery."

He sounded as reluctant to go as she was to let him but she simply nodded, not wanting to appear needy in any way whatsoever.

As he pushed the stool back and stood, the phone on the wall began to ring and Chelsea's heart leaped up into her throat at the thought it might be her frequent caller. She scrambled across the kitchen, yanking the cord out of the wall before her answering machine had the chance to request a message.

Callum raised an eyebrow and she summoned a carefree smile to her face. He was the kind of guy who would freak out if he heard her heavy breather, and she didn't want him to worry about her. The police didn't seem overly concerned, so why should she bother him with it.

"I've been getting all these sales calls lately. I'm over it," she said, and then to distract him she closed the distance between them and kissed him.

"Jeez," he said, running a hand over his beard when she pulled back, "if you kiss me again like that, I'm not going to be able to leave."

She shrugged apologetically. "And the problem with that is…?"

He shook his head and smiled. "*Vixen.* I really have to go before Sophie sends out a search party, but I won't be staying away for long. And that's a promise. Are you free tomorrow night?"

She was of course—her social calendar was as bare as a newborn's bottom—but she didn't tell him that. "How about Friday night?"

He nodded. "Okay. I'll pick you up, we can go out for dinner or something."

The speed at which this was going made her head spin. She felt the need to call a few shots. "How about I come to you this time? We can order pizza. I still feel like it's a bit early to be seen out in public with you. I know Bailey was the one to end your engagement, but… well, I don't feel like we should rub this in her face."

"Fair point. Scrap the pizza. I'll cook for you."

It was her turn to raise an eyebrow. "I thought Lachlan was the chef in your family?"

"I'll concede he's not bad, but wait till you see me in an apron!"

"Now that is something I can't wait for," Chelsea said as she and Muffin escorted Callum to the front door. There she kissed him goodbye, the both of them pulling back just as things threatened to get out of control again. She couldn't help grinning as she stood on the porch waving him off.

This feeling probably wouldn't last long but she was damn well going to make the most of it while it did. With that thought, she went inside and headed to her computer to answer inquiries for breakups.

Callum couldn't remember the last time he'd looked forward to something as much as cooking dinner for and hanging out with Chelsea on Friday night. Sophie had caught him honest-to-God whistling at work today, and even a grumpy old man he'd had to deal with on the tasting floor couldn't take the spring out of his step. It might only have been two days since he'd seen Chelsea, but that felt far too long.

Although his house was usually neat and tidy thanks to his cleaning guy, this afternoon he'd left the office early to cook dinner and make sure everything was perfect. He'd checked for any lingering evidence of Bailey and done a few more pieces of the puzzle he'd dug out of his mom's games cupboard yesterday. Okay, so having a puzzle on the go was perhaps a little try-hard but he wanted to make Chelsea feel comfortable in his space. So much so that when buying the ingredients for dinner, he'd even bought a big, juicy bone for Muffin. The way to a man's heart might be through his stomach but he reckoned the way to Chelsea's was through her dog. Luckily, he liked the mutt almost as much as he liked her.

Half an hour before she was due to arrive, with his lasagna in the oven and the garlic bread ready to go under the grill, he had a quick shower. He was toweling himself dry when the doorbell rang. He peeled back his bedroom curtain, which gave him a view of the grounds in front of his cottage, and he saw Chelsea's little car parked out front. Perhaps she was as eager as he to get this evening started.

About to pull on his boxers, Callum paused and thought again. Then, his grin still wide, he walked through to the kitchen, grabbed his apron off the hook, wrapped it around his waist and went to open the door.

Muffin burst inside before either of them could say anything to each other. Callum chuckled and called over his shoulder, "Make yourself at home, buddy." Then he turned all his attention on Chelsea. She was holding a small gift-wrapped box and was dressed from head to toe in warm weather-appropriate attire. The only flashes of skin he could see were her face and hands. He shivered as the winter breeze whooshed inside.

"You're early."

"I am." She smiled and glanced slowly down his body; his skin heated as if she'd touched him. "And you're wearing an apron."

"I warned you I would."

"You did. I just imagined you'd be wearing something else, as well."

"Do you have a problem with nudity?"

She shook her head. "Not yours."

"Good." And then he pulled her inside, kicked the door shut behind them, took the box from her hands, dropped it onto his hall table and pulled her into his arms. She tasted so good—if anything, even better than he remembered—and he wanted to devour her. If the hands that landed on his buttocks were anything to go by, Chelsea's thoughts were heading in the same illicit direction as his.

As much as he'd happily take her right there against the wall, he summoned some restraint.

"This is a nice place you've got," she muttered, glancing around as he took her hand and led her down the hallway. "It's got a lovely warm vibe to it."

"Thanks. It was my grandparents' place when we were growing up, but when my grandma died a few years ago, my granddad moved out. Too many memories or something." That was all the history he gave her before closing the bedroom door behind them and lifting his fingers to the buttons on her shirt.

Later, when they lay beneath his bed covers, arms and limbs still entwined, Chelsea's head resting on his shoulder, Callum tried to recall a moment in time when he'd felt like this before. There was just something about Chelsea that got under his skin, but he still wondered if it actually meant anything more than sex. After everything with Bailey, he no longer knew whether to trust his own feelings.

"Is something burning?" Her question interrupted his thoughts and he sat bolt upright.

"Shit. The lasagna."

Chelsea laughed as he shot out of bed and hurried to the kitchen. A few moments later as he stared into the oven at what *was* going to be their dinner, he felt like weeping. He'd slaved all afternoon over a hot stove to impress her and now all he had to offer was carcinogen poisoning.

"Dammit." Ignoring the smoke that wafted out of the oven, he grabbed a tea towel to stop from burning himself and lifted the disaster out onto the stove top.

Chelsea chose that moment to come up beside him. "Hmm…" was all she said.

"Sorry." He shook his head as he turned to look at her—she'd taken a moment to pull on the shirt that he had hanging over the end of the bed and she looked amazing in it.

"That'll teach you to open the door to me wearing nothing but an apron."

"At least I haven't killed the garlic bread. And I have cupcakes."

Her lips curled at the edges. "You made me cupcakes?"

And dammit, he wanted to say yes. "I… Okay, no, I

bought them. There's a bakery in town and you haven't lived until you've tasted their cupcakes."

She laughed. "Garlic bread and cupcakes for dinner sounds good to me then. Truly, it's the company that matters and I'm quite enjoying yours."

"The feeling is entirely mutual."

They got dressed again for dinner, taking turns watching the garlic bread cook to avoid any further culinary disasters.

"I had set the dining room table for us to eat in there," Callum said, when the garlic bread was nice and crunchy, "but it seems overkill for what is essentially toast."

Chelsea agreed so they took their dinner of cupcakes, garlic bread and soda into his living room and set the feast down on his coffee table. It felt all kinds of wrong not to offer a guest in his home an alcoholic drink but he knew her well enough already to know her answer and he didn't want her to feel any kind of uncomfortable.

"Where'd you get this?" Chelsea asked, eyeing the barely started puzzle that also sat on the coffee table.

"You inspired me the other day, so I came home and raided Mom's cupboards. Feel free to help. I'm not very good."

"Back in a moment." She stood and went into the hallway, returning as promised a few moments later with the box she'd brought when she arrived. "Here," she said, handing it to him.

He took the box and unwrapped it to find a jigsaw puzzle of a glass of whiskey. The image, which consisted mostly of clear glass and amber fluid, sat on an oaky grained table. It was simple but beautiful and would be very tricky to do.

"I love it," he said. "Thanks, but do ya reckon you could help me finish this one first?"

"I'd love to," she replied, settling in beside him.

For the next few hours, they sat together on his sofa, eating, finding pieces of the puzzle and talking about everything from favorite bands to the history of the McKinnel Distillery. For someone who abstained from drinking alcohol, Chelsea showed a great deal of interest in his family business. She listened eagerly as he explained how his father and his father's twin brother had come across from Scotland in their early twenties to travel the US.

"They both got lucky over here—Dad met Mom and on impulse Uncle Hamish bought a lottery ticket and won a bit of money. When Dad decided to move to America for Mom, Hamish came too and they used his winnings to buy the land we're on right now. Coming from the Scottish Highlands region, the boys had been surrounded by whiskey distilleries all their lives. Hamish worked at a local one, where he started as a grain flipper, but he'd always had the ambition to start his own. They were two young men with a dream and because Mom was the reason for the move to America, they decided to use some of her family history in the label. One of her ancestors was a bootlegger—it's his face on our label and our signature bottle is also named after him.

"Not long after they barreled their very first batch, Hamish was killed in a car accident and Dad threw his heart and soul into fulfilling their dreams on his own.

Mom took up the trade, as well—she learned to live and breathe distilling, and when I was born, her parents moved into this cottage to help look after me. By that time Mom and Dad had built the main house with the last of Hamish's winnings."

"Such a sad story," Chelsea said, "but I bet Hamish would be very proud of what your parents achieved. From what I can gather, they've come a long way from those early days."

Callum nodded. "I wish I'd known him."

"What about your father's parents? Are they still alive? Do they still live in Scotland?"

"Yes. They're in a nursing home now but we take turns going across to visit them. All of us except Sophie, Annabel and Mac have done a stint living in Scotland and working in a distillery there that is owned by Dad and Hamish's mentor."

"It must be wonderful to have something that glues your family together like this. I can see why you love this place so much."

He could see the sadness in her eyes when she said this and it made him realize just how lucky he was. "Yes, it is. Do you not see any of your family now?"

She shook her head. "Mom was never in contact with her parents and Dad's mom died before I was born. I was never much more than a burden to anyone in my family, and I haven't seen nor heard from any of Dad's family since he died."

He was racking his head for what to say to that, but she spoke first, directing the conversation back to him. "Do you guys do tours here?"

He nodded. "Yep, Sophie and Blair take turns running them twice daily."

"I'd love to go on one."

"Seriously?" Considering her stance on alcohol, she couldn't have surprised him more if she'd said she'd love to swim naked in the Deschutes River in the middle of winter.

"Yep. I'm interested in what you do."

He grinned. "In that case, why wait for Sophie or Blair to show you through, when I can give you a private tour right now?"

Chapter 10

Why Chelsea found herself so fascinated with the workings of the distillery she didn't understand. But she found herself hanging on Callum's every word as she followed him to the distillery for a private tour and he told her about its history.

They'd put on their winter coats and boots and decided to leave Muffin in the cottage, chewing on the bone Callum had given him earlier.

The distillery was only a short walk from his place and he held her hand the whole way as they trekked across the frosty grounds toward it. This place was magical at night. Someone had strung fairy lights across the trees and the garden was lit up with hundreds of little lights, as well.

"Who looks after the grounds?" she whispered to

him, not wanting to alert his family as they passed his mom's place.

"Mom, actually. She's never happier than when she's in the garden, although some of the heavy work is getting a bit hard for her lately."

The farther away they got from the cottage, the stronger the smell that permeated the air here grew. The aroma of whiskey had always turned her off in the past, but she found herself warming to it. She guessed it was a little like those people who didn't drink coffee but adored the smell.

Only a hundred or so yards in front of the main house was the beautiful building she'd been in the first time she came here. Callum had explained that in addition to his office, the building also held the tasting room, shop floor and small café. Off to one side of this building was a large barn-type structure.

"This is the actual distillery," he said, as they approached and he shone his flashlight at the massive oak entrance doors. "And behind the distillery is our storage and bottling facility. Not all distilleries bottle their own whiskey but it's something we pride ourselves on here at McKinnel's. As you know, I'd like to go one step further and farm our own grain, as well, but I might be getting a little ahead of myself."

If anyone could do it, Callum could, she thought as he took a big ring of keys out of his pocket and dropped her hand in order to open the door. Darkness engulfed them when the door swung back, but he flicked a switch that flooded the building with bright lights. In here the smell of alcohol was so strong, she screwed up her nose, thinking she might get drunk on the fumes.

Callum laughed. "You get used to the smell after a while. I must admit I barely notice it now." Now that there was light, he went over and closed the big doors behind them. "Temperature is very important when it comes to distilling, so we don't want to let the cold air inside."

She visibly shivered at his words and he laughed. "Right, let's get this tour started before we both freeze to death."

"Sounds good." She half laughed, but it didn't quite come out that way as nerves threatened to swallow her whole. The smell of whiskey was so potent, it brought back memories of her father and the rages he used to go into when he'd been on a bender. Which was pretty much every night.

"Are you okay?" Callum asked, a frown creasing his brow.

She nodded and lied. "Just cold. Tour away."

Still looking a little hesitant, Callum gestured for her to follow him and they crossed to the far end of the building. He cleared his throat. "Now, I warn you, I can get carried away when talking about this stuff, so feel free to interrupt or tell me to shut up."

She smirked. "Just get on with it, will you?"

"Yes, miss." He rewarded her with one of his tantalizing smiles and she made the decision to focus on that, on *him*, rather than where they were. "Okay, first thing is the grain and this is where we store it." He pointed to some large silver tanks. "All whiskey is made from some kind of grain—wheat, corn, rye, barley or a blend of these are the traditional ones, but anything goes these days. And lots of boutique distillers are trying other cereal grains."

"Would you ever consider doing so?" she asked.

He nodded. "It's one of the many ideas in my five-year plan, but Dad was dead set against it, so I need to tread carefully as I try to win the others round to the idea."

"Why is the type of grain so important?"

He smiled at her question. "The grain and how we treat it is the first step in determining the flavor of the finished product."

"I see."

"All you need to make whiskey is grain, yeast and water, but that doesn't mean it's easy to do."

Chelsea glanced around them at the rows of tanks, barrels and other large machinery she had no idea of. She could quite believe it.

Over the next little while, Callum walked her around the building, explaining each step of the distilling process in layman's terms so she could understand but also with the kind of passion that made her want him to speak forever.

He taught her about milling and mashing, fermentable sugars, brewing and the two types of stills used.

"Essentially whiskey is just distilled beer. First you make the beer from the grain, water and yeast, then the beer goes into the still for boiling. The alcohol and some flavor evaporate, leaving the water behind. Dad always used to say that beer is for impatient people who don't want to wait for moonshine, and moonshine is for impatient people who can't wait for whiskey."

He'd already mentioned that moonshine—baby whiskey—was what went into the barrel, and whiskey (or bourbon or Scotch, depending on where it was made and what grains were used) was what came out.

"Does it take a long time to make whiskey then?" she asked.

"Whiskey isn't genuine until it has been aged for a minimum of two years, so yes, it takes a while."

"Wow, I don't think my family ever appreciated the effort that went into making it when they were drinking it."

"Well, to be honest, as a distiller, I wouldn't want people to take as long to drink it as we do to make it, or we'd go out of business, but it's nice when connoisseurs take the time to do a tour and learn what they can."

They continued on to the area where the barrels were stored, each one stamped on the end with the McKinnel logo and the date the batch was barreled. The room felt a lot warmer than the rest of the building and was positively temperate compared to outside. "And did I mention all these barrels must be new American oak? That's the law—you can't call it a bourbon unless it's aged in new oak."

Callum's smile dazzled her as he spoke and every word that came from his mouth was so full of fervor that she couldn't help grinning.

He caught her looking and frowned. "What's so funny?"

She shook her head. "Not funny. Wonderful. You really love this stuff, don't you?"

He shrugged a shoulder. "Yeah. I guess I do. I've been feeling a bit jaded lately, but sharing it with you reminds me this is who I am. This distillery, it's in my blood. Without it, I wouldn't know what to do."

"Can I taste some?" The question surprised her almost as much as it did him.

His eyes widened. "What? You serious? I don't want you to feel pressured just because we're here. I wouldn't want to make you do anything you don't feel comfortable with."

She swallowed. If someone had told her a few weeks ago that she'd be voluntarily tasting whiskey, she'd have laughed in their face. But Callum made her want to push boundaries, to step outside her safety zone.

"You're not," she said. "I don't feel pressured at all. Watching you, and seeing your family at Thanksgiving, has shown me that alcohol isn't black and white. I don't want it to scare me anymore. Does that make any sense?"

"Yes, it does." He stepped closer and took her hand; his hand was warm despite the frosty temperatures. "Come on, let's go over to the tasting room."

As they left the actual distillery, Callum let go of Chelsea's hand only long enough to lock the door again, then he led her across to the building she'd gone into that first day they'd met. She'd been nervous the first time she stepped inside, but her heart beat wilder now than it ever had before.

What the heck was she getting herself into?

"Take a seat at the counter," Callum instructed. "Are you warm enough? Do you want me to get the fire going? There's something about tasting whiskey with a roaring fire in the background, I always think."

"That would be great," she said, more to delay the

tasting than anything else. As she looked around this gorgeous building—brimming with McKinnel family history—she fought to control the urge to turn and run away.

Callum shrugged off his coat and threw it across the black leather sofa by the fireplace. Chelsea watched, inhaling and exhaling deeply as he brought the fire to life. Pity she was far too apprehensive to appreciate the lovely view of his tight behind as he squatted low. When he was done, he straightened again, wiped his hands on his jeans and then crossed over to where she was perched on a stool. Smiling at her, he went behind the tasting counter, retrieved two funny-shaped glasses— like a bowl at the bottom but narrower at the top.

"Nosing or snifter glasses," he said. "These are for tasting whiskey, not generally for drinking it—the narrow rim helps channel and concentrate the aromas toward your nostrils, if you know what I mean."

She nodded and only just managed to reply, "I think so."

"Take your coat off, you should be relaxed when tasking whiskey."

Chelsea raised her eyebrows. Relaxed might be asking a little much, but she slipped off her coat and draped it over the stool beside her anyway.

Next Callum took a couple of bottles off the shelf on the back wall. "Remember how I said we have a few different varieties. I'll start you on our signature line— this is a bourbon, which means…"

"It's mostly corn," she interrupted, "and aged in charred new-oak barrels."

"I'm impressed." As he spoke, Callum poured a

small amount into both glasses, then lifted one, swirled the liquid around inside and then handed it to her. "One of the first rules of drinking whiskey—or any alcoholic beverage for that matter—is that you must never do so alone. Drinking is a social thing. Or it should be."

Her stomach flipped as their fingers brushed, but she wasn't sure if it was his touch or the fact she was about to do something she'd always sworn she never would. He noticed her fingers shaking and reached out to steady her hand, wrapping his around hers and the glass as he looked right into her eyes. "Chelsea, you don't have to do this if you don't want to."

"I *do*." She wanted to *and* she needed to. Tasting Callum's whiskey would be like flipping her past the bird. Proving that no matter what happened between them, she would no longer let her past have such a strong hold on her.

"Okay, then," he whispered, easing his hand away from hers. "Take it slow. First look at the color—this will vary depending on the oak of the cask and how long the whiskey has been aging. Then stick your nose in the glass and have a smell. Then do it again and again. A whiskey's nose tells you a lot. If the smell intoxicates you, you're more likely to enjoy the drink."

She did as he said, aware of his eyes fixed on her. Not a sound could be heard except the crackling of the fire behind them. "I can actually smell caramel," she said after a few long moments.

A proud grin spread across Callum's face. "Not many amateurs smell anything the first time. You obviously have a nose for this."

Her stomach flipped at his compliment, giving her

the courage to lift the glass to her mouth. "Okay. Here goes nothing." She sucked in a deep breath and then took a sip. As the liquid hit her tongue, it burned and she screwed up her whole face, spluttering as she swallowed.

"Yuck." She wiped her mouth with the back of her hand as if that would eradicate the aftertaste. "That's *ghastly*! It doesn't *taste* like caramel. How can anyone ever get addicted to *that*?"

Callum had never in his whole life seen anything quite as delightful as Chelsea's reaction to the whiskey. Her beautiful grimace would be imprinted on his mind forever.

"You know not all people who drink alcohol become alcoholics," he said, stretching out his hand and wrapping it around hers, "but I'm sorry that's mostly been your experience."

She shook her head. "Please, don't apologize. My past isn't your fault, but you're showing me the other side of the coin and for that I thank you." And then she lifted the nosing glass and took another sip.

Again, that grimace. This time, he couldn't help laughing.

"Does it get any better?" she asked, a smile blossoming on her face.

"Bourbon can be an acquired taste," he admitted, scrubbing his hand over his beard.

"I'm sorry." She rubbed her lovely lips together. "I'm being rude. This is the produce of your family's love and hard labor. I wonder if I'd like it better with soda or ice? Or is that a big no-no?"

He swallowed, almost losing focus on what she was

saying because he was staring at her lips. "There are no rules. Some folks say you shouldn't drink whiskey anything but straight, some say even adding ice is sin, but I say—and this is one thing my father and I agreed on— that there is no one way to drink whiskey. Saying that, I don't want to force you. We can stop now if you like."

After all, he could think of many other ways to pass their time together.

"No." She shook her head and held out her glass. "Hit me with the next one."

He took the glass and put it to one side. "New whiskey, new glass. This one is our single malt, made with 100 percent malted barley," he explained as he poured her a measure. "It's basically a Scotch, but you can't call it that if it's made outside of Scotland. It'll taste quite different to the bourbon."

Chelsea took the glass, swirled the liquid and then lifted it to her mouth as if she'd been born tasting whiskey. "I can definitely taste the grain in this one," she said after taking a sip. "It's a lot more…"

"Malty?" he suggested.

"Yes," she shrieked. "That's it."

They both laughed.

"Do you like it any better?"

"No, I'm sorry but I don't. Although I never thought I could have this much fun tasting alcohol, the good news is, that after doing so, I think it's safe to say I'll never become an alcoholic. No offence but I much prefer hot chocolate or coffee."

"No offense taken." He wasn't sure any words that escaped *that* mouth could ever be offensive. "Now, shall we go back to my place and do the jigsaw puzzle?"

She raised an eyebrow and leaned a little across the counter toward him. "Is *jigsaw puzzle* code for something else, Callum?"

Heat flooded his body at the suggestiveness in her tone. "Do you want it to be?"

In reply, she leaned even farther forward and pressed her lips against his. This time when they kissed, he tasted McKinnel's own sweet whiskey on her tongue and the combination of Chelsea and the liquor he threw his heart and soul into turned him on like nothing ever had before. Taking her home would take too long. She didn't seem to have any complaints when he all but hauled her over to the rug in front of the still-burning fire and pulled her down onto the ground beside him.

"Oh, *Callum*," she whispered over and over again as he slowly undressed and seduced her. His name had never sounded so sweet as it did on her lips, no woman had ever tasted so good and he couldn't recall ever feeling as alive as he did when he was inside of her. It felt as if he'd known her forever, but a quick calculation revealed they'd barely been acquainted two weeks.

"I hope you don't have security cameras," Chelsea said, still resting her head on his chest and distracting him from his thoughts.

His arms tightened around her. "Shit. We do." He'd been so desperate to have her, he hadn't given a thought to such things.

"Oh no," she squealed, sitting upright and scrambling around them for her clothes.

As much as he enjoyed the view, he chose to put her out of her misery. "Relax, sweetheart, I'm the one who checks the cameras."

She paused in her frantic efforts and turned back to look at him, relief flooding over her face. "Can we go look now?"

He pretended to misunderstand. "You want to watch us in action? I didn't peg you for the kinky type."

Chelsea swatted him with her bra and glared. "I. *Meant.* To. Delete. It."

"I don't know." He shrugged. "That seems a bit of a shame, don't you reckon?" Although he was stringing her along, there was no way he'd ever leave evidence of this night lying around for his family to find. It was hard enough getting them to take him seriously as boss without a sex tape doing the rounds.

"Show me where the recordings are. Now!" Chelsea demanded, standing and dressing quickly. "Or I'll… I'll…"

He laughed and pulled her back into his arms. "Relax. We'll delete them right away."

They took longer to get dressed than they had to get naked, possibly because Callum kept getting distracted. Then, like a couple of naughty teenagers, they headed down the hallway and snuck into his office to erase all evidence of their sordid shenanigans.

Chapter 11

After wolfing down a bowl of Froot Loops, Chelsea opened her door and stepped onto her front porch right into a pile of... She looked down and screwed up her nose in shocked disgust.

Is that horse manure?

Trying not to vomit, she lifted her foot out of the mess and shouted at Muffin, who had all but buried his nose in the pile, to get back. She shoved him inside, closed the door behind her and yanked off both her boots, which were going immediately into the trash. Then she stepped around the poo and peered left and right, trying to see if there were any signs of whoever had left it there.

Nope. Nothing. Not even a car on the road. It was almost eerily quiet out the front of her house. Maybe she should be scared, but right now Chelsea was too furious about her favorite pair of boots to be anxious. She yanked her cell phone out of her purse and almost gagged as she snapped a few shots of her morning delivery, the pungent smell wafting upward as she did so. Knowing she'd need to clean it up before she went out, which would likely make her late for today's job, she went back inside first, shutting the door and then double-checking that she'd locked it. Muffin looked up at her with big wide eyes as if wondering what he'd done to make her punish him.

"I'm sorry, sweet pea, but I think our heavy breather has struck again." As she admitted her fears out loud, her heart raced a little faster. The last couple of weeks she'd spent a fair few nights at Callum's house. The nights she didn't, he often came to her place. However she'd had an early appointment today and Callum an important meeting, so last night they'd only spoken on the phone. Exhausted from night after night of little sleep, she'd slept like a baby, but the idea that while she'd been slumbering some creep had been lurking around outside her house, leaving presents, took the edge off that sleep. It brought back the fears she'd been trying to swallow since the phone calls had started—the fear that someone was watching her every move.

Not wanting to feel like she couldn't sleep soundly in her own home, Chelsea called up Officer Fernandez, hoping he'd take this latest thing more seriously than he had her reports of threatening calls.

He answered after a few rings.

"Hi, Officer, it's Chelsea Porter here." She paused a moment, giving him the chance to place her.

"Hello, Chelsea. Have you had any more calls? Has

the caller identified themselves or made any actual threats yet?" he asked, his tone a little condescending, as if he really didn't have time for this and would much rather deal with something more exciting. Perhaps a murder? Should she try to speak to someone else? Demand Sergeant Moore get back on her case? At least he'd been kind and seemed to take it seriously when Muffin had disappeared.

"I disconnected my home phone, so haven't had any more calls—" Thankfully whoever was behind all this hadn't gotten hold of her cell number yet. "But this morning I got a delivery and I'm sure it's linked to the heavy breather."

"What was this delivery?" He sounded marginally interested.

"A big, smelly pile of horse poo."

This announcement was met with a few moments' silence and then the moron exploded into laugher.

Chelsea raised her eyebrows and her grip tightened on the phone. "I fail to see the amusing side of this, Officer. How would you like it if I delivered said pile of manure to your desk?"

He cleared his throat. "I'm sorry. Quite right."

"I've taken some photos I can send through to you if you like."

"Send away." He chuckled again. "Nothing I like better than a few good photos of shit to start my day."

Chelsea's jaw clenched. "Are you actually going to do anything about this?"

"Of course. I'll come over today and knock on some doors, ask the neighbors if they saw anyone suspicious and then you can let me know if any of the descriptions sound anything like any of the people you've previously done *business* with." Again, he couldn't hide his amusement when speaking about her work, but at least he'd agreed to investigate this time. Still, she was tired of people not taking her work seriously.

"I've got to go out now to…do some *business*…but I'll be back in half an hour or so. Shall I leave the evidence on the porch or will the photos be enough?"

"I'm sure one pile of horse manure is much the same as another," Fernandez said. "I'll make do with the photos."

"Okay." She uttered reluctant thanks, then said, "I'll send them through in a moment."

"Great. Have a good morning, Ms. Porter. I'll be in touch."

Having no confidence whatsoever that Fernandez would even look at the photos, she emailed them to him and then set about removing the evidence and disinfecting the entire length of her front porch. Perhaps she should take comfort from the fact the cops didn't seem overly concerned about her problem. As she hosed down the porch, she decided that if whoever was doing this was a real threat, surely they would have done something more drastic by now.

Chelsea finished the cleanup, then went inside, showered and changed into a whole new outfit. She glanced at her watch, hoping today's dumpee was still at the gym—according to Garth's soon-to-be ex-girlfriend, he was a weight-lifting junkie and, without fail, went every morning. She was glad she'd arranged today's meeting for a public place—she didn't always insist on this, but what with the burglary, the phone calls and now the poo, she didn't want to be alone in private with anyone she didn't know.

After the short drive into town, she parked in front of the gym, then checked his photo and the details of the breakup on her phone, before getting out. She left Muffin in the front seat of the car with the window down for air and went over to wait outside the entrance. Somehow she'd made it here five minutes before Garth's girlfriend had predicted he would leave.

Exactly five minutes later, the door to the gym opened and out strode one of the bulkiest guys Chelsea had ever seen. While he had a classically handsome face, she had to try hard not to grimace at the sweaty, bulgy muscles that weren't hidden at all beneath his sweatpants and sweatshirt. Bulky dudes just weren't her cup of tea. Tall and lean like Callum—that was how she liked them.

Garth saw her looking and smiled warmly. "Hey," he said as he continued on his way.

Chelsea bit her lip and hung back, almost paralyzed. Although Garth seemed like a friendly bloke, she had a vision of exactly what he could do if he wanted to hurt her. But unease wasn't the only thing holding her back. The last week or so, for the first time since she'd started her business, she'd found herself beginning to dread the face-to-face meetings where she had to deliver the bad news to someone's boyfriend or girlfriend. It was hard to be stoic about ending a relationship when she herself was living in a bubble of bliss.

Because that was the only definition for what she had going on with Callum. Granted it was early days—

generally she didn't feel the need to detach herself from someone until the two-or three-month mark—but this thing with him felt different already. The shine of her new relationship hadn't even begun to wear off. Her attraction toward him was strong, if not stronger, than that first moment she'd laid eyes on him. But it was no longer simple chemistry that drew her to him, it was much more—they had fun together. She didn't even care that he made his money from making whiskey— and this scared the hell out of her.

For the first time, Chelsea found herself thinking of a future with a man. For the first time, she felt the risk of getting hurt.

Callum and her relationship was still a national secret, due mostly to her fears that her professional reputation would be sacrificed if it got out that they were seeing each other. Of course that wouldn't be a problem if she stopped doing this and did something else instead. But what would she do? She'd enjoyed waitressing but she wasn't passionate enough about it to want to make a career out of it. And, although Callum undoubtedly savored her company, he'd not given any indication of wanting anything more serious. Since Thanksgiving, he'd made no suggestions she meet his family again nor mentioned anything more than red-hot fun.

Muffin barked as Garth passed Chelsea's car on his way to hers and the sound jolted her back to the present. No matter if she was questioning her career, she had an obligation to follow through on all current jobs and Garth was one of them. Spurred into action, she called out his name as she started jogging toward him.

* * *

As they didn't have a private room big enough to accommodate the whole family in the distillery buildings, Sophie had called the family meeting at their mom's dining table. It had taken almost a month to find a time when everyone could attend, and Callum was biting at the bit to get started. Unfortunately, the rest of his family didn't appear to share his urgency and right now only his mom and Sophie were here.

"I'll go gather the troops," Sophie said, pushing back from her seat at the table and hurrying out.

Callum tapped his fingers on the dining room table.

"Relax," his mom said from across the table. She poured him a glass of orange juice and then pushed it toward him. "They'll be here soon. How's that lovely girl you brought to Thanksgiving? Is it her car I've been seeing parked outside your cottage late some nights? I can't help but notice on the nights her car isn't there, your SUV is often absent also."

He took a sip of juice and leveled his eyes with hers. "You ever considered a job with the FBI?"

She laughed. "I only notice what matters to me, and you, my darling, matter. While I'm sorry to see you and Bailey go your separate ways, Chelsea seemed lovely. If things are getting serious in that department, maybe you should bring her over for dinner again soon?"

Callum spluttered. "Serious? Who said anything about serious, Mom? I know you're desperate for more grandbabies but my focus right now is the distillery. You know that." He'd meant it when he said he didn't have time for a relationship—he'd barely seen Bailey the last few weeks they'd been together—but he was making time for Chelsea and enjoying every moment of it. Nora opened her mouth to say something more and Callum prepared himself for a lecture on the balance of work and play, but the dining room door swung open again and Sophie returned, all her siblings bar one in tow.

"I called Mac," she said, taking her seat at the table again. "He's only a few minutes away." Mac had a massive, architecturally designed house on one side of the formation in the mountains that gave Jewell Rock its name—from his front porch, he overlooked the whole town—but until recently he'd barely lived there.

"Good," Callum grunted and took another sip of orange juice as he checked the PowerPoint presentation for the umpteenth time.

While his siblings helped themselves to drinks and Nora encouraged them all to devour the feast she'd laid out on the table, Callum glanced over at the photo of his dad on the mantel.

I promise I'm doing all this for the greater good, he said silently, knowing that if Conall McKinnel were still alive, none of what he was about to propose would stand a chance.

"How's Hamish doing? I haven't seen him since Thanksgiving," Annabel said to Lachlan before shoving a piece of Mom's chocolate brownie into her mouth. Hanging around all the guys at the firehouse had taken the edge off her femininity, but he'd heard she had plenty of admirers so it didn't seem to be doing her any harm.

"He's great." That proud grin Lachlan got whenever he talked about his son came onto his face. "He's just joined the school chess club, so we're living and breathing it at home at the moment."

Annabel smiled. "I'll have to give him a game. But you'll have to warn him, I'm pretty good—we often play it while waiting at work."

Listening, Callum bit back a smile. For some reason the idea of all these big, burly firefighters sitting around playing chess caused him amusement.

At that moment, Mac entered the room—looking as grumpy as he had every day since quitting the team. "Sorry I'm late," he muttered, as he sat down beside Blair and surveyed the table. "Have we got anything else aside from OJ?"

"I can get you some water if you'd like, Owen," Mom said, and although she sounded perfectly warm, the fact she'd used his proper name let everyone know it was a reprimand. Nothing escaped Mom's notice and, like Callum, she'd observed that Mac had been drinking a fair amount of late.

"Let's get started," Callum said, clearing his throat. He looked to Sophie sitting beside him and she nodded, pushed a few buttons on his laptop and the first slide of their presentation appeared on the wall behind them. "Thank you all for coming today. With Sophie's help, I want to show you a few ideas I have for the business. We've divided these into four main areas and created a five-year plan, showing how we would like to roll them out. Area one is merchandise, which will be Sophie's baby, so I'll let her talk about that more in a moment. Area two is entertainment and hospitality. You know I want to expand the café into a restaurant and I'm pleased to announce that Lachlan is willing to come on board as head chef. The restaurant, how it runs, its style, et cetera, will all be his vision, but," he turned to look at Mac, "the café area we currently have is too small, so we'll need someone to oversee the building of an extension. Mac, I'd love you to head this project if you have the time."

Mac's eyes widened and then he blinked as if he wasn't sure whether to be offended or appreciative of the offer.

"No need to give me a definitive answer right now," Callum said, "I'd just like you to think about it. And if you're interested, then Lachlan, you and I can talk more later."

Quinn piped up. "You make this all sound like a done deal. Is there any point the rest of us being here?"

"Quinn," Nora chastised, "stop being a spoiled brat and listen to your brother's ideas."

Callum tossed his mom a grateful smile. "Also in the area of entertainment and hospitality is the option of holding events such as weddings and other celebrations on our grounds. We've got plenty of space for a marquee in the summer months and with the new restaurant, we'll be able to offer catering, as well." He didn't mention that this idea had been Chelsea's, but her face came into his head and he couldn't help smiling at the thought of her.

"This all sounds fabulous," Annabel said, reaching for another brownie. "I'm almost a little sad I don't work here."

"You just say the word and we'll find a job for you."

Annabel grinned. "I'll give it serious thought." But they all knew she'd never leave the firehouse.

"Area three is distilling." Callum continued quickly before Quinn could make a snide remark about their whole business being distilling. "I've been talking to Blair about the possibility of expanding our range— maybe starting to sell white dog, marketing it as a good replacement for vodka in cocktails. In the restaurant, we can have a range of cocktails and even the odd demonstration about how to make them. There's also the option of experimenting with more grains and…"

"White dog?" Quinn scoffed. "Dad would never have gone for that. In fact, he'd have hated all of this. He hated change."

Callum clenched his fists. "And that was fine twenty, thirty or forty years ago when we were the only one of our kind around, but you'd have to be blind not to have noticed all the other boutique distilleries popping up in the region. We're not only competing with the big-brand bourbons now, we're up against the beer, rum and vodka guys to name a few in our own backyard. If we don't start to make a few changes, we'll go under. Is that what you want?"

Quinn glowered back, his cheeks flushing red. Callum realized he was practically shouting and he glanced apologetically at his mom, but she smiled encouragingly and spoke for the first time since the meeting had officially started.

"No one wants that, Callum, and I have to say I'm liking all these ideas. Go on, please."

He took a quick breath and then hit them with area four. "Grain production. Now hear me out," he said, when a few of his siblings made noises of surprise. "I've been looking at the farming land adjacent to ours and am in discussions with the owner, who is wanting to ease into retirement. If we lease some of his land and grow our own grain, in the long term, we'll save a huge amount of money and have more control over the quality of the grain we use."

"I love the idea," Blair said, "but, just one question— who is going to farm this grain of ours? Aside from Mom, none of us is exactly a green thumb."

Callum looked across to his sister and winked. "Annabel?"

When the laughter had died down, he took heart that, except for Quinn, everyone seemed enthusiastic about his ideas. "We'll hire a farm manager of course."

Quinn, although sounding more resigned, had one final bugbear. "All this sounds mighty expensive."

Callum opened his mouth to reply but Mom got there first. "What's that saying about having to spend money to make money?"

Her enthusiasm surprised him; he'd thought she'd be more reluctant, hold on to the distillery as her husband and his brother had envisioned, but if anything, she sounded as excited as him.

Quinn held his hands up in surrender. "Alright, you've almost convinced me, but can I make one suggestion?"

"Anything," Callum said, thrilled that it had been a lot easier to win Quinn around than he'd thought.

"These events you want to run? Do you think we could outsource the planning to Bailey? She's hoping to quit working in Bend to start her own events-management company."

"Really?" It was the first Callum had heard of it, and

he couldn't help but wonder why Quinn knew so much about Bailey. Then again, they'd been in the same year at school and still had a number of mutual friends, so that probably accounted for it. Whatever, he didn't have the time or inclination to think about this any further.

"Sure," he said, "if everyone else is agreeable."

His family nodded in unison. Working with Bailey could be a good thing—they could reestablish a professional friendship—and if not, well, she'd mostly be dealing with Lachlan and Sophie he imagined.

"Just one more thing, I also had this idea about how we could promote responsible drinking among our customers and patrons of the restaurant."

Quinn, back on form, scoffed, "You want to encourage our customers *not* to drink?"

"No." He shook his head, annoyed. But the thought of Chelsea and her background made him continue. While he wasn't about to take responsibility for all the alcoholics on the planet, being with her had reminded him of the vulnerability some people had where alcohol was concerned. "But being seen to be aware of alcohol abuse could be good for business. I was thinking about partnering up with the local taxi company to offer a discount for restaurant diners, or maybe even offering a free dinner to the driver."

"Another innovative idea, big brother," Annabel said. "I'm in favor of anything that might reduce the number of motor vehicle accidents we have to attend."

"Thanks. But right now, it's just a thought. I know this has been a lot to take in at once, but does anyone have anything they want clarified?"

It was a stupid question. His mom, brothers and Annabel all opened their mouths and spoke at once. Even Mac seemed to show more enthusiasm for the future of the distillery than he had for anything in quite a while. Callum and Sophie spent the next hour or so answering questions and explaining various things in greater detail.

Then came the vote.

They'd always been an open family, so there was no secret ballot. However, the rules of the distillery were that every member of the family must be agreeable before anything new could go ahead.

Nora took on her role as matriarch. "All in favor of going forward with the five-year plan presented today, raise your hand."

Callum held his breath, glancing around the table from face to face as one by one hands shot into the air. As he suspected, Quinn was the only one to hesitate, but just when Callum thought all was lost, a slow smile crept onto his younger brother's face and he raised his hand.

"Okay. Let's do this," Quinn said, and happy cheers burst all around them.

Callum pulled Sophie into a tight hug and whispered his thanks for everything into her hair. There were exciting times ahead for the McKinnels…he could feel it in his blood.

Chapter 12

"How was your day?" Callum asked after greeting her with a smoking-hot kiss. The way his green eyes glowed and the smile that stretched almost from ear to ear told her his day had been a great success and she couldn't wait to hear about it.

Her *day* flashed before her eyes in a series of snap-shots—there was so much to tell him, but something held her back from including the whole horse manure thing. Not wanting to alarm him or make him feel obliged to protect her, she still hadn't mentioned the phone calls or the fact she felt like she was being fol-lowed, so this latest installment would come out of the blue.

"Okay." She sighed, still feeling a little heavy in her heart. While she was eternally single, her work had felt important, as if she was doing a service to others like herself who were unlucky in love, but now she wasn't so sure whether she *was* single or how she felt about her work. "I dumped a guy…"

"And?" he prompted, leading her into the house and down the hallway into the living room. Muffin had already collapsed on the rug in front of the fire.

"*And* it's hard to explain, but I didn't get the same satisfaction I usually do."

He frowned.

"*Satisfaction* isn't the right word," she said, frustrated that she couldn't explain herself well. "But when I'm spending time with someone after I've broken the bad news to them, I usually feel that it is time well spent. That I'm somehow helping them get through a tough time and that, by listening and talking to them, I'm giving them hope for a future. Today, when I told this poor guy, he was fighting back tears, and I felt like… I don't know…a tax collector or something."

Callum chuckled and pulled her down onto the couch with him. He caught her face in his two big palms and smiled down at her. "You do have an unusual career, but if it's not making you happy, maybe you should think about doing something else."

She blew air out between her teeth and felt her bangs fly up a little. She felt more unsettled than she had since those days when she'd had no real place to call home.

"But what would I do?"

Chelsea wasn't exactly expecting him to have an answer, but he surprised her by offering one. His expression turned serious and his tone matched. "Remind me again why your friend suggested you start a business of breaking up for people?"

"Because I have personal expertise in dumping men."

He half smiled. "I meant the other reason. Wasn't it because you were a good listener?"

She rubbed her lips together and nodded. "Yes. That too."

"I've certainly found that to be true," he said. "You've listened to me ramble on and on about the distillery for hours and always acted interested."

"That's because I am interested."

"Even though you come from a long line of alcoholics?"

And she nodded, realizing the terrifying fact that Callum could be talking about toilet paper designs and she'd still hang on his every word. How many nights over the last few weeks had they stayed up until the early hours of the morning talking? It was no longer just his body she craved when they were apart, but every single thing about him. The way he bit his lower lip and his brow creased when he was concentrating over a puzzle, his devotion to Muffin, his love for his family, his ambition, the way he looked in an apron—she could go on and on.

"You are an excellent listener," he said, and she took a moment to remember what they were talking about. "That gives you a fair few other career options."

"Oh?" Chelsea tried to focus on what he was saying when inside her heart was threatening cardiac arrest having just been told by her brain that she'd fallen in love. *Really?* She could hardly believe this alien concept, but it was the only explanation for the way she felt about Callum. The only reason the shine hadn't even begun to wear off their fling.

He counted off the possibilities on his fingers. "You could become a hairdresser or you could host your own talk-radio show."

She felt her lips lift at the edges. "Are you simply plucking random careers from nowhere?"

He shook his head. "No, these are jobs where you're required to be a good listener. Or you could become a counselor and really make a difference with your wonderful talent for listening and knowing the right things to say to make people feel better."

"A counselor?" She tried the words on for size. "That would involve going to college or something."

"Which you'd excel at, I'm sure." Callum gave her an encouraging smile that not only melted her insides but boosted her confidence. He sounded like he actually believed in her. Aside from Rosie and her grandfather, when he wasn't blind drunk, no one else ever had.

"Hmm… You know, I would love to work with kids and teens who come from similar backgrounds to my own. Maybe you're on to something."

"Of course I am." He pulled her into his arms and kissed her, which resulted in all sensible thought vanishing from her head. She could barely think straight, never mind seriously plan her future when Callum's lips and hands were bestowing such attention upon her.

As was the way whenever she came to his place or he to hers, conversation waned for a while as other things, *wonderful*, *earth-shattering* things, took over. She let the physical sensations wash through her and tried to forget about the disquieting emotional ones.

After thoroughly ravishing each other, they turned their attentions to food. Callum outdid himself this time, managing to throw together a satay beef and noodle stir-fry without burning any of it. While they ate, she finally remembered to ask him about *his* day.

"Hey, how was your family meeting?" she asked between mouthfuls.

"Magic." He grinned, sounding like an excited schoolboy as he told her all about it.

"Everyone was really open to the new ideas. I feel awful admitting this, but it was such a different vibe to those meetings when Dad was at the head of the table, pooh-poohing anyone else's suggestions. I think I could have been sixty-five and he still wouldn't have given me any real responsibility; I just wish he didn't have to die to give me the chance."

"I guess it was hard for him to relinquish control of the company he and his brother had put their everything into. Maybe handing over any part of the business would have felt like losing even more of his brother?"

"Yeah, I get that, but it felt more like he didn't trust or believe in me. Sometimes I think he still saw us all as little kids. Hell, I was willing to get married to prove to him I was a grown-up."

"What do you mean?"

He blinked and ran a hand through his hair as if he hadn't meant to admit this, but then said, "I'm not proud to admit it, but I doubt I'd have asked Bailey to marry me if I hadn't thought maybe it would help Dad see me as more of an adult. He was very traditional, and I got this idea in my head that if I had marital responsibilities, he'd see it as time to hand me some of the business responsibilities, as well. Don't get me wrong—I like Bailey and we had fun together, but there wasn't enough between us to build a lifetime. We were both going into marriage together for the wrong reasons. Thank God she saw sense."

Chelsea swallowed, uneasy at the reference to her client, but at the same time wanting to pry deeper. Was he against marriage in general? Or just marriage to Bailey?

She forced those questions from her head. "You know, I'm sure your dad is looking down from wherever he is up there and he'll see the success you make of the distillery and he'll be proud."

Callum chuckled. "I'm not sure I believe in all that 'up there' stuff, but right now he's probably turning in his grave at some of the things I'm planning to do.

"Sounds like you're going to be very busy indeed."

He winked. "Don't worry, I'll make time for you."

And then he stood and began clearing the table. As Callum carried their dishes over to the sink and started filling it with water, Chelsea watched, wondering if his feelings for her were growing at the same crazy rate as hers were for him. She refused to ask him, because if he ever confessed his love to her, she wanted him to do so of his own free will. She never wanted to feel like a burden or an obligation to anyone ever again.

She'd wondered if he might ask her to Christmas dinner with his family, but Christmas was only a week away, and he hadn't mentioned it once. It was quite obvious that turning the distillery around was his prime focus right now.

As was becoming their habit, after dinner they retreated to his bed to watch late-night television until Callum finally drifted off to sleep. Chelsea took a while to fall asleep—instead, she took the time to admire his naked form beside her. He truly was a work of art and this felt more like a relationship than anything she'd been in before. Usually when things started to head this way with a guy she was dating, she freaked and ended it, but the closer she got to Callum, the more she didn't want it to end.

After a taxing day, which included a long drive to do a face-to-face breakup in a town on the very boundary of her face-to-face region, Chelsea returned to her place exhausted. She and Callum had made no official plans to meet that evening. In fact, he hadn't sent her so much as a text message today. She guessed he was just busy with all the new plans for the distillery, but she missed the messages he often sent her, which brightened her days. And she couldn't help worrying that maybe there was more to his silence. Was he getting bored with her? This feeling of anxiousness in relation to a man was a new one and she didn't like it one bit.

Not knowing whether he'd turn up later or not, she'd bought enough Indian takeout in case he did and a big tub of their favorite ice cream for dessert. Their love of nutty coconut was another one of the many things they'd found in common.

"Muffin, come inside," Chelsea called to her dog. He was sniffing something over by the fence and eventually trundled over to her with a raw piece of meat in his hands.

"Gross," she exclaimed, leaning down to grab it out of his mouth. She hurled it toward the street, then with her unbloody hand opened the door. Muffin skulked off to the kitchen, obviously angry at her for stealing his treasure. Chelsea followed, dumped the takeout on the counter and the ice cream in the freezer and then went into her bedroom to change into more comfortable clothes.

She'd taken two steps into her bedroom, when the door slammed shut behind her. Frowning, she looked to the window, wondering if she'd left it open and the breeze had blown the door shut, and then her heart thudded in her chest at the sight of broken glass. Someone had thrown a brick into her house; it now lay in the pile of shattered glass on her bedroom floor.

"Hello, Chelsea," said a menacing voice, and she spun around to come face-to-face with a man she vaguely recognized. He smiled creepily at her and she suddenly placed him as a guy she'd dumped a few months back. A man who'd been on the list she'd given the police of people who could potentially bear a grudge against her, but who, like all the others, had been ruled out as dangerous. She remembered his girlfriend had cited his neediness as one of the main reasons for the breakup.

"Finally I have your attention," said the guy.

Her whole body trembling, Chelsea somehow managed to say, "Freddie, isn't it? What are you doing here?"

"You hurt me" was his reply and she swallowed, not knowing how to respond. "I loved Lara and *you* split us up."

On the other side of the closed door, Muffin started barking like a crazy dog and Chelsea silently prayed her elderly neighbor Maureen didn't have her television turned up too loud and would hear him.

"Did you leave that piece of meat out front for my dog?" she asked, her tone equally as accusing as his. Her heart turned icy as she wondered exactly what this lovelorn man was capable of. "Was it poisoned?"

"It wouldn't have killed him, just made him sick. I'm not an animal hurter. I just…"

His voice trailed off and, hoping her words wouldn't aggravate him further, Chelsea changed her form of attack. "I'm sorry you've been hurting," she began. Her spray deodorant was only an arm's length away from her on the dresser. If she could grab it without him seeing, then she could spray him in the eyes, which would hopefully stun him enough to give her time to escape.

"My life isn't worth living without Lara in it," Freddie said, his unnerving gaze on her never wavering. "Since you told me it was over, she won't take my calls or see me. How am I supposed to win her back if she won't even talk to me?"

You're not. That's the whole idea of breaking up. Of course Chelsea knew better than to say this to him.

"Do you want my help? Is that why you've been calling me?" she asked.

Freddie blinked, as if wondering whether to admit to this or not. Then he said, "Yes. But also to make you stop doing what you're doing. You're going to hurt other men too. But you didn't listen. You didn't stop. Even after I broke into your house a few weeks back and left poo on your porch yesterday, you still keep dumping men like me. I've seen you."

She failed to see how she was supposed to get his message from a pile of horse manure, but that didn't matter now. What mattered was that he knew about the breakups she'd done lately and had all but confessed to following her. So she hadn't been imagining it after all. This thought brought little comfort, and she glanced again at the deodorant. "If you'd left a message instead of hanging up all the time, I could have talked to you, Freddie. We could have worked something out."

"It's not *my* fault you do what you do!" he shouted, spittle shooting from his mouth.

"I didn't say it was," she said, taking the tiniest of steps toward her dresser. The way he shouted at her, reminded her of the way her dad had shouted at her and her mom whenever he was drunk. It was hard to tell if Freddie was an actual threat or just a really sad guy, but as he'd broken into her house twice and tried to poison her dog, she decided to take him seriously. "You seem like a great guy. Lara has obviously made a terrible mistake."

"Thanks to you," he spat, as she took another almost imperceptible step.

"Yes, thanks to me," she agreed, her palms so sweaty she could feel the perspiration running down them. "Tell me about your relationship with Lara. What is so special about her?" If she could get him talking, maybe she could make him see that the breakup was a good thing. At the least, it would hopefully distract him so he wouldn't notice her dive for the deodorant.

Freddie stared at her a moment as if trying to work out if this were a trick question, then his stance relaxed a little and he started to talk. He told her about how Lara and he met at a soup kitchen where they both cooked for the homeless and how she was the kindest, prettiest girl he ever knew. He told her of dates they'd been on and how he wanted to move in together but she'd thought it was too soon.

"She sounds very special," Chelsea agreed, "but you know what? All those romantic dates you planned show that you're a pretty amazing guy yourself. You deserve someone who really appreciates all that, and it doesn't sound like Lara is that girl. I know you're hurting—losing someone you love is the worst feeling ever—but if you accept Lara's decision and let her go, I believe there's someone even better out there waiting for you."

She knew these words were risky and couldn't imagine any woman wanting a man who would break in and trash another woman's apartment, but there was some truth in her message.

Finally, with his head cocked to one side, Freddie spoke, "You are kinder than I imagined." He sighed and wrung his hands together. "I'm sorry. I'm not really a bad dude, I can't believe I—"

At that moment the door behind him burst open and Callum exploded into the room, his nostrils flared and his eyes cold as he launched at Freddie, grabbing hold of him and yanking his arms behind his back so he couldn't move.

Chelsea let out a long breath she hadn't realized she'd been holding as Muffin jumped up at Freddie's knees, barking louder than he ever had before.

"Are you okay?" Callum looked to her, speaking over the top of Freddie's head.

She nodded, blinking back the tears that threatened now that the danger was over.

Callum turned his attention to Freddie. "Who the hell are you? And what do you think you're doing?"

Freddie looked terrified and Chelsea's heart went out to him. He was misguided, yes, but deep down she didn't think him evil. "You're hurting him!"

Callum glared at her. "And what the hell do you think he would have done to you if I hadn't turned up when I did? Call the police!" Ignoring her, he turned back to Freddie. "Are you the one who broke into her house before? You better start talking!"

Her hands shaking and her heart still racing, Chelsea knew there was no point arguing with Callum right now. Besides, although she believed she'd almost had the situation under control, she couldn't deny the relief she'd felt when Callum had appeared like a knight in shining armor to rescue her. She staggered past the men into the kitchen, grabbed her cell from her purse and dialed 911. Part of her felt sorry for Freddie and didn't want to get him into trouble, but she hoped if he were charged for the phone calls and the break-ins maybe the authorities would get him the psychological help he needed.

Chapter 13

Callum didn't let the intruder go until two uniformed police officers arrived and cuffed him. Finally, and only then, did his muscles start to relax and his breathing return to normal.

He'd arrived at Chelsea's place and heard frantic barks the moment he'd climbed out of the SUV. After a few weeks of being in Muffin's company, he'd come to identify his different barks and recognized instantly that this wasn't a good one. Although there was every chance Chelsea hadn't heard his knock on the door over the noise of the barking, when it went unanswered, Callum's hackles had risen, an uneasy feeling settling in his gut. He'd tried the door handle and, after discovering it unlocked, hesitated only a few moments before letting himself inside. The fact the little dog hadn't abandoned his pursuit to welcome Callum only increased his anxiety. He'd stormed into the hallway and found Muffin on the wrong side of Chelsea's closed bedroom door. There was no logical reason why she would lock the dog out and that was all the encouragement he'd needed to fling open the door and barge inside.

It had taken him all of two seconds to analyze the situation—window broken, glass shattered all over the room, Chelsea over by the dresser, an oily-haired sleazy-looking man standing threateningly before her, blocking her passage to the door.

And Callum had seen red. He'd launched himself at the guy and barely managed to control the rage blustering inside him. In hindsight, he reckoned he deserved a medal for the self-control he'd displayed by *not* ripping the man's tonsils out and feeding them to Muffin for dinner.

But, thankfully, the man was now gone and the danger over. A whimpering mess when the cops questioned him, Freddie had confessed to a whole host of offenses relating to Chelsea—most of which were news to Callum. He couldn't believe that while they'd been sleeping together, she'd never thought to mention she was getting threatening phone calls and was worried about someone following her. He could have *done* something.

They stood on the porch, Muffin still barking, as they watched the police car reverse into the road. Then Callum turned to Chelsea and yanked her into his arms.

He inhaled the vanilla scent of her hair and relished her soft loveliness pressed against him. She felt so damn good, she fit so perfectly, and the thought of anything bad happening to her made him crazy.

"Move in with me," he begged.

"What?" Chelsea pulled back from his embrace and looked at him as if he were as mentally unstable as Freddie.

He was almost as surprised as her by his question, but it made sense, didn't it?

They'd been spending practically every night together anyway and after coming upon Freddie in her bedroom, Callum wouldn't ever be able to sleep soundly knowing she was home alone.

"You'll be safe with me, out at the distillery," he said, his thoughts storming ahead, "and while you're studying to do counseling, you could work with us. Sophie was only saying the other day how she's struggling with the social media side of things since taking on the extra merchandise planning and stuff."

When Chelsea simply stared at him, he continued, "You'd be great at that. You're good online since you've run your business mostly through the internet. And, the job will be flexible, so you can—"

Chelsea held up a hand to interrupt him. "Let me get this straight. You want me to move in with you and work at the distillery."

He nodded. "It makes perfect sense."

"To whom?" She took a step back and threw her hands up in the air. "I don't need your protection, Callum McKinnel. I might have been handling things differently than you would have with Freddie, but I almost had everything under control when you stormed in there all heavy-handed. And I already have a job, one I can do while I'm studying, *if*—and I haven't decided on that yet—I go the counseling route."

Her words were like venom and he couldn't understand why she was angry at him. He was only trying to help, only looking out for the woman he cared about. "Yesterday you said you were starting to question your career."

She snapped her hands to her hips and glared at him. "Well, today I'm remembering how important it is. How helping people end a relationship when those in it have different priorities, different needs and desires is a very worthwhile profession. In fact, I think it's time to tell you that this thing we have going on has met its expiration date."

"What?"

"It's over, Callum. You can stop feeling like you need to protect me from danger, because that was never what this was about. I warned you that I didn't do relationships, this was just a charade that got out of hand, so don't pretend this is a big surprise. Thanks for the fun. Merry Christmas and good luck with the distillery. I'm sure you'll make it a great success."

And with those words, Chelsea grabbed Muffin's collar and hauled herself and the dog inside. She slammed the door shut in his face, leaving him standing out on the porch in the freezing evening air wondering what the hell had just happened.

He'd been starting to think this was something real, something more than just sex between him and Chelsea, but the moment he took a step toward commitment, she'd all but thrown it in his face. He stared at the closed door for a few more moments, dithering about storming right back inside and kissing some sense into her, but she'd made her feelings perfectly clear. If he barged in and tried to plead his case, he'd be no better than Freddie, unable to accept that she didn't feel the same way about him as he did about her.

He'd sliced open his heart and bared his soul talking about his family and his hopes and dreams, but now he realized Chelsea had been very reticent about sharing much about herself. That showed exactly how she felt about their liaison. For a guy who hadn't thought he wanted a relationship right now, her rejection cut deep. Much, much deeper than his breakup with Bailey had.

It was with this thought in his head that he managed to drag himself off the porch, over to his SUV and drive slowly home where he immediately headed for the sofa to drown his sorrows in a bottle of McKinnel's finest whiskey.

"Well, that's it then." Chelsea spoke to Muffin as she peeked through her curtain to watch Callum's SUV disappear into the night. "I've done it again, although for a different reason than usual." She sounded far more nonchalant than she felt, but despite the aching in her heart, which was growing by the second, ending things with Callum was the right thing to do.

While she'd been fantasizing about him offering her more than the no-strings fun they'd been enjoying, he'd only asked her to move in with him out of a perverted sense of duty. And that was the last thing she wanted. She'd spent her childhood and most of her adolescence with people who'd felt obliged to look after her and no way was she going down that path again as an adult.

She had too much self-respect for that and as much as her heart might hate her right now, in time it would recover and so would she. She was the breakup expert after all—she knew all the tricks for recovering from a broken heart, even if she'd never actually had one herself. Until now.

"First step ice cream."

Muffin barked his approval, then tottered after her into the kitchen.

Ignoring the scents of India wafting from the take-out bag on the counter, she went straight to the freezer, retrieved the ice cream she'd bought for their dessert and then grabbed a spoon to eat it with. She took these things to the couch, switched on the TV, peeled off the lid and then dug her spoon right in. But when the first spoonful melted on her tongue, it didn't offer any of the comfort she'd been hoping for. This ice cream, which she'd now shared with Callum numerous times, tasted like their late-night kisses.

A tear slipping down her cheek, Chelsea dumped the ice cream—spoon and all—on the coffee table in front of her. Had he broken her heart *and* ruined her favorite ice cream for her? She didn't think she'd ever be able to enjoy nutty coconut again. She swiped at the tear, but it was no good as another one replaced it almost immediately. Then another and another and another until she found herself curled in the fetal position on her sofa bawling her eyes out.

Every inch of her ached, as if the pain was seeping from her broken heart and spreading like wildfire through her body. She started to shake and Muffin came up beside her and shoved his head into her face, licking the salt from her cheeks. She pulled him into her arms, seeking the comfort his warm, furry body had always given, but this time it didn't work.

Yes, she still had Muffin, but he was no longer enough. She wanted Callum more than she'd wanted her parents to stop drinking when she was a child, and she wanted *him* to want *her* with that same desperation.

Taking a deep breath, Chelsea tried to imagine sitting across a table from herself—what would her professional persona say to her right now? She thought of her words to Freddie earlier in the evening but, now that she was in his position, they felt empty and she could understand why he'd acted the way he did. Love messed with your brain, it made you think crazy thoughts and want to do crazy things. No wonder it was sometimes referred to as a drug.

In her two years of being the breakup girl, she'd handed out numerous pieces of advice on how to recover. Aside from the ice cream, there were many practical steps one could take in this process.

Find your independence again. How many people had she encouraged to go pursue a new hobby or interest in order to distract them from their hurt? She thought of her hobby—jigsaws—and let out a gut-wrenching sob. They'd never be the same again either.

Help someone. This involved donating your time to a good cause—like helping out at a homeless shelter or something. The idea being that helping someone else through hardship might help you forget yours or realize it's not as bad as you think.

Get out of the house and meet new people—you'll soon learn there truly are more fish in the sea. Or simply get online and do so.

As Chelsea ticked through all the steps in her head, she stumbled across one major problem. Right now, she didn't know how she'd ever be able to summon the will to leave her couch ever again and, unfortunately, moving on required effort.

Maybe she should have said yes. Callum wouldn't have asked her to move in with him if he didn't at least like her, and like could turn to love, couldn't it? If she'd said yes, right now she'd be in his arms and they'd be…

Jeez, listen to yourself. The nostalgic voice in her head sounded exactly like the kind of desperate she despised. How the heck had one man made such an imprint on her life, on *her*, in such a short time?

She'd fallen hard and fast, and now her only hope was that the time needed to get over him was equally as short.

Chapter 14

Callum stared at the range of sample merchandise Sophie had spread over his desk and tried to feign some kind of enthusiasm. As she rattled on about each item and how it would work to enhance their new image, he rubbed a hand against his forehead, wishing like hell his damn headache would take a hike. He'd drunk too much last night. Hell, he'd drunk too much every night since Chelsea had dumped him. Always with the aim to obliterate thoughts of her—it worked to an extent for a fraction of a time, but in the mornings he always regretted it.

If he wasn't careful he'd be sliding down the same slippery slope he worried about Mac traveling, and after all those conversations about Chelsea's parents, he should know better. He needed to get a grip or all his innovative ideas for the distillery were going to be ruined in the aftermath of his self-destruction.

It was time to find another vice. He'd thought work enough but...

"And this," Sophie said, pointing to a little box with a postcard-perfect image of the distillery printed on the top, "is quite possibly my favorite product."

Positively beaming, she lifted the box, removed the lid and upturned it. He watched in horror as what looked like hundreds of little pieces of card fell onto his desk, scattering across everything else.

"What the hell is that?"

Sophie half frowned, half smirked. "It's a puzzle, brother dear. They're very popular at the moment believe it or not. They're experiencing some sort of resurgence, a bit like adult coloring books, which I also think we should consider selling—McKinnel branded of course. A guy Storie knows has started up this company in Bend, creating high quality, personalized gifts and he can do these puzzles for us at an awesome price."

Callum heard nothing of what she said—glancing down at all the puzzle pieces, his heart squeezed so hard he was certain he was having a heart attack. Whatever he did, wherever he went, there were reminders of Chelsea and they were suffocating him. He pushed back his office chair, opened his desk drawer and grabbed his car keys.

"I need some fresh air" was all the excuse he gave his sister as he strode past her and out of his office. He barely registered the customers milling around the tasting room or Mac and Lachlan outside starting to take measurements for the restaurant extensions—all he could think about was his escape.

He crunched over the frosty ground to his SUV, climbed inside and then he drove, having no destination in mind, simply needing to get away from the distillery and from the memories. Less than a month he'd known Chelsea and now wherever he looked there were memories of her—in his house, in the distillery, even in his goddamn office where they'd laughed their heads off together as they'd erased the footage of their naughty night.

Callum drove aimlessly—or so he thought—until he found himself slowing in front of the animal shelter where he'd rescued Muffin. He recalled his thought to get a dog a few weeks back and it made more sense now. A dog would make his house less empty when he stepped inside, and taking it for runs would be a better way to spend his spare time than staring into a bottle of bourbon. Besides, he'd gotten used to having a dog around the last few weeks. And he'd liked it.

His decision made, he parked his vehicle and as he strode toward the building, he felt a sense of déjà vu. The little bell above the door ding-donged as he stepped inside and he inhaled the scent of disinfectant mixed with animal smells. As he crossed over to the counter, he passed by the row of cages holding cats and paid no attention whatsoever until a paw stretched out and some claws snagged on his woolen sweater. Frowning, he stopped and turned to see a mammoth ginger cat peering at him with big, pleading, green eyes. It let out a long meow, which sounded so sad it shot right to Callum's heart.

"Hi there, how can I help you?" An elderly woman, her clothes covered in animal fur, appeared beside him. "You seem to have made friends with Bourbon. Would you like to know more about him?"

He shook his arm free of the cat. "Bourbon?"

The woman smiled warmly. "That's what we named the ginger cat. Are you looking for a new feline friend?"

"Definitely not." No matter what the cat was called, he was in the market for a dog. "Have you got any German shepherds?"

"We're a refuge shelter, sir," she said, narrowing her eyes at him and crossing her arms over her large bosom. "If you're looking for a purebred—"

"I'm not," he interrupted, setting her straight. "I'm just looking for a dog who needs a lot of exercise. I want a friend and a running partner."

The lines around her eyes softened again as she smiled. "I'm not sure we have anything that fits your bill exactly, but we do have a lot of lovely dogs. Come and have a look."

He followed her through a door, down a corridor and past rows and rows of cages filled with more cats. It was like an animal prison.

"Why is the ginger cat out front?" he asked, racking his head for anyone else he knew who could do with the company of a pet.

"Bourbon?" She sighed. "He's been with us a long time. We rotate the animals in the foyer so they're always ones in dire need of a new home."

"Right." Callum ignored what felt like barbed wire twisting around his heart and followed her outside to even more cages. The noise of yapping dogs assaulted him, yet after doing two rounds of the canine yard, he hadn't found any animal that met his requirements. Most of the pups available barely stood taller than his ankle and no way in hell was he getting a dog that would fit in a purse. He might end up stepping on it in the dark.

"I'm going to need to think about this some more," he said.

"Of course." Although the woman smiled at him, her shoulders sagged and the sparkle left her eyes. "I'll see you out."

Chelsea had lived on her own a long time and had become accustomed to quiet nights in; in fact, she loved nothing more than coming home at night, cooking herself some dinner and relaxing in front of the TV with a jigsaw puzzle to stimulate her mind and Muffin warming her feet.

Loved as in past tense.

It had been a matter of days since she'd said goodbye to Callum for the final time and now she dreaded coming home at night almost as much as she dreaded leaving the house for work. She'd done two face-to-face breakups in that time and made a total botch of both of them. One poor guy had ended up comforting her when she'd burst into tears while telling him his girlfriend didn't want him anymore. She felt other people's pain more strongly than she ever had before.

Her little house no longer filled her with joy and a sense of achievement. Muffin, still his energetic adorable self, no longer satisfied her craving for company. It was Christmas in a few days and the prospect of spending it alone left her cold. She was desperately close to falling into a black funk that would be almost impossible to climb out of. Nothing she could think to do felt like it would cure her. She couldn't even summon the enthusiasm to put up a Christmas tree when no one but she and Muffin would see it.

Finally, deciding it was unhealthy to spend the holidays alone in her little house, she called Rosie in Portland to ask if she could visit.

"Long time no speak," Rosie said when she answered the phone in her usual jovial tone. She was such a vivacious soul and Chelsea only hoped a few days with her friend would be the boost she needed.

"Sorry, I've been busy with work." It wasn't a lie. The breakup business was booming—unfortunately she found no solace from the fact that hers was only one of hundreds of broken hearts floating around.

"What's wrong?" Rosie's tone turned serious and Chelsea's grip tightened on her cell.

"Nothing," she said, trying to sound like she meant it.

"I know you and I can tell from your voice that this isn't just a friendly catch-up. What's the matter?"

"How do you *do* that?" Chelsea asked.

"It's a talent. I have a sixth sense where my best friends are concerned."

So Chelsea hit her with it: "I've fallen in love." This announcement was met with protracted silence. "Are you still there?" she asked eventually.

"Yes. Sorry. Just give me a second to pick my jaw back up off the floor."

At Rosie's words, Chelsea almost smiled, which proved that some friend therapy was exactly what the doctor ordered.

"So let me get this straight," Rosie said. "You have met a guy you still want to be with after a few months?"

"Yes. Well, it hasn't even been a month yet but…it's different this time." Chelsea sniffed as she tried to fight the tears that threatened at this confession.

"Oh. My. Freaking. God! Tell me all about him. Who is this man of men? When do I get to meet him?"

"That's just it," Chelsea admitted, "I dumped him." And then she succumbed to more tears.

Callum stared at the cat, who had made itself at home from almost the moment he let it out of its box and now sat on the kitchen table, surveying the sights around him as if he were a king. He'd totally lost his head thinking that a cat could fill the void Chelsea had left in his life. He guess this proved his worst fear—he hadn't been with her because he was lonely, he'd been with her because he didn't want to be without her.

"At least you have a cool name," Callum said, reaching out and rubbing Bourbon under the chin. In adopting a fat cat instead of a manly dog, he'd basically given his brothers an open invitation to tease him for the rest of his days. He could hear them now—*Callum the crazy cat lady*—but he didn't care. That would take effort. And, although he'd gone out today to get a pet in the hopes that it would distract him from his continuous thoughts of Chelsea, it hadn't worked.

And thinking about her all the time was simply exhausting.

He turned back to his laptop screen and tried to exorcise her from his mind for the hundredth time that evening.

A knock sounded on his front door and he groaned. "Shh," he told Bourbon. "If we're very quiet, maybe they'll go away." He guessed it might be Sophie come to confront him about his weird behavior today and, although he owed her an apology for running out, he couldn't face that right now.

Instead, it was his mom, which was far, far worse. Her knock was merely a formality and two seconds later she let herself into the house. "Callum!" she called as her boots click-clacked along the corridor toward him. "It's Mom. Are you in here?" He closed his eyes and wished he'd thought to lock the door.

"No," he shouted. "Go away."

She appeared in the doorway and frowned at him. "That's no way to speak to your poor old mother. Sophie warned me you were in a mood. What's going—" Her question died on her tongue as her eyes came to rest on Bourbon.

"Is that a cat?"

"No, Mom, it's a horse." It appeared his wounded heart amplified his tendency toward sarcasm, but she ignored this and crossed to the feline, stooping down to stroke him.

"Hello, gorgeous girl," she cooed as she scratched under his chin.

"*He's* a boy," Callum said, although judging by the sound of Bourbon's purrs, he wasn't too fussy about little things like gender.

Nora looked back to Callum. "I do like him, but if you're hoping he'll fill the hole in your heart left by Chelsea, I think you'll be sadly disappointed."

"What?" he scoffed, instinctively glancing down at his chest, almost expecting to see a gory wound there.

She smiled tenderly at him. "I should have realized that you and Bailey weren't marriage material because being near her didn't light up your whole face the way Chelsea did when you sat beside her at Thanksgiving. I'm sorry if I pushed you into that. And I know you don't think you have time for a relationship—I admire your dedication and commitment to McKinnel's— but…" She paused and cleared her throat. "I don't want you to make the same mistakes your father did."

"Huh?" Callum frowned at her—that wasn't the direction he'd been expecting.

"I loved your father," Nora said, "but he was single-minded. He did love us in his own way, but the distillery was all that ever mattered to him. I'm not sure, in the end, if it made him as happy as he wanted us to believe."

"What?" His mom's words stunned him. It was the first time in all his life he'd ever considered that his parents hadn't had the perfect relationship.

"I want you to have more in your life than work," she continued. "Was that the problem with Chelsea? You didn't think you had room for her?"

He shook his head and found himself confessing everything. "Maybe at first I didn't think I had time for a real relationship, but I guess I'm not quite as driven as Dad was because Chelsea got under my skin in a way I never imagined. And now, no matter how much I try to focus on work, I can't forget her."

"So what happened then? Why are you sitting here alone with a big, gorgeous furball when you should be with her?"

"My feelings weren't reciprocated. She dumped me," he confessed. "That's two times in a month—I guess I'm not much of a catch after all."

His mom frowned and then sat down at the table, all the while tickling Bourbon under the chin. "Tell me everything, sweetheart."

And the way she looked at him had Callum opening up like he hadn't done since he was a kid with a scraped knee sobbing for his mom to make things better. He told her about Chelsea's work, the way they really met and about Freddie and his threats. And how seeing her in danger made everything real for him.

"You love her." It was a statement more than a question.

"Yes." He nodded—it was the first time he'd admitted it to himself, never mind anyone else. It was the only explanation for the way she made him feel. "More than I thought I ever could."

"And did you tell her that?"

He ran a hand through his hair. "Not in so many words, but I asked her to move in with me; if that didn't make my feelings pretty damn obvious, I don't know what will."

"Callum, Callum, Callum." She sighed. "Women need to hear the words. And from what you've just told me, she probably thought your invitation to move in was a reaction to her break-in. Women don't want…"

And suddenly something clicked into place inside his head.

He didn't know about women, but he knew about Chelsea! Hadn't she told him about the burden she'd been for most of her childhood? His heart had broken every time she let down her guard long enough to talk about her past, about how it felt to be passed from one unwilling family member to the next. Yet he'd gone and made her feel the way she never wanted to feel again—asking her to move in with him in a way that made it feel like a reaction to the break-in. Yes, the burglary had instigated his question, but the moment he'd asked her to share his home, he'd known he wanted to share everything with her. His home, his life, their pets and one day children. He loved her—with absolutely everything he had to give—and deep down, he thought she loved him too.

He didn't blame her for saying no to the way he'd asked, but why-oh-why had he ever taken no for an answer? He didn't accept no easily where the distillery was concerned, and Chelsea meant even more to him than it did. He should have made her listen. He should have made her see the truth.

An idea started to take form inside his head.

As if his mom could read his mind, a warm, encouraging smile spread across her face. "Why the hell are you still sitting here pining for her like a wounded teenager? Grow some balls, go be a man and tell that girl how you feel."

"I will," he promised, "but first I have to arrange a few things." This time when he asked her to be with him, he was going to give her an offer too good to refuse. And he was going to make exactly what he wanted clear, and what he wanted was Chelsea.

He reached across the table, picked up his cell and phoned his sister. "I'm sorry about today," he said the moment Sophie answered the phone; he continued on before she had a chance to accept his apology. "But I need your help. You know that guy who makes the jigsaw puzzles? How long does it take for him to design and make them?"

Chapter 15

As Chelsea headed for the front door, Muffin ran ahead and started barking like a crazy dog. Since she'd been taking him with her everywhere, he'd become almost uncontrollably excitable whenever she prepared to leave the house. She chuckled at his antics, thankful she still had him for company.

"Settle down," she said as she opened the door.

Standing on her porch, his hand raised as if he'd been about to ring the bell, was the reason for Muffin's noise. The reason for her melancholy. The dog leaped at Callum as if it had been years rather than days since they'd seen each other and Chelsea's heart leaped into her throat. She felt a tad put out that Muffin was no longer content with just her company, but seemed to have missed Callum as much as she had.

"Hey, buddy," he said, dropping to his haunches to give the dog the attention it craved.

Chelsea took the opportunity to pull herself together, to try to slow the erratic racing of her heart and, if she were honest, to soak up his gorgeousness just a little. She'd thought she would never see that beautiful face and body again and now here he was, standing on her porch on Christmas Eve, and well, she couldn't waste the opportunity.

"What are you doing here?" she asked, self-protection kicking in. Perhaps he'd left something here. Although she was pretty certain if he had, she'd have seen it by now.

Callum straightened and it was then that she noticed the small gift-wrapped box in his hands. "I got this for you." He held it out to her but she didn't take it.

"Why?" she asked, glaring at it like it were a bomb about to explode. What was he playing at? If this was some kind of let's-still-be-friends gift, he could shove it where the sun didn't shine. Then again, what if it was some kind of attempt at making amends? What if he were here to ask her out again? Her heart kicked a little at this thought.

"You'll see when you open it. *Please*, open it."

"I'm on my way out. To Portland. To go stay with Rosie." She didn't know why she was telling him all this; after all, she didn't owe him an itinerary, but she felt the need to fill the space between them with words.

"Please," he said again, and something in his eyes made her heart slow a little. "It won't take long."

Against her better judgment, she stepped aside and gestured for him to come on in. She took the box,

dumped her luggage, then marched into the kitchen
and laid his gift on the counter. Her fingers shook as
she opened it, and the way he stood there watching only
made her more nervous. Beneath the wrapping was a
plain brown box. Curious, she lifted the lid to discover
it was filled with puzzle pieces.

She glanced over at Callum and he nodded at the
box. "Would you do it for me?"

"Now?" This visit was getting weirder by the second.

He nodded. "It's important, please."

She squeezed her eyes shut and felt her resolve wavering. There weren't that many pieces so it wouldn't
take her long to do, and she wouldn't be that late getting
to Portland. Call her a sucker for punishment but a few
moments with Callum could be her Christmas present
to herself. Yep, she was a sad case if ever there was one.

"Okay." She opened her eyes again. "But where's
the image?"

"There isn't one. But a puzzle pro like yourself
should be able to handle it, right?"

Never one to resist a challenge like that, she began to
sort the outer pieces—all those with straight edges. In
spite of the company, the buzz of doing a puzzle kicked
through her veins and she had to admit she was curious about what she'd find when she'd put it all together.

"Are you going to help?" she asked, when she'd com-
pleted the border and Callum hadn't moved an inch.

He shook his head. "I'll leave this to the experts. In
fact, why don't I take Muffin outside for a bit of exercise while you do it?"

Chelsea frowned, totally perplexed by his odd behavior. "Okay, whatever." This situation was so bizarre

that she'd welcome a few moments' reprieve from his intoxicating proximity.

You could have just told him to take a hike, said a voice in her head. She ignored it because, however needy and desperate it made her, she'd been happy to see him. Hope that maybe they could pick off where they'd left off, but take things slower this time, filled her heart.

Callum grabbed Muffin's lead and promised to be back soon. Chelsea sent a quick message to Rosie saying she'd been delayed and then returned to the puzzle, which was starting to take form and appeared to be mostly some kind of writing. Like a newspaper's masthead. The word *missing* appeared. Then *my*. As the puzzle neared completion, Chelsea's fingers began to shake again—the words had to mean something, there had to be a message. Frantically she fit one piece after another so that within a few more moments she could read it.

Every cell in her body froze as she eyed the words on the counter in front of her: *You're the missing piece of my puzzle.*

There were footsteps behind her and she turned to see Muffin and Callum had returned. He dropped to one knee and she sucked in a breath, her hand rushing to cover her mouth.

"You're the missing piece of me," he said, his eyes and tone earnest as he repeated the sentiment on the puzzle. "Please, marry me, and make me whole."

Chelsea's head spun as his words ricocheted around it.

"Marry you?" she finally managed to whisper. Was this some kind of dream?

He nodded. "I know you think I asked you to move in with me because of the break-in, and there might be a smidgen of truth in that, but the rest of the truth is that in a few short weeks you've become as much a part of me as breathing is. I can no more live without you than I can without my lungs."

She grabbed hold of the countertop, feeling as if she might faint at any moment.

"Until you came along," he said, "I didn't realize that I wanted more out of life. I thought a good career and a relationship based on a solid friendship was all I needed, but you've shown me how much more life has to offer if you open up your heart. I've only ever proposed to two women in my life—the first time was for all the wrong reasons, but this time I'm asking because I truly mean it. I want you to be my wife more than anything."

"Those are beautiful words," she whispered, her voice shaking like a leaf on a stormy day. "You're quite the romantic, you know."

Of course, she couldn't bring herself to believe him. She must have fallen asleep while packing. This Callum standing in front of her, offering himself as her husband, had to be a figment of her imagination.

"Trust me, I wasn't the slightest bit romantic until you," said the illusion. "You've brought out a lot of things in me. Hell, because of you, I even got a cat."

Muffin's ears perked up at the word *cat*—who said dog's weren't smart?—but Chelsea shook her head. Yep—he was speaking gobbledygook—this was a dream indeed. Still, she persisted in talking to him. "You've lost me. You got a cat? What's that got to do with me?"

He sighed and shifted as if it was getting uncomfort-able down there on one knee. "It's a long story. I was lonely without you, so I went to get a dog and ended up with a big, ginger, tomcat named Bourbon, so I think it's only fair that you become co-owner. A single man with a cat gives off the wrong kind of vibe, but a cou-ple with a cat, that's perfect acceptable. Anyway I'm sure you'll love him."

She blinked, struggling to keep up, and Callum smiled up at her. "So what do you say? Will you marry me? Because my knee's going numb down here and if you're going to break my heart by saying no, then you may as well get it over with."

She blinked again. "Oh my God, you're serious?" So much for taking things slower. She could never in her wildest imaginings have come up with this.

He turned and gestured to Muffin's collar. "I wouldn't have bought this if I wasn't."

Following his hand, Chelsea's eyes caught on some-thing glistening on the dog's collar. Her jaw dropped as she peered closer to see a beautiful diamond ring dan-gling next to his dog tag. It was a white-gold setting with a large square-cut diamond, surrounded by lots of smaller ones. Muffin looked proud to have been charged with its care. She'd never seen anything as stunning. Her ring finger twitched.

"I took Muffin outside and we had a man-to-man chat," Callum explained. "He wants you to know you'll make us both very happy if you just say yes. I love you, Chelsea. I think I started falling in love with you that day you walked into the distillery and tried to break my heart."

A half laugh, half sob escaped her mouth at the absurdity of his words. "Say it again," she asked, wanting to be sure her ears weren't playing evil tricks.

His lips curled into a slow, sexy smile. "What? That I love you?"

"Yes, that." A tear slid down her cheek—no one had ever said they loved her before, not in a way that made her believe it anyway. And the most wonderful thing of all was that she felt exactly the same way.

"Oh, Callum." Her words choked, she rushed forward and dropped to her knees in front of him. "Yes, I'll marry you. I love you too. I've missed you so much. I didn't think—"

Callum's need to kiss her overcame the need to hear the rest of her sentence. Nothing else mattered except the fact she loved him too and soon she'd be wearing his ring. He cupped her face in his hands and drew his lips to hers, never ever wanting to let her go again. The past few weeks had been a whirlwind but they'd held the best moments of his life and it was all because of her.

He couldn't wait to make more memories and a whole host of plans for the future, but right now having her in his arms was enough.

After what might have been one of the longest liplocks in history, Muffin's bark broke them apart. Laughing, they looked sideways to see the dog watching them, his head cocked to one side like a confused puppy.

Callum reached over and ruffled Muffin's fur, then he unclipped his collar and removed the ring he'd spent hours choosing today while Sophie's acquaintance had done a rush job on the puzzle for him.

"I hope you like it," he said as he lifted her hand and slipped the ring onto her finger. It sparkled as they both gazed down at it.

"Like it?" She wiggled her fingers and giggled. "I love it. You have very good taste, you know that?"

"Of course I do. I chose you, didn't I?"

"Yes, you did," she whispered, and then she said, "Can you pinch me?"

He frowned. "What for?"

"So I can know this is real."

"It's real, sweetheart. Nothing has ever been as real as this, so how about I just kiss you again instead?"

And he did.

Epilogue

Chelsea stared at the little white stick in her hand, almost unable to believe the two blue lines looking up at her. *Pregnant.* The last few days she'd noticed changes in her body but didn't dare hope too much that this was what they meant, so she'd kept her suspicions to herself until she could get into town to buy a test kit.

She and Callum were getting married in spring—they were going to be the first couple to use the distillery grounds as a venue, Lachlan had planned an amazing menu to showcase the new restaurant, and she'd picked out the most beautiful dress imaginable. It was ice-pink and far more girly and princess-like than she'd ever thought she'd choose, but Callum brought out the feminine side of her and she couldn't wait to see the look on his face when he saw her. Then, in private, later in the evening, he would slowly peel it off and…

Her cheeks heating at this thought, Chelsea glanced in the bathroom mirror and palmed her hands against her flat stomach, something glowing inside her at the thought of the tiny life beneath them. A life that she and Callum had created out of their love. She never thought she could be so lucky. So blessed.

Would she be showing by the wedding? Would the dressmaker have to alter her dress? Whatever. She didn't care. This was wonderful news and she racked her mind for the perfect way to break the news to Callum. Maybe she could have a personalized jigsaw puzzle made like he'd done when he'd proposed, although that would take time and she knew she wouldn't be able to keep this secret long enough. Right now, she felt like going outside, spreading her arms wide and shouting her news to the whole world.

While they hadn't been trying for this baby, they hadn't exactly been not trying for it either and they both wanted children. In the past few months, she'd fallen in love with the McKinnels almost as much as she had with Callum. *Almost.* Sophie and Annabel were going to be her bridesmaids alongside Rosie who had yet to meet the McKinnels but was coming for the wedding. All Callum's brothers were going to be groomsmen.

Finally Chelsea was part of a big, happy family—the kind of family she'd always fantasized about—and the news that she'd soon be adding to the McKinnel clan filled her with warm fuzzy glee.

A bark coming from the living room interrupted her happy thoughts, so she put the pregnancy test down on the vanity and went out to investigate. Sure enough, she found Muffin beside the coffee table, nose to the ground trying to entice Bourbon, who was hiding under there, out to play. The cat made low mewling noises and occasionally stretched out his paw, claws readied, and took a swipe at Muffin.

"Leave Bourbon alone," Chelsea warned, stooping to take hold of Muffin's collar and encourage him to back up. The poor dog only wanted to play and had been trying to win Bourbon's affections since he and Chelsea had moved into Callum's cottage a couple of months ago, but she feared Muffin was fighting a lost cause. Whenever he got within an inch of the cat, Bourbon narrowed his eyes and looked as if he wanted to scratch the dog's eyes right out. It was surprising there hadn't been any blood spilled yet, but they had the local vet on speed dial just in case.

As she was trying to separate the animals, the front door opened and Callum strode in, sleeves pushed up to the elbows just the way she liked them. "Hey, gorgeous," he said.

"I didn't expect you home this early." Her heart leaped into her throat at the thought of him going into the bathroom and seeing the test. She wanted to tell him. She wanted to see the look on his face when he found out he was going to be a dad.

"Sorry, did I interrupt your studying? This is just a quick visit. Truth is, I couldn't wait till tonight to do this." With those words, he crossed the room and pulled her up into his arms. She let go of Muffin's collar and, as Callum kissed her, the dog returned to his pursuit of the cat.

"These two fighting like cats and dogs again?" Callum asked when he finally tore his mouth from hers.

She rolled her eyes at his lame humor, but couldn't help smiling. He could tell the world's most awful joke and she'd still laugh her head off.

"They'll get used to each other eventually," he said, "and I suppose it's good practice for when we have kids. My brothers and I used to bicker so much I'm quite surprised we didn't kill each other."

"About kids," Chelsea began, thinking that now was as good a time as ever. She mightn't have come up with some dramatic, exciting way to tell him, but then again, this news was dramatic and exciting enough in itself.

"Yes?" He stared down at her. "What about them?"

She placed a hand on her stomach again and smiled. "In two years' time Muffin isn't the only problem Bourbon is going to have—he'll also have a toddler trying to chase his tail."

It took a moment for Callum to register what she meant. She watched, amused, as his expression changed in slow motion from confusion to one of absolute joy. Then he grabbed hold of her again and met her gaze. "Are you saying what I think you're saying?"

She nodded. "I'm pregnant. The evidence is in the bathroom if you don't believe me."

In reply, he leaned forward and kissed her again. There was just as much heat, just as much passion, as before, but there was also something else in it. Something Chelsea couldn't describe but liked very much indeed.

"Mom is going to be over the moon," he said, pulling back.

"What about you?" she asked. "Are you…over the moon?"

"Sweetheart, my darling…" He cupped her face in both his hands. "I'm so high I've gone way past the moon. This is the best news I've heard all… Ever. We're going to be parents."

"We are."

"You know, I've heard a rumor that a woman's sex drive increases when she's pregnant," Callum said, his expression suddenly serious. "I wonder if this is true?"

Chelsea rubbed her lips together and wriggled her eyebrows at him. "Hmm…perhaps that accounts for why I suddenly have an urge to strip you of all your clothes and have my wicked way."

Callum grinned and held his hands out in surrender. "Who am I to stand in the way of a pregnant woman's needs? I'm all yours, baby."

Never had any words been sweeter. "And I'm all yours too." Chelsea reached up and sealed this promise with a kiss.

* * * * *

Christy Jeffries graduated from the University of California, Irvine, with a degree in criminology, and received her Juris Doctor from California Western School of Law. But drafting court documents and working in law enforcement was merely an apprenticeship for her current career in the dynamic field of mommyhood and romance writing. She lives in Southern California with her patient husband, two energetic sons and one sassy grandmother. Follow her online at christyjeffries.com.

Visit the Author Profile page
at Harlequin.com for more titles.

THE MAKEOVER
PRESCRIPTION

Christy Jeffries

To my Monkey Roo. Your superfast race-car brain has been such a blessing and continues to amaze me every day. You are so smart, creative and incredibly witty. Even though I can't wait to see what kind of man you'll grow up to become, you will always be my little boy. I love being your mommy.

Chapter 1

Captain Julia Calhoun Fitzgerald had no problem commanding a full surgical team in the operating room during an emergency decompressive craniectomy, but she could be naked, standing on her head and yelling from a bullhorn, and nobody in the Cowgirl Up Café would give her a second look.

"May I get some…" Julia's voice trailed off when she realized she was talking to the back of the busboy's turquoise T-shirt. He'd unceremoniously dropped the plate of food off on the counter between her seat and the empty one next to her, not bothering to ask if she had everything she needed.

She looked down the counter and saw an unused place setting two seats over. She could either sit here, going unnoticed for another twenty minutes—which was how long it'd taken for the waitress to take her order in the first place—or she could reach over and grab the neighboring paper napkin and utensils. She decided to do the latter.

After centering the newly acquired napkin in her lap, Julia neatly cut her oversize breakfast burrito in half with surgical precision, then clamped her lips shut at what looked to be sausage gravy oozing out of the center. This couldn't be right. She lifted her head and looked around the restaurant, hoping to catch the attention of the lone waitress who was darting between several crowded tables, fumbling with her order pad before picking up a stack of dirty plates from an empty table.

Was this place always so crowded? Since being stationed at the Shadowview Military Hospital last month, Julia had come into her aunt's restaurant only twice, and both times were right before closing when most of the small town of Sugar Falls, Idaho, shut down for the night.

And speaking of Aunt Freckles, where was she anyway? Julia could've sworn the calendar app on her fancy new smartphone said they were supposed to meet at the café at eight this morning.

She glanced at her gold tank watch—one of the more modest pieces she'd inherited from her mother—and noted that she had only about fifteen minutes before she was supposed to meet the contractor at her new house.

Julia used her fork and knife to probe at the contents of the flour tortilla on her plate, then leaned forward and sniffed at the batter-covered meat inside. This was definitely not what she'd ordered. She carefully set her utensils down on either side of her plate and took a sip of her orange juice while observing the other customers and trying not to eavesdrop on the intense conversation going on in the booth to her right.

"There's no way the Rockies are going to make it to the play-offs this year, let alone win the pennant." One of the older-looking cowboys slammed his fist on the table, making the salt and pepper shakers rattle as the equally elderly man beside him nodded in agreement. "And if you try to tell me their bull pen is stronger than the Rangers', I'll call you a liar."

Julia squirmed in her seat, trying not to listen to the heated discussion but unable to tear her gaze away.

"Now settle down, Jonesy," said the younger man sitting on the opposite side of the booth. He was holding up his hands, the sleeves of his gray flannel shirt rolled up to reveal strong, tan forearms that could only be the result of years of outdoor physical labor. His short auburn hair was messy—probably due to the green hat precariously hanging on his bouncing knee—and his square jaw and smirking lips made Julia's pulse want to do the opposite of settle down. Luckily, though, his quiet voice, or maybe his overall size, had the proper effect on Jonesy, who took a couple of deep breaths before nodding. Sexy Flannel Shirt continued, "Nobody said anything about their pitchers. All I said was..."

Out of the corner of her eye, she saw the server approach, and Julia turned away from the conversation, slightly lifting her hand in an attempt to get Monica's attention. At least, she thought the name tag read Monica. She couldn't be sure since the woman kept passing by in a blur, not even glancing in Julia's direction.

"Excuse me." Julia tried again when Monica rushed behind her side of the counter, this time balancing three plates of food in one hand and a carafe of coffee and a bottle of syrup in the other. But the young woman still didn't look her way.

Sighing, Julia decided that she'd settle for eating what she could off the plate. She hated being late, and since the contractor was a good friend of her aunt's, Julia wanted to make a good impression. She picked up her fork and began eating the home fries, which she had to admit were delicious, if a little greasier than her usual breakfast fare. Just as she swallowed the last bit of potatoes, she heard a choking sound coming from the booth beside her.

Sexy Flannel Shirt had his hand covering his mouth, and Julia sprang into rescue mode. Within four strides, she'd pulled the man out of the booth and wrapped her arms around his torso, locking them in place directly above his upper abdomen. His chin almost collided with her forehead when he whipped his head back quickly to look at her.

"You'll be okay," she said in her most authoritative tone. "Try to stay calm."

"I would be a hell of a lot calmer if I knew why you were latching onto me like that," the man replied. If he was capable of speaking, he was capable of breathing.

Oh no.

Julia rose awkwardly to her full height, her hands disengaging so slowly, she could feel the softness of his flannel shirt under her fingers. And the tightness of the muscles underneath. Obviously her senses were on high alert because of the quick adrenaline rush she got whenever she was in an emergency situation like this. Even if it was a false alarm.

She quickly clasped her overly sensitive hands behind her back.

"Sorry," she said to Mr. Flannel, as well as to the two older cowboys sitting with him at the table, their eyes as large and round as their stacks of blueberry pancakes. "I thought you were choking."

"I thought so, too," the man admitted. "Then I just realized that I was being poisoned by whatever was inside my chicken-fried steak burrito."

He pointed to his plate, and Julia suddenly realized where her breakfast order had ended up.

"It looks like you got my egg white and veggie delight wrap." She picked up the plate and walked back to her seat at the counter, then returned with his meal, the spilled gravy not yet congealing. "I think I got yours by mistake."

"What happened to my hash browns?" he asked, looking at the empty space alongside his burrito.

A defensive heat rose up from the neckline of Julia's hospital scrubs, all the way to her hairline. Who put chicken-fried steak in a tortilla, anyway? "I, uh, ate them when I realized that the burrito wasn't what I ordered."

"Most people would've just sent the order back if it was wrong," he said, his lips twitching, giving her the impression that he found her mistake hilarious.

Oh really? She wanted to ask. *They wouldn't gasp and choke and pretend to be poisoned?* But she didn't know this man, or the rest of the people in this town. Yet. And Julia didn't want to start off on the wrong foot with her new neighbors. Although she had a feeling that with all the eyes—including Monica's, *finally*—in the suddenly quiet restaurant staring at her, she'd already made quite an impression.

The pressure on her sternum felt as if someone were trying to save *her* from choking…on her own embarrassment and she had to silence the whispers of one of the other few times she'd been so foolish. She returned to her seat and picked her leather satchel up off the floor, retrieving her wallet out of the front pocket before walking back to his booth.

"Here. This should cover the cost of your breakfast." Julia's voice wobbled as she pulled two twenty dollar bills out, setting them on his table. Then, before she walked out the door, she decided someone had better tell him. "And just so you know, there's a piece of spinach stuck in your teeth."

Julia dodged the waitress and her tray full of food as she made her way to the front door. Several shouts of laughter reached her ears right as she exited, but she didn't pause or turn back to see who was making fun of her. Instead, she squared her shoulders and walked down the sidewalk of Snowflake Boulevard, wondering how long it would take for news of the embarrassing scene she'd just caused to make its way down the shops and businesses lined up along this main road through town.

This was why she was more comfortable in the background. Out of the way. Being ignored.

She'd just climbed in her car when her cell phone chirped to life. Seeing her aunt's name on the display screen, Julia quickly answered it.

"Sug, where are you?" Aunt Freckles asked.

"I just left the café." No need to tell the woman about

how she'd accosted one of the customers by mistakenly performing the Heimlich maneuver. Her aunt would probably find out soon enough, anyway.

"Why would you go there?"

"Because we were supposed to meet there at eight."

"No, we weren't. We were supposed to meet at the bakery. Why would I have you come to my restaurant when I'd already taken the morning off?"

Well, that would explain why the café was so understaffed. But how could Julia have gotten the location wrong? She tried to tap on her calendar app to confirm that she hadn't screwed up twice this morning, but she accidentally ended the call. Ugh. She squeezed the phone in frustration, then took a deep breath and reminded herself that she was smarter than this. She tried to pull up Freckles's number, but before she could find the right button, a text message from her aunt popped up saying they could just meet at the new house, so Julia put her MINI Cooper in gear.

Turning onto her street, Julia gazed up at the ramshackle old Victorian that stood at the end of the culde-sac on Pinecone Court, a proud smile making her cheeks stretch and alleviating her lingering shame over that awkward encounter just a few moments ago. If one didn't count the Federal-style mansion in Georgetown, the summer cottage on Chincoteague Island in Virginia or the countless commercial properties still held in the Fitzgerald Family Trust, Julia had never owned her own house.

She parked her car in the driveway, biting her lip and staring out the window, trying to envision all the possibilities spread out before her. Unlike Julia, this house was anything but practical and understated. But all thirty-two hundred square feet of it was hers.

There were no interior designers to suggest beige color palettes and overpriced modern art. No maids to rush in and make up her bed the moment she'd robotically woken up at five thirty every morning to practice the cello. No private tutors waiting in the informal library—the formal library in the Georgetown residence being reserved for when Mother invited her university colleagues over—to ensure Julia's MCAT score was high enough. After all, they needed the med school admission counselors to overlook the fact that she wasn't old enough to buy liquor, let alone cut open cadavers to research the long-term effects of liver disease. And there was no personal chef here to tell her that her parents had already instructed him on the week's menu, so she would *not* be eating processed carbs for dinner, no matter how many of her classmates were cramming for finals over pizza and Red Bull energy drinks.

A horn blasted behind her, and she turned to see her elderly Aunt Freckles behind the wheel of a slightly less elderly rusted-out 4x4 that Julia didn't recognize. Freckles was actually her great-aunt on her father's side, and while Julia only had sporadic contact with her relative until her parents' joint memorial service several years ago, it didn't take a neurosurgeon to figure out why the flashy waitress and former rodeo queen had been estranged from their conservative and academic family.

"Morning, Sug," Freckles hollered—there was really no other way to describe the woman's cheerfully brash voice—as she patted the Bronco emblem near the driver's-side door. "Ain't she a beaut? My second husband, Earl Larry, had one just like it back in '73. We hitched an Airstream to it and cruised all over Mexico."

She brushed her aunt's weathered and heavily rouged cheek with a soft kiss as Freckles wrapped her in a bear hug that threatened to crush several ribs. Julia was still accustoming herself to the woman's hearty displays of affection. "Whatever happened to Earl Larry?" she asked, always interested in hearing about her aunt's series of past relationships.

"His grandpappy died and left the family business to him. Earl Larry went corporate on me, and after that *Forbes* report came out with him on the cover, I told him I wasn't made for that kind of life. I couldn't stand being married to some stuffy old three-piece suit, no matter how many capital ventures he sank our RVing money into."

It was hard to imagine anyone named Earl Larry wearing a suit, let alone having a grandpappy who left him a company that would be featured in a well-respected financial magazine. Of course, it was just as difficult to imagine seventy-eight-year-old Eugenia Josephine Brighton Fitzgerald of the Virginia Fitzgeralds wearing orange cowboy boots, zebra-printed spandex pants and an off-the-shoulder turquoise T-shirt emblazoned with the words Cowgirl Up Café—We'll Butter Your Biscuit.

"Whose car is this?" Julia asked.

"It's Kane's," Freckles said. "I saw him pulled over on Snowflake Boulevard, and he said he'd eaten something that hadn't agreed with him. I told him he just needed some fresh air, and since I've been itching to take this old Bronco of his for a spin, he agreed to let me drive it so he could walk the rest of the way. It's only a couple of blocks, so he should be here any sec."

Julia had yet to meet Kane Chatterson, the contractor Aunt Freckles suggested she hire to remodel the house. But if this derelict hunk of junk on wheels was any indication of the man's rehab skills, her once-stately Victorian abode was in serious trouble.

Of course, if her overzealous impromptu CPR skills back at the restaurant were any indication, Julia's medical career as a Navy surgeon might be in serious trouble, as well.

"Would you like to see the inside of the house?" Julia asked.

"You bet," Freckles said in her mountain drawl.

"I have only an hour before my shift at Shadowview, so I might ask you to give Mr. Chatterson the tour if he isn't here soon. I can email him some of my notes and suggestions later."

What Julia didn't say was that it would certainly be a load off her mind if she could just skip all this formal meet and greet business and fire off a quick note to the guy. Especially after the disastrous morning she'd already had. But Aunt Freckles's quick shake of her dyed and teased peach-colored hairdo was enough to suggest Julia shouldn't keep her fingers crossed.

"Kane's a good boy and dependable as sin. He'll get here in time. Besides, I'm holding his baby ransom." Freckles dangled the metal keys above her head. "And men have an unnatural attachment to their cars. If you ever took the time to go out on a date with a decent fella, you'd find that out for yourself."

Julia rolled her eyes, a practice that she never

would've dared in the presence of her parents when they'd been alive. But, seriously. Her aunt referred to every male under the age of sixty as a boy and never missed an opportunity to suggest Julia's social life was too date-free—at least by the older woman's standards. Freckles liked men almost as much as she liked sequins and comfort food.

"I'm in and out of surgery all day, and when I do get the occasional time free, I usually spend it swimming laps or sleeping at the officers' quarters near the base hospital."

"You work too hard, Sug," Freckles said, rubbing her niece's shoulder. Julia, who normally tried to remain as reserved as possible, had difficulty not leaning in to the comforting motion. "And you gotta eat sometime. In those blue hospital scrubs and that cardigan, you look like you haven't got a curve to your name. Isn't there a nice doctor or admiral or someone you could go out to dinner with?"

"I don't need a man to take me to dinner."

"Hmph." Had her aunt just snorted? "I don't know if I mentioned this yet, but the town of Sugar Falls puts on a big to-do at the end of the year to raise money for the hospital. Since you're one of the new surgeons and an official resident of Sugar Falls, the committee is going to expect you to be there as a guest of honor. With a plus-one, if you know what I'm saying?"

Guest of honor? A plus-one? Julia's stomach twisted and her forehead grew damp, despite the fact that the early November sun still hadn't peeked out of the clouds. She was pretty sure her aunt was suggesting she'd need to find a date, which was much easier said than done. Besides, Julia never wanted to show her face in the town of Sugar Falls again.

"Oh, look," Freckles continued. "Here comes Kane now. Smile and try not to look so dang serious."

Julia's insides felt tighter than a newly strung cello as she turned around to await the contractor who would be doing the remodeling work on her new home—if his estimate was reasonable. Yet before she could formulate her plan to refrain from shoveling out piles of her inheritance to someone in order to avoid the hassle of negotiating, she recognized the familiar gray flannel shirt, and her heart dropped.

Oh no. Please, no. This can't be happening to me.

The man hadn't seemed quite as tall when he'd been sitting in that booth back at the Cowgirl Up Café, but his broad shoulders and chest looked just as muscular as they'd felt twenty minutes ago. He moved with long, purposeful strides that ate up the sidewalk, and Julia didn't know whether she should meet him halfway and beg him not to mention the choking incident to Freckles, or whether she should hide in the overgrown azalea bush.

In the end, she was too mortified to do either. Her aunt motioned the man up the uneven cement path and onto the porch. "Kane Chatterson, meet my favorite grandniece, Dr. and Captain Julia Fitzgerald."

The pride in her aunt's voice blossomed inside Julia's chest, nearly shadowing the lingering shame. Or was that just her elevated heartbeat?

"I'm your *only* niece," Julia said, trying to lighten things up with a joke, but she succeeded only in making her nerves feel more weighed down. She cleared her throat and looked at Kane. "We weren't formally introduced earlier."

God, she hoped this man didn't spill the beans to her aunt. His sunglasses shaded his eyes, and he certainly wasn't smirking now, making it impossible for Julia to figure out if he was annoyed, amused or biding his time until Freckles left and he could tell her that she and her contracting job weren't worth the trouble.

But Kane Chatterson simply gave her a brief, unsmiling nod before asking, "Do I call you Doctor or Captain?"

"Call me just Julia. Please." She reached out her hand to shake his, and he gripped her fingers quickly, his warm calluses leaving an imprint on her palms. As a medical professional, she had no rational or scientific explanation for the shiver that vibrated down her spine. As a woman, her only explanation was that this new sensation was most likely the result of her aunt's fresh lecture on dating. And possibly the fact that she hadn't been this attracted to a man since…ever.

"Just Julia," he replied. But still no smile.

She looked at her watch. She'd be out of here in ten minutes. Surely, she could pretend to be a normal, successful woman for another ten minutes.

"What do you mean, you weren't formally introduced earlier?" Damn. Aunt Freckles didn't miss a thing.

"We, uh, spoke briefly at the Cowgirl Up Café when our orders got mixed up this morning," Kane told her aunt. The faint dusting of copper-colored stubble on his square jaw made it too difficult to tell if the man was actually blushing.

"Yeah, I figured the new waitress I hired wasn't quite

ready for me to leave her on her own," Freckles replied, then turned to Julia and gave her a wink. "Seems like lots of people are getting stuff wrong this morning."

"Here." Julia handed the cell phone to her aunt, determined to prove that she hadn't made a mistake. Or at least two of them. "It says right here on my calendar app that we were supposed to meet at the café."

Since Freckles was busy tapping on the screen and Mr. Chatterson's attention was on the yellow paint chipping off the wood siding of the house, Julia stole another look at his dour face. She'd been trying to save his life back at the café. Surely he couldn't be irritated with her over that—unless the laughter she'd heard as she left the restaurant was directed at him. Maybe the guy's ego had taken a hit. Or maybe his feet were cold and tired from walking all this way from the restaurant.

Julia glanced down at the scuffed cowboy boots. No, that sturdy, worn leather looked like they'd been walked in quite a lot. So his stiff demeanor most likely wasn't the result of sore feet. She allowed her gaze to travel up his jeans-clad legs, past his untucked shirt and all the way to his green cap with the words Patterson's Dairy embroidered in yellow on the front.

That funny tingling made its way down her spine again.

What was wrong with her? She didn't stare at unsuspecting men or allow her body to get all jumbled full of hormones, no matter how good-looking they were. Julia reached up and tightened the elastic band in her hair, hoping he wouldn't look over and catch her checking him out.

"Sug," Aunt Freckles said, holding up the smartphone. "Somehow you managed to program the Cowgirl Up Café as the location for everything in your calendar this month—including five surgeries, two staff meetings, a seminar on neurological disorders and the Boise Philharmonic's String Quintet."

"Oh. Well, I haven't had time to go over the new software update. Yet." Julia waved her hand dismissively before powering off her screen. That wasn't a real mistake. She had much more important things to accomplish than mastering some stupid scheduling app—like getting this tour underway if she wanted to report for duty on time. She pulled a key from the pocket of her cardigan sweater, the one Aunt Freckles said did nothing for her coloring or her figure, and asked Mr. Chatterson, "Would you like me to show you around inside?"

"I could probably figure it out on my own," he said, then used the top step to wipe his boots as she unlocked the door. "But it wouldn't hurt for you to tell me some of your ideas for the place."

Well, wasn't he being generous?

"Shouldn't you grab a notepad?" Julia gestured toward his run-down truck-vehicle thing.

"Why?"

"So that you can take notes?"

"Don't need to."

"What about measurements? Surely you won't be able to remember every little dimension."

"No, ma'am. I probably won't. In fact, there's probably a lot of stuff I won't remember. But I'll get a sense of the house and what it needs, which is something no tape measure can show me."

"But how will you give me an estimate?"

"*If* I decide to take the job," he said, looking up at the large trees, their pine needles creeping toward the roof she was positive needed replacing, "I'll come back and take measurements and write it all down neat and tidy for you."

"Sug," Freckles interrupted in a stage whisper. "Kane here knows what he's doing. He doesn't come into the operating room and tell you where to cut or how to dig around in someone's brain." Then, as if to lessen the rebuke, Freckles turned to the brooding contractor. "Julia's a neurosurgeon in the Navy. Smart as a whip, my grandniece. Did I mention that?"

"I believe you did. Should we get started?" he asked, wiping his hand across his mouth. Then, without waiting for a response, he walked through the door as though he couldn't care less about Julia's abilities in the operating room or her whip-like intelligence. Not that she wanted the attention or expected him to be in awe of her, but it was one of the few times somebody hadn't been impressed with her genius IQ.

The guy strode into her front parlor as though he owned the place, and Julia resented his take-charge attitude and her unexplainable physical response to him. However, he was the expert—supposedly—and she was intelligent enough to know that this old house needed much more than her surgical skills.

The trio made their way from room to room, and Julia lost track of the amount of times she had to tell Aunt Freckles that she didn't love the idea of glitter-infused paint on the walls or a wet bar added to each of the three floors. When they finished the tour in the kitchen, Julia was already in jeopardy of being ten minutes late for her shift. Unfortunately, she didn't trust her aunt not to suggest something outlandish in her absence.

"I say you get some of those cool retro turquoise appliances and redo all these cabinets with pink and white paint." Freckles waved her arms like an air traffic controller. "Then you can do black-and-white-checkered tile and give it a real fifties' vibe. If you knock out this wall, it will open up the kitchen to the family room."

"Which room is the family room?" Julia rubbed at her temples before tightening her ponytail. Again.

"I believe that's the room you referred to as the study," Kane told her. His smirk gave off the impression that he was laughing at her for some reason. Again. "Or was that the informal parlor?"

"Either way," Julia said. "I don't want a fifties-themed anything in my house. Besides, remodeling the kitchen is my last concern."

It was difficult to not startle at Freckle's loud, indrawn breath. "Sug, no, no, no. The kitchen is the *heart* of the house. That should be the first thing Kane works on. How're you gonna cook or eat if you don't have a decent kitchen?"

"I don't intend to do much cooking here. I eat most of my meals at the hospital, and as long as I have a refrigerator to store all the leftovers you give me, I should be just fine."

The woman tipped her head back, then rubbed her fingers over her eyes. Julia feared her aunt was going to smear her purple eye shadow. "It's just that with the Pumpkin Pie Parade coming up and then ski season right after, I'm going to be so busy at the café. I worry about you being all alone, not eating right and withering away to nothing."

"I assure you, I value my health too much to allow myself to wither away," Julia said. "But I know you worry about me, and if it makes you feel any better, I'll buy a cookbook and teach myself some basic recipes. After all, how hard can it be?"

"Sug, I know most things come easy to you," Freckles said, wrapping her thin arm around Julia's waist. "But there're a lot of things in life you just can't learn from a book."

Unfortunately Julia knew the truth of that statement all too well. Freckles was her last living relative and the reason Julia had transferred duty stations and moved to Idaho. If it would ease the woman's mind to know that her only niece would have a fully functional kitchen, then Julia would give Sexy Flannel Shirt permission to start tearing out the old rotting cupboards today.

Julia leaned into Freckles's one-armed embrace. She didn't even have to look at the contractor's estimate to know that no matter how absurdly high his price might be, she would end up hiring him just to appease the affectionate woman.

"Fine," Julia said. "First things first, though. I need my bedroom to be in habitable condition. Then Mr. Chatterson can start on the kitchen. But no turquoise appliances or checkered floors. All design ideas need to be approved by me."

"Of course, Sug."

"Now I *really* need to get to the hospital," Julia said, glancing at her watch. "Take your time looking around."

"You want me to lock up afterward?" Kane asked after she hugged her aunt goodbye.

"That would be great, if you don't mind. Do I need to sign anything?"

"Not until I send you the estimate. Like I said, I haven't decided if this project is something that will fit into my schedule yet."

Julia collected her leather satchel on her way to the front parlor, then glanced out of the glass-paned entryway toward his old car parked in her driveway. His schedule was probably chock-full of appointments involving lots of smirking and consultations on how to give strangers the silent treatment. Unfortunately for her, that kind of work likely didn't pay his bills. Which meant she'd be stuck convincing herself that she could easily handle this unexpected attraction to her new contractor.

Chapter 2

Kane let out a long breath, feeling some of the nervous energy leave his body. This was exactly the kind of job he loved—taking something so run-down and bringing it back to its former glory. But Dr. Captain Julia Fitzgerald was exactly the kind of client that he most assuredly did *not* love.

He'd first noticed the blonde woman the second she'd sat down at the counter of the Cowgirl Up Café. It was hard not to notice a pretty face like that, despite the fact that she'd kept mostly to herself and didn't make eye contact with any of the other customers.

Not that he'd been in a real friendly mood himself these past two years. But before he knew it, the woman had her arms wrapped around him, her small, firm breasts pressed up against his back, and suddenly he hadn't cared about the vegetables he'd accidentally bit-

ten into because all he could think about was his desire
for her clasped hands to travel downward. He'd reacted
so quickly, almost knocking his head into her face, that
he wasn't quite sure what they'd even talked about after
that. He'd seen a flush of embarrassment steal up her
cheeks, and she'd pointed at something in his teeth before the entire restaurant broke out into laughter. Then
she was gone before he could find out who she was.

An hour later, he still hadn't recovered from the unexpected shock of seeing the same woman standing
next to Freckles on the front porch. Nor had he stopped
anxiously wiping his mouth or checking his teeth for
residual spinach every time he'd passed his reflection
in a window. So maybe he'd put on his game face when
he'd been formally introduced to her, but she hadn't
exactly been real comfortable in his presence, either.

"You sure she's your niece?" Kane asked Freckles
now, looking out the kitchen window at Dr. Smarty-
Pants sitting in her car, frowning at her cell phone.
Yeah, he got the message loud and clear. The young
woman was a doctor. She saved lives for a living. Apparently she even tried to save lives during her breakfast. He didn't need a college degree to see that no
matter how beautiful she was, she thought she was way
too good for the likes of him.

"What? You don't see the family resemblance?" the
café-owner-and-sometimes-waitress asked.

He glanced back at the seventy-something-year-old
woman, noting that her purple eye shadow was an exact
match to the geometric pattern on the scarf tying up her
orangeish hair. Just Julia, on the other hand, didn't wear
a lick of makeup, and her only accessory had been an

ugly beige cardigan covering up the hospital scrubs he hadn't noticed earlier at the café.

"Well, she's almost as pretty as you, but she kind of reminds me of one of those Lego people I had when I was a boy," he said, then tried to offer the woman his most charming smile. His mouth and his opinions had often gotten him into trouble before, and he hoped Freckles didn't object to his honesty.

But the sassy older lady just beamed a crooked grin, then sauntered over to join him by the window. "Yeah, she's a little stiff and formal, but she'll come around once I give her a good makeover."

Actually, Kane would've used the words *cold* and *inanimate* to describe her. Just Julia was exactly like those academic decathlon snobs Kane had avoided in high school. The ones who were standoffish and thought less of him because he was some dumb jock. Not counting the high-handed way she'd talked down to him at the café, the woman had barely said three words to him, directing most of her comments to her aunt.

"What's she doing to that poor phone?" he asked when he saw Julia shake the device before throwing it onto the dash of her car and backing out of the driveway.

Freckles sighed. "Poor girl's not so good with technology. But don't you dare tell her I said that. She's used to being the best at whatever she sets her mind to."

"I'll bet that doesn't help much when it comes to interpersonal relationships," he said.

"You're one to talk, Kane Chatterson," Freckles responded, and he could see the disapproval in every wrinkle on her face. A wave of remorse lodged in his gut. As usual, he'd said the first thing that popped into his mind, not thinking that it might come out as an insult. He was always too quick, too impulsive. "We all have our flaws, son."

Kane didn't want to think about the reasons that he'd practically been hiding out in Sugar Falls for the past few months. So he wiggled his eyebrows and shot a grin at Freckles instead. "And what exactly are *your* flaws?"

"None of your beeswax, you little charmer." She smacked his arm lightly, and the playful gesture helped loosen the knot in his gut. "And speaking of charm, don't you get any ideas about putting those famous Chatterson moves on my Julia, you hear?"

"Ha!" Kane tried to laugh. "What famous moves?"

"She's not real savvy when it comes to people, especially anything involving business and dating. She's too trusting. She needs worldly people like us to look out for her."

"I think you're doing a fine job of looking out for her." *All on your own*, he thought, but didn't dare say out loud. In fact, Kane pitied the man who was stupid enough to get on Freckles's bad side. And not just because they'd be banned from her restaurant and the best chicken-fried steak in Idaho.

"You keep that in mind. Julia's nothing like those major-league groupies you got used to when you were playing baseball."

He tried not to roll his eyes. How could he get anything from his notorious past out of his mind when everywhere he turned, it was getting brought up? Most people in town knew not to bring up his past career as a major-league pitcher or the scandal in Chicago if they wanted to engage Kane in more than five minutes of conversation. And usually five minutes was his max. Which meant this little chat with Freckles had gone on way too long.

"Don't worry. I'll give your niece a fair price, and you can rest assured that I have absolutely no intention of bringing the so-called Chatterson moves out of retirement." He pulled the antique watch out of the pocket of his jeans and clicked the cover open and closed a few times. "Come on. I'll give you a ride back to the café so you can make me a new burrito."

"Fine, but you're paying full price for a second meal." Freckles sighed and hopped up into the Bronco. She was much sprier than most women her age—whatever age that was. "So, you're saying my niece isn't attractive or smart enough for you?"

"That's not what I said at all, and you know it." He slammed the door a little more forcefully than necessary, wanting to cut off any further discussion on this subject. People with half their eyesight could see that Just Julia was drop-dead gorgeous, even if she kept her classic beauty hidden underneath those ugly hospital clothes and an aloof exterior. He wasn't about to admit to Freckles—or anyone—that every muscle in his body hardened the moment she'd reached out and shaken his hand. Kane hadn't been remodeling homes for long, but he already had a few rules for himself.

Rule Number One. He worked alone.

Rule Number Two. He always packed an extra sandwich in case time got away from him and he found himself on the job after dinnertime, which happened nearly every day.

Rule Number Three. He wouldn't work for a client

who didn't have the same vision he did for the outcome of the property. Some people might think this was bad business sense, but it wasn't as though Kane was in this line of work for the money. He didn't believe in working for free, but his past salary and careful investing pretty much negated the need for him ever to work again. He'd started this business because he loved to build things and see his ideas come to life, not because he loved being around people.

Today, he would add Rule Number Four. He wouldn't date a client, no matter how attracted he was to her. That would be an easy enough rule to follow. Unlike Just Julia, Kane's heart wasn't in need of protection. It was retired, along with his pitching glove.

"So, what do you see for the house?" Kane asked her aunt as he climbed in and started up the classic car he'd been refurbishing in his spare time.

He listened to Freckles's chatter as he steered the Bronco back into town, noting that all of her suggestions were the complete opposite of what her niece wanted. Which, actually, made following Rule Number Three rather easy. He and Just Julia definitely saw eye to eye about keeping the same features of the stately old house and just repairing and refinishing everything to bring it back to its original splendor.

Kane turned onto Snowflake Boulevard, the street that ran through downtown Sugar Falls, and pulled in front of the Cowgirl Up Café to let Freckles out. Neither his stomach nor his still-tense muscles were settled yet and he promised her he would stop in for lunch instead. He waved to a few of the locals, keeping his green cap pulled down low just in case there were any tourists out and about looking for an autograph or a sly selfie with the elusive "Legend" Chatterson.

God, he hated that nickname. And he'd grown to hate the celebrity status that came along with it.

What he *did* like was the slower pace of the small town, along with the refuge and the anonymity it had provided him. So far. The scandal of Brawlgate was finally dying down, and he didn't want to challenge fate by coming out of hiding too soon. Plus, Kane was finding that as much as he missed pitching, there was something to be said for living out of the spotlight. Despite fielding the occasional calls from his sports agent and former coaches, he was free to do whatever he wanted. Like tinker on his old cars and rebuild homes. And right now, there was a deteriorating Victorian on Pinecone Court calling his name.

As he drove back to the house, he reached under his seat and pulled out a notepad. So maybe he hadn't been completely honest about not needing that. Kane parked the car and grabbed a tape measure from his tool bag in the backseat. Because he had issues focusing, Kane had a tendency to get so absorbed in a project that he would forget about his surroundings and tune out everything and everyone around him. And when that happened, he preferred not to have potential clients think he was off his rocker.

Since he hadn't given the key back to Freckles yet, he could spend some more time in the house on his own, exploring it and making notes.

He just hoped that when he made those notes and calculated the costs, he didn't spell anything wrong or add incorrectly on the formal estimate.

Concentrating on schoolwork had never been his strong suit, and he'd rather have a busload of newscasters from ESPN roll into Sugar Falls and reveal his hiding spot than have Just Julia look down her cute, smarty-pants nose at him.

By the time he pulled into a visitor parking spot at Shadowview Military Hospital the second Thursday in November, Kane was already five minutes late for his group session. Well, not *his* group session—one run by his brother-in-law, Drew.

He stopped by the Starbucks kiosk in the lobby and ordered a decaf Frappuccino because he hated sitting still in those introductory meetings with nothing to do, nothing to hold on to. Unable to wait, he stuck his tongue through the hole of the domed plastic lid to taste the whipped cream, then kept his head down as he walked through the large, plain lobby. Kane navigated his way down the fall-themed decorated corridors of the first floor until he found the psychology department, which was directly across from the physical rehab department.

Dr. Drew Gregson had explained that he wanted his patients with PTSD to understand their therapy was no different than someone learning how to walk again after losing a limb. Tonight he was meeting with a new group in a classroom-like setting—and Kane hated classrooms. They would eventually meet out on the track, in the weight room and on various courts and fields.

When Kane had been doing physical therapy after his shoulder surgery, his sister, Kylie, had talked him into coming to work out at the hospital. Drew had been looking for innovative ways to assist his PTSD patients in their recovery, and helped his wife convince Kane that exercising with them would be a great motivator for some of the men and women who used athletics as a physical outlet. Especially since most of the group's sessions ended up in some challenge that usually provided one of the patients with bragging rights that they'd competed against Legend Chatterson.

Good thing his ego could take it. Being at Shadowview—seeing the world through the eyes of the wounded warriors and the staff who helped them—always put things into perspective for Kane. These people were dealing with legitimate life-or-death situations. Brawlgate, his former baseball career, being attracted to his new client...none of that seemed as important when he was faced with real obstacles to overcome.

Kane looked at the number he'd written on his hand to make sure he was going to the right meeting room. Which was why he didn't see the shapely blonde exiting the gym facilities until she'd bumped into him.

"Sorry, darlin'," he said before thinking about it. The flirtatious endearment sounded as out of practice as his pitching arm. His first instinct was to pull an orange pumpkin-shaped piece of construction paper off the nearby bulletin board and hide his face behind it, but then he recognized those round green eyes.

Whoa. His hand flew to his mouth to make sure he didn't have any whipped cream stuck to his face. He hadn't seen her since she'd signed off on his estimate and he'd started work on her old house a few days after they first met. Neither time had she looked so flushed, and sexy, and...hell, feminine, as she did now.

Not that he wasn't well aware of how attractive she was. But Just Julia in her boxy hospital scrubs only served as a reminder that she was some smart doctor with a fancy education. In this outfit—he let his eyes travel down her form-fitting workout clothes—she looked like the kind of woman who would hang out in hotel bars and throw herself at the visiting professional baseball team.

"Mr. Chatterson?" she asked, and Kane tried not to look at the straps of her sports bra as he shifted the cold drink to his other hand, then back again.

"Sorry. I didn't recognize you dressed like…" Dressed like what? One of Beyoncé's backup dancers? Nothing he could say at this point would make him sound like less of an infatuated idiot. "Anyway, I wasn't expecting to run into you here."

"Sorry for running into you at all," she said, then held up her smartphone. "I wasn't paying attention to where I was going because I have this new fitness monitor on here, and I somehow programmed it wrong. It's telling me that I've only burned thirty calories but that my heart rate is 543. Now, I'm trying to just delete the whole thing, because really, I know how to check my own pulse and multiply and… Sorry. You probably don't want to hear about this."

She tapped harder on the display. Kane, always a sucker for video games and electronics, eased the phone out of her hand. "Here, let me."

She leaned in and watched over his shoulder as he made a few swipes and closed out the app. He didn't have the heart to tell her that touch screens didn't seem to be her forte. Or that standing this close to her still-damp skin made him think of a different type of physical exertion he wouldn't mind engaging in with her.

He finished and handed the device back to her, cursing to himself for having such an inappropriate thought. "What are you doing here, anyway?"

"Well, I *do* work here." It might've come off as defensive or stuck-up from any other woman, but Just Julia's response seemed more like a schoolteacher trying to explain a new concept to a first grader.

And Kane Chatterson had always had a soft spot for his first-grade teacher, who'd been the only one who hadn't treated him like a below-average student with problems sitting still in class.

"Are you working now?" He finally allowed himself to look down at the form-fitting sports tank that tapered down to her small waist. He brought his straw to his lips, needing something to relieve the sudden dryness in his mouth. He got the paper wrapper instead.

"I had back-to-back surgeries this morning and needed to loosen up and relieve some tension before I started on my post-op reports. Normally I do laps in the pool, but there was a water aerobics class going on, so I used the cardio equipment instead and accidentally set the program for the inverted pyramid. The incline level got stuck on high, which is why I tried to use my phone to calculate my heart rate. Wait. Why am I explaining all this to you?"

"Because I have the kind of face that makes people want to open up?" Why was he being so damn flirty? It was as if he couldn't stop the asinine comments from flying out. But she'd caught him off guard, looking like that. Plus, she was much more down-to-earth and endearing when she rambled on about nothing.

"Your face is perfect. It's your eyes that make people feel as if they're strapped to a polygraph machine." That was an interesting revelation. Did he make her nervous?

"So you like my face?" He reached up to stroke his trademark beard, then remembered he'd shaved it several months ago when he'd moved to Sugar Falls. Instead he touched a bristly jawline that felt like eighty-grit sandpaper.

"I'm not going to answer that." But he could tell by the blush rising up from her neckline that she probably liked his appearance more than she wanted to admit. An alarm bell went off inside his brain. And then, as if she'd heard the same warning, she straightened her back and crossed her arms, her haughty stance effectively putting him back in his place. "What are *you* doing here?"

"I'm here for the…" He stopped. Kane couldn't very well tell her he came as a guest to help boost troop morale. That might give away his celebrity status.

"I'm here for a meeting," Kane finally said, then shifted his drink in his hands again and prayed she wouldn't look at the big Psychology Department sign behind him.

She looked, and he saw her green eyes become round with realization.

"Therapy is nothing to be ashamed of," she said, surprising him. No, he didn't suppose it was, for a brain doctor like her. The only thing he was embarrassed of was the fact that he'd called this uptight, intelligent woman *darlin'* and that she might connect the dots and figure out who he really was. Assuming she hadn't already.

"Oh really?" He seized on her mistake. "Do you go?"

"As a matter of fact, Aunt Freckles suggested I start talking to a professional about my... Well, that's not really relevant."

Oh boy. The smart doctor had a secret. Besides the fact that she'd been hiding all her sexy curves under those blue scrubs and ugly cardigan sweaters. Now Kane was more than curious about what else the doctor was keeping under wraps.

"Actually..." She shifted back on her sneakers and stood up straighter. "I've been meaning to call you and see how the progress is going on the upstairs bedrooms."

Bedrooms. Bedrooms. He tried not to think about the fact that this Lycra-clad woman had just said the word *bedrooms* to him. "Progress? Well, the flooring is all done in two of them and down most of the hallway. I should have the stairway finished by next Wednesday. I'm still waiting for you to get back to me on those tile samples so I can start the master bathroom. Why?"

"I was just thinking that with the colder weather approaching, I'd like to move in soon so I can appease my aunt. She's worried that since I'm living close to work, I don't have much of a social life and... Sorry. I'm rambling again."

"You mean you want to move into the place while it's still under construction?"

"I promise I wouldn't be in your way or anything. I'm usually at the hospital all day and would keep to one bedroom and bathroom upstairs."

"Stop saying *bedroom*," he muttered.

"What was that?"

"I said 'spraying bedroom.' As in, I need to use my paint gun to finish spraying the last coat on it. The bathroom will still take at least a week once I order those tiles. But I haven't even started on the kitchen yet, and your aunt was pretty convinced that you needed a fully functional kitchen before you could move in."

Julia sighed. "Aunt Freckles is convinced about a lot of things that I don't actually need. You should see the liquid eyeliner she bought me so I could practice something called the cat-wing technique." Kane didn't reply that Just Julia's aunt was probably right about the kitchen and most definitely wrong about the eyeliner. Or the fact that he preferred working on empty houses where the pretty and distracting homeowners weren't coming and going anytime they pleased. Especially if this was her normal after-work attire. "Anyway, I'll head back to my office now to look over those tile samples, and then we'll plan on me moving into the house next week."

She didn't wait for his response as she nodded at him, then walked away. Her expensive-looking sneakers squeaked along the pristine hospital floor with each step. He had a feeling brain surgeons—not to mention military officers—were used to telling people what to do and having their orders carried out.

Apparently the boss lady didn't understand that Kane Chatterson wasn't a lower ranked recruit or some unemployed laborer in a small hick town perfectly content to do her bidding. He might not have a bunch of letters after his name, but he had two championship rings and had been on the cover of *Sports Illustrated* three times. Even if one of those times was a shot taken during Brawlgate and wasn't the most flattering image.

No wonder she didn't have much of a social life, if this was how she talked to people. He definitely wasn't some nobody to be so easily dismissed. And if the good doctor thought she was going to move in and start ordering him around as he remodeled her home, she'd better think again.

Chapter 3

Julia hadn't minded when Freckles had hired a personal shopper who emailed links containing possible dresses for Julia to wear to the hospital's fund-raising gala in December. After all, shopping was an easy enough task to delegate since Julia didn't exactly care what she wore to the event, which was still four weeks away. The thing she wasn't looking forward to, though, was finding a suitable date to accompany her, which Aunt Freckles insisted was just as necessary as a new pair of strappy heels.

Julia sat at her desk, looking at the dark screen of her cell phone, and groaned when she was unable to open the message her aunt had sent when she'd been downstairs working out. Then she squeezed her eyes shut and sent out a prayer that Kane Chatterson hadn't seen the embarrassing text when he'd helped her reprogram her phone twenty minutes ago.

Heat stole up her cheeks as she squeezed her eyes shut and gave her ponytail a firm shake. Julia refused to think about how her contractor had stared at her when she ran into him outside the gym. Especially since she had many more pressing matters to worry about—like how to make Aunt Freckles proud of her without allowing the woman full access to her sparse wardrobe and even sparser dating options.

Setting boundaries was usually easy for Julia because she didn't tend to socialize much anyway. But this was uncharted territory for her. How did Julia politely tell her well-meaning relative that she absolutely did not need a makeover or a professional relationship coach—as the last text suggested?

Surely it couldn't be that difficult to find her own date. All she needed to do was figure out what kind of man she wanted and then go out and find one. She shoved a few chocolate-covered raisins in her mouth as she wrote "Qualities I Want in a Man" at the top of a notepad.

But the only image that came to her mind was Kane Chatterson standing there, all perceptive and broad-shouldered and rugged. Sure, Julia had come into contact with plenty of men since joining the Navy, but dress whites and blue utilities were utterly dull compared to the faded jeans and soft flannel uniform her hired contractor filled out. The man was broad, but lean and muscular in that athletic way of someone who was always on the move. He was also more intense than a college freshman studying for his first midterm, looking around as if he was taking in every detail of his surroundings and then memorizing it for future use.

Besides the condescending smirk, she'd only seen Kane wearing a constant frown, barely addressing her unless it was to ask about paint colors or refinished hardwood floors. So she'd been shocked an hour ago when she'd heard the man call her *darlin'* in that slow, sexy drawl of his. Shocked and then flushed with embarrassment when she realized he'd been staring at her body as though he'd spilled some of his iced coffee drink on her and wanted to lick it off.

Then she'd said something about therapy and the guy's whole demeanor had changed. Julia had tried to come up with something else to talk about, but she'd just ended up blabbering about bedrooms and moving in and eyeliners, then tried to walk away with her head held as high as the uncomfortable, tingling tightness in her neck had allowed.

Stop. Stop thinking about what happened in the hospital corridor earlier. No wonder her aunt didn't believe she was capable of finding a suitable date on her own.

This was ridiculous. She could do this. Julia had never failed at a task, and she wasn't about to get distracted and fail now.

She looked down at the empty page and began to write.

Must look good in flannel.

Must speak in a slow, sexy drawl.

Must look at me like I'm the whipped cream on his Frappuccino.

No, *this* was ridiculous. She tore the yellow sheet off and tossed it in the small trash can by her desk.

She rotated the pencil between her fingers, twirling it like a miniature baton. After a disastrous relationship with one of her professors a few years ago, Julia didn't want a man at all, let alone another person to help her find one. She knew that her solitary upbringing and current avoidance of social activities was anything but ordinary. She'd never let it bother her before now. But her fitting in seemed important to Aunt Freckles. And if she wanted to be normal, or at least create the appearance of being normal on the night of the hospital gala, then she would need to put forth more effort. She looked down at a fresh piece of paper and started her list all over again, this time leaving off any references to Kane Chatterson.

She had just finished and put her pencil down when a knock sounded at her office door. Chief Wilcox, Julia's surgical assistant, entered. "Do you have those post-op reports done? The physical therapist is already asking for them."

"Yes, they should be in the patient's online file," Julia told the corpsman, who had a pink backpack slung over her shoulder and was apparently leaving for the day.

"I looked there and didn't see them."

"I finished them after my workout," Julia said, pulling up the screen on her iPad. "Oh. I must not have clicked on Submit. Okay, they should be in there now. I'll call the physical therapist and let him know." She looked her assistant over. "You look like you're off for the weekend."

Even to Julia, the observation came out sounding a little too obvious. She didn't want the woman to think she was crossing the line from professional to overly social, but how else was she supposed to get to know her staff? She told herself this was good practice.

"Oh, yeah. A few of us are doing a camping trip up near the Sugar River trailhead. I still need to pack my gear, and Chief Filbert put me in charge of KP duty, so I need to get all the food ready, too."

Julia had no idea who Filbert was, but she was more than familiar with the hollowness circling her chest. Not that she was much of a camper, but it was her weekend off, as well, and nobody had thought to ask if she'd like to go on the trip. Same thing with happy hours or lunches in the break room. It was easier to act indifferent than to make other people see that she, too, wanted to be included in the ordinary adventures of life.

At a loss, Julia simply said, "I hope you all enjoy your trip, then. I'll see you back here on Monday at 0600."

"Aye, aye, Cap'," Wilcox said before closing the door. Julia fell back against her chair and squeezed her eyes shut at how ridiculously pathetic she must've sounded. She remembered her first day of high school and how the students patted her on her twelve-year-old head when she'd foolishly asked several of the cheerleaders if she could sit with them at their table. Nobody had been rude to her outright, but the novelty of having a child genius as some sort of odd little mascot soon wore off when Julia easily outscored several of the seniors on their honors English midterms.

College hadn't been any better, especially since she was studying adolescent brain development while her own brain hadn't finished the process. Guidance counselors who didn't know what to do with such a young scholar told her things would get better for her socially once she got older. But by the time she started med school, she no longer cared about what others thought of her and found it easier to simply hang back and observe. She had her cello, she had swimming, she had her books and her studies. She didn't have time for homecoming games and celebratory drinks after final exams—even if she *had* been old enough to be admitted into the bars with the rest of her classmates.

A career in research had been on the horizon until she'd seen a documentary about women in the military.

She'd attended Officer Development School soon after her parents died, the order and regulation of the Navy reminding her of her regimented childhood and serving as the perfect antidote to Julia's hesitancy to fraternize. She easily told herself that she wasn't jealous of her staff's camaraderie or the fact that she looked for reasons to sit here in her office and work instead of going back to the lonely officers' quarters and microwaving a frozen Lean Cuisine before falling asleep on her government-issue twin-size mattress.

So why was she all of a sudden starting to worry about any of it now? She undid her ponytail and massaged her scalp before turning to the tile samples she'd set on the credenza behind her.

Julia ran her fingers over the glazed surfaces of the

colorful porcelain pieces. Kane had suggested neutral colors because they added to the resale value. While some of the decorating magazines she'd perused pushed the idea of an all-white bathroom, the surgeon in her worried that she would grow tired of the sterile and clinical feel of such a contrast-free environment.

Julia brought the blue-and-green mosaic strips to her desk and propped them against some medical texts so she could get a better look at them. If they laid the glass tiles in a running bond pattern in the shower, she could use both colors, but would it overpower the white cabinets and the large, claw-foot tub in the center of the room?

She shook some more Raisinets out of the box as she contemplated the color scheme. Not that she was the type who turned to food for comfort—Fitzgeralds didn't need comforting, after all—but during med school, she'd found that she thought better when she snacked.

Unfortunately, no amount of snacking could get Kane's voice out of her mind. She tried to ignore the warmth spreading through her at the memory of her body's response to his assessing stare outside the gym.

The sooner she made a selection, the sooner she could get back to more important things—like picking a dress for the hospital gala and finding an appropriate date to take with her. Preferably one that didn't look at her as though he knew exactly how much she wanted those sexy, smirking lips to …

Julia snatched another handful of candy, determined to distract herself from thinking of his mouth, only to have her focus shift to the blue-green glass tiles that were the exact same shade as his eyes. If she chose that color, would she be sentencing herself to a lifetime of showers feeling as though his penetrating gaze was surrounding her naked body?

She reached for the plain white subway tiles before changing her mind and grabbing her smartphone. After taking a quick picture, she fired off an email to Kane in an effort to prevent herself from wasting any more of her time with such dangerous and unproductive thoughts. And to stop the sound of his slow drawl calling her *darlin'* replaying over and over again in her mind.

It was after eleven o'clock, and Kane's brain had yet to slow down enough to make going to bed an option. Usually a day's physical labor followed by a long, mind-numbing run after dinner was enough to tire him out sufficiently so that it would take only about thirty minutes for him finally to drop off into his standard six hours of sleep. But images of his client in all her spandex workout glory wouldn't stop popping into his overactive mind, and he decided he might as well pull out his laptop and do some invoices in an effort to bore himself to sleep.

He could go out to his garage and work on his Bronco, but because of his attention issues, once he got hyperfocused on a project, he would lose all sense of time and end up exhausted and cranky the following day.

So, it was either crunching numbers or watching a late-night edition of *SportsCenter*, which he knew from past experience would only get him more frustrated.

Picking the mentally healthier and more productive

option, he sat up and switched on his bedside lamp before opening his nearby laptop. He logged onto his email and, in his inbox, he saw the very name of the source of his late-night thoughts. He clicked on the attached image and stared at her tile selection. He had to give credit to Just Julia. She wasn't too outlandish in her remodeling requests. In fact, Kane had originally suggested white just because the doctor seemed like a plain vanilla kind of person. But seeing the bold colors of the tiles she'd picked—as well as the snug fabric of her high-end athletic wear—made him rethink his original opinion. She'd typed information about the brand and tracking numbers in the body of the email. But he squinted at the bottom left of the picture, seeing notes written on a yellow notepad off to the side.

Although today's encounter at the hospital made it a total of three times they'd seen each other in person, he'd emailed her with updates, and she'd stopped by the house in the evenings when he wasn't there and left pictures carefully cut out of magazines along with handwritten descriptions on lined paper taped to the walls. Usually her notes were detailed instructions of what she liked or wanted, and even though they were long and tiresome to read, Kane would much rather deal with a client on paper than one in the flesh.

Especially one whose curvaceous, damp flesh he'd been thinking about all evening.

So when he saw the note by the bluish green tiles, his first instinct was to zoom in and see what special instructions she had for him now. Instead, he leaned closer as he read the words "Qualities I Want in a Man."

What in the world was this? His finger vibrated over

the mouse pad, but refused to click on the button that would close the image.

By the time he got to number three, he tried to tell himself that this obviously wasn't meant for him to see. Yet like a pitch in midhurl, he couldn't stop now. Why in the world would she write out such a ridiculous and pointless list? Or one so personal?

Assuming she was the one who'd written it in the first place.

It was her handwriting, though. He'd exchanged plans and inventories with her long enough to know that the woman put a ton of thought into *every* list she created. Freckles had made several offhand remarks this past week regarding her niece's single status and lack of a social life. Maybe Just Julia was feeling inadequate in that department and was making an effort to step up her game.

His eyes bounced around the enlarged image, trying to take all the information in at once while he told himself that there was no way he'd make the cut. Not that he *wanted* her looking in his direction, anyway. Kane had to take a few deep breaths to focus on what he was reading. Hell, were there any qualities on here that he even remotely possessed? He read it through again.

Must be social.

That certainly wasn't him. Sure, it used to be, before his career had taken a nosedive, but nowadays, Kane viewed social situations like most batters viewed a curveball—confusing and oftentimes unavoidable.

Must be educated and able to discuss current events.

Nope. Kane Chatterson barely sat still long enough in class to make it out of high school with a diploma. He had a feeling even that accomplishment was the result of sympathetic teachers and his dad's generous donation to the library building fund.

Must be patient and not lose his temper.

Kylie once told him that he had the patience of a hummingbird, which said a lot, considering his sister's only speed was overdrive.

Must enjoy swimming or similar civilized athletic pursuits.

Sure, baseball could be civilized if compared to rugby or ice hockey or cage fighting, for instance. But as any of the three million YouTube viewers would attest, the swinging bats and punches and profanity involved in the Brawlgate scandal two years ago were anything but civil.

Strong.

In terms of what? Before his shoulder injury, Kane could bench-press two-fifty and hurl a fastball ninety-nine miles per hour. But Erica, his ex, had once called him emotionally unavailable and a weak excuse for a boyfriend. So he was fifty-fifty in the strength department.

Good with his hands.

Kane looked at his palms, trying to imagine how his work-worn, callous hands would compare with the uppity doctor's long, graceful fingers that meticulously saved lives. Meh.

Flannel.

He glanced at his open closet and the soft plaid shirts hanging in order by color. He had a feeling the prim Navy captain meant the man she was looking for must prefer wearing flannel pajamas or some other conservative outfit to bed.

Kane stretched out under his quilt and tried not to grin at how shocked Just Julia would be if she could see the complete lack of flannel between his sheets right now. Or the complete lack of any material, for that matter.

The sudden thought of the attractive woman seeing him naked in bed caused an unexpected response, and Kane had to shift his computer lower on his lap.

Speaking of lists, maybe he should rethink the set of rules he'd laid out for himself. Specifically, the one about him not dating his clients. Or thinking about their damp blond hair pulled back away from their high, flushed cheekbones.

Kane shook his head, trying to envision Just Julia in plain blue scrubs and an oversize white coat. If he concentrated hard enough, maybe he could imagine her green eyes looking through him, instead of being dilated from physical exertion and rounded in surprise when she'd glanced up from her cell phone and collided with him in the hospital hallway earlier today.

He slammed the laptop closed in frustration, then remembered their conversation and her plan to move into her house in a week. Kane needed to get as much work as possible done before then so he wouldn't have to risk running into her upstairs. Near her bedroom. He opened the computer again and logged on to the building supply store's website to place an order for the tiles.

That done, he set his laptop off to the side and turned out his lamp, knowing he wouldn't be able to fall asleep for a long time. After a few minutes, he pulled the laptop over again, opened his email account and finally sent her a reply, using as few words as he dared.

Ordered tile. Should be in stock next Wed. Then, at the last second, he couldn't help adding, Kitchen not done. Maybe that would stall her and he could buy himself some more time. And avoid running into the pretty doctor at all costs.

Julia carried the last box down the stairs from her officer's quarters and shoved it into the backseat of her red MINI Cooper. How sad was it that all of her personal belongings fit into a car with the cubic space of a safe-deposit box? Well, technically, the attic at the Georgetown house was filled with family heirlooms and photo albums and her parents' personal effects. Yet none of that had ever really felt like hers.

Still, she would have to face that mess eventually, or have one of her attorneys face it for her and send her an invoice. She looked at her watch and estimated that the sun would set before she made it to Sugar Falls.

She'd purposely timed her move-in day to be more of a move-in evening. That way she wouldn't have to see Kane Chatterson and risk him asking her in person if she'd gotten a cookbook like she'd promised her Aunt Freckles.

By the time she pulled onto Pinecone Court thirty minutes later, her stomach was empty, yet she was eager to see what progress had been made on her house. When she saw the Ford Bronco parked along her curb, now sporting a dull gray paint color instead of its usual rust spots, she wanted to throw her gearshift straight into Reverse.

Instead she took a deep breath and ordered her tummy to quit thrashing around. She would really need to become accustomed to seeing Kane sporadically. After all, she'd hired the guy to remodel her house. She couldn't very well let her abdominal muscles get all tight and contracted anytime she saw his ugly old car.

She wasn't some lovesick nineteen-year-old anymore, thinking an affair with her college professor was the real deal. In fact, technically speaking, *she* was *Kane's* boss. She was a Navy officer, trained to issue orders. And she was an accomplished surgeon, known for her steady hand and her even steadier nerves. If she could command an operating room full of experienced hospital staff, Julia could certainly handle one small-town contractor who barely said more than a few words to her—even if his eyes drank her in as though they knew every inch of her body intimately.

She parked in the narrow driveway, then grabbed her leather satchel and one of the boxes out of the backseat and made her way up to the front porch and inside. She heard music coming from upstairs and smelled something garlicky drifting out of the kitchen area. She set the box down in the front parlor and climbed the newly finished stairway, uncertain if she should be walking on the freshly stained steps. But then she realized they must be dry, since someone was upstairs and had to have walked on them already.

She followed the sound of Duke Ellington—her classical cello instructor would've frowned at her recognizing the piece—toward her bedroom and stepped into the well-lit area, relieved that the antique chandelier had been installed already. When she got to the bathroom door, she froze. Kane Chatterson, wearing faded jeans and nothing but paint splatters on his torso, was standing behind her claw-foot tub, one well-defined muscular arm poised with a paintbrush above the top sill of the window frame.

With an effort, she ignored the weakness in her legs and drew in one ragged breath after another.

Each stroke of his hand matched the swaying tempo of the music coming from the cordless speaker propped up on the bathroom vanity. The muscles of his back moved in an orchestrated rhythm with the jazzy strains of a piano. The darkness outside made his reflection in the window almost mirror-like, and she saw the deep-set focus in his eyes, his concentrated brow and the hard lines of his set jaw. She could also see that he was completely transfixed in his own little world and had no idea she was there.

The professional in her wanted to cough or turn down the jazz music or do something to draw his attention to the fact that he wasn't alone. Unfortunately, her body wasn't behaving so professionally. Desire curled around her, squeezing so tightly it threatened to cut off the oxygen supply to her brain. Thank God the man was focused too intensely to witness her intrusion on his workspace because Julia didn't think she could've taken a step.

She had no idea how long she stood there, just as absorbed in his movements as he apparently was in his painting. A softer, slower saxophone-based song switched on the moment his eyes met hers, and Julia wasn't sure if the dizziness in her head was from the paint fumes or from the way he looked at her.

Chapter 4

Kane was so engrossed in what he was doing, he had no idea how long Julia had been standing there waiting for him. He struggled to get those old feelings of embarrassment in check before turning away from the window and pretending not to care that she'd caught him completely off guard. Noting her surgical scrubs were covered by a soft purple cardigan sweater, he let out a breath, equally relieved and disappointed that she wasn't wearing her exercise outfit.

"Hey," he said, before coughing and clearing his throat. He set the paintbrush down in the tray and walked over to his iPhone to turn off his playlist. "I wasn't expecting you so soon."

"It's seven o'clock," she said, her green eyes round and fringed with spiky lashes.

Kane pulled his late Grandpa Chatterson's antique

gold watch out of his pocket and snapped it open—more as something to redirect his focus than to actually check the time. "Wow. I must've really been in the zone."

At least, that's what his dad called it whenever Kane would tune out the rest of the world to the point that someone could ask him if he wanted a million dollars and he'd ignore the question. His mom called it hyper-focusing. He called it a pain-in-the-butt symptom of his ADHD.

"I, uh, didn't mean to startle you," she said, but he noticed she wasn't looking at him when she spoke. Correction: she was definitely looking at him, just not at his face. The skin across his bare chest tightened, causing his pectoral muscles to flex slightly. He remembered her list and wanted to suggest she add something about physical attraction as a quality she might appreciate in a man. Not that he considered himself all that attractive, but after several years of playing professional sports and living out of hotels, plagued by groupies and jersey chasers, he knew when a lady was sizing him up. Or at least when he *hoped* she was.

"That's a decently sized incision, there," she said. Not cut. Not wound. *Incision.* So maybe the doctor wasn't sizing him up so much as taking a professional interest in his anatomy. An unexpected feeling of disappointment washed down his torso. "When did you have a full shoulder replacement?" she asked.

He squinted at his shoulder before looking at her doubtfully. Maybe she *did* know who he was after all. She'd have to be living under a rock to not know, but the few times he'd met Just Julia, he'd gotten the impression that was where she liked to keep herself hidden. "So you heard about my surgery?"

"No. I can tell from your incision."

Of course she could. Otherwise she wouldn't have asked when he'd had it. Rather than making himself look like more of an idiot, he tried to concentrate on her words as she kept talking. "Your surgeon used the extended deltopectoral approach, which is normally only suitable for total shoulder replacement with an open reduction and internal fixation of a proximal humeral fracture."

He ran his hand across the lower half of his face, but that didn't make him resent her easy use of fancy medical jargon any less. "You sure like to use a lot of big words, doc."

"Here," she said, walking toward him. He tried not to flinch when she traced her finger along the pink scar tissue. "Your incision extends from the outer end of your clavicle to the coracoid and follows the medial edge of the deltoid muscle."

She must've mistaken his annoyance for a lack of understanding since she was now restating the obvious as though he hadn't been the one to undergo the procedure. However, he couldn't be sure since he could barely hear her voice over his own heartbeat pounding in his ears. The soft caress of her cool finger was making gooseflesh rise on his exposed skin.

"Why would someone your age need such an extensive surgery?" she asked, and he could feel the warmth of her breath.

Would she believe him if he said "car accident"? Probably not. Dr. Smarty-Pants was proving to be too damn intelligent for Kane's own good. But right this second, with her finger still tracing his scar and sending shockwaves throughout his body, he really didn't want to think about the pissed off player who'd charged the mound and attacked him with a Louisville Slugger. "Random baseball bat injury."

"Hmm." His eyes were drawn to her mouth. She didn't wear an ounce of makeup, not even lipstick, but the pink fullness of her upper lip was enhanced by the deep bow in the center. "That must have been quite a baseball bat. Still…"

When she shook her head, Kane caught a whiff of her shampoo, and he was reminded of the coconut and mango smoothies he'd loved as a child when his family used to vacation in Hawaii. He leaned in, his face hovering closer to hers. "Still, what?"

"It's just that even blunt force trauma from a bat wouldn't necessitate a full shoulder replacement. Usually a humerus fracture is associated with pathological fractures and osteoporosis. You must've been diagnosed with early-onset osteoporosis."

It was as if she'd dumped a bucket of cold Gatorade over his head. He immediately took a step back, already regretting how close he'd let her get. Of course his shoulder had already suffered extensive damage just from the long-term wear and tear he'd put on it as a professional pitcher, but he hadn't been willing to listen to the professionals. He had no one to blame for that but himself. Arturo Dominguez and his temper were the icing on Kane's arthritic cake.

"I guess so," he said and pivoted on his booted heel. Not wanting to talk about his career-ending injury or the preexisting condition trainers had warned him about, and definitely not wanting to breathe in the heady fragrance of her tidy blond ponytail, Kane walked over to the corner where he'd left his tool bag and pulled on his discarded T-shirt. "I was just finishing up with the bathroom so it would be all set for you to move in. As you can see, the rest of the house is still a work in progress."

He grabbed the tray of paint and almost slammed his finger shut in the ladder before hauling it out of the room, bumping it on the banister as he hurried out. He didn't have to turn around to know that she was following him downstairs, to a less intimate part of the house. Thankfully.

"The master bedroom and bath are perfect," she said, and he tried not to let the compliment go to his overthinking head. "They're way better than I could've hoped for. You even got the stairs done, so I won't have to worry about my clogs falling through any of that rotted wood."

He looked back at her purple shoes, thinking those things needed more than a hole in the floorboards to cover up their ugliness. Instead, he asked, "Do you need some help carrying your stuff inside?"

"No, that's okay. I only have a couple more boxes in my car. Besides, I saw the pizza sitting on that table thingy in the kitchen and I wouldn't want to keep you from your dinner."

"Actually, that's *your* dinner," he said, following her gaze toward the plywood-covered sawhorses and the white cardboard box with the name Patrelli's stamped on top. "Your aunt picked it up from the Italian restaurant in town and dropped it by here a while ago. She said to keep it warm in the oven for you, but as you can see, no oven yet."

Julia didn't respond and he hoped she was rethinking this whole move-in-while-he-was-still-working-here idea. Not that she needed an oven to heat things up in here. Kane doubted his body could take any more intense encounters like the one in the master bathroom a couple of minutes ago. Her face had been inches from his, her mouth way too close for comfort. His blood was still on fire from the way she'd been staring at him.

Leave, Chatterson, he thought. *Get out before you do something else you'll regret.* He dropped off his supplies in the mudroom and, on his way back through the kitchen, gestured toward the custom-ordered cabinets wedged together under a few drop cloths. "I planned to start installing the cupboards tomorrow, but you'll still need to pick out the appliances before it'll be up to Freckles's standards."

She squished up her nose, making the bow shape of her upper lip more pronounced. "I've been putting that off because I'm really not much of a cook. Yet. But I guess a refrigerator would come in handy."

Was it cockiness that made her think she could master cooking just as easily as she mastered his orthopedic diagnosis? Playing baseball professionally, he'd encountered his fair share of arrogance, and something about Just Julia's demeanor didn't give him that impression about her. Still, her aunt had suggested Dr. Smarty-Pants wasn't used to failing at anything, and because Kane knew firsthand what it was like to fall from grace, he didn't say anything else on the subject.

He walked over to the small cooler he kept near the pantry. "Can I offer you some water or a Gatorade?"

It sounded odd for him to be offering the woman anything in her own home. But judging by her man list, she probably wasn't used to entertaining male guests. Yet. No doubt that was simply another task Just Julia would attempt to master.

The thought of her bringing a guy here made his fingers squeeze the extended water bottle so tightly, the sealed lid threatened to pop off.

"No, thank you. I have a bag of drinks in my car." Then, as if a lightbulb had popped on in her head, she asked, "Would you like some of this pizza? I won't be able to eat it all."

His stomach answered with a small rumble, and Kane realized he hadn't had anything to eat since before noon. Another side effect of his attention deficit disorder—forgetting to stop and take breaks usually caused his body to punish him later.

Plus, he had a sneaking suspicion, probably fueled by Freckles's pointed comments, that Julia might be a little lonely. Not that he'd expected a moving truck and a parade, but it seemed kind of sad that on a Friday night, nobody was here to help her move into her new place. "Sure. Why don't I help you get the rest of your stuff out of your car, and we can eat after we unload."

"I'd appreciate that. Thanks."

It was asinine to stay another minute under the same roof as the woman, let alone share a meal with her. But if Julia was determined to live here during the remodel, then Kane would have to get used to seeing her and not acting upon this impulse to pull her into his arms and show her exactly what her presence did to his self-control.

He followed her outside and almost tripped on a cardboard box partially hidden by the overgrown grass. "Damn, it's the showerhead I ordered for the master bath. I was going to install it this afternoon, but I must not have heard FedEx delivering it."

Julia shrugged. "Don't worry about it. At least the tub is working. I was actually looking forward to taking a long, hot bath tonight, anyway."

And with that seemingly innocent statement, Kane was again brought back to that moment in her bathroom a few minutes ago when he'd caught her reflection in the window above the tub. His body hardened before he could command his brain to relax. He had absolutely no business imagining Just Julia stripped down naked, submerged under a cluster of bubbles. He had no business imagining her in any way at all.

"Here," she said, handing him a small grocery bag. "This should be light enough for you to handle."

He immediately felt the sting to his pride. "I can carry more than this."

"But what about your shoulder?"

"My shoulder's never been better." To prove his point, he grabbed another box and a bag of what he assumed was more hospital scrubs. "Where's the rest of your stuff? Is it coming later?"

"This is it." She loosely waved at the already half-empty car.

Was she serious? Most of the women he'd dated, including Erica, would pack twice this much for a week's vacation.

"What about furniture?" he asked, trying to balance the load in his arms as he walked up the porch steps.

She shrugged. "I'll have to buy some, I suppose."

"Wait. You don't have a bed. Where will you sleep tonight?"

"I'm going to have a campout."

"A what?"

"A campout." Her excited smile nearly blinded him. "I always wanted to have one when I was younger— you know, with blankets and pillows, building forts in the living room—but my parents didn't like the idea of me messing up the house. I decided that there's no better way to start my new life in my new home than by declaring my own set of rules."

Boy, her parents sounded like a pair of buzzkills. No wonder Dr. Smarty-Pants was so formal and stiff. Growing up in the Chatterson house meant sheets, quilts and toys scattered all over the floor. Having four siblings was fun and kept things interesting, but it was certainly chaotic and… Wait. A basset hound had just lumbered up her driveway and through the side yard. Had she bought a dog, too?

He turned to ask her if they allowed pets in the officer's quarters near Shadowview, but his bad shoulder bumped into the front door frame and he let out a strong curse instead, dropping the armload of stuff he'd bragged would be easy to carry.

"Are you all right?" she asked, those big green eyes looking scandalized by his choice of words.

"Yep. Just wasn't watching where I was going."

"Let me take a look." She set her box on the floor,

and he had to hold out his hand to stop her from coming closer.

"No, really. It's fine." The last thing he needed was the sweet doctor touching his body again—even if it was clothed this time. "I've always been a little accident-prone, so I'm used to a few bumps and bruises. How about some pizza?"

Julia looked doubtful, but Kane rolled his shoulder and held back a grimace at the stab of hot pain. "See? It's fine. No big deal."

He walked to the makeshift table and opened the white cardboard box, his lips curling down at the contents. "Uh-oh. We're oh and two with restaurant orders. Looks like Patrelli's forgot the meat."

Her blond ponytail shook back and forth. "No, they didn't. I'm a vegetarian."

Kane couldn't stop the involuntary shudder. "Does your Aunt Freckles know?"

"Yes. She's not too happy about it, either, and says I'll outgrow it by the time I'm in my thirties."

Kane was looking so intently at the pizza, he almost didn't catch her admission. "Your thirties? How old *are* you?"

"Twenty-nine." Her shoulders elevated several inches with the straightening of her spine, and he suspected he'd just hit a nerve. But he didn't care. The math wasn't adding up, and he hated it when problems didn't add up.

"But I thought you were surgeon. Doesn't medical school and all that take a long time?"

"The average is four years for medical school, and depending on your specialty, the neurosurgery residency is another six or seven years."

"But that would be impossible," he said, then saw her eyes turn a darker shade of green, reminding him of that superhero cartoon he used to watch as a kid— the Hulk, where the good guy would get angry and turn green all over.

Not wanting to rile her past the point of no return, he tried to get his brain to calculate the numbers. But she beat him to the punch. "I graduated from high school when I was fourteen. I had a bachelor's in science by age seventeen. I finished med school early, and did my residency right after being commissioned an officer."

He kept staring at her, this obvious genius who truly was a Dr. Smarty-Pants. By the time she was in her mid- teens, she'd already far surpassed the level of education he had now. That familiar baseball-size knot of shame grew to the size of a basketball, and again he wanted to change the subject as soon as possible.

"Why do you always touch your mouth and chin like that?" she asked. He'd been unaware he was doing it, and he shoved his hands in his pockets. "Is it a nervous tic or something?"

"Of course not," he said, then screwed up his face in annoyance, because that's exactly what it was. Damn, for someone who supposedly didn't socialize much, the woman had picked up on one of his most obvious tells. The involuntary gesture was the reason he'd had to grow his beard when he played baseball, making it appear as though he was simply smoothing down his facial hair rather than alerting the opposition to his dis- comfort. But he wasn't about to admit that to her. "Actu- ally, ever since a woman tried to give me the Heimlich maneuver and then pointed out that I had spinach stuck in my teeth, I've been a little self-conscious about having something on my face."

Her face grew red. "I am so sorry about that. I really did think you were choking." There was a note of insecurity in her voice, and he cursed himself for being the cause of it. Especially since he'd made the joke to deflect from his habit of touching his former beard.

"Don't worry about it. Scooter and Jonesy thought it was hilarious. I don't suppose you have any plates packed away in one of those boxes?" he finally asked.

"Plates? Oh. Right." She tightened her already perfect ponytail. "I guess I'll need to get some of those, too. I've never had to furnish an entire house before, and I was so focused on getting the upstairs bedroom and bath livable, I didn't even think about how the rest would all come together."

Was she serious? She'd been studying for her med school entrance exams at the same age when he'd been studying for his driver's license test, yet she hadn't thought about the most basic necessities of a house. How could she be so naive?

"Most women I know wouldn't dream of moving into a house and roughing it without some long-term plan in place."

"Well, I'm not most women."

He forced himself not to look her up and down and confirm her obvious statement. Instead, he handed her a cold slice of pizza loaded with...what were those? Carrots? Who puts carrots on a pizza?

"Thank you," she said, looking anything but grateful to hold her food in her bare hands. Well, Just Julia should've thought that one out a bit more. Then he wanted to kick himself for being such an insensitive jerk. He took a bite of veggie-covered congealed cheese to keep himself from saying something he'd regret.

Big mistake, he realized when his throat refused to welcome a piece of broccoli. He coughed several times before getting the bite down. Then waved his hand at the concerned look on Julia's face. The last thing his extra tense, hyperaware muscles needed was for her to wrap her arms around his chest again.

"I'm okay. But would it have killed Freckles to order an extra pizza for your poor contractor? One with a little pepperoni and sausage?"

"Let me get you something to drink," Julia said, walking toward the grocery bag he'd dropped by the front door. She pulled out a yellow-green soda and twisted the top off for him.

He felt his eyebrows shoot up to his hairline. "You won't eat meat, but you'll drink that?"

"I know it's a contradiction, but growing up, I wasn't allowed to have any junk food. Yet I was able to convince my parents that it gave me an extra boost of energy so I could study longer."

Ma and Pa Fitzgerald sounded like a real barrel of fun, and again Kane found himself experiencing a sense of pity rather than inadequacy. As much as he hated the fact that his grades had prevented him from going to college, at least he'd had loving and supportive parents growing up.

He shook his head as Julia handed the drink to him. The neon color was about the least healthy shade he'd ever seen, and he had to wonder if the genius gene had skipped a generation in her family. "No, thanks. If I drink that, I'll be up all night."

He picked off the more offending vegetables and threw them in the black trash bag he'd set up in the corner of the room. With nowhere to sit, they ate their cold meal standing up, Kane growing more and more restless by the second. By the time he'd gotten down to his third piece of crust, his legs were so fidgety, he'd begun pacing the room.

"It's getting pretty late," he finally said. "I'm going to run back upstairs and get my tools and stuff out of your room so you can get settled in."

"All right," she said, "I'm just going to wash my hands." He sure hoped she'd brought some soap with her.

Then the thought of soap made him think about bubbles, which made him think about her in the bath and…

Man, he needed to get out of here. He took the steps two at a time and grabbed his tool bag and portable speaker in record time. He was halfway out the front door when her voice stopped him.

"Do you think you could help me with a list?" she asked.

He froze. What list? The man list? Was she seriously asking for his help with something so personal? "Um. Depends."

His voice sounded like he still had broccoli stuck in his throat, and his once restless feet felt as though they were encased in concrete as he forced himself to turn and face her.

She bit her lower lip before explaining. "I'm only on call tomorrow, so I planned to go shopping as long as no emergencies come up. There are so many things I need for the house. I was hoping you could tell me what I should buy. I'd ask Freckles, but the café is usually packed on the weekends, and besides, she'd probably talk me into stocking up on a bunch of kitchen supplies I won't ever use."

Aw, hell. Kane knew his answer long before he said it. He'd been a protective older brother for too long, and he was instantly reminded of what her aunt had said about Julia being too trusting and needing someone more worldly to look out for her. Besides, he was going to be working here for a couple more months and could probably benefit from her having a better stocked kitchen.

"Sure, I'll make some notes and bring you a list tomorrow." Of course, that would mean a lot of writing and concentrating, and it would just be far easier if he went and picked up all the stuff at the store himself. He thought of something else Freckles had said about her niece's business sense. "You'll also need to get those appliances ordered."

"I know I've already asked so much of you, but do you think you could help me navigate that, too? After the whole furnace fiasco, I think I may need some refreshers on how to negotiate."

Kane clenched his jaw at the reminder. He'd wanted to kick that heating and air-conditioning salesman's ass for the price he'd quoted her last week. Instead, he'd called in one of his own subcontractors to do the installation. Sending Julia alone to one of those appliance warehouses would be like throwing her to the wolves.

"You know, my shoulder will probably still be a little

sore tomorrow," he said, rotating it, this time not trying to hide his wince. "And I doubt I'll be able to get those cabinets in with just one good arm. Maybe I should go to that appliance place in Boise with you, and we can stop by one of those big department stores afterward and get you some of the basics you might need."

"Oh my gosh. I would appreciate that so much. Are you sure you won't mind?" He'd mind more if he had to watch her be taken advantage of by some salivating salesmen looking to pad their commissions. And it would keep him from having to write out a list of his own. Really, it was a win-win. As long as he managed not to touch her. Or smell her shampoo. Or look at her sexy lips.

Man, his senses were out of control. Especially his common sense.

"I'll pick you up at eight." His voice sounded a bit more gruff than he'd intended.

He saw her peek around him and look out the front door at his Bronco before saying, "Why don't I drive? After all, it's not fair for you to have to use up your gas money on an errand for me."

Gas money? Did she think he was some broke guy down on his luck?

"Besides," she continued before he could take too much offense at the assumption he was purposely hoping people would make about him. "You should give your shoulder some rest, and steering on those steep mountain curves will do more harm than good." She tossed the crust of her pizza into the trash, wiped her hands on a napkin and stood up. "All right, then. I'm going upstairs to soak in my new bathtub. See you to-morrow."

He blinked twice. Despite another awkward dismissal, he was touched that she was taking his well-being, and his gasoline budget, into account. He was also slightly annoyed by her presumption that he couldn't afford to take her somewhere and Kane didn't know how to reconcile his conflicting feelings.

He told himself that her concern was a refreshing change from many of the women he'd dated in the past who seemed to be more interested in his celebrity status and seven-figure income than in him. Not that she was interested in dating him. But if Just Julia truly was clueless about who he was, then she was proving herself to be a thoughtful and kind person. Judging by her list and her determination to excel at everything, she'd make some guy damn lucky once she got herself settled.

Which was a good thing for him, as well. The sooner she got off the market, the sooner he'd be able to get her and her damn bathtub out of his mind.

Chapter 5

Kane was surprised that his six-foot-two body was able to scrunch into the passenger seat of Julia's MINI Cooper the following morning. He'd voiced his concern out loud when she'd walked out her front door carrying her key fob and another yellow-green soda for the road, yet she insisted that the inside of her car was deceptively roomy.

Kane had a thing about arguing with a determined woman so early in the day. He also had a thing about zippy little cars, especially the kind that didn't come with a six-figure price tag or a midlife crisis ego boost. His muscles were already clenching at the thought of being stuck in the passenger seat for the next hour or so. He didn't need the added stimulation of being this close to her out of her surgical uniform. Granted, she wasn't wearing the sexy workout gear, but her dark jeans encased her long, athletic legs and as she sat behind the wheel, her well-tailored blouse slightly gaped open where the top two buttons should've been fastened to prevent him from catching a glimpse of the curve of her left breast.

"How long have you had this?" he asked as he buckled his seat belt. He could still smell the faint traces of new car scent.

"I bought it about four months ago," Julia said, proudly smiling as if she'd just told him it was her first Nobel Prize. They had those things for doctors, didn't they? "I've never owned a car before. Or at least, a car that didn't come with a hired driver."

His brain picked up the clue to her implied wealthy background, and maybe he'd remember that tidbit of information later, but he could only focus on the more important admission that this was her very first car.

"What did you drive before this?" he asked.

"Oh, I didn't get my driver's license until I was stationed at Shadowview. I always lived in a city with a mass transit system or on a military base and never really had to drive anywhere before now."

She reached forward and tried to program something into the GPS system, but her thumb hit the speakerphone button. "Name, please," the electronic voice said.

"Directions to Boise," Julia called out, and Kane had to look out the passenger window so she couldn't see him trying not to laugh.

"Contact not recognized," the speakerphone replied.

Julia repeated the command again and got the same response. She shrugged and said, "I don't think the navigation system recognizes my voice."

"Let me try," Kane said, pushing the menu button before typing in the address.

"Calculating route," the electronic voice announced, and a map popped onto the screen.

"Thanks." Julia smiled, then snapped her seat belt into place. "There's supposedly an instructional video to learn how to use that thing, but I haven't exactly had time to take a look at it. Yet."

Everything was *yet* with this woman. He studied her from behind the dark lenses of his Ray-Bans, while she fiddled with the radio dial, sending the volume skyrocketing and forcing Kane to cover his ears.

"Sorry," she said. "I'm still getting the hang of this stereo system, too."

"Is there an instructional video for that, as well?" he murmured, but because her finger had accidentally hit the mute button at that exact second, she ended up hearing him.

"Probably. But I might have to look online for it. With the house remodel and taking on some of Captain Karim's patients while he's on deployment, I just haven't had any extra time. But I'll figure it out eventually."

They set out down Pinecone Court. Julia was in fact a better driver than he'd expected, considering the way she handled her smartphone and the other devices in the small, well-equipped car. But by the time they were heading south on Snowflake Boulevard, Kane's left knee was doing its hummingbird imitation and he had to use his hand to hold it steady. He should've insisted on driving. Focusing on the road would've given him something to do. Being the driver gave him freedom to be in control of the car, of something bigger than him. He was a horrible passenger because he felt like a prisoner, trapped.

When she reached for the thermostat controls, he practically pushed her hand out of the way before she could accidentally set the seat warmer on high. "Let me help you with that so you can concentrate on driving."

"Thanks, but I've got it. I'm a surgeon, remember? My hands are used to multitasking."

He stared at her palms placed precisely at the ten and two positions. She might have phenomenal surgical skills, but her inability to master electronics was making his own fingers twitch with the need to commandeer something. Anything. Man, he hated just sitting here, being this far away from the steering wheel.

"So, why neurology?" he asked, his eyes squeezed tightly shut behind his sunglasses. Not that he was one for idle chitchat—or any kind of chitchat, really—but if they were going to be stuck in this car that he couldn't drive with a radio she couldn't operate, he might as well get the woman talking about herself before she decided to ask him any personal questions.

"Because it's the hardest," Julia said.

"You mean, it's hard working with patients who have so much to lose?"

"Well, that, too, I guess. But I meant it was one of the more intellectually challenging medical specialties. The central nervous system is the control pad that makes all the other body parts function."

He didn't want to point out that in the few times he'd been around her, she hadn't exactly been all that great with any other types of control pads. Instead he asked,

"You chose your specialty because you wanted to be at the top of the field, not because you have a special affinity for the brain?"

"Well, of course I'm fascinated by the brain. And the cerebrovascular system. I mean, who wouldn't be?"

Kane wanted to raise his hand and claim, *Me! I wouldn't be fascinated by any of that.*

"Kind of sounds like you're a bit of an overachiever," Kane suggested and saw her fingers tense up on the wheel. Whoops. "Uh, did I say something wrong?"

"No," she answered. "I guess I'm just a little sensitive to that word."

"To what word? *Overachiever?*"

"Yes. I know that being a child genius may sound all unique and fun, but it also has its drawbacks."

Actually, it didn't sound fun at all. It sounded like a lot of weight to carry in the expectations department. "What kind of drawbacks?" Kane asked.

"Being teased by older kids who are embarrassed that you scored higher than them on the AP Calculus exam or that you got into a better college. I know it's just jealousy on their part, but it can wear on a person after a while."

A warm dart of sympathy shot through Kane's rib cage. "I wasn't making fun of you. I meant *overachiever* as a compliment. You're talking to someone who took typing as an elective, even though I can't spell worth a damn, because the wood shop teacher made students write essays on the different species of wood."

"But if you enjoy being a contractor, why wouldn't you want to excel at it? It would be such a waste not to try, at least."

Kane rolled his shoulder against the tight restraint of the seat belt and thought about his own waste of talent now that his athletic career was over. Her words were hitting home better than any coach's ever could. In baseball, he was notorious for going against the best and beating the odds. He used to revel in the challenge, in the competition. So why did he always take a backseat to real life when it became too difficult?

"Speaking of careers," he said, hoping she would be too polite to say anything about his cop out of a response. "Why did you join the Navy?" he asked.

"My parents were in a train crash when I was twenty-one. My mom died at the scene, but my father was in the ICU for several days before he passed. I was sitting in the waiting room, and a documentary came on about the WAVES, the naval reserve for women during World War II. I was completely fascinated. Really, I was fascinated by all the shows I saw in there because I'd never been allowed to watch much television growing up, but the series on the WAVES really made me think that I could dedicate my brain and my knowledge to something besides science. Here were all these women who'd volunteered to go into the military for the good of the country rather than for personal gain, and I wanted to be like them. I wanted to help others."

She was not only a genius but also a damn do-gooder. How could he compete with someone like that? Not that they were in competition, but if they were, he wouldn't even be in the same league.

"I'm sorry about your parents," Kane offered, not knowing what else to say without pointing out more of his own inadequacies.

"Thank you." She'd reverted to that formal, stiff tone that made him want to tell her to stop being so damn proper. At least not for his benefit. "Aunt Freckles suggested I not make any big decisions while I was still grieving, but I was so used to the schedule my parents had set for me that I thought the order and discipline and routine of the Navy would actually be a comfort."

Hmm. Those were the same reasons Kane *hadn't* joined the military. He'd had a hard enough time following orders in high school. In fact, baseball was the only team sport he could manage because, as a pitcher, he was able to be somewhat on his own. Kane scratched at his chin, mentally calculating how much longer he would be stuck in this seat.

"Has anyone ever told you that you're very fidgety?" she asked when she finally hit the off-ramp.

"Only when I don't like sitting still."

"Hmm. Interesting," she said, reminding him of a therapist making notes in a patient's file. Kane should've known nothing good would come of them going into town together, but last night he'd let his mouth engage before his brain. He was still pretty sensitive about his childhood diagnosis and would've asked if she was trying to assess him. But he preferred that she focus all of her concentration on her third attempt to reenter their destination address after she'd accidentally switched off the navigation system when she'd picked up her bottle of soda.

He could offer to show her how to do it again, but he had the feeling Dr. Smarty-Pants wouldn't like the implication that she couldn't accomplish something herself after the first try. It was going to be a long day.

* * *

As the automatic glass doors swished open, Julia watched Kane pull his green ball cap lower until the brim nearly touched his sunglasses, which he didn't seem inclined to put away once they entered the store. She'd worked alongside plenty of men in the Navy, but that didn't mean she understood when one was being so frustratingly moody. Or secretive. What was up with his whole stealth disguise? He was one video camera still away from looking like a convenience store robber at large.

"Hello, and welcome to Land O'Appliances." A large voice boomed out from an even larger man dressed in a trendy pastel button-up shirt. The name tag pinned crookedly over the man's orange paisley tie read Paulie. Julia immediately took a step back, bumping into Kane's injured shoulder. The only things louder than Paulie's greeting and his taste in neckwear were the painful-looking injection sites from what her medical training told her was a recently botched Botox treatment.

"Is there anything in particular I can help you two find?" the salesman asked.

She looked at Kane, waiting for him to tell Paulie what they'd come to buy. But her quiet contractor said nothing, one hand gripping a half-used notepad and the other shoved deep inside the front pocket of his jeans. While Julia was accustomed to taking charge in classrooms or in surgery, she wasn't as experienced as she would have liked when it came to negotiating.

"I need a new refrigerator," Julia finally said to the eager salesman with his bleached white smile, before shooting Kane an imploring look to chime in. She couldn't very well be rude and just stand there saying nothing.

"Well, you've come to the right place," Paulie said. She tried not to flinch at his volume, which hadn't lowered when he came closer. "All our fridges are back against this wall. Do you have a price in mind?"

"Oh, I suppose we're more concerned with the style than the pri—"

"We want inexpensive," Kane interrupted. So *now* he decided to grace them with his input. Then he raised his rudeness another level when he told Paulie, "We'll take a look around and let you know if we have any questions."

Kane lightly gripped her elbow and steered her toward the refrigerator department. She caught the scent of spicy shower gel and coffee when he leaned in close to her and whispered, "When you're negotiating, never tell the opposing side that you're not concerned with the price."

Manners had been instilled in Julia since before she could speak, which was why she cast a nervous look over her shoulder to the abandoned salesman before directing her quiet reply toward the plaid-patterned flannel covering Kane's shoulder. "But we weren't at the negotiating part yet."

"We were at the negotiating part the second we walked in the door and Paulie Loudmouth over there was calculating how many extra tanning bed sessions he could buy with our commission."

"I didn't realize you knew the employees here already."

"I don't," Kane said. "But all these salespeople are the same."

"Then why didn't you take the lead when he approached us?"

"I did."

"How? By being rude and not saying a word?"

"I wasn't being rude. I was being hard to read. If I came in looking like an eager beaver, Paulie would've had us right where he wanted us."

"I see," she said, not seeing at all but willing to go along with his reverse psychology strategy. For now.

He didn't release her arm as he successfully maneuvered her in front of a nondescript white unit that didn't even have an ice maker. While she wasn't used to being touched—or, some might argue, manhandled—so intimately, she didn't attempt to pull away. But only because she didn't want to thwart what might be part of his negotiation tactic. It certainly wasn't because she liked the feel of his strong fingers through the thin cotton of her white blouse.

"But Kane, I don't want to look at these plain refrigerators. I thought we agreed that the stainless steel ones over there would look better with the granite countertops."

"Don't point," he said as he dropped her elbow, causing her tummy to sink in disappointment. He reached across to pull her pointing hand back, and his bare forearm brushed across her chest. Julia's cheeks flooded with heat as her nipples tightened in response. Logically, she knew the movement was inadvertent on his part, but that didn't stop her from feeling as though an electric current had been shot through her body.

Thankfully, Kane must not have noticed her reaction to his touch because Mr. Controlling Contractor leaned in and gave her another order under his breath. "Make them think we're interested only in the cheaper models. He'll still try to upsell us, but his expectations won't be as high."

Oh, for the love of all things good. She'd asked for Kane's support and experience. Not for his high-handedness or a lesson in power-play maneuvers. And she especially hadn't asked for his full lips to practically caress her temple as he whispered in her ear.

She'd never been so aware of a man's nearness and tried to chalk this overpowering sensation up to her inexperience in being in this type of situation.

But just because she'd never been shopping for appliances before didn't mean she couldn't figure out how it was done.

"Kane, this is a store. Not a fine art auction house. There are huge price tags on everything. Clearly there's a set price. So let's just pick the one we want and pay for it."

"Come on, Dr. Smarty-Pants. This isn't how businesses like these operate."

"What did you just call me?" She turned toward him and crossed her arms, not sure if she was more offended by the nickname or by the implication that she wasn't capable of doing something so simple as buying a refrigerator.

"Sorry. I meant it as a compliment." He did that little smirk thing again, not even having the decency to look sheepish or remorseful.

"Smarty-pants? Overachiever?" She put her hands

on her hips, trying to figure out if he was patronizing her or if this was how friends teased each other. "You sure have a funny way of delivering a compliment."

"Can we shelve the arguments right now? Paulie is walking this way to check on us, and we need to appear to be on the same team."

Julia thought they *were* on the same team. Until he'd started "complimenting" her. Something about his teasing tone triggered that underlying desire in her to prove that she wasn't completely in the dark. Perhaps it might benefit him to realize a little something about his so-called teammate. "I'll have you know that I took a global business concepts course my sophomore year in college."

One side of his mouth quirked up, making her brain go all fuzzy and forget why she'd been so annoyed with him a second ago. "I'm guessing that, based on your recent history with the furnace, you aced that class."

Oh yeah. His sarcasm was why.

"It was more theory than practical approach, but I still passed," she whispered out the side of her mouth right as the salesman arrived, glad she didn't have to admit that her passing score was the lowest one on her undergrad transcripts.

"I saw the missus pointing to one of our most popular models," Paulie said as he walked up. He attempted a wink, but the Botox in his forehead made the gesture seem more like a mild focal seizure. "Everyone is buying stainless steel these days."

"Oh no, I'm not the… I mean not *his*…" Julia broke off when she saw Kane pull his sunglasses off—finally—and pinch the bridge of his nose. Maybe she should've stuck with being on Kane's team, but she didn't want to give anyone the impression that they were a couple. Or together...in *that* way. It would've been misleading. Mostly to her. And she'd learned long ago not to be misled by a man who wasn't actually interested in a serious relationship.

"Here's the thing, Paulie." Kane shoved the sunglasses in his shirt pocket, and Julia tried not to stare at the slight rise of his pectoral muscle underneath. Was it getting warmer in here? "We're remodeling a house and are actually in the market for several kitchen appliances, as well as a washer and dryer. Now, I have a pretty good idea of what models and styles are going to work best, so we don't really need your assistance in that regard. However, my *missus* and I will require your help in making sure we get the best deal. Think you can do anything to help us out?"

Julia would've pointed out how ridiculous Kane's lie was if his words hadn't made Paulie's collagen-plumped lips smile in anticipation.

Or if his reference to her being his "missus" hadn't made her legs buckle and her heart beat so hard, she could feel it pulsing behind her unblinking eyes.

Chapter 6

Julia walked out of Land O'Appliances with the promise of a Monday delivery and the loss of her car keys. She wasn't quite sure how her moody contractor had been smooth or charming enough to manage either. She blamed her easy acquiescence and light-headedness on the fact that she'd skipped breakfast.

"Are you hungry?" she asked Kane as they walked toward her car.

"I'm always hungry." He pulled that gold watch out his pocket and flipped it open. His use of the antique timepiece struck her as such a stunning contrast to his rugged construction worker look. "Besides, it's almost eleven, so we have time to grab something before we hit Bed Bath & Beyond."

"Great. You brought the shopping list, I hope? We can go over it while we eat."

"Don't need a list," he said, pointing to the side of his head. "I've got it all up here."

Julia would have rolled her eyes at his confident bragging, but she was too busy trying to pull up the restaurant locator app Chief Wilcox had downloaded to her phone last week.

"What are you doing?"

"Trying to find a place to eat." She showed him the screen. "See, it recommends the Aztec Taqueria, which is only a few hundred yards from here on Callejon Road."

"Julia, I'm pretty sure there isn't a Callejon Road around this part of Boise."

"Yes, there is." She pointed to the small map. "We're the blue dot right here next to it."

The sound of Kane's deep, rumbling laughter shocked her, then sent an unexpected vibration through her bloodstream. "What's so funny?"

"You have the current location set for Taos, New Mexico."

She was relieved that the man actually had a sense of humor buried somewhere deep inside his aloof shell, but that didn't stop the back of her neck from bristling with embarrassment that he was actually laughing *at* her. Or was it tingling at the sight of his straight, white teeth flashing with actual mirth?

"Whatever," she said, slipping the dumb phone back into her purse. "That restaurant across the parking lot looks like a good place to eat. And it's close enough to walk."

"The Bacon Palace?" He raised one of his auburn eyebrows at her, and Julia decided she liked quiet, brooding Kane much better than smug, teasing Kane. "I thought you were a vegetarian."

Gulp. "Oh, I'm sure they'll have something there that will suit me just fine."

Of course, judging by the sizzling aroma wafting across the asphalt as Julia walked beside him, she had a feeling the words *hold the bacon* would be an addendum to her order.

Kane held open the pink door painted to look like a pig's snout and Julia kept her opinions about the swine-themed decor and the misleading signage to herself. The proprietors got half of the restaurant's name correct, but this place was definitely no palace.

After making a pretense of intently studying the trough-shaped wooden menu above the cash register—she'd had no idea that a breakfast meat could flavor everything from pasta sauces to milkshakes—Julia ordered a basket of plain french fries and a garden salad, minus the bacon ranch dressing. She pulled out her wallet before Kane finished ordering his triple-stacked BLT and handed her American Express card to the cashier.

"No," Kane said. "You're not paying for my lunch."

"Well, you're certainly not paying for *my* lunch. It's not like this is a date."

His eyelids lowered as though he was trying understand a foreign language. "I'm not poor, you know."

"I never said you were," she replied, then walked over to the soda machine so he couldn't see that her cheeks were the same shade as the pink plastic drink cup she'd just grabbed. Had she messed up? Had she offended his pride? Ugh. It was times like this when she hated her social awkwardness.

This was why she was single. She couldn't even carry on a normal conversation with a man she wasn't dating. A man she wasn't the slightest bit interested in. Attracted to, maybe, but that wasn't the same thing. Which was why Julia had made that comment about this not being a date. More to remind herself of the fact since, judging by his annoyed expression, Kane Chatterson certainly didn't need reminding.

In fact, he didn't say another word as they sat down across from each other at a small booth in the crowded restaurant. She'd heard his laughter outside only briefly, and though it had been at her expense, she regretted that it had been short-lived. Julia was accustomed to being on her own, and silence was pretty much standard in her house growing up. So she didn't mind him not speaking. But she hated the fact that she might've offended Kane or done something to ruin the good mood he'd been in a few minutes ago.

"Are you okay?" she finally asked when he didn't say more than two words to the friendly server who'd brought them their food.

"I don't like big crowds," he said before hunkering down over his plate and taking a large bite of his sandwich.

Then it *wasn't* her or something she'd said. She was no expert on cognitive behavior therapy, but perhaps if she got his mind on something else, he would be able to relax and enjoy the meal, at least.

"So, you were in the military," she started, thinking they could discuss something they had in common.

His brows shot up. "No. Why would you think that?"

"Because I saw you at Shadowview. Why would you

be a patient there if you weren't a veteran or on active duty?"

"What makes you think I'm a patient?"

Julia couldn't very well ask him why he was in the psych department the other day. Perhaps he'd been there visiting someone, but she could have sworn that the room he'd gone to was where the PTSD group held their sessions. She squirmed slightly in her seat. "No reason."

Sharing a meal with such an attractive man—even in a location such as the Bacon Palace, of all places— wasn't something that happened to her all that often, and this was why. She didn't have anything to talk to a good-looking man about. Julia picked up a french fry, racking her brain for another conversation starter. But before she was forced to ask him about the wainscoting in her downstairs bathroom, she recognized another doctor from the base hospital coming toward their table.

"Kane, it's good to see you out and about," Dr. Drew Gregson said as he reached out to shake Kane's hand.

"Shh, Drew." Kane pulled his hat lower and sank deeper into the vinyl booth seat. "Do you have to be so loud?"

She had met the Navy psychologist at the hospital during one of the bigger admin meetings and seemed to recall that he also lived near Sugar Falls. But that didn't explain why Julia's surly contractor was on such familiar terms with him. Unless they were encouraged to use first names in those PTSD sessions.

"Sorry. I guess I was just surprised to see you making a rare public appearance." The psychologist, who'd inadvertently just given Julia some insight into the man spending every day working on her home, turned to her. "Hi. I'm Drew Gregson."

"I know," Julia said, returning his handshake. "We both work at Shadowview."

The man took off his wire-framed glasses, probably fogged up by the bacon-tinged air around them, and wiped them off. She didn't blame him for not recognizing her out of uniform and without her standard surgical scrubs.

"Julia Fitzgerald. I'm in Neurology."

"Of course. That's right. Kane's remodeling that old Victorian on Pinecone Court for you, right?"

Apparently Kane told his therapist all kinds of information about himself. Maybe she should ask Dr. Gregson for some tips on how to get the man to open up more when he was with her.

Wait. Where did that thought come from? She didn't want Kane Chatterson opening up to her about anything but carpet samples and light fixtures. It was already bad enough that her heart rate accelerated every time his lips gave off the slightest grin. She'd probably suffer from a full blown case of tachycardia if he actually engaged in a friendly conversation.

Julia gave him an exaggerated nod, trying to shake loose the unwarranted analysis of her contractor's personality. "That's right. We came into Boise to pick out some appliances, and Kane was kind enough to offer me his expertise at Bed Bath & Beyond next."

Julia wanted to make their relationship sound as businesslike and professional as possible. But something about the other doctor's quirked smile made her think she'd done just the opposite.

"Is that so?" Gregson asked. "My twin brother and his fiancée, Carmen, just registered at Bed Bath & Beyond for their wedding gifts. I'm sure Luke would've loved your *expertise* with that, Kane."

Julia wasn't positive, but she could've sworn Kane's shoulders visibly shuddered at the word *wedding*. She wiped her mouth on the pink paper napkin—seriously, pink?—and pushed her salad plate away. If there was any other way to signal it was time to exit this odd conversation, she didn't know how to go about it.

"You know what else I'm an expert at?" Kane spoke so low, Julia didn't know if it was annoyance in his tone or something more sinister. "Taking all your winnings at poker. Get ready to pay up next Thursday, doc."

When Dr. Gregson let out a loud burst of laughter, Julia finally released the breath she'd been holding, feeling more out of place than she had back in the appliance store.

Today was a perfect example of the reason Kane avoided cities, shaved his beard and kept his hat firmly in place—even when he was indoors. He didn't want to be recognized. Of all the people they had to run into at a crowded restaurant, why did it have to be his know-it-all brother-in-law? And what was up with Just Julia's insistence on paying for lunch for him?

Was she under some impression that Kane was poor? First she'd paid for his breakfast at the Cowgirl Up when she thought he'd been choking. Then she'd made that comment about not wanting him to use his own gas money to drive into the city. And just a few minutes ago, she'd swiped her credit card before he even had a chance to do the gentlemanly thing and offer to pay. He hadn't had a woman pay for one of his meals since…well, since ever. Not that he and Julia were on a date or anything, which she'd made more than clear. But still.

It had felt cheap. As though he was simply the hired help—which he was currently acting like as he pushed the nearly full shopping cart behind her down the kitchen gadget aisle of the big home goods store.

Worker, employee, someone to pay. That's what he was to her, after all. What he *should* be. Hell, they weren't even friends, which was too bad, because the woman's rear end looked more than friendly in those expensive, curve-hugging dark jeans. His chest tightened and for the hundredth time that day, he asked himself why couldn't she have worn her boxy hospital scrubs. Kane was no expert on women's fashion, but today, Julia's outfit was serving up one contradiction after another. Her clothes were simple, but obviously high quality. Preppy, but sexy at the same time. Like she wasn't trying to flaunt her good looks, but they were still so obviously there. It was distracting, and he'd been having a difficult time keeping his eyes off her. Worse, it drew too much attention to her from other people.

Not that he cared if slick salesmen or overeager waiters were checking her out. The problem was that it also drew attention to *him*. Kane ran his fingers under his bottom lip. Erica used to love it when they'd get all dressed up for a dinner event or a fancy cocktail party with the team owners. Once Kane had been horrified to overhear her telling the cameraman to make sure to capture everyone's reactions when the hottest couple in the sports celebrity world walked into the room. Once upon a time, he hadn't minded the attention to his skills on the mound, but he'd never been comfortable with being recognized in public. Now, he simply avoided it at all costs.

"Do you think seven hundred dollars is too much to pay for a set of knives?" Julia had her back toward him, her cute blond ponytail bouncing as she took in the variety of displays. "Maybe they'd be willing to give us some sort of discount, like Paulie did over at Land O'Appliances."

"Jules, this isn't the kind of place where you can negotiate prices." *Jules?* He squeezed his eyes shut in an effort to clear his mind. Where had that name come from? Like most of the stupid things he'd said in his life, it'd impulsively popped out before he could think about the inappropriateness of giving his client a nickname.

"Of course it's not," she said, not noticing his slip, he hoped. "Even I know that. What I meant was that maybe they offer some sort of coupon or sale on certain items. Anyway, Aunt Freckles says to never scrimp on kitchen equipment, but I have no idea if this is a fair price. What do you think? Would you pay seven hundred dollars for 'VG-10 supersteel blades with durable pakkawood handles'? It says they were handcrafted in Japan."

"I wouldn't pay that much if they came with four wheels and their own engine."

"No, I don't suppose you would." She picked up the midprice brand instead and put it into the shopping cart on top of the sixteen-piece glassware set she'd selected twenty minutes ago.

There she went again, thinking he couldn't afford

something, and a knot of shame wedged itself in his throat. What with his poor grades, his career-ending injury and being cheated on by his ex-girlfriend, Kane had experienced plenty of embarrassing moments in his life. But having a lack of money had never been the subject of any of his pity parties. In fact, he had almost as much money as he did pride, which was why he didn't want her thinking he was just some busted, broke-down contractor who couldn't pay for his own meals or buy his own set of fancy Shun double-bevel blades.

"Actually, I think you should get the nicer ones. Your Aunt Freckles would have a fit if she thought I was letting you purchase substandard tools." When he saw the doubt fill her green eyes, he said, "In fact, consider it a housewarming gift from me."

"Oh no. I couldn't accept such a generous gift from you."

He thought about the limited-edition Bentley he'd bought for Erica—before he found out she'd been sleeping with his nemesis while Kane was undergoing shoulder surgery. "Trust me. It's not that generous a gift."

"No, you don't understand. It would be wasted on me. I spend hardly any time in the kitchen. My aunt inherited all the culinary skills in the family. She wouldn't even let me help her slice peaches in the café last August when she was perfecting her recipe for the Cobbler Festival or one of those dessert themed events Sugar Falls always seems to be putting on."

"Maybe she thinks you need more practice with sharp instruments?"

"Are you kidding? I use scalpels and bone-cutting saws with as much precision as a laser. In fact, I use lasers, too. Steady hands, remember?" She placed her palms up, and he tightened his gut to keep from laughing at how unsteady those fingers had been at programming touch screens. Who in the world would've let this woman anywhere near a laser?

"All the more reason you should own a good set of knives," he said, sincerely hoping she wielded the sharp tools better than she operated a cell phone. "Speaking of Freckles, when I went in for breakfast this morning, Monica, that new waitress she hired, told me she was gone for the day. That's three Saturdays in a row that I haven't had my chicken-fried steak made the way I like."

"I think she might have a boyfriend," Julia whispered as though the thought of Freckles dating was some big secret. It wasn't.

"Is that a bad thing?"

"Not for her, no. But she thinks everyone should be paired off. In fact, she told me I needed to bring a date to the Sugar and Shadow Shindig next month."

"What in the hell is that?"

"Apparently, it's some annual fund-raiser dinner and dance that the town puts on to benefit the hospital. Get it? Sugar Falls and Shadowview? I think it's supposed to be a play on words."

"Oh, I get it all right. I just hadn't heard that was the theme the committee had come up with for it this year."

"So you're familiar with it." Julia's eyes lit up, reflecting a hundred questions that Kane did *not* want to answer. "Are you going?"

"No way," he shook his head. "I stay far, far away from those kinds of dog and pony shows."

"Normally, I do, too." Julia leaned forward as though she were confiding in him. "But my commanding officer said that most of the doctors are expected to attend. Even if it wasn't a work-related function, Aunt Freckles would want me there so she could introduce me to most of the town all at once. I don't know if you've noticed, but my great-aunt can be a bit of a show-off."

"Yeah, it's hard not to notice. So…uh…have you found a date yet?" There he went, engaging his mouth before his brain again. He had no business asking her such a personal question, especially when his lungs froze as he waited for her answer.

"Pshh." She swatted her hand in the air. "Are you kidding? I barely have enough free time to go to a Laundromat, let alone go out looking for man. But I'll get to it."

"Huh." Kane leaned on the handle of the cart, struggling not to show his relief. "I'm surprised Aunt Freckles isn't doing your laundry for you."

Julia sighed. "She offered to. Unfortunately, she'd also spearhead the Find Julia a Man Committee if I'd let her."

Kane started to rub his chin, then thought better of it and pinched the bridge of his nose instead. "You're not going to let her, are you?"

"Do my laundry or set me up with a date for the hospital gala?"

"Either."

"Listen, if it were up to me, I'd be happy living alone and doing everything on my own. However, I promised my aunt I'd try to become a little more social, which isn't exactly one of my strengths. Yet."

With that, Julia moved toward the bedding section, and Kane walked beside her with enough questions to fill the shopping cart he was pushing. Personally, he didn't blame her one bit for not wanting to get dressed up and schmooze with all the bigwigs from the hospital. But he also understood about high-handed family members who thought they had your best interests at heart. While Kane could hold his own with the rest of the Chattersons, he doubted Julia would be tough enough to oppose her aunt. Hell, Kane himself had a hard time standing up to a determined Freckles. But there must be something he could do to help the underdog. He might not be great at studying, but he'd always been good at coming up with ways to fix things.

"Do you have a plan in mind?" he asked.

She stared at a shelving display and tapped her bow-shaped upper lip, making his mouth go dry. "I think the plan is to hold off on the new sheets until I order a real bed. But I might need a down comforter for my air mattress in the meantime."

"No, I meant do you have an idea of how you're going to get out of the Sugar and Shadow Shenanigans?"

"You mean the dance?" she corrected him, but a smile twitched at the corners of her lips. "Of course I'm not. Why would I try to get out of it?"

"Because you supposedly have a high IQ?"

Julia crossed those arms primly across her fitted white blouse, making Kane's veins pulse at the sight of her breasts pushing up against the fabric.

"I'm assuming that you don't plan on attending," she said as though he was beneath fund-raising galas. Or maybe he was just being extra sensitive since his energy level was at an all-time high. His teeth ached from clenching together so tightly. "Don't get me wrong, I wish I could be like you and write the whole thing off. But the way I see it is that it's something I have to do. I might as well give it my best shot to find a date and try to make the evening a success."

Kane forced his jaw muscles to loosen. "It must be so easy to decide to master something and then snap your fingers and, boom, it happens."

She tilted her head and squinted. "I didn't say it was easy. In fact, I know I've got my work cut out for me. I just haven't found the time to put the effort into it. But I've set a goal for myself, and I've even made a list."

"A list? Of what?"

"Of…" She hesitated. "Of what I'd want in a date."

Oh no. Kane tugged his ball cap lower on his head. He really didn't want to think about what was on that stupid piece of paper again. Or the fact that he didn't meet any of those qualifications. But the impulsive demon inside him was overriding his common sense. Besides, it didn't help that they were standing in the middle of an aisle full of plush bedding and all he could think about was her bedroom. "What's on the list?"

Julia blushed, a deep scarlet to match the rose-printed decorative shams on display. "Just a little of this and that."

She was normally so confident, he felt his lips quirk at seeing her a bit flustered. But he also didn't want her thinking he was applying to be her date. At least not the kind her aunt would approve of. His eyes lowered to her soft pink lips and he briefly toyed with the idea of putting on a tux and taking her to the gala himself if it meant he'd get a good-night kiss.

Her head was tilted up and it would be so easy to slide his hand around her neck and pull her toward him…

He took a step back, bumping into a stack of fleece blankets. He needed to lighten this discussion up, fast, before he did something stupid. "Forget the details. So you make the ideal-man list. And then what? You go out shopping for a guy like you would a refrigerator?"

Julia inhaled deeply, then tested the satiny softness of a down-filled pillow above her head. The motion caused her shirt to pull against her chest again, and he saw the faint outline of her lace bra underneath. Maybe they should make their way to the bath department to look at something less inviting. Like toilet plungers.

"Wouldn't that be nice and simple?" she said, a dreamy look on her face. "I could just bring in my notepad and show it to Paulie, the salesman, and poof!" She snapped her fingers. "He could fix everything for me. No more being the wallflower and not fitting in at parties."

Kane would've been saddened by her words if his blood wasn't pumping in disgust over the thought of someone fake and phony like Paulie Loudmouth seeing to her needs. Which led to him thinking about the slimy salesman or some another jerk sharing that pillow with her. Taking advantage of her natural innocence. Her naïveté with people could really get her into trouble in a dating situation…

The runaway train of thought made his chest constrict with concern—and his lungs fill with jealousy.

And before he could consider what he was saying, Kane heard himself suggest, "You know, I could help you find a guy."

Chapter 7

Thankfully, Julia's cell phone rang and she'd been called in to assist with a complicated emergency surgery seconds after he'd made the impulsive offer. Well, not thankfully for Corporal Rosenthal, who had been touch and go for a while after the removal of the blood clot in his brain. But at least she'd been saved the embarrassment of taking Kane up on his offer to find her a plus-one for the hospital gala.

Especially after she'd caught him staring at her lips in the bedding aisle and had held her breath, hoping he would volunteer to go as her date. Oh, who was she kidding? Standing so close to him, she'd been hoping he'd offer a lot more than that.

But he hadn't even touched her, let alone kissed her, and the hollowness of disappointment was just as fresh several hours later.

Julia stood in the middle of the officers' locker room, stretching out the muscles in her lower back. When she got the call earlier today…wait. She looked at the clock on the wall. It was after oh four hundred. Make that yesterday. When she'd gotten the emergency call *yesterday*, Kane had abandoned the loaded shopping cart in an empty aisle and had driven her straight to the hospital. He didn't say a word—not that he could've spoken much since she'd been on the phone getting briefed by the head ER doctor—and she hadn't allowed herself to think about anything beyond what awaited her in the operating room.

In fact, Julia wasn't even sure what had happened to her car until she'd gotten out of surgery and saw his text message, before she'd accidentally deleted it. Apparently he'd parked it in long-term parking and called for a ride home. The fact that he'd volunteered to help her "find a guy" made it pretty clear that he was of the same mindset she was when it came to dating. Or at least, when it came to dating her. Still, after with the deal he'd gotten on her appliances yesterday, as well as the extra time he'd had to put in, she found herself in Kane's debt once again.

Julia wondered who he possibly could've called to pick him up at the base hospital. Sure, he probably had a family or maybe even friends nearby. But he seemed like even more of a loner than she was. Which made it all the more odd that he thought he could help her find a suitable date. Actually, he'd never said suitable. Her mind flashed back to the angry old cowboy he'd been arguing with in the Cowgirl Up Café that morning he'd acted like he was being poisoned by vegetables. She could only imagine what kind of guy Kane would come up with on his own.

And that brought her back to her original thought. Her emergency call had saved her from having to decline his offer. Although she would decline it, eventually. If she could figure out a way to do it without making her sink into a hole with shame. She was already having difficulty explaining to her Aunt Freckles about boundaries and registering an online dating profile in Julia's name. Misreading Kane's intentions and crossing the line of professionalism was too big of a risk for her to take.

She took a quick shower before heading out to the parking lot, where she'd found the key fob under the front passenger-side tire, right where Kane's text said it would be.

The leather interior smelled of his spicy, masculine scent, and when she started the engine, the satellite radio shot to life, the volume at a much higher decibel level than any audiologist would recommend. The display screen told her that Louis Jordan was playing on the jazz station. Not that Julia was one to categorize people or rely on stereotypes, but this was the second time she'd found herself surprised at the musical choice of a simple contractor from a simple town. But she tapped her fingers against the gearshift and let the piano and trombone melodies carry her up the mountain toward Sugar Falls.

Kane was proving to be quite a contradiction of what she'd first expected and she made a mental note to find out more about him. After all, the last time she'd allowed herself to be so naive about a man she'd been dating, Julia had been devastated by the truth.

Wait. She and Kane weren't dating. They weren't even friends. She forced her fingers to relax on the steering wheel as she chastised herself for comparing her contractor—who didn't owe her any explanations because she was not in a relationship with him—to Stewart Morsely, who'd purposely kept her in the dark about his real life.

Ella Fitzgerald was fittingly crooning when Julia was at last turning off Snowflake Boulevard. The sun had barely crested the twin pine trees behind her house, and though she was relieved finally to be home, Julia sighed at the realization that she still needed to go back to the store and finish shopping today.

When she pulled into her driveway, she saw several cardboard boxes broken down and stacked next to her recycling bin. Upon closer inspection, she recognized the box from the knife set she'd wanted yesterday, as well as several others that had once contained measuring cups, dishes and even a KitchenAid stand mixer in pale blue.

Her cell phone rang, and she headed toward the front door, answering her aunt's call as she fumbled with her house keys. "Morning, Aunt Freckles."

"Morning, Sug. Did you get the introductory email from the An Apple a Day website?"

"Actually, I got it but I barely had time to glance at it."

"The ad said it's the premier dating service for singles in the medical profession. They even have a little apple-shaped app icon. We can download the app to your phone, and you can get suggested matches no matter where you are."

Julia didn't have the heart to point out her concerns with the marketing strategy behind naming a company after an old adage that promised to keep the doctor *away*. "I'll try to check it out when I get a moment."

"You don't *have* a lot of free moments, Sug. The gala is only a few weeks away. That's why I'm taking the liberty of speeding up this date-finding business for you." Oh great. It was a business now? "Anyway, I got your text yesterday about getting called into surgery and not being able to finish your shopping trip. You want me to come by this afternoon after the breakfast rush and we can have a second go-round?"

"Uh…hold that thought." Julia walked into her kitchen, the temporary sawhorse table cleaned off and the overhead cabinets snugly installed. She opened a cupboard door to find it filled with glasses. If Freckles hadn't gone back to the store to buy the stuff Julia had picked out, then who had?

She made her way into the butler's pantry and saw the top-of-the-line knife set sitting on a shelf, along with several other small appliances. There was a note next to the expensive-looking toaster that said "Put stuff in here till I get countertops installed. Maybe Monday." It wasn't signed, but she recognized Kane's scratchy handwriting.

"Sug? You still there?"

"Oh, yes. Sorry, Freckles. No, I don't need to go shopping today. It looks like Kane took care of it."

"You're kidding," her aunt said, and hearing the cackling laughter, Julia could almost picture the woman slapping her jeans-clad thigh. "I guess there's a lot more to that boy than a good throwing arm. No, Monica, those are the bowls for the fruit cups, not the oatmeal."

"Listen," Julia said, before her aunt became too engrossed in training the new waitress while she waited on the other end of the line. "I'm going to catch a little bit of sleep. Maybe you can tell me what you mean by 'good throwing arm' when we get together for dinner tonight?"

"Uh, tonight won't work for me," Freckles said, her voice pitched lower than normal. "I have, uh, plans."

Julia would've pressed her aunt for more details on what those plans might be—and whom they might involve—but she was still trying to figure out when Kane had time to play the home-goods fairy *and* install half of her kitchen cupboards.

So instead, she said goodbye, then fired off a quick text to the mysterious man. Did you buy all this?

She didn't get a response. It was then that she noticed someone had also made a run to Duncan's Market—the only grocery store in town—because one of the pantry shelves was stocked with cereal, crackers, granola bars, pasta and jars of gourmet vegetarian sauces.

Julia's sigh was almost as loud as the rumbling coming from her stomach. She would have to pay him back, of course, or maybe he'd bill her in a future invoice. Either way, she hadn't eaten since that meal at the Bacon Palace. She was excited just to have a bowl to pour some cereal into. Until she realized she still wouldn't have her refrigerator until it was delivered tomorrow. Which meant no milk.

Just then, she spied the cooler at the opposite end

of the kitchen. Unless…nah…he wouldn't have taken the time to—yep. There was a quart of milk nestled on some fresh ice, along with a six-pack of her favorite soda.

Bless Kane Chatterson. Julia found a spoon in a silverware tray near the sink in the mudroom, which was the only functioning source of water downstairs. The man had even washed everything before putting it away. She was going to have to pay him a bonus.

She carried the bowl of raisin bran upstairs, trying not to wonder how he knew her preference for raisins, but stopped in her tracks when she saw a new down comforter spread out over her air mattress in the center of the bedroom. She knew she hadn't even made her bed before leaving the house yesterday. Mostly because it had been the first morning she'd woken up without a maid to do it for her or without a higher-ranking naval official directing her to do it.

But also because she was positive that she hadn't actually selected a comforter yesterday at the store. In fact, if she remembered correctly, she was still looking at sheets, thinking about kissing him, when Kane had made his impractical offer—which, suddenly, after Freckles's An Apple a Day suggestion, didn't seem so silly.

She looked at the crisp Egyptian cotton pillowcases covering what she suspected were brand-new fluffy pillows. Yet before she could think of the intimate implications of Kane Chatterson selecting her bedding, her cell phone rang again. She sat down at the edge of the air mattress as she spoke with the on-call neurologist who was following up on Corporal Rosenthal's care. After being reassured of her patient's condition, she didn't give her pillows or her inappropriate attraction to her handsome contractor another thought as she sank onto her freshly made bed and promptly fell asleep.

Kane saw Julia's text message when he woke up late Sunday morning. But he had a feeling she'd stayed up much later than he had, and he didn't want to disturb her with what was an obvious answer. Who else would have gone back to buy the stuff in her Bed Bath & Beyond cart and then spend all evening installing her overhead cupboards?

Not that he had anything better to do on a Saturday night. Two years ago around this time of day, he would've just been rolling in from a night of drinking and celebrating, catching a couple of hours of sleep before being expected to pitch the opening of a Sunday afternoon game. Once he committed to something, Kane didn't believe in doing anything half-assed. And partying had been no exception.

Not that he missed that particular aspect of his former life. In fact, toward the end of his career, he'd been spiraling more and more out of control. Like a foul ball spinning its way into the cheap seats. And he'd always known baseball wouldn't be forever. His body currently appreciated the slower pace of small-town life, but his restless mind sometimes needed more stimulation than what Sugar Falls had to offer.

He was itching to finish the lower kitchen cabinets at the Pinecone Court house, but he didn't want to disturb Julia if she was sleeping in. Plus, after that near kiss and his unexpected reaction to the thought of her dating, he didn't think it was a good idea to be too close to her right now. Knowing in his head that there was no way he'd actually act on his attraction was one thing. Communicating that rational thought to his nerve endings was another matter.

Just thinking about the way her lace bra had cupped the perfect shape of her breasts had Kane's palms sweating. Today it'd be much safer for him to get out of his house and do something that would get him refocused.

Maybe he'd go over to his sister's house, and offer to babysit his twin nieces. Or maybe he'd stop in at Russell's Sports and he and his buddy Alex could take a couple of the guys from the support group and a raft down the Sugar River rapids. Hell, if he really wanted to live dangerously, he could call up the nine-year-old Gregson twins—who technically were Drew's nephews, not his, but still called him Uncle Kane—and offer to take them on a mountain bike ride.

Deciding he needed a healthy dose of adrenaline and fear, he called Drew and made arrangements to do all three.

When Kane showed up at Julia's house on Monday morning, his injured shoulder should have been in a sling. But he'd swallowed down a few ibuprofens with his morning decaf and hauled his tool bag out of his backseat. Today, the kitchen would get done even if it killed him.

He needed to finish working on Dr. Smarty-Pants's house and move on to the next job. That way, he wouldn't be distracted by thoughts of her waking up wrapped up in that stupid down comforter he shouldn't have bought.

The basset hound he'd noticed the day she moved in was sitting on her front porch, and he moved toward the dog slowly, not knowing how friendly Julia's pet might be with strangers. He hadn't seen it that night he'd installed the overhead cupboards, but he wasn't paying attention to a lot of things lately. Or maybe Freckles took care of the animal when she was gone.

It let out a low growl. Kane, knowing he needed an ally if he was expected to work alongside the animal, reached into the white bag he'd picked up at the bakery on his way over and tossed a doughnut to the dog. The yeasty treat was gone in a second, and the pooch was licking its sugar-covered snout when Julia opened the front door.

"Oh, hi," she said, shifting the strap of her black bag higher onto her shoulder. "I was just heading off to work. But I'm glad I got to see you before I left. I wanted to thank you for…" Just then the hound walked over to its owner and sniffed Julia's hand.

"I think he's hoping for another treat," Kane explained when Julia seemed puzzled by her pet's response to her.

"A treat?"

"Yeah, Mr. Donut and I were just having a little manly breakfast out here before getting to work."

"Oh. Um, okay." Julia scrunched her nose as the dog wiggled its butt and waddled inside the house. Maybe she was one of those people who didn't give animals human food and didn't appreciate strangers taking liberties with their pets.

Kane wasn't taking a chance on making his work environment any more awkward than he'd already made it when he'd brought up the subject of dating and almost kissed his client. "I hope you don't mind."

"No. Of course not. You and Mr. Donut should eat whatever you like. But back to what I was saying. I wanted to thank you for returning to the store on Saturday and getting all that stuff for the house. I couldn't find a receipt, but let me know how much it all cost and I'll write you a check."

His throat constricted with annoyance at her money reference and he waved his hand. "We can settle up later."

She pursed her lips as if she was biting back an argument. Instead she said, "I'm so sorry I left you stranded at the hospital like that."

"No problem. Really. Don't even give it another thought." *Please*, Kane pleaded silently. *Let's not talk about that day anymore, or how I wanted to press you up against that display of seven-hundred-thread-count sheets and kiss you until you couldn't think of a single quality on your damn man list.*

To distract them both, he outlined his plans for what he hoped to get accomplished by this afternoon, and she nodded, stepping closer to him as her eyes followed the dog, which would occasionally walk by the open front door as he sniffed his way from room to room. Kane heard the lurch of a loud engine, and his sore arm brushed against Julia's soft sweater as they both turned to look at the delivery truck lumbering down the street.

He had no idea she'd been standing that close, and despite the sturdiness of his flannel shirt, Kane could feel the hair rise on his chest. It was all he could do not to think about the tingling sensation or the fact that he'd now accidentally touched her like that twice. Even he had to wonder how much of an accident it could be.

"I hate to run off like this, but do you think you can show them where to put everything?" Her breath was warm and tinged with the lemon-lime smell of her morning beverage of choice. He could only imagine how sweet she would taste.

Focus, Chatterson.

He cracked his knuckles, then put his hands in his pockets before pulling them out and crossing his arms over his torso. "No problem."

When he heard the dog let out another growl toward the delivery men, Kane tossed him a second doughnut. *Attaboy.* At least he knew someone was protecting her.

"Okay, I guess I'm leaving you two in charge," Julia said, giving the hound another pat on his smooth head. Then she bolted toward her car and waved before driving off to the hospital.

"Well, big guy," Kane said to the pooch before walking down to help the men from Land O'Appliances unload. "Your mom didn't leave me any rules, so I guess she expects you to stay put and not get in my way today."

Yet all day long, the dog was close on his heels. Unlike its owner who couldn't seem to get away from Kane fast enough.

The sun was setting and Julia's stomach was already rumbling with hunger when she pulled into her driveway and saw the thickset basset hound sitting on her front porch. She sighed. It wasn't that Julia minded dogs. She just hadn't been around too many. In fact, she'd always wanted a pet of her own, but her father had been allergic to nearly anything with fur and four legs.

She supposed it might be kind of nice to have an animal around the house, and if Kane wanted to bring his dog to work with him, who was she to object? Especially after the guy had already gone above and beyond for her at the home goods store the other day.

Besides, Mr. Donut seemed relatively well-behaved enough, even if Julia did have some concerns about the healthiness of his diet. And the fact that the animal could probably benefit from a good scrubbing. But it wasn't any of her business—unless she found muddy paw prints on her new white comforter. She'd maybe have to say something to Kane at that point.

If she could get herself to stop sounding like a tongue-tied teenager in front of the man every time his heat-filled gaze turned in her direction. Speaking of which, why was he still working this late?

She set the parking brake and shoved the open box of chocolate-covered raisins back into her purse. When she walked in the door, she almost crashed into Kane's chest, making him drop his tool bag on the floor before he reached out a hand to steady her. And then her tongue twisted itself into a neat little knot again and a tingle shot from the base of her scalp to the back of her knees.

"Sorry. I meant to be gone by now," he said, and she tried not to notice the way the antique chandelier in the front parlor cast a fiery glow along the bronze stubble covering his jawline. "I was trying to get the kitchen sink installed before you got home. But when I heard you pull up, I threw in the towel and figured I'd get out of your hair for the night."

"You don't have to leave on my account." Although it probably would be better if he *and* his sexy five o'clock shadow left so that she could get back to avoiding all the sensations that got stirred up whenever he was near her.

"No, I need to leave on my own account. I'm going to drive myself crazy if I waste any more time on those antique pipes." He gestured toward the kitchen, and she saw the makeshift bandage on his thumb.

"You're hurt."

"What? This?" He shoved the injured digit, which appeared to be wrapped in a paper towel and duct tape, into his pocket. "Just busted my knuckle while I was trying to show that brushed nickel faucet who was boss. And lost."

"Oh no. Will the replica farm handle pump I picked out not work?"

"No, it'll work. But it's beyond my pay grade. I have a friend who specializes in plumbing, and I'm going to call him in to handle it for me. I hope you don't mind."

"Why would I mind?"

He shrugged his shoulders and did that chin wiping thing again. Which only drew her attention to his full mouth. "Some clients are funny about having subcontractors come into their houses without vetting them first."

"I'm not. I mean, I don't want just anybody working on my home, but I trust your judgment."

He gave her a questioning look and didn't respond. Julia couldn't tell if that meant *Of course you should trust my judgment* or *Why in the world would you trust my judgment*? Either way, she still had a lot to do to-night, and none of it would get done by standing in her entryway making small talk with the hard-to-read Kane Chatterson.

Her phone vibrated, and the screen indicated a new text message from Freckles. "Speaking of vetting peo-ple," Julia announced, glad for the excuse to look at something other than his chiseled face. "My aunt signed me up for one of those online dating sites today. She already filled out the application and paid the dues, but I need to log in there and change her answers and the profile she wrote for me before some romantic hopeful gets the wrong idea and messages me. It's going to be a long night cleaning up her potential mess."

"Online dating?" he asked, and she felt heat rise into her cheeks. *Now* he wanted to ask questions? He was supposed to take the hint and leave her alone to deal with her awkward social life. The one she didn't want.

"Embarrassing, right?"

"Not necessarily." He shrugged. "But how'd your aunt get you to agree to that? Never mind. I've met Freckles, and I've witnessed your negotiating skills."

The smallest hint of a grin danced along his lips, and suddenly Julia wanted to experience the full ef-fect of Kane Chatterson's smile again. Even if it was at the expense of him teasing her. "You're never going to let me forget that trip to the appliance store, are you?"

"Not if you end up matched with a knucklehead like Paulie the Salesman, I won't."

"I would think I'm smart enough to have learned my lesson after dating one of my—" She cut herself off at the curious tilt of his head. Really, the fact that she'd foolishly been romantically involved with one of her charismatic college professors—before finding out he had a wife and a history of sleeping with most of his female TAs—was none of his business. Julia wasn't proud of the fact that her first, and only, intimate relationship had been built on her inability to see through Professor Mosely's lies. She didn't need Kane's curiosity or his pity, nor did she want to point out that she'd always had trouble with interpersonal skills. "Anyway, I promised Freckles that I would go out on three different dates to screen a candidate for my dreaded plus-one."

"With three different guys?" His tone made her think that three was too lofty an aspiration.

"I assume that's what she meant," Julia said, wishing his eyebrows would stop lifting like that, mimicking her rising apprehension over what she'd agreed to.

"That's your problem, Jules. You see the world in black and white and you think everyone and every situation is going to go exactly by the book."

She crossed her arms and ignored the warm sensation that fluttered in her tummy at the nickname he'd now used twice. "They should. It makes more sense, logically, to take things at face value. It would be a lot easier to understand what people are thinking and fit in with them if we were all on the same page."

"It would be nice if it *were* that simple, but the real world doesn't work that way."

"I know." She sighed. In fact, nobody knew that better than her. "Which is why I'd rather go to the hospital fund-raiser alone. It's difficult enough feeling out of place at a social function with coworkers. Now I need to make sure I don't pick a date who is equally inexperienced and out of place."

Kane pulled his hands out of his pockets, used his bandaged thumb to click his gold watch open and closed a couple of times, then shoved the timepiece back in his pocket. Just when Julia thought she'd made him uncomfortable with all this dating talk, he said, "If you want, I could take a look at these guys before you decide to settle on the top three."

"Top three? I'd be lucky if I could find one who matched my list of requirements and wasn't old enough to be my grandfather."

"This would be your man list, right?" Kane asked, his eyebrows lifted.

Julia's cheeks couldn't get any hotter. Why had she allowed him to refinish the floorboards in the entryway? Now there was no chance of the glossy hardwood planks swallowing her up. "Please forget I ever mentioned that thing to you. Truly, it's not a serious list. And certainly not one that Aunt Freckles would likely follow."

"Let me take a look at it, and I'll help weed out the candidates that don't match. I'd hate to see you end up with some loser who wasn't good enough for you."

She'd been wrong about her cheeks. Flames of embarrassment rushed up Julia's neck and heated her entire face. There was absolutely no way she would ever show Kane Chatterson that pointless piece of paper where she'd written down what she was looking for in a man, especially since half the requirements were inspired by him.

"How do I know that you'd be any better at picking

one?" She hoped that didn't come out too defensive, but she needed to get the subject off her list and her crummy dating life—or lack thereof.

"Because I have plenty of experience when it comes to this kind of thing."

He did? Curiosity was building inside her like a snowball rolling downhill, cooling her blush and causing her to forget all about professional boundaries. "So you date a lot?"

"I used… I mean, no. I don't date a lot, nor do I want to. But I'm the oldest of five kids, so I've got the protective older brother role down to a science."

And there was her answer. Disappointment threatened to crack her rib cage into a million pieces. Kane had never been interested in her that way. He was offering out of pity for her. Or brotherly concern. On the other hand, he might just want to make sure she didn't pick a sociopathic serial killer so that nothing happened to her or to the payment of his hefty remodeling fee. There was also the chance he just wanted a front-row seat to watching her fail epically at the one area she'd never been able to master in life—

Dating.

Sex.

Although, Julia had a feeling that sex with Kane Chatterson wouldn't feel like a failure at all.

Now where did that *thought come from?* she wondered.

She waved a dismissive hand and held open the front door. "I'll let you know if anything even comes of the process. Fingers crossed, nobody will even select me as a match and I'll be off the hook."

Kane's near-smile clamped into a tight line, and he bent to retrieve his tool bag off the floor. "Just make sure *you're* the one doing the selecting. Not the other way around."

"That's another lesson on negotiating. Got it."

"I'd better take off," he said, passing by her to get to the front door she'd left open. "Stay," he said to the hound thumping its tail against the battered planks of the front porch. Then he continued down the steps without his seemingly obedient canine.

Wait. Was he leaving his dog here?

"What about Mr. Donut?" she called out when he was climbing into his Bronco.

"What about him?" He slammed the heavy door closed, then rolled down the window.

"Doesn't he want to go with you?"

As though to answer for himself, the hound plopped down on his sizable belly—which wasn't too far off the ground, considering his short little legs—and rested his chin on Julia's foot.

"I don't know why he would," Kane said. "I'm all out of pastries. And to be honest with you, that old boy could probably benefit from one of those low-calorie brands of dog chow. I'm sure whatever you pick up at the feed store will be fine."

Julia tilted her head as he started up his engine. Was she missing something here? Had he sent her a text or an email about watching his dog for him, and she'd accidentally replied to it? She really needed to learn how to use that new cell phone.

"So, just to be clear," she called out over the sound

of revving. "You want me to go buy him some diet dog food tonight?"

"That's up to you, but I think he's had plenty to eat already today, so you might as well grab it on your way home tomorrow. Also, I couldn't find a water bowl anywhere, so I just filled up one of the new baking dishes. I hope you don't mind."

Mind what? That he was using her brand-new bakeware to feed and water his dog? Well, to be honest, it wasn't like she was going to be cooking anything in it anytime soon—if ever. Or did she mind that in the space of five minutes, Kane Chatterson had implied that he thought of her as a sister and his personal pet-sitter?

She squatted down to stroke Mr. Donut's soft fur. He really was a sweet animal, and it might be kind of fun to play doggy owner for a day or so. It could be like a trial run of sorts to determine if she should get a pet of her own. Plus, it might be kind of nice not to be alone with her disillusionment tonight.

"I guess not," she said.

Kane's only acknowledgment was a small nod before driving off and leaving the basset hound happily drooling on her clogs.

"Come on, boy," she said, sliding her ugly but functional footwear out from under the dog's chin. His droopy brown eyes looked up at her as he followed her inside. "I'm not sure where you're supposed to sleep, but it seems you've already made yourself at home. I sure wish your owner would've at least left me some instructions."

Maybe people in Sugar Falls did this sort of thing all the time. Perhaps she should be flattered that he trusted her with his pet. Julia had no idea if any of this was normal, but sometimes she got the feeling that her hired contractor wasn't normal, either. Which left her with another question.

Should she really be talking about her dating life with Kane Chatterson, let alone wishing he were a part of it?

Chapter 8

"I knew I'd catch Legend Chatterson in here this morning," Kane heard Kylie Gregson say a week later as she gracefully sat down across from him and swiped a piece of his buttered rye toast.

He looked around to make sure there were only locals in the Cowgirl Up Café. The place might be decorated similar to the inside of Dolly Parton's horse stables, but it was also one of the few restaurants in town where he felt comfortable enough to let down his guard. "You know I hate it when people call me that, Kylie."

"Of course I know. But I'm your little sister. My job is to do stuff that you hate."

"Like volunteering me to hang out with your husband at his group therapy classes?" He took a sip of his decaf coffee.

"Please. You don't hate that, Kane. Just like you don't hate coming over for Thanksgiving dinner at my place."

He raised a questioning eyebrow at her before moving his plate out of her reach.

"That's why I stopped in this morning when I saw your old truck parked outside," his meddling sibling continued. "To make sure you're willing to run interference for me when Mom and Dad come to town next week."

"Have you suddenly learned how to cook?"

"No. But Luke and Carmen are bringing the boys, and she promised to help me in the kitchen. I figure we could do it potluck-style. So what will you be bringing?"

"If Dad doesn't promise to behave, some antacid and an excuse to leave early."

"You know what, Kane Chatterson? Because I'm your sister and I think our father has been too soft on you lately, I'm going to tell you straight up what everyone else has been too afraid to say. Ever since you've stopped playing baseball and exiled yourself to Sugar Falls, you're no fun anymore."

"Says the new mom of twin babies." He redistributed some of the sausage gravy onto his hash browns. His sister was worse than his agent, Charlie, who Kane really needed to bite the bullet and fire once and for all. But he didn't even like to think about his former career, let alone talk about it out loud. In a public place. "Where are my nieces, anyway? I'm surprised you could get away this long."

"Drew has them this morning. I have a lot of work at the office I need to catch up on, and he wanted me to stop in and see you because you can't refuse the invitation in person."

"Fine. I'll come to your Thanksgiving dinner, and I'll even bring something."

"Perfect. I already put you in charge of beer and wine."

"That's about all I'm capable of these days." In fact, a few years ago, nobody would've put Kane Chatterson in any position of responsibility. So at least he was improving.

"Not from what I hear." Kylie's singsong voice rattled around his head, just like she'd probably intended for it to do.

"You of all people should know better than to listen to gossip."

"Oh please. I'm a psychologist's wife with two kids under nine months and a full-time accounting practice. Unless Drew has an afternoon off and we manage to luck out by getting both girls down for a nap at the same time, small-town gossip is the only entertainment I've got left."

"Ew."

"Anyway, I heard you've gotten a lot done over at the Pinecone Court house."

He grunted and then shoved the plate of toast in Kylie's direction when it became evident that she wasn't going to leave him in peace anytime soon.

"How's the new boss lady?" his sister asked breezily, as if he didn't know exactly which direction she was headed with this.

He grunted again, wishing the beard he'd shaved several months ago was still there to hide the heat rising in his cheeks. It had been a couple of days since he'd called in the plumber to finish her kitchen, and with the roofing company he'd subcontracted at her place every day trying to lay new shingles before the typical late November snowstorms, he and Julia hadn't had any more awkward moments alone where they talked about dating and one of them ended up high-tailing it to their car before they did something they'd regret. As much as he wanted to see her again, it was a good thing he'd been making an effort to avoid her because it forced him to focus on the house remodel and not on the woman who hurled his common sense into the off-season.

"Drew said he ran into you guys in Boise not too long ago and she seemed friendly."

Another grunt.

"I hear she's a hotshot brain surgeon over at Shadowview. Doesn't seem like the kind of woman you normally go for." Kylie, along with the rest of his family, knew how to rattle him into giving them even a small sliver of information. And he felt his tight-lipped determination slowly slipping.

"Who said I was going for anybody?" Kane asked after swallowing a bite of scrambled eggs. Not in a burrito this time, though, as he'd learned that he preferred his breakfast in plain sight.

"You want a menu, Kylie?" Freckles asked before setting down a glass of orange juice in front of his sister. The café owner's question was rhetorical since menus were usually used only by the tourists who filled up the place on weekends.

"No, thanks. I think I'll have a ham biscuit. To go,

please. I can't remember the last time I actually had time to sit down and eat a real meal."

"Babies and jobs will do that to a woman." Freckles winked. "Speaking of jobs, Kane, has my niece been getting home from work at a reasonable hour?"

He kept his eyes locked onto the plate of food before him, not wanting to witness his sister's ears physically perk up at that information the way Mr. Donut's floppy ones lifted whenever a delivery truck rolled down the street. "I wouldn't know, ma'am. I'm usually gone by the time she gets there."

"That's what I was afraid of," Freckles said, leaning against the side of their booth. Now both Kane's and Kylie's ears were at full attention.

"Why's that?" Kylie asked Freckles, and he was thankful he'd be able to get more information without having to be the one to get his gossip-free hands dirty.

"She works crazy hours and has absolutely no social life. It ain't normal, I tell you." Freckles shook her head.

Kane glanced at the woman's neon-green sneakers, snakeskin leather pants and fuchsia polka-dot suspenders. Freckles really wasn't the best one to be defining *normal*.

"Is she happy, though?" Kylie asked before taking a drink of orange juice and settling back in her seat. Since the chatty waitress hadn't put in her order yet, nobody was going anywhere for a while. At least, that's what Kane told himself to alleviate his guilt at sitting here like some nosy busybody instead of asking for his check and hauling butt out the doors painted to look like the entrance to a saloon.

"I can't really tell," the older woman said, then

put her hand on her hip. "What do you think, Kane? You probably see her more than me. You think Julia's happy?"

He scrunched his nose, not wanting to be a part of this conversation at all. "How should I know? I barely talk to her."

"See?" Freckles said. "The girl doesn't talk much to anyone. Probably because her parents were big on that whole 'children should be seen and not heard' child-rearing method. I tried not to be too opinionated since I rarely made it out there except for the occasional holiday, telling myself that they were doing what they thought was best, pushing her to excel all the time. But kids need to play, to have fun. And they were just so structured with her. Not that Julia knew any better. I just wish my sweet little niece knew how to cut loose now and then."

Kane thought of Julia's regularly unmade bed and the dishes she'd left in the sink each morning after heading for work. Apparently her housekeeping skills were something she'd decided to cut loose on. But mentioning that seemingly personal tidbit of information to her aunt, who ran a tight ship in her kitchen, would be somewhat of a betrayal to his client. Plus, he liked holding on to a bit of knowledge about Dr. Smarty-Pants that no one else was privy to. Oh, the secrets one discovered when given unrestricted access to another person's house.

"It sounds like we need to get her out more," Kylie said, and Kane recognized the mischievous glint in his sister's eye.

"Not everyone is a party girl like you, Kylie," Kane

grumbled, more to himself than anything, because he could see Freckles quickly warning up to the irresponsible suggestion.

"That's what I've been telling her." The waitress wagged a long purple-painted fingernail in the air. "I even signed her up for an online dating website."

"Any success with that?" Kylie leaned forward. He had to wonder if these women realized they were trying to manage Julia's life as much as her parents once had. Only in the opposite direction.

"Just between me, you and the fence post..." Freckles looked around, and Kane decided that Scooter and Jonesy, the two old cowboys sitting at their usual booth and blatantly listening in to the conversation, must be the fence posts. "She met a man for coffee two days ago and said he was nice enough. But since I set up her account, I have the password and decided to go onto the website and do a little snooping. I looked the guy up and found out that he had no job and claimed to be in what he called an 'open relationship.'" Freckles used her fingers to add air quotes to the last part.

Kane found his fingers clenching again. She was supposed to be a doctor. A genius. Didn't the woman know how to screen these guys? This was why he'd offered to help her meet someone in the first place. Julia didn't know a blasted thing about men or how they thought. At the rate she was going, best case scenario was that she'd get matched with some sleazy dirtbag who would embarrass her at the hospital fund-raiser.

Worst case scenario, she was setting herself up for someone to take advantage of her. The woman's heart was as big as the third-story turret on her home. She was prime pickings for some gold-digging, power-hungry loser who would come into her life and start changing things around. Like putting in a tacky man cave where the formal library should be, or wanting to knock down the gabled roofline to install a satellite dish. Or sending Mr. Donut off to doggy reform school—which, frankly, wouldn't be a bad thing since the pooch had been sneaking into Kane's tool bag whenever it was unattended and, so far, had ferreted out a crescent wrench, two Phillips screwdrivers and a tape measure. He'd even blamed the basset hound for eating one of the paintbrushes he'd been using to stain the balustrade along the second floor and had been about to rush the poor, senseless animal to the emergency vet in town. But then Kane realized he'd accidentally left the brush on top of the stepladder when he'd gotten a phone call from one of the guys in Drew's therapy group.

Which was why Kane now went through Julia's house every morning after she'd left, making sure she hadn't left any food or other dangerous items sitting out where the dog could get them. Besides, Kane needed an organized workspace. He didn't do well with messes or distractions.

He was in his own world, having no idea how he'd wandered down the mental road from Julia's asinine online dating plan to his missing tools, when he overheard his sister say to Freckles, "I have a great idea. Why don't you and your niece come for Thanksgiving dinner?"

Wait. What Thanksgiving dinner? The one Kylie had just roped *him* into attending? The one his sister had said she needed him at to run interference on his domineering parents? Well, just their father, really. Mom always took a backseat to his old man's crazy schemes.

But before Kane could suggest that subjecting anyone to the overbearing presence known as Bobby Chatterson would swear poor Julia off social gatherings forever, the older woman gave Kylie a grateful smile. "We'd love to, hon. Thanks for the invite."

"I'll ask Drew and Luke to invite one of their single Navy friends. There's bound to be someone we can set her up with."

"You'd do that for her?" Freckles's heavily lashed eyes opened wide.

"Of course. If you promise to bring a few dozen of your famous buttermilk biscuits for dinner. Maybe a dessert or two?"

"You're on," the waitress said, five inches of jangling silver bracelets clinking together when she stuck out her hand to shake on the deal.

The sound reminded Kane of what shackled prisoners must have heard as they were being marched to their execution.

"Are you sure I'm not underdressed?" Julia asked her aunt when they drove up and parked in the circular drive of the Gregsons' lakefront house.

"You look beautiful, Sug." Aunt Freckles reached over and patted the knee of her niece's black tailored slacks, which were expensive and well cut, but also very understated.

When Julia was growing up, formal dinners meant long, elegant dresses and heirloom pieces of jewelry from the built-in safe in her mother's dressing room.

However, judging by her aunt's choice of a brown leather miniskirt and tall moccasin boots, the people of Sugar Falls celebrated the holidays a bit more casually. Freckles's orange sweater with the words Gobble Gobble stitched on the front was a far cry from any of the fancy clothes in Julia's own sparse closet.

"Now help me get these biscuits inside. I hear Kylie and Drew had Kane install one of those fancy double ovens in the kitchen, so I hope she won't mind me popping them in to bake before dinner. We can come back for all the pies."

Kane? Would he be here? Julia's hand trembled slightly as she reached for the passenger door handle. Certainly Drew wouldn't invite one of his patients for dinner. Not that Julia knew how they did things in smaller towns, but she couldn't imagine her mother ever entertaining her own patients.

She looked around at the other cars in the driveway and didn't spot his Bronco anywhere. Maybe she should've made more inquiries ahead of time. Not that she minded seeing him. But she hadn't had an actual conversation with the man in almost a week. Just notes in passing about built-in bookcases for the den or the delivery of the mahogany armoire she'd bought at an antiques shop in downtown Sugar Falls.

After the way her body had been responding to him lately, she hadn't even trusted herself to speak to him on the telephone. Which was maybe an overreaction on her part, because there were quite a few things she needed to speak to him about—like the way he assumed she wouldn't mind taking care of his pet.

She'd made the mistake of leaving a note for him regarding the low-calorie dog food she'd picked up for Mr. Donut, and Kane had apparently taken that as an invitation to leave his dog there overnight indefinitely. Then she'd come home from a grueling eighteen-hour day last Wednesday to find that he'd also taken the liberty of bringing over some fancy stuffed pillow for the basset hound to sleep on. Perhaps she should've told him that his pet didn't bother with the bed at all when it seemed more comfortable using her air mattress.

She exited the car and walked toward the rear of Freckles's turquoise Ford Flex, still brooding about the dog. It wasn't like she could blame Mr. Donut. The bedding Kane had picked out for her temporary bed was very plush and luxurious, even if she had learned the hard way to check under the down comforter for various tools that the animal liked to hide there.

"So, who else is coming for dinner?" Julia whispered to her aunt as she balanced a tray in one hand and straightened her necklace with the other. The pearls had been in her family for generations and, besides her mom's watch, was the only piece of jewelry she'd brought with her when she'd moved to Idaho. It was also the only thing she had to liven up the pale gray cashmere sweater she'd opted for rather than accepting her aunt's offer to buy them matching turkey-themed tops.

"Just the Gregsons and the Chattersons," Freckles replied before an oversize teak door opened and a boy with curly blond hair launched out of it.

"Did you bring the chocolate pie, Miss Freckles?"

Wait. Did she just say the Chattersons?

As in, her moody contractor?

Before Julia could question whether she was seeing double, a duplicate boy darted out.

"What other kinds of pies did you bring?" The other boy asked. In less than a second, two bouncing blond heads were on either side of her and peeking into the rear hatch. "You want us to help you carry stuff, Miss Freckles?"

The older woman, who could match anyone in energy, didn't miss a beat. "Yes. And yes. Sug, allow me to introduce Aiden and Caden Gregson, two of the finest dessert connoisseurs the town of Sugar Falls has ever seen." Her aunt patted each twin's head as she said his name, but Julia had no idea how anyone could tell them apart. "Boys, I'd like you to meet my niece, Dr. Julia Fitzgerald."

"Our Uncle Drew is a doctor," one of the boys said. "But he's just the talking kind. He doesn't even have those plastic gloves in his office, so he can't make cool balloon hands or nothing. What kinda doctor are you?"

"Okay, monkeys," Drew Gregson called from the front porch, his arm wrapped around the waist of a tall redheaded woman. "Let's allow our guests to come inside the house before you ask them a million questions."

The boys ran back and forth as the striking couple made their way to their car.

"Hi, I'm Kylie Gregson," Drew's wife said, her smile and handshake almost as exuberant as the constantly moving twins. "We're so glad you could join us for Thanksgiving, Dr. Fitzgerald."

"Please, call me Julia," she started, but before she could thank her hosts for their invitation, her voice trailed off as her eyes were drawn back to the front of the house where a hatless, clean-shaven Kane Chatterson stood.

He was here. And he was dressed up. Her vocabulary went on sabbatical and her muscles felt about as firm as the yeasty circles of raw biscuit dough lining the baking sheet she was trying not to drop.

"Is *Fitzgerald* one word or two words?" Caden—or was it Aiden?—asked as he grabbed Julia's hand, breaking her out of the frozen trance she'd fallen into the moment Kane had appeared on the front porch. "Because when Carmen marries my dad, her new name is going to be two words. But we won't have to call her Officer Delgado Gregson on account of she'll be our mom."

Julia blinked several times. Who were these kids and what in the world were they talking about? If her overwhelmed head hadn't been spinning at their rapid-fire sentences, she might have been tempted to command her unsteady body to retreat inside Freckles's car and get her pulse under control. Julia wasn't used to children, and she especially wasn't accustomed to ones who were so welcoming and friendly. Kane smiled at her as he grabbed the tray of biscuits from the hand not enclosed in the smaller, damper one of Aiden or Caden Gregson.

"Welcome to crazy town," he said low enough for only her to hear. "You want to come inside and meet the rest of the circus?"

Her heart fluttered up into her throat and all she could manage was a nod. The proximity of his voice, coupled with his rare smile, was enough to make her agree to jump into a cage of dancing lions with him if that's what he'd asked.

"Miss Freckles brought a ton of dessert, Uncle Kane," one of the twins said as they led the procession of baked goods up the front steps. "Which means we can have that pie-eating contest, after all."

Uncle Kane? He was related to these people? The assumption that he was Drew's patient, along with every other preconceived notion she'd made about the man was suddenly replaced by an empty void, leaving her anxious to figure out the answers to refill it.

"I hope you boys know better than to challenge your Uncle Kane to *any* kind of contest," said a man who looked exactly like Drew Gregson, minus the glasses. "They don't call him 'the Legend' for nothing." He turned to Julia and grinned. "Hi, I'm Luke and these little pie-eating chatterboxes are mine."

The name Legend would imply that Kane was legendary at something. Unless it was for his ability to go hours without saying a single word or ever mentioning the fact that he had family living nearby, Julia couldn't imagine what kind of contest Kane might win. Instead of asking for clarification, though, she shook hands with the boys' father, and then with more people once she was ushered inside.

Drew and Kylie's Craftsman-style home boasted an open floor plan with a long counter separating the great room from the elaborate kitchen, making it easy for the guests to interact with each other over the chaos of pots and pans. A pair of matching pink baby swings swaying out of sync, the blaring television and some sort of board game were set up in front of it.

Julia had never been more thankful for her uncanny ability to remember names and faces, because there were a lot of twins in this extended family. And some-how, Kane was related to them all.

Luke, a Navy recruiter and Drew's twin brother, in-troduced her to his fiancée, Carmen, an officer with the Sugar Falls Police Department.

The connection that surprised her most was that Kane and Kylie were siblings. Although now that she finally saw Kane without his usual hat, the physical resemblance between the vivacious mom and the quiet contractor was apparent as they both got their hair color from their father.

Bobby Chatterson was a bear of a man and kept young Aiden and Caden engaged in what appeared to be a high-stakes game of *Battleship*. From what Julia could tell, the man wasn't technically their grandfather, but the boys lovingly called him Coach, and he would launch a full tickle attack when he caught one of them sneaking looks at the coordinates of his small plastic submarine and destroyer.

As soon as Mr. Chatterson found out that Julia was not only in the Navy but also an officer he was quick to enlist her as his teammate against the two adorable but sneaky opponents.

"Are you sure I shouldn't be helping cook or some-thing?" Julia asked when Freckles and Carmen joined Lacey Chatterson, Kane's mom, near the double oven.

"Nah." Kane's dad waved a thick, freckled hand as if he were swatting a fly. "Drew already did most of the cooking, anyway. Lacey and Carmen are just hid-ing out in there because these two little hustlers here beat them double or nothing, and nobody else is willing to give these young pups a real run for their money. I need a teammate with a solid background in military subterfuge."

"And I don't have a solid military background, Coach?" Luke said from across the room. "You *do* know that I was team leader of my SEAL unit, and I'm currently the commanding officer of recruiting for the Western Idaho district, right?"

Bobby Chatterson rolled his eyes. "We've been over this, Luke. I don't care how many push-ups you can do or how many airplanes you've jumped out of. Your poker face is a worse giveaway than that nervous tic of Kane's when he rubs his chin. The boys can read a play from you two from a mile away. So what do you say, Captain? We allies or what?"

Julia looked at the older Gregson twins, her fellow Navy brethren who were probably much better equipped to handle an intense strategist like Kane's father, yet seemed equally reluctant to do so. "I've never played *Battleship*," she began. "Besides, I'm mostly trained for what happens inside the infirmary, not for complete naval warfare."

"Good point," Mr. Chatterson said, then turned to his daughter, who was nursing one of the babies. "Hey, Kylie, do you guys have that game *Operation*? Julia's on my team."

"Sorry, Dad. We just have that one and chess."

"Yeah, figures your shrink of a husband would only prefer the head games."

Julia sucked in a startled gasp at the insult, but the rest of the adults laughed.

"You're just jealous that you've been on a sound losing streak since your granddaughters were born," Drew shot back at his father-in-law.

"I have a feeling my luck's about to change with this one." Mr. Chatterson used a tree-branch-size thumb to gesture in her direction.

"Dad, leave Julia alone." Kane spoke from behind the U-shaped sofa. "If she doesn't want to play a board game with you guys, she doesn't have to."

Julia squared her shoulders, not needing Kane to protect her. She wanted to fit in with this fun-loving and quick-bantering family. "I'd be honored to be your teammate," she said, sitting on the plush wool rug beside the older man and folding her legs under the dark pine coffee table, which served as the command post.

Apparently Julia was in fact good luck for Mr. Chatterson, as they won the next two games against the Gregson boys, who were surprisingly cutthroat in their precision and execution of moves. She knew her upbringing had been unique, but how many families got to sit around playing games and watching football on television during the holidays? Maybe it was routine for the Chatterson gang, but this was a first for her.

When the kids ran off to play outside, Julia stayed where she was, comfortable but out of the way. Kane had stopped pacing long enough to sit on the sofa behind her. She could feel his restless leg brush against her back every time one of the sportscasters on television made a reference to some exclusive baseball interview coming up after the game. While the occasional contact was seemingly inadvertent on his part, Julia found herself leaning back slightly to put pressure against his jostling knee, which would cause him to pause, even if only momentarily.

She was well-versed in neurobehavioral disorders as well as neurological matters, and it wasn't the first time she'd suspected that Kane Chatterson's many nervous gestures and his inability to sit still or stay focused were ongoing issues for him. But because he never talked about himself—or about anything, really—she didn't want to diagnose him so readily.

What she *wasn't* well-versed in, however, was family dynamics. Despite the easy camaraderie between the seemingly tight-knit group, Julia immediately sensed that there was something about Bobby Chatterson that had his son on edge. Of course, Kane often seemed on edge to her anyway, so maybe she was overthinking things. But while all the other men seemed comfortable teasing each other and talking about people Julia didn't really know, the elder Chatterson kept giving his son pointed looks, and the knee behind her back would spring into action again and again.

Trying to solve the riddle kept Julia's brain from contemplating her physical reaction to Kane's continued closeness and accidental touch. But no matter how much she was conditioned to think logically, she was having difficulty commanding her body to remain neutral. Being this close to him alternated between a pleasant fluttering feeling in her lower extremities and involuntarily being stuck in one of those vibrating massage chairs at the mall.

"Here," Bobby Chatterson said to Kylie when one of the babies started crying. "Let me take her."

"Thanks, Dad," Kylie said. "Carmen said dinner's ready, so let's make our way to the dining room."

After a minor argument between the boys over whose turn it was to sit by Coach and three rounds of rock-paper-scissors, Carmen and Luke put one son on each side of the patriarch and newly crowned *Battleship* champ.

"Divide and conquer," Carmen whispered to her, and Julia was again flattered that this group had welcomed her so willingly into their personal lives.

The large family sat down at the even larger table, which was decorated just as stunningly as the rest of the house. They might have openly teased Kylie about not being a good cook, but Julia had to admit that Kane's sister was at the top of her class when it came to decorating skills. In fact, Julia was tempted to ask for the new mom's input when it came time to furnish her own house.

She'd gathered that the Gregsons had just moved here after renting out Kylie's much smaller condo. The sizable home was done mostly in neutrals of beige and stone with strategically placed green shades throughout to liven things up. The food was perfect, and the wine flowed along with lighthearted conversation and slightly competitive banter. Kane even made a couple of jokes about his father, who apparently had recently added some poundage to what was already a thick frame.

Kane had taken the seat next to Julia and passed her only the dishes that he knew were vegetarian-friendly. She was touched by his consideration and the fact that nobody had treated her like an outsider for eating differently.

"So, you still happy living out here in Idaho and just being a contractor?" Bobby Chatterson asked his son, and Julia looked around the room to see if she was the only one who'd heard the emphasis on the word *just*.

Kane leaned behind her back to send the gravy boat to Luke. "As happy as I could expect."

That was an odd answer, but Bobby simply nodded before reaching across one of the boys to fork a piece of white meat onto Lacey's plate, then taking a few slices of turkey for himself. Julia noticed that with each dish coming his way, the man served his wife first—just like his son was doing for her. She shifted in her seat, not wanting to dwell on the similarity.

Kane's dad stared across the table at him. "You know what I want to say, right?"

Apparently the entire table—including the nine-month-old girls, who both looked up from the mashed potatoes and peas they were exchanging across their high chair trays—knew what the elder Chatterson wanted to say. Julia took a sip of her wine, wishing she could be clued in.

"Yes, Dad. We talk about wasting talents and meeting my potential every time you call me. You aren't telling me anything new."

"Then I won't push you, son."

"You won't push me?" Kane asked, his eyes narrowing. "What's the catch?"

"No catch. I just want my kids happy. Even you, sourpuss."

"But…?" Kane took a sip of his pale ale. Julia's calf muscles clenched, reminding her she was practically sitting on the edge of her chair.

"But your mom would like to know when you're going to settle down and give us some more grandkids."

Julia heard several snorts, along with a chorus of snickering coming from the end of the table near Luke Gregson and her own Aunt Freckles.

"Bobby Chatterson, don't you go putting words in my mouth," Lacey said before spearing a bite of green beans her husband had just spooned onto her plate.

"Okay, so *I'd* like to know when you're giving us some more grandkids. Your mom's not getting any younger, you know."

Mrs. Chatterson responded with a sharp elbow to her husband's rib cage. Either Aiden or Caden asked if this time they could have a boy cousin.

"I don't know, Dad." Kane replied, shrugging one shoulder as if he didn't intend to give the subject any thought. "Why don't you ask Kaleb when *he* plans to settle down and give you grandkids?"

"Oh, you know your brother Kaleb. I think he relishes being the black sheep of the family. He marches to the beat of his own drum, that one."

"If by that you mean he runs a successful multimillion dollar gaming company, then beat away," Drew said. "Actually, Julia, you'd probably like Kaleb. He's very intelligent, very well-read. Do you know if he's dating anyone right now, Kane?"

"How the hell should I know?" Kane took another drink and, seeing the tablecloth rustling, she could only imagine the way his knee was bouncing beneath it. "I'm the only one in this family who seems to mind his own business."

"Last time I talked to him, he wasn't seeing anyone

special," Kylie said. "When he comes out for Christmas, we should introduce him to Julia."

Julia gulped, then gave a noncommittal murmur, unsure of what her response should be. Were they trying to set her up with Kane's brother? Or were they just being polite and trying to include her in the conversation? These were the kinds of social intricacies she wished she could better navigate.

She remembered auditioning for the District of Columbia's youth chamber orchestra when she'd been nine years old. She'd practiced the Vivaldi concerto on her cello for hours a day and knew the piece forward and backward. But when she'd gotten on stage, her mother had told the conductor Julia would be performing the Tchaikovsky instead. Later, her mom had explained that it was important for her to learn to be adaptable and to overcome her insecurities, despite being so unprepared.

Sitting around this table reminded Julia of that experience. She had the feeling there was a performance going on, but she'd practiced for one situation and was thrown into another, one she was utterly unprepared for.

"You know who else we should introduce to Julia?" Luke Gregson said, his fork poised in the air as if he was about to start a PowerPoint presentation of eligible bachelors. Julia's stomach dropped when everyone's eyes turned his way. "My buddy, Renault. He was on the SEAL team with me and just moved to the area a few months ago, too. He's supposed to stop by later tonight, after he gets done serving dinner at the homeless veterans' shelter."

"You guys are making Julia uncomfortable with all your matchmaking talk," Kane said. She suddenly realized she was sunk down so low in her seat, her chest was inches away from the marshmallow-covered sweet potatoes on her plate.

"Sorry, Captain," Bobby Chatterson said. "I only meant to steer my boy into the right direction. We didn't mean to bring your single status into any of this."

"Well, Dad," Kane said defensively, "you shouldn't be trying to steer anyone."

Looking down the table at Aunt Freckles, who was on her third glass of cabernet sauvignon—not counting what she might or might not have consumed in the kitchen before the meal started—Julia saw her aunt following the conversation as though she were watching a match at Wimbledon.

"I don't know, Lace." Bobby finally said to his wife. "It seems like no matter how hard we try to plan out their lives for them, these kids of ours have their own minds."

Julia knew firsthand what it was like to have parents pushing you into their idea of perfection. Luckily she'd been able to meet their expectations. But she could practically feel the annoyance in Kane's tense leg beside her. She wondered if he felt like the failure in the family compared to his recently married CPA sister and an apparently wealthy younger brother. While none of them had come out and criticized Kane directly, the stirring need to defend him and his life choices caused her to speak up.

"Kane is doing a fabulous job remodeling my house," she said, then wondered if her off-the-cuff pronouncement sounded more like an unexpected toast. "He is extremely skilled and dedicated. Personally, I don't think he's wasting his talents at all."

Nobody made a sound, and Julia felt the weight of everyone's stares—minus that of one of the babies, who'd fallen asleep with homemade applesauce smeared all over her tiny face. But the only gaze she met was Kane's. His entire body had shifted so he was facing her, his head tilted to the side as if to ask her to repeat what she'd just said.

"Hey, guys," Caden said, interrupting the awkward silence. "Now that we're all done with dinner, who wants to try out the new double bike Uncle Drew bought us?"

"Uncle Drew is going to get payback for that little gift," Luke Gregson vowed, and the unexplainable tension shifted just like that, returning the conversation back to a playful banter.

"That's the same thing you said when Uncle Kane bought us that bow-and-arrow set for our birthday," Aiden said.

She looked at Kane and saw his face slowly relax into a smirk. A bow-and-arrow set for nine-year-olds? Maybe his family was right to question the man's ability to make good decisions.

"Good point," Luke said, one arm around Carmen's shoulders. "I'm sure Uncle Kane would like to try out the new tandem bike."

"What about you, Dr. Julia?" Caden asked. "You wanna take a turn with Uncle Kane?"

"Oh, I don't know. I've never ridden a bike before."

"Never?" Aiden asked. "Like ever?"

"Well, I've used a stationary one at the gym," she

clarified as she squared her shoulders, not willing to admit to the table, or to herself, that she couldn't do something. "I can't imagine it'd be much different to ride yours."

"It's way different." Kane shook his head. "This one actually requires balance."

"I can balance," she said. She'd practically balanced on the edge of her seat throughout the entire meal.

"You're saying you could just hop on a bike and start riding it, no problem?" Kane rested his arm on the back of her chair, his chest appearing to be a bit more puffed out than usual—as though he were throwing out a challenge.

"If I wanted to, I could," she said, almost convincing herself.

"It's not that hard," Bobby Chatterson said. "I've taught my share of kids, and you look like a sturdy enough gal to me." Julia wasn't sure, but she thought that coming from the opinionated man who resembled a lumberjack himself, it was meant as a compliment.

"I don't know, Sug." Aunt Freckles suddenly took a break from sipping her wine to speak up. "If you take a nasty fall, you'll end up in a cast right before the Sugar and Shadow Shindig. Think of how that would look in the evening dress you just ordered."

"I'm not going to break a limb," Julia said, rolling her eyes. "How hard can it be to hold on to the handlebar and pedal at the same time?"

"Okay then," Kane said, his smooth chin lifted in such a way that he had to look down his nose at her even though they were sitting side by side. "Let's go outside and you can prove it."

She didn't want to prove anything. At least, not in front of witnesses. She looked at the ceiling, wondering how she was going to get herself and her pride out of this situation. "I should probably stay here and help clean up the kitchen."

"So you can't do it?" The corner of Kane's mouth was tilted up.

"Kane, last week I used a robotic arm to conduct a laser ablation of a deep-seated tumor on a patient's brain. I think I can manage a bicycle," Julia said.

"Care to make a wager?" he asked, and Lacey Chatterson looked to the ceiling while her husband smacked his palms together.

Oh boy. Betting was another thing Julia had never done. But she wasn't about to confess that to this group. "What kind of wager?"

"Ooh, I know," Aiden—or was it Caden?—said. "Whoever loses has to do something embarrassing, like dress up in a pig costume and do a funny dance in the gazebo at Town Square Park."

"Where are we going to get a pig outfit on Thanksgiving?" his nine-year-old brother responded. "A turkey one would probably be easier to find."

While Freckles and Kylie chimed in with suggestions about available costumes, Julia looked at Kane and knew exactly what she wanted if she won the bet. "If I prove that I can ride the bike, then you have to go to the Sugar and Shadow Shindig."

"What about the plus-one?" Kane asked.

"You can bring a date if you want. It's up to you."

"No, I meant what about *your* plus-one?"

"I don't know who that is yet, remember?"

He slowly smiled. "That's right. Which means, if you can't ride the bike, *I* get to choose your date."

Chapter 9

Kane wished he'd never challenged Julia to learn how to ride this blasted tandem bicycle. Then, to make matters worse, he'd popped off and issued the most idiotic wager in the history of all idiotic wagers. If she won, he'd be stuck attending the stupid hospital fund-raiser dance next month. If he won, he would have to sit home alone and wonder about whomever he ended up picking as Julia's date and whether the jerk was treating her well and keeping his hands to himself.

It was a lose-lose situation.

"Stop leaning to the left," he called out behind him. "You're going to make us fall over."

"But the boys said I need to lean left when I want to go right."

"Jules, you're the stoker. I'm the captain."

"So?"

"So, when you're the person in back, you can go only where the person in front steers you."

"Maybe I should try being in the front," she suggested. "That way, I can steer."

"For the eighteenth time, until you can learn how to hold yourself upright, I'm not letting you near the front seat."

"Has anyone ever told you that you have control issues, Kane Chatterson?"

That was an understatement if ever there was one.

As they pedaled clumsily around the driveway, Kane's thoughts kept turning to the idea of Julia...dating. And how distasteful the idea was. He'd be damned if he'd let his family set Just Julia up with his brainiac younger brother Kaleb. Or, for that matter, Luke's macho navy SEAL friend, Renault. The guy sounded like a total loser, if you asked Kane, and not at all the type of man Julia should be interested in. What kind of name was Renault anyway?

He'd almost volunteered to go as her date himself, but knew better than to set himself up for rejection with his family there to make fun of him. Plus, her suggestion that he bring his own plus-one was all the evidence he needed that she'd rather give someone the Heimlich maneuver again than go to a social function with him. So now he was stuck trying to teach her how to ride this stupid tandem bike, completely unsure of whether he wanted her to succeed or fail.

All he knew was that if she didn't start maintaining some sense of balance, he was going to fall and break his other shoulder and wind up doubly screwed—with all of his family witnessing the potential crash.

"Hmph," he said as he overcorrected to the right. "Now that you've met my family, you can see that I came by my control issues naturally."

"That's definitely a fair assessment." He heard her chuckle from behind him. "Hey, did it bother you when your dad was asking you all those questions about your future?"

Julia was more likely to pedal while she talked, and the only way to remain upright was to keep her pedaling in sync with him. Which meant he had to keep her distracted with conversation.

"Not really," he admitted. "I know they all worry about me, but I guess I've given them plenty of reason to in the past."

"Why would they worry? Because they don't think you're meeting your true potential?"

"That and the fact that I went through a lot these past two years."

"Any chance you want to tell me about it?" she asked.

They'd successfully made it around the driveway twice, and Kane wanted to venture onto the asphalt road now that their audience was slowly trickling into the warmth of the house, taking Julia's discarded coat inside with them.

"Not while I'm trying to keep us from falling on our faces."

"I think I know what your problem is," Julia said, and he felt the pace of the pedals pick up tempo, along with his heart rate.

"Trust me, I'm dealing with more than just one hang-up."

"You're afraid to fail." He heard the smugness in her

voice and didn't want her thinking she was right. Or worse—him to start believing it.

"And you're not?" he asked.

"I'm not afraid of it, no. I simply refuse to."

"Have you ever failed at anything?"

He felt the bike jerk ever so slightly and wondered if his question had surprised Dr. Smarty-Pants. He knew from past experience, both on the mound and from participating in Drew's group therapy, that now was the time to push for an answer. "C'mon, Jules. You can tell me."

"I think it's no secret that I don't do so well at personal relationships." He could barely hear her admission as a minivan whizzed by them along the neighborhood street.

"Yeah, I don't know how you define *personal relationships*, but you handled yourself just fine back there with my spectacle of a family, including my old man."

"That's different. That's simply blending in and keeping a low profile. Besides, your dad was grateful that I saved his patrol boat from being blasted out of the water on that last round of *Battleship*."

Kane wasn't one for pep talks, receiving them or giving them. But he had a feeling there was more to this failure story of hers, and the only way he was going to hear it was if he assured her that he was on her team. "Plus," he continued, "you've managed to make it through the ranks as a naval officer. I doubt you could do that if you had some serious personality flaws."

"Actually, all I have to do is be a good doctor and follow orders. So the Navy has been pretty easy for me."

"Then help me figure this out. What kind of relationships are you talking about?"

"You know," she said, and he could almost hear her blush. "The one-on-one kind."

"Like with friends?"

"Well, that and…" Her voice trailed off.

Kane pulled off the road. They'd gone at least a mile by now and were almost at Snowflake Boulevard. Although Julia was finally able to maintain a steadier pace and they'd had only one near miss when they'd had to swerve around a raccoon darting past them, he definitely didn't want to tempt fate by steering them into a higher traffic area. Plus, he wanted to look at her. He planted his feet on the ground and pivoted his torso around.

"That and what? Dating?"

"Yes, dating." Her head slumped forward, and her whole body probably would have followed suit if she hadn't had to stand on tiptoe to balance on the still bike.

He wasn't sure if the rosiness on her cheeks was from exertion or from embarrassment at him blurting out something she wasn't an expert at. Remembering the vision of her in her spandex workout pants that day at the hospital, he doubted the bike ride had been too strenuous for her. Which meant Just Julia wasn't comfortable with him seeing a perceived weakness. And he couldn't blame her. Not that he knew her all that well, but he was on a first-name basis with inadequacy and recognized the feeling when he saw it.

"Have you dated much?" he asked.

"I dated a man in med school."

Just one? That long ago? "So what happened?"

"He was my professor. I was a little out of my element and he knew it. I'd never been in a relationship before, and he convinced me that what we had was special."

"And it wasn't?"

"Apparently not. After a couple of months, I found out that he not only was married but also had a history of sleeping with his students, and I was just one more in the books for him. I felt like such a fool when I finally figured it out. I vowed never to be in a relationship again without knowing every single detail about the man I was with."

"So you're just bad at picking the right guys." He reached out and lifted her chin from where it had sunk. What he really wanted to do was pay an office visit to this professor and bust a textbook over his scholarly, philandering head. "That doesn't mean you're a fool."

"Really? Because the way I was raised, lack of knowledge is the same thing as foolishness. I let my emotions rule my head and wound up completely in the dark about the type of man he was."

"Trust me. You won't be a fool again. I already told you I'd help."

"Actually, I think I'm doing pretty well on this bike, which means you don't get to pick my date after all."

"What about your Aunt Freckles? Is she still pulling out all the stops to get your dating life up and running?"

"Don't even get me started on that. Last Wednesday, I met one of my online matches at the hospital cafeteria during my lunch break, and—"

"Hold up. You had some guy you don't even know meet you where you work?" Kane was stunned. He knew she was inexperienced, but this was just careless. He didn't remember jumping off the bike, but he was pacing back and forth along the shoulder of the road before he realized she was clearly not as bothered by the situation as he was.

"Did I break some secret dating rule?" She crossed her arms over her chest, and he tried not to stare at the way the gesture forced her thighs to balance the bike between them.

"Of course you did. The rule is Stranger Danger 101." His legs grew tense and his stomach dropped at the potential risk she'd put herself in. "Why didn't you just give him directions to your house and provide him with duct tape and the blueprints to your basement so he could hide your body?"

She tightened her blond ponytail. "Don't you think you're overreacting a bit?"

"Better this reaction than the one I'd have if I found you buried underneath your back porch inside a fifty-five-gallon drum."

"Maybe you shouldn't watch so many serial killer documentaries."

"And maybe you shouldn't set yourself up to become a victim." Okay, even he knew his outburst was over the top. But sometimes his imagination got the best of him, and more than sometimes he spoke without thinking. Plus, seeing her straddling the red lateral tube was doing something funny to his blood flow. And his jeans.

"Kane, I was in a public place. With plenty of people around. And Aunt Freckles taught me how to do background checks after that coffee fiasco with the open relationships man. The guy from Wednesday was harmless. In fact, he was a seventh-grade science teacher."

"Then what was wrong with him?" Kane asked, stopping himself from firing off more inappropriate questions. *Was he ugly? Had he lied about his height? Did he chew with his mouth open? Did he completely lose his cool and overreact at the thought of her going out with another man?*

"How do you know something was wrong with him?"

Kane tilted his head forward and raised an eyebrow.

Julia let out a breath. "Okay, so he was a little too full of himself. But in his defense, I didn't quite meet his expectations."

Now *that* was hard to believe. If you asked Kane, Julia probably exceeded most guys' expectations. She was definitely out of Kane's league, for sure. Of course, given his track record, it seemed like only gold diggers and wannabe starlets were the types of women in his lineup. Good thing he'd retired from relationships when he'd retired from professional baseball.

"How could you possibly not be what he was looking for?" He pulled off his wool sweater and handed it to her when he saw her shiver. Then he thought of a better way to warm her up and mentally kicked himself. "Actually, let's get this thing turned around and you can tell me on the ride back. It's getting pretty cold."

He climbed back on, and as they pedaled more fluidly, Julia kept him entertained with the story of her lunch date who had talked nonstop throughout their meal and had regaled her with tales about the importance of science and how he thought it was very commendable that she was studying to get her nursing degree and how he'd almost gone into premed but he thought he could do more good molding young minds.

"Wait. Why did he think you were getting a nursing degree?"

"Apparently, when I'd used the dating app to change my profile questionnaire, I checked some wrong buttons. My smartphone is really frustrating. It's always deleting texts and mismarking my entries and doing that autocorrect thing. I'll never figure the damn thing out."

He doubted it was an issue with her phone so much as her fingers. "So, did you correct him and tell him you were a neurosurgeon?"

"I did."

"And?"

"And he laughed and didn't believe me at first. Then he spouted off some statistics for med school and how hard it was to get accepted to a good program. He went on to inform me that he'd been rejected by several of them, so he was pretty sure they didn't just let any pretty face in. I was wearing my surgical scrubs, so I had to pull out my hospital ID badge to prove it."

Good. Served the pompous knucklehead right. The only thing that didn't make Kane want to throw a fastball at the guy's stomach was his agreement with the assessment of Julia's pretty face. "How'd he take it when you put him in his place?"

"Let's just say some men are intimidated by my education and my job. At least, that's what I have to assume, since he hasn't contacted me since then. Well, not including the email he sent me right after lunch saying

I should have been more honest and he didn't think we had enough in common."

"Sounds like it was his loss." Kane sure hoped Julia didn't think she'd done anything wrong. Other than apparently giving Freckles her passcode so her aunt could download that ridiculous app, knowing full well Julia's limited abilities with electronics. Of course, he'd had to fix her phone several times and now knew her passcode, as well.

"Maybe. The good news is that I only have one more date to go before Aunt Freckles will let me call it a day with this whole experiment of hers."

"Is that what it is? An experiment?"

He couldn't see Julia, but imagined her shrugging. "Experiment, charade, demonstration of why I'm better off being alone. I prefer to refer to it as anything that doesn't imply my failure."

"Oh, we're back to that word again?"

"We are. Which means it's your turn now to tell me about your shortcomings."

He turned in to the driveway, and he was half hoping the twins were outside to beg for a ride or a wrestling match or even a tutorial session on advanced mathematics—anything to distract Julia from finding out what a disaster he'd made of his life.

"Too bad I can't go into more detail about that right this second," he said. "Now that I've lost this bet, I've got a pie-eating contest on the line as my last shot at redemption." He parked the bike and held it steady while she climbed off.

"I hope that someday you will tell me," she said, not

making any move to walk away from him. "Or if not me, maybe a professional therapist."

"I don't need a shrink to tell me what's wrong with me. I already know. I've made my choices, and I'm moving on and trying to be happy with my new job. My new life."

He began walking toward the house and was shocked when her delicate hand grabbed under his biceps to pull him back. Her lips pursed in seriousness. "Kane, I meant what I said in there at dinner. I really think you are incredibly talented. What you've done to my house is just amazing. I hope you can put to rest all those ghosts that are haunting you and take some pride in your work."

It was more than ghosts haunting him. Growing up, he knew that, in his family, he wasn't the smart-est—like his brother Kaleb—or the best-behaved—like his brother Kev—or even the toughest—like his sister Kylie. He definitely wasn't the friendliest—like his brother Bobby Junior. Sports were the only thing Kane'd been good at—the area where he excelled. The feeling of his long-standing inadequacy in all other aspects of his life had been relieved only on the pitching mound. When he'd lost that, he'd lost himself.

Julia's bad luck with relationships was nothing compared to Kane's career setback. How could he explain that as much as he wanted to be successful like the rest of his siblings, he didn't have the brain power or the patience to do so? He could never make someone like Dr. Smarty-Pants, who learned to remove brain tumors with robotic arms because challenges were fun for her, understand what it was like for someone who'd barely graduated high school.

He couldn't.

But he could still appreciate her going to bat for him and trying to make him feel like he wasn't some old has-been. "You know, I meant to thank you for what you said at dinner. Nobody's ever defended me like that before. I appreciate it."

"I don't think anyone else appreciated it. They were all so quiet after I spoke up. I hope I didn't offend them."

He laughed. "They were quiet because they've never heard anyone defend me like that, either. At least, not anyone who isn't related to me."

"Well, it *does* make me feel better to know that your family is willing to stick up for you."

Just then the front door opened, and Aiden launched himself off the porch. "You won the bet, right, Dr. Julia?"

"I sure did. My bike-riding instructor was a little bossy, but after a while, I got the hang of it," she said, winking at Kane over the nine-year-old's head.

"Our new bike was fun, right, Uncle Kane?" Caden jumped down three steps in a single leap.

"Once she finally learned to relax and trust me, it was fun," Kane replied, winking back.

It was true. Riding the bike with her had been exciting, to say the least. He thought about his sister Kylie's accusation in the café the other day. His family was right. Kane hadn't been fun for a long time.

But today he was actually enjoying himself. At least, he had been, before he saw the headlights of Renault's Jeep pulling into the driveway.

* * *

"Are you sure you don't wanna go door-bustin' with me?" Aunt Freckles asked when she dropped Julia off in front of her house later that night.

"Positive. I'd rather go against Bobby Chatterson and Aiden Gregson in a pie-eating challenge than fight off a line of people in a crowded department store."

Freckles chuckled. "Kane was certainly giving them a run for their money. That is, until he decided to shove his pumpkin pie into Lieutenant Renault's face."

"Oh, Freckles, I doubt he *decided* to do anything of the sort. Kane said it was an accident, and he looked pretty upset with himself afterward."

"It wasn't himself he was upset with, Sug." Her aunt checked her lipstick in the rearview mirror. "Kane was getting pretty territorial from the moment that Renault fellow walked in the door."

"I think he just feels a bit protective around his nieces. He was hovering over me when I was holding little Gracie, too. When he squished his way onto the sofa and sat down right between me and Lieutenant Renault, I had to remind him that I've taken classes on pediatrics and knew how to hold a baby."

Julia couldn't be positive because the only light in the car was from the overhead dome, but she was pretty sure one of Freckles's painted-on eyebrows was much higher than the other.

A howl rumbled from inside her house, and Julia saw Mr. Donut's black nose pressed up against the fogged-up glass of her living room window. For a dog with such stubby legs, he sure had an impressive ability to jump onto the white plastic patio chair she was temporarily using in place of an actual sofa.

"When are you going to tell Kane to take his dog home?" Freckles asked.

"I keep meaning to. But every time the subject comes up, there's always some sort of distraction, and we get to talking about something else." She didn't want to say out loud that the distraction was usually the way he looked in his sexy flannel shirts. At least on her end. She was beginning to suspect Kane had some issues with his attention span. The poor man changed the subject every time she brought up therapy. He surely wouldn't appreciate her diagnosing him with ADHD, even if she was a neurologist.

"If you ask me, Sug, I think you like having that grumpy ol' guy around a lot more than you let on."

"Kane's not that grumpy... Oh. You meant the dog." She hoped her aunt couldn't see the flush of heat blossoming on her cheeks. "Yes, I do rather like having Mr. Donut for company. You know my father was terribly allergic to animals, so I'm finally getting to fulfill a childhood dream with only half the responsibility. Maybe I'll wind up getting one of my own if my schedule ever allows it."

Freckles tsk-tsked. "That blasted schedule of yours. If I've said it once, I've said it a bajillion times. You need to make time for the important stuff, Sug."

"Important stuff like what?"

"Like making your house a home."

"You're right, as usual. In fact, Kane brought over a few decorating catalogs for me, and I've been meaning to visit that furniture store in Boise."

"Ugh. That's not what I meant, child."

Julia knew she was supposed to pick up on some hidden meaning here, but she preferred things in black and white. Why couldn't everyone just speak more literally?

"How's the An Apple a Day dating service going?" her aunt asked.

"Not bad." She shrugged, thinking Freckles had the same tendency as Kane to switch conversation topics before Julia could figure out what message they were trying to convey.

"*Not bad* isn't the same thing as *good*."

"That's why I said *not bad*. But do I really have to take a date to that hospital gala?"

"Unless you want people to talk, you should go with someone. Now that Kane lost that bet to you, I wonder if he is taking anyone."

"I wouldn't know. He made it pretty clear that he has no interest in dating or socializing in general. Then after I proved that I could ride a bike, I didn't want to be a poor sport and bring the subject up."

"Well, let's try to find out, shall we?"

"Why?"

"Because...oh, never mind. You let Aunt Freckles worry about it. But right now, those sales aren't going to shop themselves. I've got to get going to make it to the Midnight Madness Blowout."

Julia gave her aunt a hug and exited the car. Maybe she could approach the subject with Kane by appeasing his ego and telling him he could still pick whom she took as her plus-one. Lord knew she wasn't finding anyone suitable on her own and now that Freckles brought up the idea of him bringing another woman to the gala, the last thing Julia wanted was to have to sit at some table all by herself, watching as he bestowed that sexy little smirk of his on someone else. Forewarned was forearmed, right?

Forcing the conversation could have other advantages, as well. Like reminding her that Kane wasn't in the running himself, no matter how much she loved being welcomed by his family or how good his rear end had looked on that bike seat in front of her.

Chapter 10

"What do you mean, Freckles thinks you should go out dancing?" Kane shook his head at Julia. "Do you *know* how to dance?"

"I took classical ballet when I was younger." She squared her shoulders, ready to shoot down his arguments and his negative attitude. It had been only a week since she'd proven herself more than capable of riding a tandem bicycle. He of all people should know she wasn't one to give up. "And I've been watching a few videos on YouTube. I think I'll be able to manage."

Julia passed Kane an opened cardboard container, and he grimaced at its contents. "So, who's the lucky guy who gets to take you dancing?"

When she'd pulled up at seven that evening, Julia had been surprised to see Kane's Bronco at the curb in front of her house, all the downstairs lights blazing.

She'd brought home takeout from the tiny Chinese restaurant near the hospital and had just offered to share some of her dinner with him when the conversation segued from the baseboards he'd finished sanding into her plans for the weekend.

"I don't know yet. That whole online thing hasn't been going according to plan. My last match was a sixty-eight-year-old pharmaceutical sales rep from Rexburg who lives with his mother. PharmBandit889 said his mom wouldn't approve of him dating a modern woman who worked outside the home and asked if I'd be willing to quit."

"What'd you tell him?" He sniffed the sweet-and-sour sauce before dipping his spring roll in it.

"I told him there's no way I'd quit my job for any man. Or his mother. Anyway, Freckles said if I get dressed up and go to a club, I'll find plenty of men to dance with."

"By yourself? No way." This overprotective big brother role Kane had taken on was grating on every one of Julia's only-child nerves. How else was she supposed to find a date and get over this stupid attraction to him? She was willing to try anything at this point.

"Not alone," she defended herself. "Your sister Kylie called me the other day and said Luke's friend Lieutenant Renault asked for my phone number. I was thinking he might want to go with me."

The chopstick in Kane's hand snapped in half. "You do *not* want to go to a bar with Renault."

"Why not? His rank really isn't that much below mine. He's an officer. I don't think the Navy will have a problem with fraternization. Besides, it's not a bar. It's a dance club."

"A dance club with a bar inside. Those places are meat markets. And going with some hotshot like Renault? It'd be like sending a lamb into a den of lions with their alpha leader as her date. What are Kylie and Freckles thinking, making a suggestion like that?"

Kane tossed a piece of General Tso's tofu to Mr. Donut, who caught it easily before changing his mind and letting the small cube roll off his tongue and onto the floor.

"You know, I really don't think you should feed him from the table like that," Julia said.

"This isn't exactly a table." Kane used his hands to jiggle the floppy plywood balanced on top of two sawhorses.

"Good point. That reminds me. Aunt Freckles invited her friend Cessy Walker to go furniture shopping with us in Boise tomorrow. Maybe I'll look for something more permanent for the dining room."

"First your aunt wants you to go to a bar with some overly muscled, overly confident, macho SEAL," he said before shoving a scoop of vegetable fried rice in his mouth. She didn't point out the similarity between Renault's build and his, although Kane definitely had the advantage when it came to making her legs wobbly. The man seemed determined to find fault with Luke's friend, so maybe he knew something Julia didn't. "And now she wants to subject you to the self-appointed Sugar Falls socialite and decorating queen?"

"What's wrong with Cessy Walker? Aunt Freckles

says she can be a bit on the snobbish side, but that she has impeccable taste and good style."

"Nothing's wrong with her, exactly. She's nice enough, I guess, and she means well. But when she and your aunt get together, their opinions become a force of nature, and you can be assured they'll steamroller right over you. A whole team of Navy SEALs like your dance partner Renault wouldn't be able to stop them."

"He's not *my* Renault. And why are you in such a bad mood all of a sudden? Surely you aren't intimidated by Cessy Walker?"

Kane rolled his eyes. "Oh please. I could handle that queen bee with one arm tied behind my back."

"Great. Then maybe you can go with us tomorrow?" Julia issued the challenge and then held her breath. The steamroller picture he'd just painted didn't seem all that appealing, and she wouldn't mind having him there for backup.

"No way. I handle Cessy Walker best by avoiding her."

"You can't tell me you're afraid of a little sixty-some-thing-year-old lady."

"Don't let *her* hear you refer to her as being in her sixties. And I'm not afraid of the woman. At least, not when it's just her. But last spring, she and your charming aunt got together and planned a bachelor auction to raise funds for the new firehouse the city's building just north of downtown."

"So? What's wrong with that?" To Julia, charities and fund-raisers were an integral part of giving back to the community, and it seemed normal that one of the wealthier socialites in town would lead the noble charge.

"What's *wrong* is that they didn't tell any of the so-called bachelors what they were doing and then tricked us all into getting up on stage when the auction started."

"Us?" Julia's lips twitched completely of their own accord. She'd bet the antisocial Kane Chatterson didn't like being thrown into the limelight one bit. But instead of feeling sorry for him, a small part of her wished she could've been a fly on the wall to see him forced out of his comfort zone like that. And to see how high the bidding got. "You mean, you were one of the bachelors?"

"Not for long, I wasn't," he said, wiping his mouth with a paper napkin. "I walked out the door before the opening bids even started. I got an earful about it the next day from my sister, along with half the women in town. They said I was being a spoilsport and uncharitable. I said I was being myself, and they got what they should've expected."

"What would it have hurt to go along with it?"

"What would it have hurt?" Kane took off his ball cap and ran his fingers through his short-cropped hair. "What if someone had actually bid on me?"

"Then you would have taken her on the date she paid for. You know—" she pointed her empty soda bottle at him, trying not to appear too giddy at the opening she'd been waiting for "—we talk about my dating life, but we never talk about yours."

He picked up their plates and carried them to the sink. "That's because there's nothing to talk about. Just like you, I'm not out looking for someone to share my life with. I'm much more comfortable being alone. Women, no offense, have a tendency to complicate things and push for more than I'm willing to give."

Wow. It was no more black-and-white than that. He was making it more than clear that he didn't return her feelings—whatever those were. Even she didn't know if this was just physical attraction or something more.

And did she sound that defensive when she'd made a similar argument? A kernel of pity wedged itself in her chest, and she wondered if he'd also been burned by a bad relationship. But at the same time, she envied him for knowing exactly what he didn't want and for not letting anyone tell him he had to be with a woman to be happy. Even if Julia lost out because of it.

"No offense taken," she said, putting her professional face back in place. "So I guess that means you won't be bringing a date to the Sugar and Shadow Shindig?"

"You guess right. I'm not about to let one of my family members talk me into online dating or going out to bars to meet people."

"Again, it's a dance club, not a bar. And it's because I promised my aunt that I'd give finding a date a solid effort. I'm not like you, Kane. I don't like to let people down or give something less than one hundred percent."

He was standing in front of the sink, making it difficult to see his expression. But there was no missing the sudden tensing of his shoulders. Without turning toward her, he asked, "Are you saying I don't give things one hundred percent?"

Uh-oh. Now she'd gone and insulted him. Maybe she should've taken a page out of his book and not even attempted to be friendly to him. Clearly she wasn't getting any better at making friends, no matter how much of an endeavor she made. She stood and crossed the room. "I didn't mean it like that. I just meant that you seem comfortable with the status quo. That's not a bad thing, Kane. I actually envy that about you. Here, let me help you with the dishes."

She put her hand on his arm, and instead of jerking it away, which would have been something she'd expect if he were angry with her, he kept it eerily still.

"They're already done," he said, his voice as tight as his motionless biceps. There went that weird tingling in her head, followed by the sensation making its way down her neck. She quickly pulled her hand from the warm flannel of his sleeve and mentally grasped at some sort of neutral topic to shift the conversation into something that would make sense to her, that wouldn't send her body into sensory overload.

"I've been noticing that you've done quite a few dishes around here since I've moved in."

"How do you know that I'm the one doing them?" He twisted a dish towel in his hands, but kept his body and attention planted firmly in place in front of her kitchen sink.

"Because I didn't think the plumber or any of the roofers you hired would clean up my messes after I leave."

"Sorry about that." He began to wipe down the perfectly spotless counters. "It's just that I don't like being surrounded by a lot of clutter or chaos when I'm working. It can be very distracting for me."

"Has anyone ever suggested that you might have some issues with your attention span?"

"Only every teacher since kindergarten."

"Have you been formally diagnosed with ADHD?"

He looked up to her ceiling, and the corners of his

taut mouth dropped ever so slightly. "Yeah. When I was seven years old and still not reading, my parents took me to the doctor. They prescribed some medicine, and it helped me focus a little better in school, but it made me sick to my stomach, and I had problems falling asleep."

"But there are so many doses and different types of medications that it takes a while to get it all dialed in correctly."

"If you say so." He went back to the counter, using the dish towel to scrub at an invisible mark. "Will you hand me that bottle of cleaner from under the sink?"

This time, though, she wouldn't let his penchant for changing topics sidetrack her. "Did you ever try anything else to help with your ADHD?"

When he saw she wasn't going to indulge him in his counter-cleaning smoke-and-mirrors routine, he let out a breath, turning to lean against the cabinet. "Mom and Dad tried it all. Behavioral coaches, tutors, breathing exercises, positive reinforcement. I could deal with it okay enough at home and when I played sports, but anything that required me to be still and concentrate was too difficult."

"That's very unfortunate," she said in her best medical professional voice. She doubted a man like Kane would appreciate her pity. "Have you done anything about it since you've reached adulthood? There are new medicines and resources now that could be quite beneficial."

"I deal with it by staying busy and keeping other people's houses clean so I can get my work done."

Julia didn't want to push him, not when he was so

close to revealing such an integral part of himself that surely had shaped his life and the way he saw the world. But she'd get her answers eventually. She always did. In the meantime, she would allow him to change the subject back to her.

"I should be better about that," she said, only somewhat remorseful. "I grew up with housekeepers and parents who wanted the house pristine enough to grace the pages of *Architectural Digest*. I never even lived in a dorm on campus. I moved straight from their house to the officers' quarters, where we would have random inspections. This is my first time living on my own, and I guess I went a little over-the-top with my rebellion against tidiness. Are you going to add housekeeping services to your invoice?"

"I should." He smirked, and Julia was relieved that the earlier tension was losing steam. Mr. Donut let out a yawn from underneath the pseudotable, drawing their attention.

"Just as long as you issue me a credit for all the pet-sitting I've been doing for you these past few weeks." She tried to form her lips into a matching smirk.

Kane shook his head. "What pet-sitting?"

"Your dog. The one you leave here every night?"

"Jules, I don't have a dog. And if I did, I certainly wouldn't bring him to work with me."

"Hello?" She pointed to the hound with the droopy ears. "What about Mr. Donut?"

"What about him?" Kane crossed his arms over his chest. "He's not *my* dog."

"Then whose is he?"

"I thought he was *yours*."

"I've never owned a pet in my life."

The animal in question let out a whiff of air, and Kane waved his hand in front of his nose. "It looks like you own one now."

"No. I only let him stay here because I thought he belonged to you and I was doing you a favor."

"What kind of person would leave their pet at someone else's house without asking?"

"I don't know. I thought it was odd myself, but you're kind of a mystery."

Kane lowered his chin. "I'm a mystery?"

"Not in a bad way. I meant you're interesting. You're not what I'm used to."

"What are you used to?"

"Obviously I'm not used to any of this." She waved her hand around the house. "Living on my own, finding a date for the hospital fund-raiser, dealing with my well-meaning aunt, who keeps buying me tacky makeup by the way, and her socialite friend." *Lusting after my sexy contractor.*

"Just tell them you're not bringing a plus-one."

"But Aunt Freckles will be disappointed."

"She'll get over it. You need to start standing up for yourself, Jules."

"Maybe."

"Not maybe. Yes. So that problem's solved. What else aren't you used to?"

"I'm not used to taking care of someone else's dog…"

"Mr. Donut isn't *mine*."

"Well, you named him," he chuckled. "And he certainly follows you around like he's yours."

"That's only because I feed him human food. He sleeps in *your* bed."

"You mean the bed with the comforter on it that you bought me?"

She'd meant to say the words jokingly, but suddenly the teasing glint in Kane's eye was gone. It'd been replaced with something she couldn't quite name, but whatever it was had his pupils dilated and made his voice grow quiet when he said, "Speaking of your bed, I don't think it's a good idea for me to be working here so late anymore."

Her heart dropped. "Why not?"

"Because every time you're around, I can't focus on what I'm working on."

He took a step closer, and she had to angle her chin to look up at him. "Do you think that has something to do with your ADHD?"

"No. I think it has something to do with your bow-shaped lip," he said before closing the distance between them.

His kiss took her by surprise. She gasped and he pushed against her open mouth with his tongue as she let him inside, allowing herself to grow accustomed to the feel of him before tentatively kissing him back.

When she responded, he groaned and slid his hands inside her cashmere cardigan, planting his palms on either side of her waist. Her breasts pressed against him and the rest of her followed suit, molding itself along each contour of his body.

She'd once had to administer a dose of epinephrine when one of her patients had suffered an allergic reaction. She imagined the shock of having the adrenaline hit one's bloodstream felt exactly like this. A burst of pure energy raced through her veins, and she had to have more. Gripping his shoulders to steady herself, Julia tilted her head to get a better angle, a better taste.

Kane must have maneuvered her against the kitchen counter, because she felt the cool granite against the back of her waist, where her shirt and sweater had lifted. He groaned again, and she heard a soft thud of something hitting the floor. But it was too difficult to think about the sounds around her when her heart was pounding so thoroughly in her ears.

Julia felt something brush against her shin, and Kane stumbled back. She looked down to see Mr. Donut wedging his thick body between them and using his nose to root around inside a to-go container that had fallen off the counter. The dog successfully slurped up the lo mein noodles, seemingly having no concern for what he'd just interrupted.

She exhaled, then immediately closed her lips to keep Kane from seeing how desperately she wanted him to return to them. But there was no need to concern herself with Kane even glancing in her direction. His eyes briefly passed over the dog before lifting to the ceiling and finally landing on the emptiness outside her kitchen window. "I, uh, better go," he said to the darkened glass behind her.

It took a second to find her voice. When she finally did, she was barely able to rasp out the word, "Okay."

He turned and walked toward the front door, giving no excuse and making no apology. And surprisingly, she didn't want to hear either. For a woman who prided herself on finding a logical reason for everything, Julia didn't think she could bear hearing his contrite explanation or facing the realization that when it came to men, she'd once again failed to see the signs and had made another mistake.

Kane would voluntarily have undergone surgery on his good shoulder if it would've meant tuning out Cessy and Freckles talking about the Sugar and Shadow Shindig at the nearby table inside the Cowgirl Up Café. Especially because he knew it was just a matter of time before they brought up Julia and who she'd be bringing to the dinner dance as her date.

Jealousy spread over his skin just as easily as Freckles's homemade huckleberry jam over the hot biscuit on his plate. And hearing the chorus for Rudolph the Red-Nosed Reindeer chirping out of the overhead speakers was making him feel anything but jolly.

Kane knew last night's kiss was a bad idea five seconds before he'd moved in for it. But as usual, his actions beat his brain to the punch. Then, instead of apologizing like a rational person would have done, he'd flown out of her house like a runner stealing second base when the catcher already had the ball. He drove home the same way he'd lived out his twenties—with reckless abandon. Nothing had been able to slow his racing pulse, his racing mind. Then, refusing to imagine how much more would've happened if the dog hadn't interrupted them, he'd gone straight to his garage and stayed up most of the night busting his knuckles installing a high-performance camshaft and valve train on the Bronco. He forced himself to do mental calculations of cubic inch displacement and to read long-winded owner's manuals rather than think of how perfectly Julia's compact body had felt against his. Or how hot her tongue had been when she'd met his demanding rhythm.

And now, twelve hours later, he couldn't forget a single sensation, a single spark.

Dr. Smarty-Pants had been warm and passionate in his arms, her hands curious, her mouth exploring his. Those lips of hers feeling as if they'd been made for kissing him...

Sleigh bells tinkled behind him, and he turned toward the doors, which were actually covered with wrapping paper and decorated with bows to resemble Christmas presents. Marcus Weston stepped inside, and most of the customers in the Cowgirl Up Café turned to look at the former point guard for the men's basketball team at a Division I college. The one scouts expected to be a first-round pro-draft pick, until he enlisted in the Marine Corps halfway through his senior year. Marcus still walked with a limp, not quite used to his new prosthetic foot.

"'Sup, Legend," the man said when he reached Kane's table.

Kane stood up to shake Marcus's hand. "Don't call me that. Not here."

"Because none of these local town folks know who you are?" Only the lower half of Marcus's body had been engulfed in flames after his fighter jet had crash-landed and exploded in a training exercise over a year ago—which meant the man's black eyebrows could still be easily raised with sarcasm. "Anyway, where's this wilderness guide we're supposed to meet?"

"Alex should be here soon." Kane took a gulp of his

decaf coffee, wishing he hadn't arranged to meet some of the guys from the PTSD group at Julia's aunt's restaurant before the mountain biking trip. But then, how was he supposed to know he'd go and ruin everything by pushing their relationship way past the friendship zone?

The bitter aftertaste of the brew burned its way down his throat, and he slid the complimentary basket of buttermilk biscuits away from him, deciding he wasn't in the mood to eat, after all. He couldn't even enjoy his breakfast anymore, knowing that the café owner talking to her friend a few tables down was only one phone call away from finding out that he'd put the moves on her niece last night.

"You're going riding with us, right?" Marcus took a seat opposite him in the booth and opened the laminated menu.

"Actually, I'm not operating on much sleep today and might skip out after Alex gets everyone set up on bikes." God, not only was his morning meal ruined, but also he couldn't even think of bicycles without thinking of Julia now.

"C'mon, man. Dr. Gregson says one of the best things for our recovery is to get outside in nature."

"And he's probably right." However, Kane didn't have PTSD, and no amount of nature would cure him from thinking about how Julia's narrow, firm body fit so well against his. In fact, he'd probably think about it so much, he'd end up riding his bike off a big rock. "But it's not like you actually need me today."

"I'm from Miami, Legend. We don't do mountains in Florida. In fact, most of the guys coming on the trip today are from the big cities and think they'll end up suffocating in this fresh air. The only reason they agreed to come is that they like hanging out with you." Marcus pointed a long brown finger at him. "Don't blow them off, man."

Kane cleared his throat, trying to dislodge the knot of guilt that had wedged itself inside him. "You said *they* like hanging out with me."

"Personally, I think you can be a real downer, and it probably wouldn't hurt for you to get laid." Marcus smiled, and Kane pulled a muscle in his neck trying to look over to see if Freckles or any of the other customers had heard what the man just said. "I only stay in the group so I can tell people that I bench-press more than Legend Chatterson."

"That's because I have a bad shoulder," Kane grumbled.

"At least you still have a shoulder." Marcus reached into the basket and pulled out a biscuit. "I'm missing a foot and still outran you last week on the track."

This was why his brother-in-law Drew had convinced Kane to come to his therapy group. He knew his patients needed motivation to regain their physical fitness. But Drew also knew that Kane needed to rise to a challenge once in a while.

"You're not going to beat me today," Kane shot back, recognizing the competitive glint in Marcus's determined eyes.

Just as Monica stopped by to take their order, the bells tinkled over the door again, and Kane gulped when he saw Julia walk into the café. Actually, she blasted in, still wearing her headphones, which obviously weren't completely plugged in, judging by the way the saxophone riffs spewed out of the tiny speaker on the iPod strapped to her arm. Kane had to give her credit for her improved taste in music, but a sudden jolt of energy crackled through his already restless muscles, and he had to force himself not to run out the door. Or worse, run straight toward her and kiss her all over again.

"Sug," Freckles hollered over the sound, making even Scooter Deets, who was hard of hearing, take notice of Julia's arrival. "Turn that dang thing off and come meet Cessy Walker."

He saw her take a step back, her eyes darting around at the audience now looking her way. Kane shot to his feet and made it to her side in under five steps. His hand reached for her arm to hold the iPod steady as he shoved the earplug cord home. Julia's arm didn't jerk back at his touch—which was a relief—but her green eyes rounded as the music screamed its way into her ears.

She pulled the headphones off and made several attempts to swipe at the device's screen before finally getting the thing powered down.

"Thanks," she said. He wasn't sure if the flush on her cheeks was from embarrassment at everyone watching them or if it was leftover from how he'd behaved last night.

Or maybe it was because she'd obviously been out running, as her workout clothes and sneakers suggested.

"No problem." He tried to smile, but it felt too forced. Too awkward. Like everyone in this restaurant would know what they'd done last night.

Well, what *he'd* done.

Before he could stop them, his eyes moved of their own accord to her lips, and he remembered exactly how active a participant Just Julia had been last night. He corrected himself again. What he'd started, but what *they'd* done. Both of them. Together.

"Sug." Freckles stood, a perfectly coiffed Cessy Walker trailing behind her, and walked toward them. Kane took a couple steps back, retreating to his table while he still had the chance. Unfortunately, it wasn't until after he sat down in the safe confines of his booth that he realized he was now trapped only a few feet away from them as Freckles stood there with her socialite best friend, making introductions and talking about formal wear and hairstyles and beauty shop appointments.

Some of the confidence had even drizzled out of Marcus's smirk when it didn't appear that the three women would be moving anytime soon, thereby allowing the new waitress to take their breakfast order.

With nothing to do but wait this out, Kane settled back in his seat and allowed his eyes to roam over Julia's body. She was wearing black spandex pants that hugged every inch of her toned legs. Her long-sleeved white T-shirt with NAVY stamped across her breasts wasn't quite long enough to cover her rear end, and Kane's right knee bounced in double-time thinking about how close his hands had been to those sweet curves last night.

"Julia, honey, we're putting you and your date at the head table," Cessy said, the word *date* hurled its way into Kane's inappropriate thoughts and snapped him back to the present.

"That's the thing I actually wanted to speak to you both about," Julia replied, but instead of looking at the two women, she was staring at Kane. Was she going to stand up to them? He nodded at her and gave his fist a small pump in solidarity. Julia took a breath and continued. "I've decided not to bring a date to the gala."

"I had a feeling it was going to come down to this." But instead of looking annoyed, Cessy's bright red lips were spread in a satisfied grin. Julia's eyes grew wide, her smile tentative as though she was surprised at how quickly she'd accomplished her goal.

But before Kane could lift his fist again in support of her victory, Cessy continued. "Your Aunt Freckles and I have been putting together a list of some single gentlemen that you can bring."

Kane braced his forearms on the table and Julia crossed her arms in front of her chest, her defensive stance actually drawing more attention to her chest. Or at least, Kane's attention. "Like who?"

"How about Carla Patrelli's brother?" Freckles asked. "He just moved here recently from Chicago."

"Isn't that the guy who got drunk at karaoke night at the VFW and asked every woman in the place to sing a Bee Gees duet with him?" Kane shook his head at Julia. "You're not going with him. He's obviously a player."

Freckles and Cessy whispered to each other before the waitress began reading off her notepad. "There's Jake Marconi's friend who has that nice animal shelter out off Highway 18?"

"Carmen arrested him last month for running a dog fighting ring," Kane responded. "Next."

"Jeffrey what's-his-name, that Navy corpsman who was one of Chief Cooper's groomsmen?"

"Ran into him at the hospital a few months ago and he got married to his longtime girlfriend."

"Alex Russell?" Cessy suggested a bit too smugly. Kane should have known it was only a matter of time before the women suggested one of Sugar Fall's most sought-after bachelors. "He's single and you certainly can't object to one of your own poker buddies."

"Julia's too pretty for Alex," Kane said way too quickly, causing Freckles to arch one of her unnatural-looking eyebrows. "I mean, Alex likes his women more…plain and not so feminine."

"Then how about Vic Russell, his dad?" Freckles asked, her dreamy expression matching Cessy's. "He looks like Hugh Jackman's older brother."

Kane scrunched his nose. "He's twice her age, Freckles."

"Then I guess that takes us out of the running," Scooter said to Jonesy, reminding Kane that everyone in the café was listening to this absurd conversation. Julia's mouth opened and closed as if she were looking for the opportunity and the right words to tell them all to butt out of her life. Yet her eyes pleaded with him to make this fiasco go away and he wanted to say, *See! I told you this is what they do when they get together. Steam. Roller.*

She'd laughed him off last night, but she certainly wasn't laughing now. He needed to do something to stop this runaway train from going completely off the rails. But before he could, the man across the table spoke up.

"I'll go with the hot doc." Marcus's smile widened even more than it had when they'd gone to the batting cages in Boise a couple of weeks ago and Kane had to remind the man that he couldn't be expected to hit *all* twelve of the balls because he used to be a pitcher, not a designated hitter.

"Hot doc?" Kane whipped his head back to the former basketball player. "Who calls her that?"

"Everyone in the physical rehab wing at the hospital," Marcus said as Freckles and Cessy began nodding in earnest and whipped out their seating chart. Then Marcus leaned across the table and put his hand up to his mouth before whispering, "Have you ever seen her in workout clothes?"

A green, jealous haze closed in around Kane and before he could ask Julia her opinion or stop the words from shooting out of his mouth, he all but shouted, "That's it. I'm going to take her my damn self."

Chapter 11

For a few days, Kane tried everything he could imagine to reconcile his desire to avoid both public events and complications with his building excitement that he was going to be taking Julia on an actual date. Of course, after he'd shot off his mouth in the Cowgirl Up Café that morning, he'd stormed out of the restaurant before the "hot doc" or her overprotective aunt could object— with Marcus Weston's laughter still ringing in his ears. Then he'd waited for a phone call, a text, a note taped to her front door or tied to Mr. Donut's new collar telling him that there was no way in hell she would be willing to attend the hospital gala with him. But no such message ever came, and he found his spirits lift each day that he'd successfully avoided her potential rejection.

In fact, he avoided her altogether, too afraid of crushing this unfamiliar feeling of hopefulness picking up speed in his chest. He waited until she left for work before going to her house. Then he'd purposely do minor repairs around the house, not wanting to become too engulfed in a project that would cause him to lose track of time so he could leave well before he anticipated her return.

Then, the following Tuesday, Freckles had sent him a text asking if they wanted to ride in the rented limo with her and Cessy. He fired off a reply saying that he would be driving them himself.

On Wednesday, when Kylie had left him a voice mail asking if he needed her to take his tux to the dry cleaner, he casually texted back that she could do whatever she wanted, but was secretly pleased to come home the following day to see it freshly pressed and hanging on his closet door.

On Friday, he'd accidentally caught a glimpse of a brand-new garment bag spread out on Julia's bed, and he'd slammed the door closed, refusing to acknowledge the way his palms itched to unzip the thing and take a peek at what Julia would be wearing to the gala.

For six days, they hadn't talked about the pending date, and they especially hadn't talked about their kiss. Actually, they hadn't talked at all. Kane had thought it was better this way, but now that he was parked in front of her house on Saturday evening, he had to wonder if not addressing the situation had only allowed his expectations to grow out of control.

He sat in his late-model Ford F-250, his more practical and comfortable vehicle, and pulled the gold watch out of his tuxedo pocket, more to fiddle with the latch than to check the time. He was still ten minutes early and couldn't very well sit in his idling truck all evening. And if he was a normal red-blooded male, he would've also decided that it was his lucky night.

But this wasn't luck. It was torture, pure and simple. He grabbed his tuxedo jacket off the front seat and slipped it on as he got out of his truck and walked up the front path to her porch. He inhaled the woodsy pine scent of the fresh wreath she'd bought—and he'd hung on her door—as he tried to regulate his breathing. He used the antique brass knocker, making a mental note to repair the doorbell, then heard a bark just before the front door opened to reveal a woman silhouetted by the golden chandelier light inside.

His breath caught at the wavy layers of blond hair framing her face and he cursed himself for not taking a peek inside that garment bag and preparing himself for how sexy she'd look tonight. But he had a feeling nothing could have prepared him for how his body would react to seeing her in that dress.

It wasn't gray, nor was it silver. It was satiny and smooth and clung to her curves. The color reminded him of his Grandpa Chatterson's antique revolver—the one Kane had never been allowed to touch. Her body was nearly as dangerous and his compulsion to break the rules for a chance to hold her was twice as strong.

Snow was starting to fall, yet he felt like he was burning up.

"Kane?" she asked, and he almost looked down at himself to make sure it really was him.

"Didn't recognize me in a tuxedo?" He tried to joke, but his voice was too raspy. His senses were too overwhelmed. This was really happening.

"Actually, I didn't recognize you in that truck. You didn't have to borrow someone's car," she said. "We could've taken mine."

"I didn't borrow it. I own it."

"Oh," was all she said.

It wasn't until he'd bent down to pet Mr. Donut that Kane realized Julia was shifting from one strappy sandal to the other. He supposed she could be uncomfortable in such high heels, but a small part of him hoped she was just as nervous about the evening ahead as he was. Not that he wanted her to be anxious, but he'd feel a lot more secure if they were on common ground.

"Are you ready?" He stood, trying to wipe some of the hound's fur off his jacket sleeves.

"As ready as I'll ever be." She grabbed a small silver clutch and a scrap of fabric before stepping out onto the porch.

"Do you have a jacket?" Kane looked at her bare shoulders, one shade darker than the snow landing on her front yard.

"I've got a wrap. Besides, after spending the last thirty minutes trying to style my hair and squeeze into this dress, I'm way too hot even to think about a coat right now." That made two of them. But his temperature had nothing to do with getting dressed. "Freckles has been dead set on this makeover since I moved here. She made me promise not to wear my hair in a ponytail tonight, and I should've had it done professionally, but I was called in for an emergency surgery this morning and didn't get home in time to do much with it."

"I like it down," Kane said, reaching out to stroke

one of the silky, wavy strands that framed her face. She looked up into his eyes and his head instinctively tilted toward hers, before Mr. Donut used his increasing bulk to nose his way between them.

The interruption caused Julia to take a step back and say, "I, uh, guess we'd better get going."

"Right." Kane shot the dog a reprimanding look, making a silent vow to never bring the interfering pooch another baked good, then used his own set of keys to lock her front door. He'd been locking this same door nearly every day for weeks, but never had it been more intimate than now, when she was standing beside him in a dress made for sin.

She pointed out the twinkling holiday lights decorating the storefronts along Snowflake Boulevard, but it took fifteen minutes to drive to the trendy Snow Creek Lodge, and during that time, he had to remind himself a dozen times to keep his hands off Julia. When they pulled up to the valet, he almost reminded the parking attendant of the same thing. Instead, he just gave the young guy a look that he hoped said, *Hands off, buddy. She's mine.*

As Kane walked around the truck, a strong breeze kicked up, and he saw her shiver. "Maybe I should've brought more than a skimpy wrap after all."

"Here." He wrapped his arm around her waist and pulled her in closer to his side, telling himself she felt too good to not belong there. And if he maybe shot the valet an eat-your-heart-out smirk, then so be it. "It'll be warmer when we get inside."

They walked into the lobby, and despite the fact that

a ten-foot stone fireplace with a blazing fire took up the center of the room, Kane kept his arm around Julia. Heads turned in their direction as they made their way to the ballroom, and Kane experienced a flashback to when he used to attend major functions like this on a regular basis. He didn't hate it back then as much as he did now, but he'd never really loved the attention. He'd gone along with it for the team.

"All we have to do is get through the next couple of hours," he mumbled, hoping this shindig had a well-stocked bar.

"Are you talking to me or to yourself?" Julia asked, sticking to his side like pine tar on a batting glove.

"Both."

The big band orchestra was in full swing when they walked into the ballroom. Freckles was the first to rush over and greet them, and through the fabric of Julia's dress, Kane felt some of the tension leave her body. But only some.

Half the people he knew from living in Sugar Falls for the past year. The other half, Julia said she recognized from the hospital. A waiter handed them glasses of champagne, but Kane slipped the guy a twenty-dollar bill and asked him to bring a beer instead.

"You doing okay?" he asked, leaning in close enough to be heard over the music.

"I think so." Her smile seemed a bit forced. "Just stay close by."

With pleasure, he thought. By the time they made it to their table, Kane was positive his hand had left a permanent imprint on Julia's waist.

* * *

"You know what your dining room needs?" Freckles asked her niece as the waiter removed Kane's salad plate. "A pool table."

Everyone at their table had been giving Julia unsolicited opinions about her home remodel and decor while Kane had sat back and enjoyed the music. Of course, it helped that his sister and brother-in-law, as well as Luke and Carmen, were seated with them, providing him with an island of friends in this sea of social sharks.

It also helped that he was already on his second beer. All they had to do was get through the rest of dinner.

Cessy Walker returned to their table with Police Chief Matthew Cooper and Dr. Garrett McCormick, who'd both delivered speeches on the great work Shadowview Hospital did for active military and veterans. Their wives, Maxine Cooper and Mia McCormick, came back from the ladies' room at the exact moment Cessy asked what she'd missed.

"I am not getting a pool table," Julia said, making Kane proud she was finally doing a better job of sticking up for herself and cementing the battle lines. "Besides, where would I put that antique armoire?"

"But men love pool tables," Freckles continued. "You can get one of those antler chandeliers to hang over it and maybe put up some classy-but-discreet neon beer signs."

"Is there such a thing as a classy-but-discreet beer sign?" Cessy challenged her.

"Another beer would be a blessing right about now," Kane mumbled, then jerked in surprise when Julia nudged him with her elbow. He chuckled, laying his arm along the back of her chair. He probably needed to get some real food in him to absorb the pale ale. He wasn't intoxicated or anything, but his fingers found the alcohol to be a convenient excuse for toying with the ends of Julia's loose hair as she turned to talk to Kylie about linen closets.

Freckles gave his hand a pointed look and then continued her campaign. "Are you saying you wouldn't want a pool table, Kane?"

"Not in the dining room, no."

"Which room would you put it in?" Luke Gregson asked.

"What about the bedroom?" Julia asked, and Kane's fingers froze.

"I dated a guy with a pool table in his bedroom once," Freckles said, then shrugged. "You could probably make it work if you skip the antlers and go for some tasteful artwork. Something painted on velvet, perhaps, to coordinate with the felt top."

"Sorry, Aunt Freckles. Are you still talking about the pool table? I thought we'd moved on to the armoire." Julia played with the stem of her champagne flute.

He remembered those same hands two weeks ago and how they'd felt against his waist when she'd been in his arms. Stroking his back, urging him closer. He couldn't remember the last time he'd held a woman so intimately.

Of course, he'd held plenty of women before, most of them unclothed, even. But with Julia it had been different. It didn't take a clinical psychologist like Drew to explain that Kane was simply wanting something he couldn't have.

If Mr. Donut hadn't interrupted them, they would've ended up in her bedroom for sure.

And if she didn't stop being so damn sexy and Kane didn't stop reliving that first kiss, they might still end up there.

Julia had once thought the guy looked hot in flannel, but nobody looked better than Kane Chatterson in a tuxedo. So good, in fact, even Chief Wilcox had given her a high five in the ladies' room earlier after asking Julia where she'd been hiding him. For the first time in twenty-nine years, she finally felt as though she could actually fit in somewhere.

Well, somewhere besides Kane's arms. His embrace had been the perfect fit. It had been almost two weeks since that passionate kiss in her kitchen and she could still feel the muscles in his waist tightening as her hands explored his torso. As his tongue explored her mouth.

When she'd run into him that morning in the Cowgirl Up Café, she'd been waiting for him to revert back to his brooding, moody personality so she could admit her failure to Freckles, then go home to her empty half-finished home and privately berate herself for falling for the wrong man. Again.

But his moodiness hadn't been directed at her, and she found herself sputtering in disbelief as he shot down one suggested date after another before declaring to the entire restaurant that he was going to take her to the gala.

After that, she threw herself into work and, as she checked her unreliable phone for a message from him calling the whole thing off, she told herself that no news was good news. She'd been so grateful to hear his knock on her door tonight, Julia had almost reenacted that reckless kiss again right there on her front porch. She made a mental note to bring home a doggie bag for Mr. Donut to reward him for his timely interruption.

The waiter had just removed their dinner plates when Kane's cell phone vibrated. He looked at the screen before frowning and mumbling something about people never leaving him alone. When the band launched into the first dance of the night, most of the couples at their table headed out to the parquet floor.

Except for when he'd been cutting into his prime rib, he'd spent most of the evening with his hands somewhere on her body. First on her waist, then in her hair and now on her shoulders. It felt as though someone had connected Julia to a morphine drip the moment she'd walked into the Snow Creek Lodge and she was floating through the evening on a dreamlike cloud of bliss.

Kane leaned closer. "I probably should have told you that I don't dance," he said. "Was that one of the requirements on your man list?"

She cleared her throat, then reached for her glass of ice water, thinking it would be more effective for her to throw it on her blushing face than just drink it. Why did he have to bring up that ridiculous subject again?

"No, but looking good in a tux wasn't on the list, either, and you aced it with that one." She clapped her hand over her mouth, mortified she'd let the thought slip out.

"Is that a fact?" His grin was all too pleased, and she had to straighten up in her chair to keep from hiding under the table. "Are you going to tell me what else is on it?"

She shrugged, the gesture not coming off as casual as she'd intended. "It doesn't matter now. I no longer need to look for any more dates."

Instead of retaining their teasing glint, his eyes stared her down, and *her* knee was now the one bouncing conspicuously under the table. The intensity of his gaze cut through her insides like a scalpel, and Julia had the sensation that she was completely exposed and raw.

Luckily his cell phone rang again, distracting him enough that he didn't see her little shudder. "Do you want to take that call?" Julia asked when he looked at the display screen.

"Hell, no, I don't want to take it," Kane said tightly. "But if I don't, he'll just keep calling me."

Cessy looked over Kane's shoulder at the screen, and Julia's eyes widened at the woman's invasion of his privacy. Well, Julia's eyes also widened at the fact that she'd forgotten they weren't completely alone at the table. But then Cessy patted Kane's arm in sympathy and said, "You might want to go outside and call him back."

"Will you excuse me?" he asked, and at her nod, he stood and left the table.

Julia's upbringing demanded that she not be so impolite as to ask Cessy who had called, but her curiosity demanded that she find out why he was so upset over it.

"Do you think Kane will be long?" Julia asked, fishing for information.

"It depends on why Charlie's calling," Cessy responded. Who was Charlie? Another client?

"He'd better not be giving our boy any grief." Freckles chimed in as she pulled off her high heels and replaced them with pink no-skid socks. "That stubborn man hates it when someone tries to force his hand."

Cessy nodded and pulled a pair of ballet-style slippers out of her beaded clutch. "He's too soft-hearted for his own good and needs someone to take care of him."

"Kane?" Julia asked. "You think Kane is too soft-hearted?"

Both women looked up from switching out their footwear. "Of course, Sug. Who else would we be talking about?"

"He doesn't seem very soft to me. Or like he needs anyone to protect him." Julia quickly peeked toward the entrance to ensure he wasn't coming this way. "In fact, last week he told me about how he managed to bail out of your bachelor auction without any assistance at all."

"Nah, we knew he wouldn't be willing to participate, anyway." Freckles used her reflection in her dinner knife to check her lipstick. "Kane Chatterson isn't exactly dating material."

"He's not?" Could've fooled Julia with the solicitous way he'd been acting tonight. But she'd been easily fooled before, and she wanted to get more information from them without giving the ladies any insight into her own feelings. "I'm sure plenty of women would have loved to go out on a date with him."

"Of course they would. But that doesn't mean they'd get their money's worth if any of them made a bid." Cessy waved at a group of elderly gentlemen.

Her aunt slightly lifted her sock-covered feet and gave them a wiggle. Oh goodness. These two ladies seemed as if they were ready to storm the dance floor. But Julia was determined to get answers before someone asked her sources of information for the next foxtrot. "So why trick Kane into participating?"

"We didn't trick him into *participating*." Freckles sighed as if she was explaining Men 101. "We tricked him into blasting off that stage with enough white-hot anger to send a rocket ship into space."

Julia didn't point out the inaccuracies in her aunt's theory about emotions propelling interplanetary probes. She was too busy attempting to connect the cause and effect of these ladies' thought processes. "I'm afraid I don't see the logic in getting him mad for no reason."

"Here's how it works." Cessy placed a heavily jeweled hand on the linen tablecloth as if she were a battle commander outlining an attack route on a map. "Kane's the impulsive type that jumps to conclusions first, then asks questions later. He's also the type that feels especially guilty when he lets people down. Since guilt equals generous donation, we all got what we wanted."

"So, you're saying you staged the whole thing to get a small donation from him? Why didn't you just ask him for one?"

"Where's the fun in that?" Cessy's red-painted unnaturally plump lips were turned up in the same smug grin as when Kane had impulsively told them all he was going to be her date for the gala. The hairs along the nape of Julia's neck bristled, but the older socialite continued. "Besides, who said his donation was small? The new Sugar Falls Fire Department is going to have a steam room, a sauna and a state-of-the-art dispatch center thanks to us and Mr. Chatterson's charitable spirit."

How could he possibly have managed that? Perhaps he wasn't as poor as she'd initially thought. Nor was the Sugar Falls Fire Department, if its sponsors were installing saunas in the building. Before she could think about this new revelation further, the man in question strode back into the ballroom.

"So, what did Charlie want?" Freckles asked him once the server dropped off another round of drinks.

Kane looked at Julia, then at the guests seated near their table. "Nothing that needs to be talked about here."

She was surprised that her normally nosy aunt and Cessy Walker, who made no secret of their vast wealth of town gossip, didn't follow up with more questions. Julia couldn't help but feel this was more than some social nuance she couldn't understand. But were they purposely keeping something from her?

Jonesy and Scooter Deets, the older cowboys Julia recognized from the café, were making their way over to the table when, out of nowhere, a boy who couldn't have been more than eighteen walked by their table and blinded them with the flash of his camera phone before scurrying toward the lobby.

"Damn," Kane said, then ran his fingers through hair that had started off the evening perfectly combed. He turned away from the table and took a few steps before pausing and returning to Julia's side. "You ready to get out of here?"

It was almost as though he was going to leave without her and then remembered he needed to give her a ride home. Something was wrong, and her stomach twisted in both disappointment and confusion. They'd been having such a great night up until now, and suddenly Kane was on edge. Her voice wobbled slightly when she said, "I guess so."

Kane grabbed her hand, and she tried to keep up with his long-legged strides as he steered them between tables and guests making their way to the dance floor. They passed Chief Wilcox so quickly, Julia was forced to turn back and give her a little wave goodbye. She saw Cessy in the center of the room, talking to Chief Cooper and pointing their way, but before she could ask Kane to slow down, she stumbled behind him.

He must have felt her slip, because he stopped only long enough to ask her if she was okay.

"Yes, but the skirt of my dress is too tight for me to take big steps, so I can't really keep up with you."

She couldn't be positive over the sound of the music, but she was pretty sure he'd made a growling sound in his throat before hauling her up against him again. By the time they made it to the resort's lobby, he had slowed his pace, but his face was set in stone-cold fury.

Julia's father had had a temper, and even though she wasn't good at reading men, she knew when to avoid someone angry. But she wasn't afraid of Kane. Despite the confusion twisting through her rib cage, she knew he wasn't angry with her, and she had a feeling that he shouldn't be alone right now.

She realized she'd left her wrap back at the table the moment they walked outside and the frigid mountain air hit her bare arms. Yet before they even made it to the valet stand, Kane had shrugged out of his tuxedo jacket and settled it over her shoulders.

Instead of waiting for the truck to be brought around,

Kane grabbed his keys from the parking attendant and held Julia tightly against him as they crunched their way across the freshly fallen snow on the parking lot. Actually, they walked so far, they were no longer in the main parking lot, but in an empty area behind the service entrance.

Thanks to Julia's open-toed shoes, her feet were damp and almost numb by the time Kane opened the passenger-side door for her. She waited for him to start the engine before she asked, "Do you want to talk about what happened in there?"

Kane's head was resting against the leather headrest, his eyes staring out the windshield as his wipers cleared off crescent shapes in the snow. "No."

"Do you want to be left alone?" It would be embarrassing and awkward for Julia to go back inside the lodge to find another ride, but she understood his need for solitude even when she didn't understand why he was upset.

"Yes, I want to be *left* alone, but I don't want to *be* alone. If that makes any sense."

"It makes perfect sense." Actually, none of this made any sense to Julia, but her heart was aching for whatever had caused the man this much pain. Since she didn't know how to fix it, the least she could do for him was stay by his side. What did normal people do in times like this? "Do you want to go somewhere and get a drink?"

"The last thing I need right now is a drink," Kane said.

"What do you need? I want to—" But before she could get the words out, his mouth silenced her.

* * *

Kane was lost. Right here in the annex parking lot behind the Snow Creek Lodge, he was absolutely lost. The second Julia had opened her lips to him, he'd been a complete goner. He curved his hand around her neck, pulling her face closer to his. She'd asked him what he needed and this was it.

He needed her. He needed to forget that he was once Legend Chatterson, and he needed to forget that Charlie, his agent, was still bugging him with assistant pitching coach offers and an insistence that he return to baseball. He needed to forget that he couldn't hide from his former life forever.

Slowly he began to forget about all of that, because being with Julia was so mind-consuming he could think of nothing but touching her. He could deal with the consequences later, the rejection when she realized that he was some old washed-up has-been, completely out of her league. But right now, her hands were caressing his face, sliding down his neck and into his collar, and he thought that just maybe, for tonight, he could be with someone who didn't know about his old life and all the mistakes he'd made.

Sure, it was unfair not to disclose his inadequacies to Julia before he took her right here in the front seat of his truck. But it was also unfair the way she'd slipped his tuxedo jacket off her shoulders and was pressing her satin-covered breasts against his white dress shirt as she used her tongue to claim his mouth.

"Jules," he said, pulling back.

"Don't apologize."

"I'm not. I was going to say that if we don't go some-where else, I'm going to end up taking you right here."

"In your truck?"

"Yes. In my truck. In the parking lot. With that dress pushed up around your waist."

She was still plastered against him, the center arm-rest between their hips the only thing keeping him from making good on the threat he'd meant to shock her back into her senses.

But instead of looking shocked, she simply said, "Technically, we aren't in the parking lot. And I've never had sex in a vehicle. Yet."

She rose up to her knees and pressed in closer to him, her lips resuming their quick work of making him lose what was left of his mind.

How long had she wondered about the feel of his hair? Would the other parts of his body—the ones she hadn't been able to stop thinking about since that night she'd found him painting her bathroom without his shirt—feel this good?

She had to find out. Right now.

Julia slid her fingers down under the collar of his white dress shirt, making her way through the buttons, only to be dismayed by the soft fabric of his white T-shirt underneath.

If only she had a pair of surgical shears to speed up the process. Perhaps in her eagerness, though, she'd come on too strong, because he moved his hands up to cradle her face, but pulled just far enough back to look at her. The only light was from the dim glow of the dashboard, yet she saw that Kane had a question in his eyes. She prayed he wasn't going to ask her if she'd lost all common sense. Clearly the answer to that was a resounding yes.

"Jules?"

"I love it when you call me that," she said, hoping he wasn't going to reject her for throwing herself at him.

He tilted his head to the side, his slightly swollen mouth grinning vaguely. "Why's that?"

"It doesn't sound so formal. I don't want to be formal with you anymore, Kane." She pushed forward to meet his lips, but after only seconds, he broke the kiss again.

"I don't want to be formal with you, either, Jules."

Her heart skipped a beat as a warm shiver spread through her. He groaned before shoving the center armrest up and pulling her onto his lap. If she'd thought his kisses had aroused her before, that was nothing compared to what his hands were doing to her. She felt the calluses on his work-roughened palms slip beneath the thin straps of her dress and gave a silent thanks that she'd forgone a bra since she didn't own a strapless one.

When his hands pulled her breasts free of the satin material, Julia couldn't remember what she was even giving thanks for. The coarseness of his fingertips couldn't mask the tenderness of his strokes as he brought her nipples to rock-hard peaks.

His tongue followed a similar pattern within the confines of her mouth, and she was forced to pull the hem of her dress up to her thighs so she could straddle him. His fingers moved away, and she gave a slight whimper at his withdrawal and the way the cool air lingered in his place. Then she realized he'd only adjusted his touch so that he could slide the rest of her dress over her waist and then her head.

She was wearing nothing but lace panties and a blush, and though she'd had sex only a handful of times with the college professor she'd briefly dated, she didn't want Kane to think she was a slow learner.

She reached for the hem of his T-shirt and lifted it off him, briefly breaking their joined lips. Kane paused and Julia, afraid he might get distracted or—worse— change his mind, grabbed his shoulders and pulled him toward her. Even if she hadn't been eager to feel his bare skin against hers, she needed to prove that she could be somewhat competent at this despite her limited experience.

It certainly felt more natural than riding a bike.

He lifted her hips slightly and settled her firmly onto his lap. She gasped at the sensation of the ridge inside his tuxedo pants pressed against her most intimate parts, and she wished she could wrap her legs around him, drawing him in closer.

"Are you sure?" he asked, and she wanted to giggle and scream in frustration at the same time. She was almost nude, nearly exposed and completely loving this reversal of her usual inhibitions. She'd never been more unsure of anything in her life. But she'd also never been as alive as she was now. She was an academic intellectual—a conventional person who did things by the book. Julia liked only things that made sense. And to her quivering body, Kane Chatterson made perfect sense. Besides, Julia Fitzgerald didn't quit. She wasn't stopping now.

"Please," she whispered.

He effortlessly lifted her and set her on the passenger seat facing him. Placing his fingers in the waistband of her panties, he worked the scrap of lace over her hips and down her legs. Then he ran his hand toward her left knee, pushed it up, leaned forward and kissed the sensitive flesh right above it. She would have clamped her thighs together if he hadn't been between them, his hands firmly on her waist and holding her in place. She was about to ask him what he was doing, but then his tongue touched the center of her heat. Julia threw back her head, her eyes closed in raw pleasure.

She'd never had sex like *this* before. It was one thing to read about this kind of thing in books, but no written definition could ever tell her how intoxicating it would be to feel the stubble from Kane Chatterson's strongly chiseled jaw rubbing against her most sensitive flesh. This was unlike any classroom she'd ever been in, and instead of taking notes, she was rocking her hips toward him. Silently begging for more.

"Not yet," Kane said, pulling his wallet out of his back pocket. She heard the rustling of plastic packaging. Then Kane shoved off his pants, and Julia barely had time to register how perfectly shaped his body was before he moved his hands under her hips and slid inside her depths.

"Kane," she said after only the third thrust. "I'm going to… I can't wait…"

He withdrew, but only partially. "Do you want me to slow down?"

"No. Yes. I don't know. I just want it to stay perfect like this."

"Aw, honey, you're perfect at everything you do."

"But it feels so good. I don't want it to be over yet."

"Don't worry." He smiled, then pushed himself in deeper, causing her to moan. "It doesn't ever have to be over."

He caught her next gasp with his mouth. When he thrust inside her again, she cried out, anchoring herself to him as the waves of pleasure crashed over her body.

"I thought you said it didn't have to be over?" Julia raised an eyebrow at Kane as he balanced himself between her trembling legs, trying to recover his breath. Despite the fact that he was usually so impatient and antsy, he'd never been one to rush sex. Yet the second he felt her release, he'd lost all control and hadn't been able to stop his own.

"I meant that we could keep going." His raspy voice sounded as though he'd made a hundred sprints around the bases. "Again. Later. After I recover a little."

"But it's never felt like that for me before."

"It's like warming up in the bull pen," he explained, pushing several blond strands away from her flushed face. Normally he liked her cute, swinging ponytail, but after seeing all the loose hair surrounding her face when she was calling out his name, he liked it down so much more. "You have to throw a few pitches to loosen you up and get the nerves out so that when you take the mound, you're ready to bring the heat."

"Is that a baseball reference?"

"Yes?" He tucked his chin and wrinkled his brow, hoping she wasn't offended. Did she think it was odd that he'd just compared sex to pitching? "I couldn't think of a more passionate sport to relate it to."

"I've never played many sports, but if what we did was just practice, I doubt I can handle a real game."

He let out his breath, along with a small chuckle. "Trust me, Captain Fitzgerald, you're more than ready for the big leagues."

"I don't know about that," she said, then blushed when she couldn't reach the discarded panties on the driver's-side floorboard. He sat up and handed them to her, along with her dress.

"So, what do we do now?" she asked, not attempting to hide the fact that she was blatantly checking him out while he wiggled his way back into his slacks. The woman was too honest and too curious for her own good.

What he wanted to say was that now they did the whole thing all over again. But slower this time. Too bad he was afraid to make the suggestion and have her laugh in his face. "Why are you asking me?"

She looked at the torn wrapper on the floor after pulling the satin over her head. "I was under the impression you were a bit more experienced in this kind of thing."

All it would take was one glance at the expiration date on that same wrapper to see that he'd been carrying the condom around for so long out of habit, he was just as out of experience as she was. They were lucky the stupid thing hadn't ripped. Although he could imagine worse things than having a baby with Dr. Smarty-Pants.

Whoa. He rubbed at his entire jawline. His brain was really getting ahead of itself with dangerous thoughts like that. He had no business thinking about any sort of future with her.

If he even wanted one. Oh God, he did. Maybe it was just the postcoital hormones talking, but he'd had sex with her only once and already he found himself thinking about a future with her. Yet the whole idea was impossible. Sooner or later, she'd figure it on her own, and all of this would come crashing down on him.

"What do *you* want to do now?" There, he'd put the ball back in her court. She bit her lip. "I've always been taught that practice makes perfect."

Something stirred in his belly, and it wasn't a lack of food. Was this what hope felt like?

"Given your opinions on failure, I bet you can't stand not being perfect at something." The corners of her mouth turned up, the same way they had when she'd been challenged to learn how to ride the tandem bike.

"I certainly like to get things right."

"Well, if you keep looking at me like that, you'll end up with a lot more practice than you've bargained for."

She traced her fingers along the scar on his shoulder, and he had to close his eyes briefly to remind himself not to let his impulses get ahead of things again. Maybe she knew exactly who he was, after all. And exactly what she was getting herself into.

"I wouldn't mind that," she said simply.

"Here?" He sounded like an overeager batboy sitting in the dugout for the first time.

"Maybe not *here*, exactly." She blushed again.

"We could go back to your place, but then we risk your neighbors seeing me parked in front of your house all night."

"*All* night?" Instead of seeing doubt, he recognized the dare in her eyes.

"Only if you want to become an expert at it."

"Do *you* have any neighbors you're worried about seeing us?" she asked.

"Not a single one," he responded. "But we might need to make a stop at Duncan's Market."

"Were you expecting to work up an appetite?" She grinned.

Kane was starting to like this confident and sassy side of Julia. It also helped ease his guilt to think that if she could make jokes, she wasn't having second thoughts. Yet. "Actually, I was going to buy more protection. That one from my wallet was a leftover from… Well, let's just say I haven't needed to stock up on those kinds of things in a long time."

"Oh." She blushed a little.

"If not, we can stop in at the Gas 'N' Mart. I'm sure Mrs. Marconi would love the firsthand gossip."

He was obviously teasing and expected her to voice an objection to anyone in Sugar Falls finding out they were involved romantically. Kane himself was uncertain how he felt about people knowing he and Julia Fitzgerald were involved as more than a contractor and a client. On the one hand, he now preferred living his life under the radar and detested the idea of anyone knowing his personal business. On the other hand, having someone as smart and successful as Julia by his side made him want to show off to the world. *See, I haven't made a total mess of my life.*

But Julia didn't respond, and at this hour, the market was probably closed anyway. He pulled the antique watch out of his pocket and clicked it open to look at the time. It was then that he realized he hadn't looked at the thing since he'd picked Julia up. Even with Charlie calling him and the kid taking the picture, he hadn't been overly antsy tonight.

Kane turned on the satellite radio, and B. B. King crooned through his speakers about being home for Christmas. They were both quiet as he drove through town, the light dusting of recent snow making the holiday decorations stand out. He stopped by the minimart at the gas station to pick up additional provisions—and a box of Raisinets for her—and instead of avoiding eye contact with the other late-night customers or the ducking from the security cameras, Kane's chest puffed out with satisfaction.

When they got to his house, an old remodeled barn nestled near Sprinkle Creek, he led her to the upstairs loft, which he'd converted into a master bedroom and bath equipped with more modern amenities than the new Sugar Falls Fire Department facility he'd been tricked into financing. Then, in an effort to be a good host, he went along very willingly when she pulled him into the shower with her. They made love against the white marble tile, and then again in his king-size bed.

The following morning, the sun's pinkish light spilled into his wall of steel-framed windows, giving Julia's pale skin a glow as she rose above him in a steady rhythm, bringing him to the edge of ecstasy and then sending him over.

When she collapsed beside him on the bed, he stroked his hand from her shoulder to her hip, outlining the contours of her curves. He kissed her and said, "I finally feel as if I'm on an even playing field with you."

"What do you mean?" She grinned.

"I'm not like you, Jules." He brought his fingers to her hair and tapped lightly at her temple. "I don't have any of this. You're so smart and so successful, and I'm neither of those things."

"How can you say you're not smart?" She sat up, taking the pale blue sheet with her. "You're brilliant when it comes to measurements and calculating materials and envisioning what a finished home should look like."

"Brilliant? Hardly. I barely graduated high school with a C-minus average."

"You have ADHD, not a low IQ."

He shook his head. "It might as well be the same thing."

"No, Kane. It's actually the opposite. I wish I could give you a baseball analogy because I know how much you relate to those, but I'm not familiar with that world. Yet. So I'll give you a driving one instead." He didn't want to point out that she didn't have much more experience with driving, either. "When you have ADHD, your brain is like a race car. A high-performance race car. It works so much faster and more powerfully than most normal brains. The problem, though, is that your race car brain has brakes made for Aiden and Caden's tandem bicycle. So when it's time to slow down or to make a turn, your brakes aren't sufficient, and you spin off the road. The ability to perform is there. You simply have to address the mechanics of it all to get it to run smoothly. Does that make sense?"

"I think so." He looked up at his motionless industrial-size ceiling fan. Suddenly his life felt as calm and as still as the blades on that fan. He had to find his own brakes, his own light switch to turn his spinning engine on and off. "Nobody's ever explained it to me that way."

"Good. Because I know what I'm talking about. I'm an expert, remember?" Julia leaned over to kiss him, but before he could pull her on top of him, a knock sounded on the door. "Do you get a lot of company on Sunday mornings?" she asked.

"I don't get a lot of company anytime," he replied. "Maybe it's someone for you."

She gulped and pulled her sheet up tighter. So much for the sassy expert. Kane laughed at her rediscovered social discomfort. "It could be Drew or Luke with the twins."

Julia let out a small squeak and dove for her dress, which lay crumpled on the floor. Kane chuckled and pulled on his slacks from the night before. He didn't bother with a shirt, because whoever was knocking at this time of day knew better than to expect a warm and friendly welcome.

Sure enough, when he swung open the door, the person on the other side made him feel anything but warm and friendly. "Erica? What are you doing here?"

Chapter 12

"I was in the neighborhood and thought I'd stop by." Julia heard the visitor's words as she walked down the loft steps. He glanced at her before looking outside at whoever this Erica woman was. "Aren't you going to invite me in? I've missed you, Kane."

That voice sounded more than friendly. It didn't take a dating authority to recognize that the sultry tone was flirtatious in nature. And intimate. It also was apparent that whoever was on the other side of that door was someone Kane didn't want Julia to see. She braced herself for the nausea sure to come. The same thing had happened after she'd found out that Professor Mosely was married.

Thank goodness she'd resisted the urge to throw on one of his flannel shirts and pulled her evening gown over her head instead. She might look a mess—perhaps even like she'd been up all night making love—but at least she was in her own clothing. Embarrassed. Potentially disgraced. Possibly even lied to. But she owned it.

"I'd better get going," Julia whispered from behind Kane.

He glanced at her quickly. "No. I don't want you to leave."

"Who's that?" the woman outside asked.

"That's none of your business, Erica. How did you find out where I lived?"

"I'm a reporter, Kane. I find things out."

Julia let out a breath. If the lady was someone important to Kane—like a wife or a girlfriend—his address wouldn't be a secret. Still, Julia wasn't convinced Erica's surprise arrival was anything but ominous.

This situation wasn't good. Why was a reporter standing outside, talking to Kane as if they had some sort of close relationship? At least, the woman was speaking that way. Kane's tone indicated he wanted nothing to do with this Erica person, which was good as far as eliminating the notion that he was cheating on another woman with Julia. However, his tone also indicated that he was hiding out from something or someone. And that was a secret he hadn't shared with Julia.

She'd finally opened up to Kane, letting down her defenses and forgetting the lesson she'd painfully learned as a second-year med student. Yet she was now in danger of finding out that the man she'd let get close to her wasn't who he seemed.

Pushing back at the irrational doubts throbbing in her head, Julia reminded herself that Kane was different than Stewart Mosely. The older professor had been an infatuation, someone in a position of authority over her who'd taken advantage of her naïveté.

Kane hadn't done that, had he? Surely, their love-making last night—and this morning—wouldn't have been the most intense and physically overwhelming she'd ever experienced if he'd been holding back a piece of himself.

Julia wracked her brain for red flags that she'd missed these past two months, but it was difficult to concentrate with the obnoxious odor of Erica's heavily applied perfume floating into the house. She'd felt like a failure after the whole fiasco with Professor Mosely because when she'd realized her mistake, she hadn't *wanted* to salvage their relationship.

With Kane, she didn't even know if there was a relationship to salvage. Julia pulled her hair into as neat a ponytail as she could manage and told herself she wasn't going to waste any more time not knowing.

"Hi." She pushed herself under Kane's arm and stuck out her hand. "I'm Julia."

"Oh my," the stunning brunette said, taking a step back instead of meeting the offered handshake. "The picture didn't lie. I didn't know you'd moved on so quickly, Kane."

"It's been two years, Erica. And I moved on the second I woke up from surgery and found out you'd spent the night with Arturo Dominguez."

"Babe." Erica tsk-tsked. "I was only trying to get the story. You'll never have any idea what it's like to be a female sportscaster in a man's world."

What picture? And what story? The throbbing in

her brain intensified as she tried to make sense of the crumbs of information being tossed her way.

Kane shoved a hand through his hair. "Don't act like there was some sort of inside scoop. The only story was that he ruined your boyfriend's career when he rushed the mound with that baseball bat."

"He didn't ruin your career, Kane. You were getting too old for the pros, anyway. It was time to hang up your glove and get into coaching. Charlie said you've had several offers from some of the top pro teams. Why haven't you taken any of them?"

"Is that how you found me?" Kane cursed. "You got my address from Charlie?"

"Who's Charlie?" Julia whispered, latching onto the name she recognized from last night.

"Charlie's my agent."

Kane had an agent? An agent for what? It had something to do with baseball and sportscasters and taking a new offer. Unfortunately, Julia didn't want to stand out here in the freezing air, trying patiently to sort this all out. Nor did she want this woman as an audience when Kane explained who he was and what he'd been keeping from her.

Julia hated secrets. They made her feel ignorant and powerless. She relied on knowledge, not intuition. Facts, not gut feelings. A long time ago, her instincts had been right about Professor Mosely, and she had only herself to blame for not paying better attention.

As frustrated as she was with Kane for not opening up to her sooner, she couldn't very well fault him for avoiding questions she hadn't thought to ask in the first place. He hadn't lied to her, as far as she knew.

And he seemed just as upset about this woman's un-announced arrival as Julia was. She had no idea what was going on, but she knew that if the situations were reversed and Julia was even the slightest bit uncomfortable, Kane would be the first one to jump into the middle of things and protect her.

So she decided to do the same for him by giving him a polite way to excuse himself. "You know, I hate to cut this short, but I'm going home so I can check on Mr. Donut."

"Crap. I forgot about him. I'll go get my keys."

Kane backed away from the door, and Julia stepped into his place, prepared to ask the woman who exactly she was. But the words never came, because, in the end, she wanted to hear it from Kane. He owed her that.

Out of the corner of her eye, she saw him take the steps two at a time. He was already on his way downstairs, his keys and a jacket in hand, when Erica asked, "Who's Mr. Donut?"

"My dog," Julia replied.

"Our dog," Kane said at the same time, his declaration causing goose bumps to rise along her skin. He put his arm around her waist.

"He's still *ours*, right?" Kane whispered into her hair, causing a shiver to vibrate down her spine.

"Depends on who *you* are, Kane Chatterson." Julia's response was not a whisper.

"I'm still me, Jules," he said, the endearing nickname flooding her with more confusion and uncertainty. "No matter what she says or what you find out, just keep that in mind."

"Oh my God," Erica clapped a well-manicured hand

to her cheek. "Please don't tell me that your little girlfriend from this little town has no idea you're Legend Chatterson."

Legend? There was that nickname again.

"Would someone like to tell me what I'm missing here?" Julia asked, feeling slightly empowered by Kane's announcement that they shared a dog and his tight grip of the car keys she was trying to pry out of his closed fist.

"I will," Kane said. "Just as soon as my ex-girlfriend leaves."

"She's your *ex*?" Okay, so that revelation took some of the sting out of Julia's growing frustration.

"You mean you don't know who I am, either?" Erica's bright white smile reminded Julia of a shark documentary she'd once seen in an oceanography course.

Julia glanced at the woman's wrap dress and Louboutin shoes, neither of which were appropriate for this weather. Her airbrushed makeup and perfectly curled hair looked professionally done and more suited to a fancy cocktail party. But she didn't care what this woman looked like. Nobody made Julia Fitzgerald feel unintelligent. "Should I?"

"Only if you haven't been living in a bubble the past two years, completely unaware of one of the biggest pro baseball scandals of the twenty-first century. My news station reported on it nonstop for twenty-eight days straight." Erica looked at Kane's stony expression, probably ensuring she had a captive audience, before continuing. "Allow me to fill you in, cupcake."

Living in a bubble? The words were like a slap across

Julia's face because that's precisely what she'd been doing these past months.

"First of all—" Julia rose to her full height in her strappy evening shoes and squared her shoulders, her years of poise lessons coming in handy "—it's *Doctor*, not *cupcake*. Second of all, no, I don't have a clue who you are because I don't sit in front of my television set all day, watching newscasters speculate about sports scandals. I'm a neurosurgeon, and I'm too busy saving lives instead of trying to wreak havoc on everyone else's."

Clearly Erica wasn't used to having to back down, because she placed her hands on her hips and shot back, "It doesn't matter how many lives you save, cupcake. Kane Chatterson was once considered the MVP of the single world. You're just another stat on his score card."

The woman turned on her designer heel and made a regal retreat to a nondescript rental car. As Erica opened the door, she looked over her shoulder and called out, "When you're ready to return to the real world, Kane, give me a call."

"Not a chance," Kane said, pulling Julia in even tighter.

As Erica's car kicked up dirt and gravel, Julia's evening bag vibrated on the entry table where she must have left it last night.

"Did you see it, Sug?" Freckles asked the second Julia answered the phone.

"See what?"

"Your picture with Kane is all over the news. He's got his arm around you, and you're all cozied up. I think the word the reporter used was *canoodling*. Don't that beat all?"

"What picture are you talking about, Aunt Freckles?"

"The one that kid snapped last night. I followed him to the bathroom, but Cessy told me I couldn't go inside to make a scene. Chief Cooper went in there to reason with the teen, but the thing had already been posted all over social media. Then Commodore Russell flushed the poor kid's phone down the toilet and all hell broke loose."

"Who's Commodore Russell?" Julia asked, then shook her head, keeping the phone to her ear as she turned toward the man hovering beside her. "Wait. That's not important. Who are *you*, Kane?"

"Did you go home with Kane, Sug?" Freckles asked. "Put him on."

"He can't talk right now," she replied, then gasped at her inadvertent admission. "I'll call you back later," Julia told her aunt, then tapped the red end button.

"I'm guessing that was Freckles?"

"You're guessing right. Now tell me what's going on. Who are you, Kane Chatterson?"

"You haven't told her?" A voice came from the cell phone and Julia realized that instead of hanging up, she'd actually put the thing on speaker.

"No, Freckles, I thought she knew," Kane said. "It wasn't like everyone else in town wasn't broadcasting it everywhere I went."

"Knew what?" Julia was cold, she'd barely had any sleep last night and she was starting to get hungry. And if she didn't get some answers soon, she'd be trembling with anger.

"I'll explain everything when we get in the car."

"I'm not getting in any car with you until you tell me what's going on."

"You're taking the car?" Freckles asked through the speaker. "Wait until I tell Cessy and Kylie. He must be serious about you, Sug, if he's taking you out in the car."

"I simply grabbed the wrong keys, Freckles. Your niece will call you back later." Kane took the phone from Julia's hand and really disconnected the call this time. "We should probably go check on Mr. Donut."

Right. Their dog. Julia followed him past his truck, over to the building she'd assumed was some sort of equestrian stable when they'd driven up last night. He punched in a code on the keypad, and when the electric door rolled open, she saw the building was actually a garage.

The Bronco was parked to the left, where there was a workshop and what looked to be an entire mechanic's bay. To the right was a perfectly reconditioned blue Chevy truck, the license plate boasting the year 1952. Next to that was some sort of green muscle car Julia recognized from a Steve McQueen movie her dad used to watch.

"You restore cars, too?" she asked.

"Yeah," he said as though this was yet another thing about him that was clearly obvious. Julia had just done all sorts of intimate things with the man only to wake up this morning to find out she hadn't really known anything about him.

"But all of these must be worth a lot of money." Even someone who'd just bought her first car a few months ago understood the value of a classic automobile.

"Yep." He turned to look at her.

"Like, a whole lot of money."

Kane lifted a brow. "Is it a problem if I'm not some poor small-town contractor?"

Just then, several alerts pinged from Kane's pants pocket, and he pulled out his own cell phone.

"Aren't you Mr. Popular all of a sudden," Julia said.

"Everyone in town is trying to warn me about the picture online," he replied, a frown deeply etched in his face. Julia hated that frown. It had been there last night when they'd left the gala, and she'd put in a lot of intense physical effort to make him forget about whatever had bothered him.

And judging from the way his phone was repeatedly vibrating, a lot of other people didn't want him upset, either.

So everyone knew about Kane's career and his exgirlfriend and his car collection. Had she been the only one left in Sugar Falls who was completely in the dark?

She put her palm out. "Give me the keys."

"Let me drive you home. We can talk about it on the way."

"I'm not going anywhere with you. Either give me the keys, or I'll call for a taxi."

"This is Sugar Falls. We don't have taxis. Sometimes Elaine Marconi's sister will use her own car for cab fares, but you don't really want everyone in town gossiping about you spending the night here, do you?"

Her response was to keep her hand extended as she glared at him.

"Jules, it's a sixty-eight Mustang GT. You know what

you said about my brain being a superfast race car? The engine in this thing puts it to shame."

Julia gave him a dark look. "Luckily, I know how to slow things down."

Watching the way she peeled out of his driveway in his prized muscle car, Kane knew she was furious. And he couldn't blame her. Julia thought he'd kept this all a secret from her. Technically, he hadn't hidden anything from her, but he hadn't been quick to parade his disastrous past in front of her, either.

He reminded himself that she'd grown up sheltered. That a woman like her was used to things being laid out in black-and-white terms. All he needed was five minutes to explain things to the woman he wanted to spend the rest of his life with...

Oh God. It was true. He wanted to spend the rest of his life with Dr. Smarty-Pants, who'd looked as though she was going to split the second Erica had shown up. Not that any explanation he had would prevent Julia from laughing at what an idiot he'd been to think she could possibly feel the same way about him. What a mess he'd made of this, too.

His gut twisted and his fingers twitched. It was too much to hope for Julia not to dump him, but did she have to do it while gunning the V-8 engine he'd so patiently restored?

Then he replayed her words in his mind and recalled that she didn't break up with him. At least not in so many words. Kane looked at the other two vehicles parked in his garage.

Should he go after her, or should he give his impulses time to simmer down?

He went back into his house to grab his cell phone and another set of car keys—just in case. Then he called the one relative that was professionally obligated not to laugh at him.

His brother-in-law Drew picked up on the second ring. Kane explained the situation, the words tumbling out in a rush as he described the confrontation with Erica and Julia's departure. "Now Julia thinks I lied to her about my past and I need you to tell me how to convince a hardheaded woman how to give me a second chance."

"I heard that," his sister yelled in the background.

Kane let out a breath. "So much for doctor-patient privilege."

"You're not my patient," Drew reasoned with his calm psychologist voice. "Now tell me again what happened with Julia."

Kane stood outside his truck, flipping the keys around his finger as he told his brother-in-law—and his sister, who had obviously convinced her husband to put the call on speaker—what had happened with Julia this morning. Of course, he did leave out some of the more personal details, but the story took long enough that he felt like he should switch to Bluetooth and get Drew's advice while he followed Julia back to her house.

"Do you love her?" Drew asked.

"Who? Julia?" Kane put his truck in Drive.

"Of course Julia, you weenie," Kylie shouted loud enough to wake one of the babies who then began crying.

He'd thought he'd loved Erica, even imagined they'd

end up married. But looking back on their relationship, her betrayal hadn't run as deep as the surgical scar on his shoulder. He'd been too busy mourning his career to give his ex-girlfriend a second thought. But Julia? Hell, losing her would do more damage than a team of doctors, coaches and meddling family members could ever repair.

"God, I really do." Saying the words out loud brought Kane a sense of calm. "Please tell me that's not the stupidest thing ever?"

"Do you feel like it's stupid?" Drew asked.

"Only if she doesn't love me back."

"Have you thought about asking her?"

"So she could laugh in my face?" Kane said, then took a left onto Snowflake Boulevard, already knowing he was willing to take that risk.

"Do you ever think you worry too much about losing?"

"Do you ever think you could just give me some advice or at least a brotherly pep talk instead of asking me all these rhetorical questions? You know what, never mind. I already figured it out for myself."

Kane disconnected the call while Drew was still chuckling.

And his brother-in-law had a good point, even if he hadn't said it directly. Kane hated to lose.

In fact, Julia was right when she'd once told him that he didn't like trying something if there was a chance he'd fail at it. Hell, she was right about a lot of things. Julia hated failure as much as he did, yet she was the opposite and would throw herself at a challenge, determined to become the best at it. Even if she hadn't wanted to do it—like going along with her aunt's make-over and dating plan.

Therefore, if Kane didn't want to lose her, he needed to convince Julia that he was a challenge worth taking on.

But just to be on the safe side, he stopped off at the bakery and grabbed a bag of doughnuts for their dog because he needed all the backup he could get.

When he pulled up to the house on Pinecone Court, he was relieved to see his classic Mustang parked behind the MINI Cooper.

He knocked on the door, rocking back on his heels while he waited for her to answer. He probably would've had to wait a lot longer if Mr. Donut hadn't pressed his wet nose against the glass-paned windows in the entryway and seen the white bakery bag before barking like crazy.

Probably figuring out that the dog wouldn't calm down until he got his treats, Julia finally opened the door. She was still in her sexy evening gown and, even with all the creases caused by it spending the night forgotten on his bedroom floor, the sight of her froze his vocal cords.

"You must've come for these," she said holding out his keys.

He shook his head. "You can keep the car."

"Then would you mind giving those doughnuts to the dog before you leave so he'll stop making all this noise?"

"I know you're upset about what happened this morning," he said, holding up his free palm to stop her from closing the door. "But it wasn't like I purposely kept anything from you. Plus, all that stuff was from my past. It's not who I am anymore."

She crossed her arms over her chest and said, "Don't you think who we were in our past defines who we become?"

"You sound like my brother-in-law, Drew."

"Stop getting off-topic, Kane. Just tell me the truth. You were a professional baseball player?"

"Yes. A pitcher. I was drafted straight out of high school and played in the minors for a couple of years before being called up to the majors."

"Were you good?"

"What kind of question is that?"

"It's just a question. I've come to the conclusion that I haven't been asking enough of those where you're concerned."

"Yes." He shifted from one foot to the other. "I was good."

"Is that why people call you Legend?"

"I guess."

"Now's not the time to be modest," she said. "Tell me why they call you Legend."

"I won the award for best pitcher in the league four years in a row. Which my dad never lets me forget, considering he won it only twice."

"Wait," she frowned. "Your father is a baseball star, too?"

"Well, he's a team manager now. He doesn't play anymore himself."

"What about you? Why aren't you playing baseball now?"

"You saw my shoulder," he said. "You also touched it, kissed it, rested your leg on it when—"

"I'm familiar with your shoulder, Kane." A crimson heat stole up her cheeks, and he was glad he'd sidetracked the conversation long enough to remind her of what they'd already shared. "But your ex-girlfriend mentioned something about a scandal, so I'm trying to figure out if that event was responsible for your drastic change in careers."

"At least you know that she is my ex-girlfriend. As in, very ex. A long-time-ago ex. A no-idea-she-was-going-to-show-up-out-of-the-blue ex."

"Yeah, I got that impression when half the population of Sugar Falls practically launched its own form of an emergency broadcast to warn you she was in town."

"I just didn't want you to think there was anything between me and her. Or that I would ever sleep with you if I wasn't completely free and available."

"We can talk about you sleeping with me after you tell me this baseball story," she said, not moving an inch, let alone inviting him inside.

Man, Julia would've been just as good a prosecuting attorney as she was a surgeon. "A couple of years ago, I was pitching in game six of the division series. We were up three to two, and there was a runner on second. Their designated hitter was at bat and hoping to set a home run record that night. But I walked him."

"Like, on purpose?"

"There's no more, buddy," he said to the dog as he brushed the sugar off his hands. "Yes, on purpose. A pitcher does that when there's a risk of someone scoring. The batter doesn't get an RBI and we stack the bases, which gives us a chance of making more outs."

"You're forgetting I don't speak baseball."

"Basically, the hitter got pissed that I walked him, and he charged the mound. That means he ran at me because he wanted to fight. But he brought his bat with him. He managed to get in a few solid blows to my shoulder before the dugouts cleared and the rest of the teams joined in. Supposedly it was one of the biggest brawls in televised history, and the news stations and broadcasters still refer to it as Brawlgate."

"What happened to the other guy? The one who hit you with a bat?"

"Arturo Dominguez? He was fined and suspended for a year. He's playing for a team in LA now."

"That's the guy you mentioned when you were talking to Erica."

"Yes."

"And she slept with him? While you were in surgery?"

"You heard her. She wanted to get the story."

Julia shook her head. "Tough crowd you used to run with."

"Nah. They weren't all bad."

"Then why not go back? Not as a player, but as a coach. It sounds like your dad and agent think you could."

"And be reminded of what I lost?"

"No. To be reminded of what you could give other players."

"I don't know. I never had the patience to coach. When I was pitching, I could focus out there because I was on my own little island. All I had to concentrate on was the ball in my hand going into the catcher's mitt."

"Do you miss it?"

"Baseball? Yeah. A little. Alex Russell and Luke Gregson talked me into umpiring a few Little League games last season. It was a nice balance, to be able to work on houses and then go to the ball field once or twice a week."

She looked him up and down, as if she were taking it all in. Taking him all in. And she still hadn't closed the door on his face.

"So, can we move on to the talk about us sleeping together?" he asked.

Instead of answering, Julia laughed and brushed by him before sitting down on her porch step. Hmm. Maybe he didn't like this sassy, confident Julia after all. Not when he was left wondering what was going through that brain of hers. The dog waddled beside her and rolled onto his back, sticking his stubby legs in the air as she rubbed its belly.

He took the smiling expression on her face as a good sign. But he would remain in suspense until he knew for certain that Julia felt at least something for him. "What are you thinking?" he asked.

"I'm thinking that I have a dog named Mr. Donut and that I just slept with a man named The Legend."

"Not *The*. Just *Legend*."

She rolled her eyes, then glanced back at him. "I'm still trying to wrap my head around all this new information I should've realized from the very beginning. I can't stand not knowing things."

"Yeah, I've been getting that feeling."

"Do you? I had no idea you were a famous baseball player. I had no idea Mr. Donut didn't belong to you." She was ticking off items on her fingers. "I had no idea that junky old Bronco of yours was a classic and probably worth as much as my MINI Cooper."

"You thought my Bronco was junky?"

"Kane, focus." She motioned for him to join her while the dog plopped between them. "What I'm trying to say is that I like knowledge. Sure, I could've found out most of that information with a simple internet search, and I'm annoyed with myself for being the last to know. But the thing I'm still trying to process—the thing nobody else can tell me—is how *you* feel."

"How I feel about what?"

"About me!"

"I'm crazy about you." He shot up and paced in front of her. "Stupid, mad, crazy about you."

"Don't say *stupid*. You're not stupid."

"Maybe not. But I have one more confession."

She tilted her head. "What else could you possibly confess?"

He immediately sat back down. "I knew about your man list before you ever brought it up."

Julia's hand flew to her mouth. "You saw that thing?"

"It was on your desk, in that picture you sent me with the tile samples. I hated the thought of you going out with some loser and thought I could steer you away from that. Plus, it helped remind me that you were so out of my league, the only criterion I met was my closet full of flannel shirts."

She started laughing. "You should've seen the first

draft. It was all about you. Besides, I don't need some silly list to tell me that I love you, Kane."

He put a finger under her chin and looked into her eyes, not sure he'd heard correctly. "You love me?"

"Even before I knew you had an entirely different life before me, I loved everything about you." His fingers moved along her face, but he remained silent, unable to talk around the lump rising in his throat. "I love your quiet brooding and your impatient knee that jiggles whenever you're nervous. I love the way you know exactly what I want to buy or eat or drink and have it here at my house waiting for me before I even have to ask for it. I love the way you clean up after me because you require a clutter-free work zone. I love the way you negotiate with salespeople and take in wandering animals, then pass them off to someone else."

"In my defense—" Kane scratched the basset hound between his floppy ears "—Mr. Donut was making himself at home here."

"Only because you would feed him baked goods every morning." She pushed playfully at his arm.

Kane took her hand and kissed her palm. "Tell me what else you love."

"I especially love the way you look in those sexy flannel shirts."

"I knew you were a smart woman."

"I think you've been the smart one, Kane Chatterson. You steered me straight into your arms."

"I love you, Julia. Just you."

Epilogue

Six Months Later

"Sug, you're supposed to slice the strawberries," Freckles said. "Not make jam out of them."

Julia hadn't quite mastered the technique. Yet. But she was getting close. Her aunt demonstrated how to use the knife crosswise along the cutting board as the Dixieland Jazz Band played a catchy tune from the gazebo in Town Square Park.

And because her aunt didn't do anything small, the sign for the Cowgirl Up Café's booth was almost as big as the Shortcake Festival banner strung up across Snowflake Boulevard. The town's main street was closed off so the townspeople and tourists could freely roam amongst the vendors and the carnival-style atmosphere.

"I can't believe that good-looking man of yours built

you that fancy gourmet kitchen and you still don't know what to do in it." Freckles tsk-tsked.

"Oh she knows what to do in it all right," Kane said as he walked up, Mr. Donut on the leash beside him. Julia blushed and Freckles threw a strawberry at him, which he caught. "I just do most of the cooking for us."

Which was true. Kane hadn't officially moved into her house yet, but he spent more nights there than he did at his own place. She waved at Chief Wilcox, who was walking across the street, holding hands with Marcus Weston.

"Kane." Cessy Walker materialized from across the street. "I'm so glad you're finally making more social appearances around town, because we could really use you to drum up business at the Chamber of Commerce's kissing booth."

Kane let out a bark of laughter. "No way. And don't even try to manipulate me into volunteering again."

"But Alex Russell and his hunky dad Vic were supposed to take this time slot and they sent over the commodore instead." Cessy pointed to the stocky eighty-year-old man with a gray crew cut and a toothpick clenched tightly between his teeth. Sitting on a stool with his arms crossed over his barrel chest, the senior Russell looked like he'd rather punch someone than kiss them. "And we're set up right next to Maxine Cooper's cookie stand. How can we compete with that?"

"I'll tell you what—" Kane pulled out his wallet and peeled off a few large bills. "—consider this my contribution."

Freckles rewarded his generosity with a paper bowl loaded down with strawberry shortcake and Kane winked at Julia, making her insides feel as creamy as the whipped topping he was licking off his plastic spoon.

A dinging bell sounded right before one of the Gregson twins yelled, "Look out, Uncle Kane!" Julia held her breath as the tandem bike narrowly missed running over her boyfriend's toes.

"Why did I start venturing out in public again?" he asked her.

"Because you love me," Julia replied. "And because we both agreed to put ourselves out there socially."

"I think I'd agree to just about anything for you." He rolled his eyes, but he couldn't hide that smirk of his.

"Hey, Coach Chatterson," the starting pitcher from the Sugar Falls High School baseball team said as he approached the booth with a crowd of teenagers. "I've been working on that curveball you taught me in May."

Julia smiled to herself as she turned to scoop up more strawberries for the new orders. Kane was still doing remodels, but he was also getting back into the sport he loved.

"Kane Chatterson," Freckles scolded. "Don't you dare feed that mutt any more of my shortcake. He'll get a bellyache from all the sugar."

When Julia turned around to remind him that Mr. Donut was only supposed to be eating the special weight control food the vet prescribed, she saw Kane down on one knee, their dog licking the bowl next to him.

"Oh my gosh," her aunt squealed loud enough to draw a crowd and it was then that Julia—and everyone else in town—saw the glittering engagement ring he was holding in his hand.

"Captain Julia Fitzgerald." Kane's voice shook as several people held up their smartphones and began snapping pictures of Legend Chatterson. She sucked in a breath, not caring about the tears filling up her eyes. Julia couldn't believe he was doing this here, in such a public place, as though he had something to prove to her. Or himself. "Will you please agree to marry me so we can get the hell out of here and go home to plan our elopement?"

"Of course she will," Freckles said, before Julia shot her the stay out of it look she'd been practicing lately.

"Of course I will," Julia echoed the words before Kane slid the not-so-discreet ring on her finger.

"I love you," he whispered so that only she could hear. And as she wrapped her arms around him, she decided that she couldn't wait to get him home. All alone.

* * * * *

*Officer Dante Santangelo doesn't "do" relationships,
but the busy single dad happily agrees to a secret
summer fling with younger free-spirited Gracie Bravo.
It's the perfect arrangement. Until Gracie realizes
she wants a life with Dante. Either she can say goodbye
at the end of the summer…or risk everything to
make this family happen.*

Read on for a sneak preview of
New York Times *bestselling author Christine Rimmer's
next book in the Bravos of Valentine Bay miniseries,*
Their Secret Summer Family.

"Gracie, will you look at me?"

Stifling a sigh, she turned her head to face him. Those
melty brown eyes were full of self-recrimination and
regret.

"I'm sorry," he said. "I never should have touched you.
I'm too old for you, and I'm not any kind of relationship
material, anyway. I don't know what got into me, but I
swear to you it's never going to happen again."

Hmm. How to respond?

Too bad there wasn't a large blunt object nearby. The
guy deserved a hard bop on the head. What was wrong
with him? No wonder it hadn't worked out with Marjorie.
The man didn't have a clue.

But never mind. Gracie held it together as he
apologized some more. She watched that beautiful mouth

move and pondered the mystery of how such a great guy could have his head so far up his own ass.

Maybe if she yanked him close and kissed him, he'd get over himself and admit that last night had been amazing, the two of them had off-the-charts chemistry and he didn't want to walk away from all that goodness, after all.

Yeah, kissing him might shut him up and get him back on track for more hot sexy times. It had worked more than once already.

But come on. She couldn't go jumping on him and smashing her mouth on his every time he started beating himself up for having a good time with her.

No. A girl had to have a little pride.

He thought last night was a mistake?

Fair enough. She'd actually let herself believe for a minute or two there that they had something good going on, that her long dry spell manwise might be over.

But never mind about that. Let him have it his way. She would agree with him.

And then she would show him exactly what he was missing. And then, when he couldn't take it anymore and begged her for another chance, she would say that they couldn't, that he was too old for her and it wouldn't be right.

Don't miss
Their Secret Summer Family *by Christine Rimmer,*
available May 2020 wherever
Harlequin Special Edition books and ebooks are sold.

Harlequin.com